THE ANTEDILUVIANS 2

MULTIPLE TARGETS

BY

ABBY BLACK

The Antediluvians 2
MULTIPLE TARGETS

© 2015 by Abby Black All Rights Reserved
www.TheAntediluvians.com
www.AbbyBlack.com

Cover Design © 2019 by Nicki Black, South Main Media™
www.southmainmedia.com, www.nickiblack.com
Illustrations © 2018 Abby Black
Editing by Tripp Black, Nicki Black, & Linda Black,
South Main Media

ALL RIGHTS RESERVED
No part of this book may be reproduced in any written, electronic, recording, or photocopying without written permission of the publisher or author. The exception would be in the case of brief quotations embodied in the critical articles and reviews and pages where permission is specifically granted by the publisher, South Main Media™, or the author, Abby Black.

This is a work of fiction. Names, characters, places, and incidents are either of the author's imagination or are used fictitiously, and any resemblance to actual persons, living or dead, business establishments, events, or locales is entirely coincidental.

First Edition - Paperback and eBook

Library of Congress Card Number: 2014919756
978-0-9909737-4-4 (This Book)
978-0-9909737-5-1 (eBook)

To contact the author or publisher:
South Main Media™, A Creative Company of Mindwatering
520 South Main Street, Wake Forest, North Carolina 27587
www.southmainmedia.com, www.mindwatering.com
contact@southmainmedia.com

ACKNOWLEDGEMENTS

Thanks to my Mom and Dad, for giving me wonderful insight and encouragement, and for always cultivating a creative environment that focuses on knowing my identity in Christ.

Thanks to my Grandma, Bide-a-Wee, for her keen eye and abundant love.

Thanks to my brother, Max, who is not only family, but also my friend. I enjoyed watching you sneaking peeks over my shoulder as I wrote, and I look forward to watching you read this continuing adventure.

And thanks to all of you for reading my books, sowing into my life, and being a part of my journey. Much love to you!

TABLE OF CONTENTS

TABLE OF CONTENTS

A red-tailed hawk looked up in wonder from its perch at the crest of the dead tree. The shout echoing in the distance was a symphony of many dialects, some of which the aging hawk had never before heard.

The hawk repositioned to a higher perch for better vision. Several miles away, a dense cloud of flying avians approached west to east. Nearby, a multitude of fellow comrades were lifting from the tree canopies to join the flock. The red-tailed hawk shuffled indecisively, unsure of the kerfuffle.

"We fly! We fly to the sea!"

"Come! Come! We must help! Come! Come with us!"

"Yes! My beak and talons are yours!"

"I'll help! I'm coming!"

The hawk bounced on its heels a few times before leaping, wide wings sweeping. It flew closer to the cloud, within shouting distance.

"Ho! What is happening?"

A great beast, unlike anything the hawk had seen before, separated from the swarm. "Our leader is allied with the humans. She has requested that we help strike the head! The snake lies in the ocean ahead. We are to gather up everyone willing to fly."

"As the winds are strong, I will help! Even though I think snakes are not what threatens the flightless two-legs."

The massive creature beat its wings victoriously. "Yes! Yes!"

With a mighty war cry, the hawk joined its brethren in the

cloud, and lent its voice to the summoning cry.

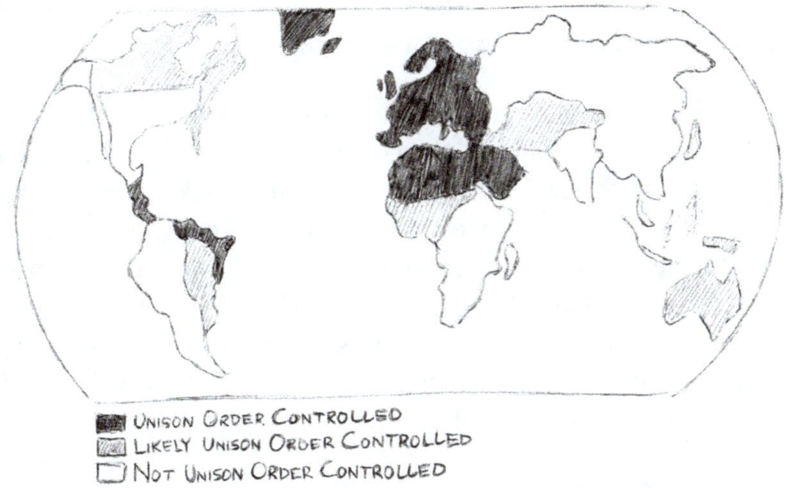

A RECENT HISTORY OF THE MODERN WORLD

In the year 2028, the United Nations Security Council unexpectedly lost their French delegate, Adrien Dubois, by cardiac arrest. Much-beloved by his people, his funeral was heavily attended by tens of thousands, while millions more watched online.

In the power vacuum, political factions fought with paper currencies and lofty promises. In the end, a dark horse woman with a message of hope won the race.

"It will be difficult for me to proceed in my predecessor's shoes," Dubois' elected successor, Lois Cornette, declared in her victory speech. "But in my love for my beautiful country of France and her people, I will work to make this world a better place; a transformed world that our grandchildren and great-grandchildren will be proud to inherit. Together, we will realize a utopia of peace and prosperity for all."

True to her promise, Lois Cornette dove into the task. The mission of rebuilding the collapsed European Union into the new Order was funded by visionary backers, men and women of great influence and global resources. Very early, they had leveraged financial opportunities from the collapses of nations and their global industries. Consequently, Delegate Cornette quickly became the most powerful U.N. Security Council member that history had ever seen. She was beloved by her own, and feared and despised by her opponents.

Using her impressive wealth and influence, she and the Council brokered immense bail-outs and bail-ins to the bankrupt European cities and nations. Seeing wealth in her shadow, the "Who's Who" flowed to her side. The people valiantly lobbied that their Robin Hood be made the permanent President. With apparent reluctance, she acquiesced.

Strengthened by populous support, the new President went before the Security Council. "Our security will be ensured utilizing the most innovative and state-of-the-art tech created by V.A.U.L.T.," Cornette said. "Our strength and unity will revolutionize the art of peace as we know it."

Vehicular Aviation Utilization and Logistics Technology lived up to its leader's promise. With an iron hand, V.A.U.L.T. cleaned up the local rampant corruption of U.N. security forces and local city-state governments with incredible expediency. On January 1, 2029, great fanfare and spontaneous celebrations burst in the streets, alongside massive spiritual ceremonies in ancient cathedrals and mosques. The U.N. assembly, with U.N. Order #B071216, formed a new nation from the European and most African nations. It was called the United Nations Unison

Republic.

Government officials and media talent, who dissented with the "Unison Order," found themselves the unfortunate victims of strange and numerous acts of God. "Even gods, if they existed, were surely backing the United Nations Unison Republic." With the new peace and prosperity, few bothered to consider hows and whys of the events.

In early March, 2031, the North and South American nations folded under their debt burdens. In a generous move, their debts were housed under the UN-backed IMF. Banks negotiated bail-outs with the failed nations. The defeated nations agreed to fall under the UNUR so long as they retained their current government hierarchy and borders. This arrangement assured their citizens that "nothing had changed."

The United States' Secretary of State met surreptitiously with UNUR President Cornette in a quiet French town in the remote countryside. It was supposed to be a closed door meeting, strictly off-the-record. Unbeknownst to the Secretary, Lois televised the meeting live.

She said, "The world has been led too long by big governmental and corporate leaders making closed-door deals to our detriment. I envision an earth where her people are united in peace. All six continents holding hands and looking forward, united under a single government."

Lois Cornette was now the people's hero. Mainline Christian denominations and their leadership praised the UNUR and the "Angel of God" for her Christlike compassion and humanity. Meanwhile, the exposed Secretary resigned, and a strong man, Frederick Gluten, replaced him.

Dissensions grew within the between-the-mountains

U.S. states who refused to fall in line. "Cornette's just too good to be true." The nation divided. Media broadcasts displayed their closed-minded protests and sign-waving with calls for secession or a constitutional convention of states.

Subsequently, the integrations of Canada and the South American nations into the new Republic stalled. Seizing the moment, previously deposed leaders scrambled to regain their lost power and control.

To ensure oversight, the Security Council moved to integrate V.A.U.L.T. into the IMF, the Federal Reserves, and the world economies. V.A.U.L.T. would become the literal ACME. The backing Cornette and her supporters provided the movement made V.A.U.L.T. massively successful, employing millions of people, distributing gadgets that ranged from elite military counterintelligence equipment to the most advanced household devices. Once again, she was the people's hero for saving the world's workers.

Rumors of wars spread from the Middle East into European and African countries. Hope eroded into suspicion and fear in the rest of the UNUR.

In the year 2038, the United Nations Unison Republic convened a summit of the Republic nations. The President was told that while her progressive vision was fantastic, it was unlikely to gain any footing. "It is no longer practical," they said, "We are sorry, President Lois Cornette, but your full vision is unachievable at this time."

Devastated, Lois Cornette removed herself from the public eye, becoming as close to invisible as a person in her prominent position would allow. The U.S.A. Secretary of State and President Lois Cornette were seen quietly convening many times. Rumors of a clandestine romance and conspiracy theories escalated in mainstream media. Political sides were taken and severed.

In the year 2039, there was a series of terrible, disastrous events:

January 1st. England's Parliament was targeted by a devastating prototype weapon during an unusual visit by the Queen. Unlike the majority of Parliament, the Queen herself survived the initial blast, but died shortly thereafter, ending her long-lived reign. The Queen's great-grandchild took the throne in her place. Representatives from all over the earth travelled to give condolences. President Lois Cornette was the most sympathetic, freely giving funds for the ailing country. Her acts of friendship gained the trust of the new rulers and Parliament.

March 11th. The United States of America's Secretary of State was on his way home, flying cross-country in his private jet. With his daughter's 13th birthday coming up, it was known that he wished to be home to celebrate. During the trip, the Secretary's jet dropped from radar. Attempts to contact it were futile. The very day of his daughter's birthday, the remains of the jet was found in the middle of a forest. A forensic report said that the plane exploded on impact, incinerating all aboard. The "black box" was apparently destroyed. Media personalities solicitously broadcasted the devastating news, lamenting the great loss to the President and the Secretary's family.

June 29th. Paris, France was struck by a small squadron of aircraft unlike anything seen before. Hundreds of tourists and native French were killed in the attack, while thousands more were injured. Reports gathered from the surviving witnesses described two different types of aircraft; The first was sleek and jet-like, the other a far smaller drone helicopter with twin outboard primary rotors. The aircrafts had approached too low to detect. There had been no warning. With the rising number of casualties came outcry against zealous religious sects.

The world waited for the next strike to come. Security worldwide was tightened. As the end of the year approached, people slowly began to relax. It was easy to want to believe that the first attack in France was also the final attack.

However, on Christmas Eve, the world received a series of new attacks. Targeting major world leader residences worldwide, the Buckingham Palace, The White House, and the Imperial Palace were included in the coordinated attacks. Few people and buildings survived. However, the new King and Queen of England were among the living.

The world reeled. No terrorist cell stepped forward to claim responsibility. V.A.U.L.T.'s UNUR keepers of peace were missing. V.A.U.L.T. military warehouses were found empty, and the production lines sabotaged or cannibalized.

December 30th. President Lois Cornette, the VA.U.LT. Security General, and her directorates, were not to be found in the aftermath. New York officials found the President's New York residence torched and the remains of an unidentifiable body. Families reported loved ones inexplicably departing in unmarked vans. Media and the remains of the governmental leaderships demanded audiences with UNUR headquarters.

A propaganda statement surfaced in Lois Cornette's name, declaring the formation of the Unison Order. "I will create a planet worthwhile for our grandchildren and great-grandchildren! With your help, we will wipe out all evil, all corruption, and all pettiness from the Earth and replace them with equality, with wealth, with truth and justice! I envision a world where our descendants will be able to walk the streets alone without fear, where wars are but tales in history books, where countries can collaborate together without suspicion, and we can journey to the stars as one people!"

January 1, 2040. The United Nations Unison Republic dissolved into disruption as countries of the earth took sides. Those that joined new Unison Order were gifted with V.A.U.L.T resources to rebuild.

The non-complying countries shifted towards war. The Unison Order preemptively struck without warning. Nations were attacked from the oceans and seas. On the United States mainland, drones came in from both coasts like a swarm of locusts, darkening the skies in an immense show of force. Citizens fled in terror to newly formed refugee camps further inland.

In the year 2041, with worldwide commerce disrupted, the economy floundered. There seemed to be no hope to be had when the elective candidates campaigned to manage the defaulted nation, but the citizens were awestruck when the new faces of government learned from history and restored principles from the early 1900s. National spending was reduced by 80%, income tax was abolished to, hopefully, never return, and a sales tax capped to the current value of US currency was implemented in its place.

Even the war on the horizon could not keep hope from surging. Inspired by opportunity, nimble start-ups employed millions, organizing the restoration of razed cities and distribution of resources. Technological geniuses young and old were swept into the development of new markets. Mere months after having taken office, the government offered military contests to anyone who could design and build defensive and tactical weaponry against the Unison Order. Although the contest monetary awards were meagre, companies leapt at the opportunity for prestige and honor.

The following year, an R&D scientist hurtled herself into a portal.

PROLOGUE

Punctuated dirt plumes formed around her as Robin somersaulted behind the nearest tree. Bullets lodged in the trunk behind her head, shards of bark and wood splaying, while she caught her breath. Dirt clods settled around her, reminiscent of falling snow, while the dust betrayed the course of the sun's rays through the canopy. Unshed tears blurred her vision, and she worked her hand beneath her visor to wipe her eyes clear.

With her helmet now askew from its rightful position, she quickly corrected. Her visor's built-in HUD, alit with a collection of sensor readings, informed her of the UO-GD drones closing in. They would surround her if she didn't move *now*.

She lunged, the grass peeling away beneath the tread of her boots. Unprepared for the slide, her knees buckled into a stumble. She hurriedly righted herself, heart pummeling her chest at the mistake. Distance lost, the drones got a clear sight of her, and her HUD flashed red. Diving behind a boulder saved her life.

She could hear the steady buzz of the drones pursuing her as she dashed from tree to tree. Rounds streaked past. She leapt off the peak of a hill, hoping that the slope would buy her a few precious seconds. Before she could descend, one of the bullets grazed her right bicep, leaving a bloody red slash across her combat suit. A gritty gasp escaped between clenched teeth as the wound seared at her nerves, pleading for care.

Setting her jaw and crouching down low, she located better cover. Scanning her HUD's readout, she bent around her cover's trunk and opened fire.

Her first shot missed, but the rest of her rounds met their respective targets. Each of the sleek dark green drones spiraled to the ground, smoke and electricity arcing visibly from their fuselages. She grunted in satisfaction as she reloaded her sub-automatic, slipping the spent magazine into a pocket.

Her HUD confirmed she was safe for the moment. With an exhalation, she granted herself the luxury of leaning against the rough bark of her shelter. She inspected her wound, pleased to find that it was minor and would hardly need stitching, although the torn edges of her uniform were already red with saturation.

"Eagle Eyes to Roost. Eagle Eyes to Roost. Fall back to rendezvous position. Repeat, fall back to rendezvous position. Affirm. Over."

"*Lima Charlie. Tapper affirms. Already at position. Over and out.*"

"*Lima Charlie. Crow affirms. Two kliks north– Eat lead, you vapid nudniks! Coming in hot. Over and out.*"

"Lima Charlie. Arcee affirms. Half klik south of rendezvous position." She paused, taking a breath. "Natter's gone angel. Over and out."

She rose to her feet and sprinted, in bursts, the 500 meters to the rendezvous point. At the peak of a hill was a tiny clearing surrounded by trees. In the center of the clearing was a sleek Manta Transport, its propellors and turbines already activated. Armed-to-the-teeth guards dressed in dark camouflage surrounded the aircraft. They only glanced at her as a ramp was lowered from the Manta Transport's underbelly. She ascended.

"Good to see you aboard, boys," she panted as she sat herself in one of the plastic chairs mounted to the hull. There was a first-aid kit attached to the wall. She grabbed it and began treating her wound.

"You look like the forest ran you over," said a teammate, glancing up from his laptop.

"And *you* look as fresh as the day you were born, fobbit," Robin shot back, aware of the grime and sweat gluing her uniform to her body. Her grazed wound was beginning to throb. The adrenaline was fading. As she applied the antiseptic spray, Robin clenched her jaw against reaction. It took several moments before the sensation of butterfly knives, kneading her flesh, faded away. "Have fun playing with code while the rest of us are hauling our tails?"

A short Asian man looked to Robin. "Conners," Commander Rick Lennox said. "What happened to Launch?"

She winced, recalling when her partner had fallen. She could not help thinking it was her fault. "The drones got him. But we did complete our objectives, sir."

She reached into her vest's chest pocket and pulled out a set of dog tags. Operatives in the field had been microchipped since the '30s, but it was tradition to wear dog tags around the neck. The set in her hand she had pulled off her friend's neck after the light had gone from his eyes. It was all she had time to snatch.

She read the inscribed indentions in the rectangular metal plates; *Launch, Jason C., 110-17-2014, O NEG, Christian.* With a small sigh, she gingerly handed them to her commander.

Lennox took the tags solemnly and placed them in his

own vest with a quiet *clink*. "Launch was a good man. Once we get back to camp, I'll write his family. You may add your own words to the message, if you wish. Takin, have you managed to scramble enemy transmissions?"

"Perfectly," Nelson "Tapper" Takin replied, fingers flying across the laptop he carried everywhere. "The firewalls protecting their drones are outstanding, but nothing I can't hack to oblivion. They won't be retrieving their drones anytime soon, Commander."

"Good," Lennox said.

A tall, blond man sprinted up the ramp, winded but unharmed. "Commander," he said, "more drones are approaching from the east. We must absquatulate." The last part was garbled before his true voice, albeit muffled, came through, signifying that the vocalizer in his helmet needed repairs.

Lennox jumped to his feet and dashed to the cockpit door. "Get this pup up and out!" he yelled to the pilots. "Drones coming in hot!"

Robin frowned. "Tapper, you said you'd gotten them all!"

The hacker bent over his laptop, frantically typing anew. "I thought I had. I'll confuse their processors long enough for us to get out of their range."

Robin wanted to press, but he was already focusing, and her words would be unheard.

"Prepare for flight," the pilot said, hands immediately flying to trigger controls. "Bring propellor power to 100 percent," he said to his copilot.

Robin hurriedly fastened the straps around her torso as the guards from outside ran up the ramp and buckled in. As the last man boarded, the ramp lifted up and sealed into place. At the same time, the muffled din of the rotors rose in volume, vibrating through the hull against Robin's back. Seconds later, the Manta Transport shifted as its skids left the ground. It briefly rocked until the twin rotors fully leveled and took the stabilized craft into the sky.

Replacing the first-aid kit, Robin was able to look out of one of the small windows in the fuselage at the rapidly falling away forest. The tops of the trees were flattened by the air forced down from the rotors, loose leaves having no chance against the gale. The aircraft quickly gained speed, pushing its occupants into their seats, and soon the ground was lost to her sight.

Robin rested her head against the wall and exhaled. Somewhere down there laid her fallen partner, left to carrion. She deeply regretted not carrying his body back to the aircraft, but, if she had tried, the team'd be down two members. It would be recovered later.

Suddenly, the aircraft veered to the port side, with protest from the engines. Hearing shouts from the cockpit, Robin peered out her window. A trio of large drones flashed by in a blur of black and yellow. Robin gritted her teeth; those drones weren't like the ones she and Natter had encountered.

No, those were UO-SDs; one of the Unison Order's speciality drones. Instead of the smaller, helicopter-styled assassin drones, the UO-SDs were six feet from nose to tail, with a nearly 10 foot wingspan. On the underside of the wings were two twin sets of compact machine guns, and hidden inside the underbelly was a lethal batch of heat-seeking missiles.

The pilots sent the Manta Transport through a series of

evasive maneuvers that seemed impossible for a craft of such design. For a moment, the ceiling became the floor, but the centrifugal force kept everything in place. Robin restrained from looking out the window, not wishing to see the ground in any other place but down. At some point, her hands had grasped the sides of her seat, but she wasn't inclined to release her white-knuckled clutch.

She fingered her weapon, its strap still slung around her neck. She didn't want to be penned in a flying metal coffin, helpless like this! If there was a way to safely dangle from the plane and return fire, she would.

The triple-barreled shock rifles pounded, vibrations echoing through the floor, and a moment later the drones aileron-rolled asunder. The Manta Transport, belying its unassuming and cumbersome appearance, took pursuit.

Robin closed her eyes, shoving away her avinosis as the aircraft abruptly and deeply plunged. Normally, she enjoyed the feeling of leaving her stomach behind, but this? It felt like her stomach had escaped to outer space. It was distinctly unnerving.

She braved a peek out the window just in time to see one of the drones flying parallel to the Manta Transport become shredded. It fell into a death spiral toward the ground with smoke billowing behind it in a black banner. The other two flew into sight, attacking the plane from the starboard side. Robin could hear the thunks of their ammunition hitting the hull, coming dangerously close to striking the fuel tank.

The onboard computer focused the shock cannons on the drones. The UO-SDs veered opposite ways. One avoided harm and found the Manta's blind spot while the other was shredded and plummeted to join the first.

The remaining drone was already firing again. Robin stifled a gasp as her stomach, just returning, plunged to the soles of her boots. The Manta Transport flew upward at an astonishing speed, with rotors pounding. Although she couldn't see the last drone, Robin still felt the juddering of the automated targeting system.

Finally, the shock cannons silenced, and the Manta Transport evened out. *"This is Captain Rex,"* came the pilot's voice over the speakers. *"Drones destroyed. Returning to previous course. ETA's nearly half an hour later than previously estimated. We can relax a bit now."*

There was no telling what else the Unison Order might throw at them. Robin couldn't relax until they were safe at the COP base.

"Is everyone all right?" Lennox asked. "Crow, are you injured?"

Maurice Williams, call-sign Crow, shook his head as he checked his magazine cartridge. "I'm quintessentially plum." He grabbed a cartridge box from a wall compartment nearby and began reloading the magazine.

"A-OK, Commander," Takin said, easing his grip on his laptop.

"I'll be fine," Robin managed.

Fortunately, the rest of the flight was uneventful. The pilots announced the final approach about five minutes before the Manta Transport landed. It was a very soft landing, barely felt. Robin unbuckled her harness and stood, stretching her muscles. Holding her rifle diagonally against her chest, muzzle pointed at the floor, she patiently waited for the ramp to lower.

Lennox trotted down first, followed by herself and Williams, and Takin took up the rear. They hurriedly crossed an overgrown parking lot, coming to a walk only when the camouflage nets were above their heads. Behind them, the Manta Transport departed for the hidden hanger.

"Team Alpha!" shouted the base's commander. "Report in for immediate debriefing!"

Robin trudged into the women's quarters with the day's events weighing on her. The base commander hadn't let anything go unsaid, and the loss of her mission partner was recounted in great detail. Robin hadn't enjoyed the process at all, but felt a little more at peace in the knowledge that the recovery of Jason's body was a priority.

Her mood wasn't improved by her surroundings. Everywhere she looked in the temporary base screamed of a past she would much rather have continued living. The base was made out of an abandoned country school. The town had been bombed several years back, and whoever hadn't been killed had evacuated and never returned.

The women's quarters just so happened to be in the southern wing, where the third through eighth grade classes used to be held.

"Class, today we have a new student with us. Honey, why don't you stand up and introduce yourself?"

". . .Hi. I'm R-Robin Conners. I. . . I'm eleven years old. I just moved here. . ."

"That's wonderful, Robin. From where did you move?"

"B-Barcelona."

"That's quite a ways from here. Do you like your new home?"

"I guess. . ."

"Well, you'll settle in soon enough! For now, let's open our textbook and begin on page. . ."

The children and teacher's desks were long gone, replaced by cots and a series of faded, colored plastic storage cubbies. There was one other woman in the room, napping.

Shoving memories into the shadowy depths of her mind, Robin quietly strode over to a cubby. She pulled out a cleaning kit, then retreated to her cot to tend to her rifle and handgun. She worked in silence for a while, taking apart her weapons, studiously cleaning them. But, finally, a tear slid from her eye and down her cheek. Her hands stilled as her head bowed.

I'm so sorry, Jason, she thought. *I could've done something. Should've done something.*

It was of no use crying over spilt milk. She would see the coffin, draped with the sovereign flag of his country, before the departure, say a few words, and move on with her life struggling with survivor's guilt.

She resumed the routine of cleaning her weapon, the tear evaporating on her cheek.

CHAPTER ONE

Nicole sat at her work desk, holding a framed photograph of a bipedal dinosaur drinking from a river. The sunlight filtering through lush tree canopies caused the *Intimidator* on Freedom's back to shine like polished silver.

Index finger tapping idly against the side of the frame, her gaze flicked to a single paper, lying on top of a nondescript envelope. She had received so many identical letters before that she could recite the text by heart. *"Miss Nicole Nike. . . consider the valuable assets over which you have jurisdiction. . . their assistance would be greatly appreciated should you consent. . ."*

Nicole thoughtfully rubbed her chin. *The* Intimidator *is short full capability only because the launchers and fuel canisters need reloading. But there is no reason to do so as Freedom is armipotent all by herself.*

Not a moment later, she berated herself for even thinking such a thing. The dinosaurs *just* came from a war. Who was she to even consider asking them to participate in a war of a completely different species? The dinosaurs were no match for long-range missiles, UAVs, and heat-seeking projectiles. They'd die before they'd come within 50 miles of enemy lines.

An idea flooded her mind. She turned on her desktop computer. Opening up the file dedicated to dinosaurian images, she viewed a section titled "Pterosaurs." Only two types had survived after coming through the time portal: Quetzalcoatlus and Pterodactylus.

She opened the file on dinosaurian data. Each glance at the Quetzalcoatlus specs caused her to wince and look away. They were too big, as large as a school bus; but the Pterodactylus was more promising. They weren't much bigger than an iguana in length, she could work with this!

She grabbed a sketchbook and pencil, her mind's eye quickly taking form on the paper. First, she sketched a Pterodactylus in a static pose. As quickly as the graphite appeared, her mind went twice as fast. She drew a vest, thick and pocketed. Then, an ammunition belt. The firearm gave her some trouble, but she came up with a suitable adaptation. Once she had finished with the pterosaur, she drew a second image of a raptor. The ammo belt was fastened around the thighs with the gun altered, handholds, and a fairly normal trigger.

At long last, she sat back in her chair and relieved her back muscles. She flipped between the two pictures, studying them intently. They were hardly similar to the *Intimidator*. The new design was without a neural linking system, laser, or jet engine, and the only weapon was a customized, fully-automatic rifle. It felt like a downgrade, but she had to consider covert aspects.

Nicole pushed back her chair as she rose to her feet. She hurried from her office, taking long steps along the halls. Interns and employees greeted her as they passed each other, and she gave them a nod in response.

"Where ya goin', boss lady?"

Nicole glanced at the young woman at the reception desk in the lobby. Jasmine was barely out of her teens and had taken the job as extra pay for college. Her thick southern drawl punctuated her speech.

"Out to check on the dinosaurs," Nicole replied, moving toward the board of key hooks that hung near the desk. She selected one for a jeep. "I'll be back in a few hours."

"Say 'Hi' to them for meh!" Jasmine cooed.

Nicole glanced down at the organized clutter on the desk, electronic pad sitting front and center. A half-drawn hadrosaur was on the screen, stenciled in blue lines. She looked back up at the receptionist and nodded. "If I get the chance."

Jasmine grinned. "Thanks."

Nicole bounced the keys in her hands as she walked out. As she descended the porch steps in a choppily bouncy gait, she waved in greeting to the guard on duty. He nodded back to her from his position in the guard hut, which was positioned on the edge of the parking lot with a direct line of sight to the driveway.

On the far side of the parking lot was a line of identical stock jeeps, all a solid shade of greenish grey with beige soft tops. She tapped the remote on the keys to see which she would be driving. One of them flashed its pale yellow headlights, the glass coverings still dustily opaque from its last few uses, and she could hear the clunk of the locks disengaging. The sound never failed to make her lips quirk; such an antique noise.

Using the roll bar, she swung herself into the driver's seat. She started the engine and carefully pulled out of the parking lot. The dirt path to the dinosaurs' territory was directly off of the paved access road to the building, cleverly hidden behind some large ferns. Once the vehicle passed the ferns, the way was unobstructed and direct.

Leaning back in the seat, she flexed her fingers over the steering wheel. She began composing a speech in her mind that she hoped was persuasive enough. By the time the path came to a dead end, she had revised her speech four times. She parked the jeep and slid out, hoping that Freedom would agree.

She consulted her compass for the right direction, twirling in a circle to pinpoint where she needed to begin walking.

"Freedom, I need your help," she muttered under her breath. "Freedom, I *need* your help. I need *your–* No, that's terrible. I need your *help*. Assistance? Reinforcements?" She shook her head.

She saw a series of large boulders up ahead, so she scaled a rock and stood straight once reaching the top. Beyond the ridge was the wide, indolent Branch River. Along one bank was an expansive clearing, lush with green blades of tall grasses. The puffy tops were shifting in the slight breeze, causing an effect like waves on water. The forest was doing its best to encroach on the open space, saplings and shrubs speckling the area. However, with the number of enormous herbivores, it was unlikely that attempt would succeed. A portion of the dinosaurian population inhabited the clearing, enjoying the brightness of the day.

Nicole took a deep breath, then let it out as a loud hooting sound, similar to what the Corythosaurus used as a locator. It came from the back of her throat and through both her mouth and nose, cracking if she shifted her tongue or tensed. She had made it a habit to hoot whenever she approached, so the dinosaurs wouldn't be startled by an unannounced appearance. They did not care for the artificial rumbling of the jeeps, the general consensus being that the engines sounded like rabid Tyrannosaurs.

Heads rose to face her. Some of them made a greeting noise in return, others had fleeting interest and returned to whatever they had been previously doing. A few of them, namely the Pterodactylus, flew toward her and circled above. Their wings cast tiny gusts of air on her, ruffling her hair and clothing.

"Welcome, Nicole!" they squawked in dinosaur-ese. "We've missed you!"

"I've missed you, too," Nicole responded in kind, tucking some wayward strands of her hair behind an ear, then reverted to English. "How have you been?" She smiled warmly at a youngling, who was valiantly working to hover in front of her.

The largest, a black pterosaur called Assail, alighted on a branch above her head. "If you mean all of us as a whole," he said in guttural, raspy English, "then we are doing fine. Food is plentiful and water is only moments away."

"Glad to hear it. And yourself?"

"Thriving. What brings you here?"

"I need to speak to Freedom. Is she nearby?"

Assail rustled his wings and pointed with his beak toward the river. "Drinking. You can see her from here."

Nicole squinted, scanning with her eyes around the shoreside. Finally, a flash of gleaming silver caught her attention. "Thank you, Assail. You've been most helpful."

"You're welcome," Assail replied.

Scaling down the boulders was a simple act of jumping from ledge to ledge until the ground was within a safe distance. Loose pebbles and stones rattled down ahead of her, disappearing into the grass, where she imagined some bugs were experiencing an apocalyptic event. Before she was able to get all the way down, a Corythosaurus moved into her way.

Before she could ask it to shift, it said, "Use my back to get down."

Nicole gingerly stepped onto its back, which was complicated. She crawled over the thin dorsal ridge and used the bump of a thigh as a step on her way down to the ground. She kept a hand on the Corythosaurus' scaly hide until she stabilized.

"Thanks," she called, waving over her shoulder as she walked on her way.

The Corythosaurus trumpeted in reply, a smile barely visible on its stiff snout.

Nicole picked her way through herds and packs, saying "Hello" at every turn. She was nudged, she was bumped, and once an overly enthusiastic Stygimoloch youngling gave her a fond pile-driver headbutt in the hip. Fortunately, none tried to engage her in conversation, and she was able to soon see the ochre Utahraptor delicately drinking from the river. The *Intimidator* gleamed in the sunlight, nary a mar on its surface.

As Nicole opened her mouth to shout a greeting, Freedom's nostrils widened and her head snapped up. She sniffed the air a few more times before searching the area. Her emerald eyes landed on Nicole, who flinched instinctively as the Utahraptor ran forward.

"You're back!" Freedom said, draping her head on Nicole's shoulder in the dinosaurian version of a hug.

Nicole felt as if she would never get used to a toothy head the size of a huge watermelon so close to her face. But, she returned the hug with a pat, feeling the sinew and muscle rippling beneath the skin. A shiver of muted fear tingled down her spine, having something so *strong* so close. "Hello, Freedom."

Freedom drew back, and Nicole's "fight or flight" instinct calmed. She hoped that her scent hadn't betrayed her. "I know that you've come here on business," the Utahraptor said, cocking her head. "What's the issue?"

This was it. "I won't beat around the bush, Freedom. We need your help."

"In your war?"

"Yes. Please, Freedom! If reinforcements don't come, the Unison Order will overwhelm our forces."

Freedom's eyes narrowed. "This is the second time you've come to me with such a request. The answer is the same. My kind is still recovering from the trauma of losing so many. We may *never* regain the numbers we once had."

"But–"

"Nicole, I've seen much more than I should've, despite my young age. You want us to go into a fight where we can be killed without ever seeing our foes." Freedom cast a look to the shallow waters, where some Utahraptor younglings played and splashed. "I have a family now, not only by blood, but everyone here is close to me."

"What happens if the Unison Order wins?" Nicole tried another tactic. "They'll invade and treat you like dumb animals, maybe even kill you all. Would you wish such a future on the youth?"

The Utahraptor looked down at the ground in rumination, then back up to meet Nicole's eyes. "And if we, the adults, the *parents*, die? They'll be left as orphans, not knowing how to hunt and live successfully. Then they'll die of starvation or foolish means they would've known how to avoid. No, Nicole, I cannot let my people die in *your* war."

Nicole was silent, gaze dancing between Freedom's alien eyes. The orbs, ebony slits in a sea of all shades of green, stared back in resolve, only the barest flickers of emotions hinted at in their depths. Not locating what she hoped for, Nicole bowed her head in submission, then turned on her heel and walked away.

"Nicole," Freedom called after her gently. When Nicole stopped mid stride to look over her shoulder, the dinosaur continued, "I. . . could gather the other sub-leaders. We'll have a meeting. I'll send you the answer tonight."

Nicole nodded. "I understand. Thank you."

The trek back to the jeep was a blur. Nicole was going on auto pilot as she drove back to the office building. She parked the jeep back in its spot, pocketed the keys, and trudged inside.

"How'd it go?" Jasmine asked.

Nicole hung the keys in their place. They jangled from rough treatment, rocking on the hook so much they almost slid right off. It was a few seconds before the keys declined into a quiet chime, then fell soundless completely.

Jasmine's hopeful grin fell. "Oh. That bad, huh?"

True to form, the television mounted on the waiting room wall decided to lend its two cents. *"Things are looking dismal as our troops on the front lines are forced to retreat sixty miles. . ."*

Nicole narrowed her gaze at the screen, not appreciating the newscast's timing in the slightest. Most of the seats were occupied by other employees or volunteers, their attention caught by the broadcast. Nicole read the scrolling text at the bottom of the screen and her heart fell. The reporter, although safe behind a desk, looked appropriately distraught.

". . .reassure that we will soon recover lost ground. Authorities predict the final encounter won't be far in the future. . ."

Not wishing to view any more, Nicole turned and trod to the break room. She went directly to the snack drawer. Rifling through its contents, she picked a box of raisins, a caramel chocolate bar, and an organic orange soda. Closing the drawer, she turned and promptly collapsed onto the nearest couch.

She indulged in the food, forcing everything but the taste from her mind. She didn't want to think about anything concerning the UO or Freedom's resistance from helping.

I understand her concerns, Nicole mused as she nibbled on the candy bar. *They just defeated an evil illegitimate king and his sycophants. It's horribly presumptuous of me to even* consider *asking them to throw themselves into another war. It's not fair to them.*

Her snack was done far too quickly, and she glumly tossed her recycling and trash in the receptacles. A dim flash of light told her that the garbage had been properly flash incinerated into ashes.

She went to her office, knowing that she still had work

to do despite how much she wished to return to her apartment and retire for the day. She closed her office door after her, a clear sign that she didn't want to be disturbed. Seating herself in her favorite chair, she turned on her computer.

Work always succeeded in drowning out everything else in life. Thoughts of evil forces and dinosaurs were overridden by updates to be made to the website, juggling her other job at the R&D center, scheduling, and paying her bills. The latter she did by hand, not trusting the online account for the state bank since their last data breach. She worked for hours, the light coming in from outside her window slowly darkening.

Finally, a pop-up window appeared on the monitor, a calendar reminder that it was 10:00. Nicole closed the pop-up and checked the security monitors. Except for the second-shift engineers, most all of the employees and volunteers were gone, and Jasmine was headed toward her office door.

Nicole looked up at the knock. "Come in."

Jasmine peeked her head in. "It's closin' time, Miss Nike. If ya don't mind, Ah'll be goin' home now."

"Go on home, Jasmine," Nicole bid with a nod. Jasmine always made sure to be the first to arrive every day. The girl deserved leisure. "Rest well."

"Ya, too, Miss Nike," Jasmine said with a smile before leaving.

Reminded of the lateness of the day, Nicole turned to her computer to run some final checks. The surveillance system was up and running, and she noticed that Jasmine safely made it onto the road. She ensured that the day's Reserve feeds were uploaded onto the main database archives.

As there were too many carnivores, the animals would wipe out a forest's population of anything mammalian. The Reserve and the government had employed a donation drive, urging farmers and hobbyists to gift livestock to the previously extinct newcomers. The dinosaurians had caught on quickly to the concept of farming.

It was a win-win-win arrangement. The herbivorous dinosaurs weren't in fear of being turned upon, the carnivores were able to eat, and the humans enjoyed their regulatory compliance paperwork regarding how the livestock lived and the minute details of each processed animal.

She wasted no time approving each and every single rating. The faster it was done, the sooner she'll be through it.

Nicole glanced at the time before scanning what she'd completed over the day. On the upper right hand corner of her desk was a stack of envelopes that needed to be mailed. The website and the events calendar for the Reserve were up to date. She made a mental note to spend more time at her other job at the R&D company.

I suppose I'm finished for today, she thought, gathering her bags. She slung them over one shoulder and shut down her computer for the night. Before she left her office, she badged out, swiping her identification card across a wall sensor.

The building was not large. There was a large front room with a hallway at the back, and off that hall were a few offices, the server room, and the break lounge. The Reserve was not a tourist attraction, so a kiosk of brochures was like an afterthought in a corner of the waiting room. As Nicole walked, she made sure that everyone was indeed gone for the day, and engaged the security system after she locked the place.

Her car was plugged into a power post in the parking lot by the nondescript jeeps. It was an old model, from when vehicles were hybrids. She used the key fob to unlock her car from a distance, then unplugged it and wound the cord into its cubby hole. She dumped her bags into the front passenger seat, and started the car.

Fortunately, traffic was scarce. Before she reached her apartment building, she passed by the complex of her friends, Pete and Anita Berg. She gave it a glance before returning her attention to the road.

Nicole and Pete were the topmost scientists in her company. As she was a focus point in the historical expedition, some of her findings and samples were being discussed in prominent journals. While also an expedition member, Pete was publicly shunned. Not long after the return, however, another research company noticed him. The gang in Room 7 was sad to see him leave.

From the Berg apartment, it was less than five minutes to the underground parking deck for her apartment complex. The noise of the city faded into an echo, as if a soundtrack from a dream. She quickly found her assigned space, illuminated by yellow, almost orange, lighting. With her bags in tow, she set the locks and alarm before heading to the glass elevator.

As the elevator quickly ascended, she looked out over the expanding view of the city. The lights from the skyscrapers and the traffic on the roads shone through the evening's haze.

She walked down the hall to her drab and unassuming door. The only thing abnormal about it were the numerous locks. She went through the meticulous process of inserting the correct keys for each, then entered.

Immediately assaulted by a mass of golden fur and slobber, her dog enthusiastically greeted her, sniffing at her clothes and shoes. If he had been any less trained, he'd be barking and rearing up to plant his front feet on her shirt.

"Hey, Compeer!" Nicole said, trying not to trip over her dog on her way to the couch. "Did you miss me, boy?"

Ruff! Compeer barked softly, panting happily. His tail was a wagging blur as he danced on his paws.

"Are you hungry? Me, too. Have you been a good dog and made dinner for me? Huh?"

Compeer bounded into the kitchen and nosed open a cabinet door beneath the sink. In the cavity was a stack of dog food cans. He tilted his head so that he could wrap his mouth around one. By the time Nicole reached the can opener, he was waiting, the can in his mouth.

"Good boy!" Nicole praised, ignoring the saliva. She opened the can and dumped the contents into his food bowl. She wrinkled her nose at the brown glop. "How can you *eat* that? It's like the mystery meat at the high school cafeteria." She felt a little guilty as she thought of her rotisserie chicken in the fridge.

Compeer didn't care. As soon as the bowl was on the floor, he attacked it, wolfing down his food.

"You'll eat it, of course." She rolled her eyes and took a few quick steps to the refrigerator. "Now, what's for me? We've got Chinese take-out from last week, the chicken, an inch of milk, and a slice of apple pie. In the freezer? Banana ice cream! I know what I'm having, Compeer."

Nicole set up the TV tray table and put her dinner on it. Leaning back on the couch, she picked up the remote and flicked through the 100-plus channels, only to eventually switch inputs and watch a recorded movie.

"You'd think that humanity would graduate from arena spectacles," she muttered to her dog, who had by then finished eating and had gone to his doggy bed. "So much for evolution, huh?"

The movie was about halfway over when something tapped at the window. Nicole jumped, almost choking on her ice cream. She rushed to the window. Pushing the curtains aside, Nicole shoved the pane of glass upward, revealing a Pterodactylus precariously holding onto the narrow exterior sill. Once the window was opened, it hefted itself onto the platform, clenching and flexing its wing-claws to loosen them.

"Hello," Nicole said in dinosaur-ese. She tried not to get her hopes up, but it was hard. *Please, let her have said yes. Let her have said yes.*

"Hi," the Pterodactylus replied, adjusting its balance. "Freedom sent me to you."

"What'd she say?"

"That we have fought our war. You can fight yours. She won't allow any of us to interfere until there is no other option."

Nicole felt mildly depressed at the news, but maintained a neutral expression. "Very well. Thanks for telling me."

The Pterodactylus squawked and flew off into the night, wing beats quickly fading off into silence. However, due to the city light's reflection off the cloud cover, she was able to track its silhouetted form for some time before it became too small to see.

With another sigh, Nicole slowly slid the window back into place, then closed the curtains. Compeer whined at her feet as Nicole trudged back to the couch. Her dessert had several bites left, but she didn't have the stomach for it anymore. She put it in a container and back in the freezer.

Chapter Two

Menial task work was a boon at times and a chagrin at others. The practiced motions, once established, enabled the mind to wander. In Robin's case, hers trod roads of memories and daydreams. The most beaten paths were of her waking up in the morning without her first thought being *Are we under attack?* Then her childish dream job that was blissfully pedestrian, like a librarian. In between shifts she could select a novel from the high, long shelves of dark rose wood and descend into a beanbag chair in a quiet corner, and no one would disturb her until she either finished or her next shift began.

She reached for the next piece of her dismantled firearm. Realizing that there were none left, she switched gears, cleaning and reassembling.

Her mind wandered to her Mam and Papa. Mornings inundated with the aroma of delectables, as her Mam was a hobbyist baker who sold her wares to whomever was interested. Of fresh wood in the garage, sawdust particles hovering in the air as Papa worked on his next commissioned piece. Breath suddenly catching in her throat, she wondered if they had made it out before the town had been razed. There had been so many bodies left in the streets, so many still exposed where they had fallen, ravaged by animals and the elements.

Robin gazed at her assembled pistol. With all that she had seen, experienced. . . she wasn't the same person.

Rising from her cot, Robin holstered her weapon and checked the clock. It was almost time for dinner in the cafeteria. She remembered the way quite well. Left, straight, pass by the gym (which now had a tree growing in the court), left. She walked through the double doors of the cafeteria and was greeted by the redolence of reconstituted foodstuffs.

She strode to the counter and looked over the selection; MREs, as always. She chose one, then walked over to the table with her teammates. She sat down at the end of the bench, adjusting her stance until the flat surface became bearable.

"Evening, boys," she said, taking a fork and digging in. Supposedly, it was beef stew. The flavors blended together to create a flat, sharp tone beneath the heat of the dish, although the stronger elements, like the corn and meat, managed to perk slightly above the conglomeration.

"Conners." Lennox nodded.

As Robin took a bite, the sound of tapping registered in her ears. A glance to her right showed Takin with his ever-present laptop, typing away with his own MRE barely touched and cooling rapidly. Robin admired his diligence, but she thought that the man needed to take a break every so often. One did not live by code alone.

"Find anything?" she asked him.

Takin cast a sidelong glance, one that told her that he heard her but most of his attention was focused elsewhere. "The French sent HQ the files on Lois Cornette," he said. "HQ forwarded them to me in the hopes I'll find a lead. None so far, though."

"You'll locate those ignoramuses, Nelson," Maurice stated past a mouthful of MRE. "You're the most nonpareil cyber invader I know."

"I swear, Williams," Robin said, "no one here needs a dictionary or thesaurus. We learn our big words from you." It was a common statement. More often than not, she only understood his speech from context, yet she was getting better over time. It was a game her comrade was fond of playing, first beginning soon after the team was established. Williams was more than capable of speaking like a normal person.

Williams took a sip of water, then put it down, his gaze distant. "Woebegone that we mislaid our compeer, Robin."

Gunfire. Rounds streaking past. Running for your life, firing over shoulders at the enemy. Too many! Sounds of bullets striking flesh. A single outcry of agony. The thud of a body striking dirt. "CLIFF!"

Robin leaned back, her eyes unfocused and glassy. "Launch was my second partner, and I'm very, very sad that he's gone. He went honorably in the line of duty." She used more force than necessary for her next bite. "Thank you for your sympathy."

Lennox moved to stand, his MRE platter empty. "Eat up, you all." He paused to cast a pointed look at Takin, who was still on the laptop. "Takin, you have patrol at 0300 hours in Section G1. Williams, you and Conners are on guard duty at 0800 tomorrow. See you at breakfast."

The peace after the monotony was simply *amazing*. Everything Nicole was working on was finished. The icing on the top was the gratifying sense of accomplishment in her latest R&D designs.

Nicole slumped in her office chair, letting her head fall back so she was looking up and behind her. It was a very interesting view of her office. The painting of the mountain looked strange, like a white and green stalactite.

Succumbing to her inner child, she pushed her feet against the floor, propelling her swiveling chair in a circle. She kept her head hanging so that she was outside the center of the spin. A moment later she braked and sat upright.

"Ooh, my stomach," she groaned, holding her abdomen. The room continued to careen around her, and she placed her forehead on the desk. "Ooh, my head. . . shouldn't have spun around like that."

"Have fun?"

The unexpected voice caused Nicole to jolt, which immediately reminded her of her nausea. "Ugh. . . How long have you been standing there?"

Jasmine smirked. "Long enough," she chuckled.

"Ever hear of knocking?"

"Ah did, but your chair's squeakin' drowned meh out."

Nicole frowned, rubbing her temple with a few fingers. "My chair does *not* squeak. Did you need something?"

Jasmine took a few steps forward and placed a bundle of papers on Nicole's desk. "The mail came. *They* wrote. Ah signed for it."

"Again?" Nicole said in dysphoria.

The young Louisiana woman nodded. "Again."

Reaching out, Nicole rifled through the mail. "Thank you. Is that all?"

"Yes, ma'am." Jasmine gave her a mock salute before pivoting sharply and striding out, closing the door behind her.

Nicole sorted the mail to different areas of her desk. Bills went in front of her computer monitor. Junk went in the far corner, closest to the trash can. Everything else Nicole kept in front of her. There was only one thing in the 'Everything else' pile, and Nicole knew that starchy envelope far too well for her liking.

Leaving that particular item until last, Nicole threw away the junk and took care of the bills. She placed the payments in an 'outgoing' container of her desk, then reluctantly returned to the envelope at hand.

What do they want now? Nicole grumbled as she opened it. She muttered the first opening lines of all the other letters she had previously received. Her fingers unfolded the crisp paper.

The first words didn't match. As she read further, none of the paragraphs matched.

"They're serious this time. . ." she assessed, frowning. She folded the letter a few extra times before sliding it into a pocket, then shoved her chair away from the desk.

Jasmine, back at her position in the lobby, looked up as Nicole snatched a set of keys from the rack. "Where ya goin'?"

"Out," was all the reply the secretary received before Nicole slipped out the front doors.

Nicole found herself in the exact same position she had been in not long ago, rehearsing a speech as she trekked through the forest. She repeated herself over and over again, but this time she hadn't settled before she came across the dinosaurs.

They had moved from the open clearing to forest, where the trees grew far enough apart to allow the largest passage. A couple younglings played a variance of Hide-and-Seek and Tag amongst the lounging shrubbery and trunks while the adults looked on and either conversed or grazed, depending on the diet type.

Announcing herself with a hoot, she looked around for Freedom.

As if anticipating her return, the Utahraptor appeared from behind a thicket, multiple hatchlings and younglings of various breeds at her tail. "Nicole!" Freedom said, coming to a stop a respectable distance away. "Welcome back."

Nicole's greeting was barely off her tongue before she was swarmed by juveniles. They leapt up on her, the tallest managing to place its front limbs on her shoulders. Claws punctured her clothes, affectionate nibbles dug shallow, bloodless trenches in her flesh. Nicole stumbled over a baby Ankylosaurus as she struggled to greet each one individually while defending herself.

"Freedom, help me!"

Freedom replied indifferently, "They're just saying hello." Her fringe twitched, betraying inner amusement.

Nicole winced as an Edmontonia stepped on her feet, and she prayed nothing had fractured. "Call off your attack greeters before I wind up as the base of a baby mountain!"

Freedom chuckled. "All right, little ones!" she rumbled in dinosaur-ese. "That's enough. Don't smother her."

The juveniles obeyed, retreated to Freedom's feet and stayed there. A tiny Bambiraptor youngling, hardly taller than Nicole's ankle, was the last to leave Nicole's side. Nicole recovered her balance and dusted off her shirt and pants. She brushed her hands over the new snags. Nicole wore an expression of annoyance, but the glitter in her eyes told a different story.

"Babysitting today, Freedom?" Nicole inquired.

"Actually, I'm their teacher. As the tribe leader, it's my duty."

Nicole glanced around at the myriad of dinosaurs of all shapes, sizes, and diets. "I'm guessing that this isn't your typical tribe."

"Tribes used to consist of only one breed, but with our numbers so small now, it would be unnecessary division." The Utahraptor shook her head, discarding a faraway look. "Discussing our traditional communities isn't your reason for being here, though. Not with that expression on your face."

"You're right." Nicole cast a meaningful glance at the juveniles.

The Utahraptor got the message. Bending down to their level, she said, "School is over for today. Go back to your families. Tomorrow we'll learn about poisonous plants."

The hatchlings and younglings sprinted off in all directions. Freedom and Nicole were now alone.

"What is it, Nicole?" Freedom asked.

Nicole pulled out the letter. "It's the government. Although I don't believe you were expecting otherwise."

Freedom's expression darkened. "Nicole, we've been over this! Several times. You know my answer. It's still no!"

As irritated as she was, Nicole was nothing if not loyal to her country, and forced herself to continue. "It's not from the military this time. It's a personal plea from the White House. It's not just a question or a demand any longer."

Freedom harshly bit the air, muttering something in dinosaur-ese that Nicole didn't know. "I'm listening," she grunted in English.

Nicole read the letter aloud, putting as much emotion into it as possible. To her, it sounded like a tear-jerker, but Freedom stood deadpan throughout. When Nicole finished, she smiled endearingly at the raptor.

Freedom sighed. "A famous man from your history once said the he didn't want to become involved with those whose only objective is to gain power. Like that hero of your past, I just want for all of us to pass through the rest of our days undisturbed while we sojourn here. It's someone *else's* turn for war."

Sometimes, Nicole thought she had taught the Utahraptor *too* well. She shook her head. "Washington was always willing to render any essential service. Any help from you would be greatly appreciated."

"I *said*–"

"Look, there's a black operations team that's just lost another member. It's their second in the span of a single year. They're on the verge of finding the means to ending this war. Just one dinosaur, Freedom. One dinosaur for each member of four Black-Ops members, tiny ones that have the best chances.

That's four dinosaurs. Just *four*."

"But what next, if I send four?" the yellow Utahraptor countered. "Your government will want more. Four will become eight. Eight, 16, 32. You humans are relentless and stubborn and refuse to acknowledge reason when you encounter matters such as this," Freedom barked. "They wouldn't be in this mess if not for insatiable power-lust and the inability to get along."

"Please, Freedom. If they want more than four of yours, then I'll refuse any requests for more. I'll even face prosecution to keep you all out of their hands."

"Will you? Can you avoid prosecution by reminding this country of its virtuous forefathers? Reasoning with people who justify any means to an end is fruitless." Freedom looked away, her jaw tightly clenched. "You know how I feel about this," she said slowly, "but I will reconsider. *But know this:* My final word will be final, and I won't want to hear another word on this subject."

"Agreed," Nicole said. "Thank you, Freedom."

The Utahraptor nodded and walked away.

Nicole typed efficiently on her computer, but her mind wasn't on her work. Every few seconds, her eyes would dart to the clock. Impatience was a great way to make time crawl, and Nicole wasn't enjoying it one bit.

She looked back at the computer screen and realized that her typing had dissolved from professional to childish.

Nicole refocused her attention to where it should be as she hit the delete key and started over. For the next half hour, she developed a rhythm and stubbornly stuck to it.

A knock on her office door jarred her from her groove. "Come in!" Nicole said, her train of thought derailing back onto the "Will Freedom agree?" track.

The door opened a crack and Jasmine poked her head through. "Ya have some visitors on the front porch," she stated.

Nicole stood so fast her chair almost tumbled over. "Visitors? As in plural?"

"Yep."

Nicole's hope heightened as she dashed past the secretary and down the hall. *Freedom wouldn't send more than one messenger to tell the same message.*

When she reached the front porch, she saw three Pterodactylus and a Bambiraptor. They had taken seats next to the stairs. The avians perched on the banister, and the raptor laid back casually in a rocking chair.

"What does Freedom say?" Nicole requested eagerly, kneading her hands.

The largest Pterodactylus, Assail, said, "We four hereby volunteer for active duty."

Thankful, Nicole gestured toward the door. "Come in, please."

Assail nodded and took flight, the other two Pterodactylus followed. The Bambiraptor slid off of the rocking chair, landing with a soft *thump* on the wood, and trotted after them. Nicole led them down the hallway back to her office. Employees who were in the way plastered themselves against the walls as if Nicole was leading her retinue. They watched the dinosaurians' passage in awe.

Back in the office, Nicole cleared off some desk space, shuffling piles to the side willy-nilly, and directed the pterosaurs to land there. The door was shut, and curious onlookers outside were thus encouraged to resume their duties. While the Bambiraptor commandeered a chair, Nicole went to her work bag and pulled out a thin, plastic measuring tape and a data-pad.

"Please, hold still," she instructed as she measured Assail. She frowned when the flexible tape twisted over itself, and she paused to quickly fix it. "I know you, Assail, but who're the others?"

Assail held very still, only his beak moving as he replied. "The brown one is Rush, my protege. The gray one is Gale. And the Bambiraptor is Shriek."

Nicole nodded as she jotted down notes. "How old is Rush? He's very small." Thinking one of the measurements erroneous, she murmured an apology as she wrapped the tape around the pterosaur's neck again.

"Almost adult," Assail replied, even as Rush's beak opened. Rush capitulated, directing his gaze aside. "He is small because he was born that way."

"Can all of you speak and understand English?" Nicole beckoned Shriek, coiling and uncoiling the measuring tape around her fingers idly as the pterosaurs made room. Shriek soon became front and center with plenty of space for maneuverability. As Assail had functioned as a sort of practice run, Nicole was able to gather the measurements expediently.

Since she had moved on from him, Assail nodded. "Yes, but Gale prefers our language over yours."

Nicole eyed Gale. "Understand that you *will* have to speak English at times. I'm the only person who can understand dinosaur-ese, and I will not be with you to translate."

Gale bobbed her head in affirmation. "Understood," she clarified in dinosaur-ese.

"Do all of you understand the risks involved in volunteering?" Nicole continued. "You're going to be partners for a black operations team with the goal of finding a way to end the war. Once you leave here, no one can guarantee your survival."

The brown Pterodactylus, Rush, appeared to collapse in on himself mentally. Nicole could see it in his eyes. This was *not* the appropriate temperament for a willful soldier. She was tempted to consult Assail about his choice, and made eye contact with him.

"Ma'am, yes, ma'am!" Shriek exclaimed with a grin, reaching up to deliver a snappy salute. "We know the risks, Miss Nicole!"

Assail met Nicole's gaze smartly, and followed her meaning when she subtly gestured to Rush. Demeanor sure, he conveyed a slow nod. Nicole demurred, but returned the nod.

A silence fell, broken only by the scratching of the pen as Nicole jotted down numbers. Once she was through, she pursed her lips in thoughtfulness while rolling the tape up. "You may go back into the Reserve. Please stay with the tribe until I come to send you off."

"Understood," Assail responded.

Chapter Three

Rush fidgeted on the hard seat. His feet and wings were not used to the smooth surface, gently contoured for a human's posterior and its relative comfort. Glancing at his companions, he could see that they didn't look nearly as nervous as he felt, not unless they were hiding it. In fact, Shriek seemed almost ecstatic that they were going off to fight. She was jittering like a hummingbird, bouncing in her chair.

Gale was not quite a friend, more of an acquaintance with whom he was friendly. He did not know her all that well, mostly trivia of the blasé kind. But they both remembered the horrors of living in the valley, Pre-Portal. Surely, *she* would have more dubiety on this entire enterprise. He was aware of how affected Gale was by the constant terror back then.

Shriek, he could only volley a broad speculation as to her undue (in his mind) vim. Pre-Portal, she would have been just too young to be directly involved in combat, and was likely regaled by woven tales of valor. Shriek was naive.

Rush was uncomfortably knowledgeable on how to bely his unassuming stature. Exhaling softly, he leaned backward, curling his neck in an elegant S so he could view the claws that protruded from his wings' wrist joint. Needle-thin and just as keen, as were the claws on his feet. If he crossed his eyes just so, he could see the profile of his beak, and the abrasion scars that had faded over time. At the tip, the exposed bone had been whittled to a fine point, so he could stab with his own beak with the surety of avian fishing. The bone would never heal.

The transference to this time was supposed to be an *escape*. A *rest*. Instead, he was subjected to a draft, merely because he declined a fishing hunt with his peers the day Assail came to him. The call was on short notice. Assail would not have had the time to drag him away, Rush was sure.

He huffed and looked around. Nothing had changed around him in the last hour. He was still in a Manta Transport with his only companions, Assail, Gale, and Shriek. The cabin seemed far too large for a few Pterodactylus the size of a large iguana and a Bambiraptor slightly bigger than a chicken. A few humans had accompanied them earlier to brief the four Squamas, but their departure before the Atlantic Ocean leg of the flight had revealed with clarity how much larger humans built their devices.

Rush did not like the sensation of being small.

Rearing back, he let his wing-claws have a rest. His movements were slightly hampered by the vest and armaments he wore. They abraded against his hide unnaturally. He still wasn't used to the feeling of wearing clothes, but Nicole had insisted.

She had made all four of them special gear. The vests were bulletproof and covered with ammunition-filled pockets. Dangling from his chest was a tiny semi-automatic. The trigger was a custom-made contraption that was tied around an ankle, so he only had to squeeze a small grip pad to fire. A tiny thingamajig the humans called a comm was fastened awkwardly around his head. The comm had a microphone by his mouth and an almost microscopic speaker located next to his ear.

"Nervous?"

Rush deadpanned. "You think?"

Gale snorted and batted him with a wing. "We'll be fine, Rush," she stated with security. "It'll be just like back in the valley."

"Harass' sycophants didn't have long-range weapons," he responded. "You heard the suited humans earlier. This is *nothing* like back in the valley!"

"We'll be fine," Gale continued, as if she hadn't heard him. But he detected a minute strain. He was not the only one she was attempting to convince.

Rush frowned, looking away.

"This is your pilot speaking," came a voice from the overhead speakers. *"Approaching COP base, one klik from the wire. Prepare for landing, ETA five minutes."*

The Squama across the way was the epitome of

anticipation. "This is it," Shriek said, grinning. Her tail wagged in her excitement.

Rush wished that he was back home.

The Manta Transport approached the base, the rotors' winds forcing the forest plants to cave and bend. It wove through the sparse tree canopy like a fish through kelp, elegantly avoiding entanglement. A few moments later, it landed in a tiny clearing. A hatch opened in the cabin, letting down a ramp. Assail was the first to exit. Rush was the last. One of the pilots began unloading their extra ammo supplies, placing the containers on the ground a good distance from the aircraft.

Now that he was outside the Manta Transport, Rush had a good view of their surroundings. Beyond the small clearing was a dense forest, something out of what Nicole called "photographs." The air disturbance made Rush's flight difficult, so he landed on a bush. As all of them exited, the Transport took off and wove its way back to the sky.

"There goes our ride home," Gale remarked.

You don't have to sound all cavalier about it, Rush groused, resisting the fanciful imagining of following the craft back to the Reserve.

Their containers were bound in straps, with a single band for carrying. Nicole had judged the Pterodactylus load bearing capacity, and ordered their supplies thusly. Rush's was, to his quiet disgruntlement, noticeably smaller. Shriek's would be able to drag her supplies behind her.

The pterosaurs circled the containers once, calculating approach. Rush glided in, waiting until the last moment so that the outstretching of his feet would not throw off his flight capability. His leg muscles strained under the weight, but he managed to lift his burden from the grass. Wings beating powerfully, he noticed that his maneuvering ability was severely limited, and flight in all directions except down would be ponderous.

"Come on, all of you," Assail said, carrying his own container with apparent ease, even though his own flight was compromised. "We need to meet up with the rest of our team."

"They just dumped us!" Shriek said, trotting after him. "In enemy territory, no less."

"Quiet," Assail whispered, looking around. "Our teammates are supposed to meet us. Since they don't seem to be here, they must be hiding."

"Very good assessment, pterosaur." A diminutive human male appeared from inside a bush, tucking some binoculars into his camouflage vest. "Welcome to COP base Beta Five. I'm Commander Rick Lennox."

Assail cocked his head. "Lennox? I'm Assail."

Lennox nodded politely. "The rest of my team are at the base. Follow me."

It was a short distance to the COP. Trees and brush had grown up in the broken asphalt of a parking lot. More were growing out of holes in the building's roof and windows. Camouflage nets dangled over strategic areas, concealing soldiers and equipment from view.

"It's lunchtime, so my teammates are going to be eating," Lennox said, entering the old school.

If he had been able, Rush would have gracefully slid through the opening in the doors. But he had to shift into a single line, following his leader. Once inside, he could see tables of ammunition and weapon racks. In the huge hall further on were shelves full of supplies. There were soldiers all about, gazing on with intrigue. Rush was positive they were quite the sight, carrying luggage almost the size of the bearers, and appearing as if they could drop like a stone at any given moment.

"What is this place?" Shriek said, looking around in awe.

"It used to be a school," Lennox replied. "It and the town nearby were attacked by an UO bombing. Everyone evacuated, and the UO's moved on. Believe it or not, one of my teammates was a student here as a child." He took a turn down a second hallway. "The DFAC is this way."

Robin, along with every other person in the cafeteria, looked up from her MRE at the sound of wingbeats. Lennox was approaching her table, followed by three pterosaurs and a raptor. She had been briefed on their unique new teammates, but even that hadn't prepared her for the sight. And, according to the expressions on the others in the room, they felt the same way.

Lennox arrived, and the pterosaurs landed atop their own burdens on the empty table-space. The tiny green raptor, crowned with a dirty tan fringe, was forced to leave its on the floor. It shoved the container slightly beneath the table so no one could trip over the box, then made its way onto the tabletop to join its companions.

Pterodactylus and Bambiraptor, Robin thought, recalling the briefing.

"Here are our new teammates," Lennox said. "The

Pterodactylus Assail, Gale, and Rush; and the Bambiraptor, Shriek."

There we go, Robin thought, leaning back in her seat. She blinked, trying to figure out which name belonged to which Pterodactylus. The briefing had not been accompanied with photographs, for the sake of confidentiality. Yet, there had been a note on the size difference between the two Pterodactylus: A case of dwarfism had rendered Rush half the size of his kin.

Rush looked at the those seated at the table. He tried not to fidget, knowing that the huge man with the buzz cut was staring holes in his head.

"And these are my teammates," Lennox continued, now referring to the humans. "My sniper and scout, Robin Conners. My hacker and field medic, Nelson Takin. And my sniper and weapons specialist, Maurice Williams." Lennox cleared his throat, adding, "To reiterate our orders, higher command has assigned partners. Assail will be mine. Gale is with Takin, Shriek is with Williams, and Rush is with Conners."

Williams crossed his arms and gazed at Robin. She returned a raised eyebrow. He cast a glance at the brown pterosaur. She looked away cooly. He meant no imputation.

Rush looked between the two, confused. "What just happened?" he asked Gale in dinosaur-ese.

"How should I know?" she replied. "Human body language is not my forte."

Robin looked at the two Pterodactylus, wondering what their interaction meant.

"Gale! Rush!" Assail barked in English. "We shall speak

their language when in their company."

"Yes, sir," Rush responded.

Gale nodded.

The two-hour time slot for lunch ebbed, and conversation nonexistent. Deciding that a change was in order, Robin stood, pushing her chair away from the table. The stilted feet screeched on the tile floor. "Commander, I request permission to better acquaint myself with my new partner."

"Good idea, Conners," Lennox said. "In fact, all of you do so over the afternoon. While you're at it, show them to their sleeping quarters. We'll assemble here, at this table, at 0500. Dismissed."

Robin strode away from the table, not looking over her shoulder. Rush hurriedly pushed off and flew after her, struggling to catch up with a weight in tow. She led him out of the cafeteria, down the halls and into a smaller room filled to capacity with cots and dressers.

"This is the women's quarters," Robin said, coming to a stop beside one of the cots. "I reside here, and this cot next to me is mine. Everything else in this room is not to be touched. Understood?" She paused to eye his strained flapping. "Feel free to put that down while we talk. Just watching you is making me tired."

Rush quickly nodded, terrified of this woman with eyes of stone, but her last instruction was welcomed. He settled the container on the ground, flexing his feet to loosen the joints before landing himself.

"I'll show you to your quarters later," she continued.

"Now, I can see your reluctance and hesitation. If those are your normal traits, then you'd better pray that you find some other ones."

Reluctance? *Hesitation?* Rush firmly believed that he was meant to be peaceful, and his own mentor had somehow divined otherwise. That did not mean Rush was some quivering hatchling.

Although, upon review of his own temperament of the past several days, it did beg the opinion that he was a spoiled, inexperienced youngling. If he kept it up, he might be sent home.

Robin began pacing. "We're going to be talking over comms, so you're going to need to know our lingo. Your name, Rush, is a good call-sign, so we'll stick with that. Same with the others, so I wouldn't be surprised if their names become their call-signs, too. Did the suits give you a jargon run-down?" At his nod, she annexed, "Good. Get ready for a pop quiz."

Throwing the sheets aside, Nicole rose from her bed. Compeer snorted as his sleep was disturbed, raising his head lethargically to watch his owner abandon her mattress and go to the kitchen. There was a work bag on the island. She opened it and peered inside, rifling through the files within twice.

"I knew it," she muttered, going back to her room. "I *knew* that I had forgotten something."

Compeer woofed softly from his seat on his doggy bed.

"I have to get my other workbag," Nicole said as she threw on clothes. "I left the R&D one at the Reserve. I'd have to get up earlier tomorrow – eh, later, I suppose, now – to go out of town, then come all the way back into town, and right back out again, and I simply can't spare the time with morning traffic. Might as well beat the other commuters to the road."

Her dog's collar jingled as he trotted to the front door. Nicole halted her brushing and looked up from the mirror to see him nosing his leash, hanging on its hook.

"You want to come with me, boy?"

Compeer wagged his tail, panting. He whined, looking at her imploringly.

Nicole sighed, tugging the brush through her hair one more time. "Fine, fine. Please, turn off the puppy-dog eyes. They most definitely work for you."

Compeer pranced in place as Nicole put on her shoes, then held completely still as she latched the leash onto his collar.

"I might as well take you, anyway," she said, going through the motions of undoing the complex locks on her door. "No telling who's out at this time of night."

The city in which Nicole lived and worked was huge. But, unlike New York, aptly dubbed "The City that Never Sleeps," hardly any cars were on the roads, and pedestrians were nowhere to be found. As Nicole drove along the roads out of town, she noticed that with the buildings' lights off, the night sky could be glimpsed through the ever-present clouds. To the east was the faintest glow of pink, but the sun wouldn't be seen for a good three or so hours. Was it the glow of fire?

The city eventually fell away to suburbia, skyscrapers descending into offices then to smaller buildings, which soon dissolved into trees and countryside. After that, it wasn't long before Nicole came to the road to the Reserve. It was marked only by a single sign of not much stature, and thus easy to miss if one was not looking hard enough.

Nicole pulled into the parking lot, which was entirely empty save for the line of jeeps and a vehicle she assumed belonged to the night guard. The lights were off in the guard post, but she could see through a window the green-tinged light of a monitor displaying security feed. She was sure that the guard had noticed her drive in.

Exiting her car with Compeer rapidly following, she waved to the nearest camera. Compeer heeled next to her as she strode to the building. When they reached the porch steps, he suddenly stopped, jerking Nicole's arm. She looked back at him. She tugged on the leash, but Compeer was a veritable statue.

Frowning, Nicole followed her dog's gaze. He was staring at the front door intensely.

"What is it, boy? Do you smell something?"

Compeer growled softly, stalking forward. Nicole followed behind, letting him lead her. He sniffed at the front door, particularly around the doorknob. After a few seconds, he lowered his nose to the porch floorboards and walked to the window. He reared onto his hind legs and sniffed the sill, then growled louder.

Nicole examined the window. At first, she could see nothing wrong, the pitch black of the night hardly helping her eyesight. She pulled out her keychain flashlight and turned it on. The tiny circle of light was a great relief, but she still didn't see anything amiss. The latch was engaged and intact, no signs of chipped paint, nothing at all unusual.

But Compeer had smelled something, and she wasn't one to doubt the dog's nose. A chill went up and down her spine, making her shiver.

She unlocked the front door and entered the building. Disabling the security alarm, she began turning on lights. She went to each room, cautiously peeking around the doorways. Her steps were silent. Compeer sniffed in each room, his nails clacking against the wood floor. Nicole scared herself more than once by mistaking shadows in dark rooms as an intruder.

After almost all the lights were on, Nicole and Compeer headed toward the last room – the server room.

"What do you smell?" Nicole whispered.

Compeer stopped, his ears flat against his head.

Nicole slowly opened the server room's door and flicked on the light. She poked her head in and looked in all directions. The only sound was the purring of cooling fans. After a thorough inspection, she turned to her dog and said, "There's no one in here that I can see."

The Labrador didn't look pleased. He snorted at the room. Nicole shook her head as she locked the door.

Once they reached her office, Nicole examined her drawers and files meticulously, checking and triple-checking to make sure everything was in place. She found her R&D workbag and looked through it, as well. Everything was in place; nothing was disturbed. Just in case, she flipped through a file that contained the names of the four volunteers and the equipment she designed for them. Everything was situated in the exact order in which she had left them. Nicole slid her arm through the bag's arm straps, still uneasy.

She noticed a translucent alert on her dormant computer monitor, blinking slowly by increasing then decreasing transparency. When she tapped the alert, it expanded into a message from the night guard. She responded promptly to the query, commending their awareness and follow-through in contacting her for affirmation, finishing with a statement that she will not require their assistance. She silenced the same alert on her smartphone, as it was now redundant.

Compeer continued sniffing, circumventing the room. His nose ultimately led him to the desk, where he reared back to investigate the tabletop. After a moment, he dropped back down and shook his head, causing his ears to flop.

"Find anything?" Nicole asked Compeer facetiously. "Come on, boy. Let's head home. I'm tired."

Compeer growled, ears flat as he patrolled around the office. Stopping at the computer tower under her desk by the wall, he stuck his muzzle into the dark crevice and sniffed. Pulling back, he barked at the opening.

Nicole walked back over to Compeer. At first, she didn't see anything, but when she felt along the side facing the wall, her fingers bumped against a lump. She hummed in interest, taking out her hand and looking down the crack. A small gray object was attached to the tower, a yellow light flashing on and off.

"Compeer," Nicole called, stepping aside. "Is this what you smelled?"

The golden Labrador stuck his nose back into the crack, growling again.

"Guess so," Nicole said. She fetched a small device from a drawer, adjusting a few knobs as she knelt on the floor. Pressing a button, she waved the device over the tower. The systems inside immediately whined in protest as the object fell off of the casing. Nicole pressed another button, and her device registered the object as dormant. She brought the object into the light and got a good look at it. Nicole turned it over and found a small screen.

Transmission Interrupted flashed repeatedly in yellow.

Nicole frowned further, now even more alarmed.

A hand slapped the keyboard in frustration. The load bar on the dimly lit screen was frozen at 57%.

Nothing. She had reviewed the past several days' camera footage of her office on fast forward. There was no sign of anyone that had even gone near her computer tower. The only occupants of her office in that time frame were herself and Jasmine.

With the object crammed into a pocket, Nicole hurriedly fumbled with the locks, clunking into place. She shoved and tugged at the door to affirm its security. To be safe, they walked the perimeter. The city was too far away to influence the night further than a slight reflective glow on the low cloud cover. Nocturnal life rattled the darkness, and she could spy bat silhouettes against the sky. The grass rustled beneath their feet, her dog's steps far quieter than Nicole's own. She shivered against the chill air as she squinted into the trees.

Compeer started snarling into the darkness. She stiffened, senses suddenly heightening. Neck hair erect, her head was on a swivel. Despite her diligence, she didn't hear it coming before it latched onto her shoulders.

She screamed at the top of her lungs, doing a wild panic dance as she grabbed at whatever it was. Compeer barked wildly, teeth flashing in the light of her phone. She pulled it off and almost tossed it away before realizing what she held. It was a Hesperonychus, no larger than a house cat.

Taking advantage of her surprise, the Hesperonychus wriggled its way out of her grip and fell to the ground. It darted

in between her legs, milquetoast. Nicole was nearly bowled over by Compeer cutting around her legs too closely, the Hesperonychus screeching as it circled around the other way.

Nicole quickly separated them, and Compeer grudgingly heeded her order to sit and stay. "Hey, hey," Nicole cooed softly to the reptile in dinosaur-ese. She knelt down and gently lifted the small raptor into her arms. Cradling it like a baby, she continued, "What were you doing here?"

"I'm so sorry," the Hesperonychus replied in dinosaur-ese, chirruping endearingly. "I wandered too far from the others and got lost."

Compeer reared back, barking loudly. He glared with absolute animosity at the tiny dinosaur in Nicole's arms. Two guards sprinted from the guard post to aid Nicole. They slowed once the scene appeared less threatening.

"Compeer!" Nicole rebuked, holding the Hesperonychus higher. "What is wrong with you? It didn't mean any harm. Look, you're scaring it." She glanced at the dinosaur, who was silently snarling. "Or maybe not." Directing her gaze to the guards, she added, "Thank you for coming to assist, but I think this was a misunderstanding, and have it handled."

"Are you positive, Miss Nike?" a guard questioned, giving the Hesperonychus a distrustful look. "You have tears in your clothes."

She readjusted the dinosaur so one hand was freed. Reaching back, Nicole realized that he was correct, and checked her fingers for signs of blood. There was none, the claws never breached her skin. "I see. But really, I believe I have the situation in hand now. You may return to the post and log this as an incident."

With some reluctance, the guards obeyed. Nicole sighed, shifting to bear the Hesperonychus in front of her and out of claw's reach. It fidgeted under her fixed stare. "Well," she said in dinosaur-ese, "what are you doing here?"

"I lost my way. I'm so happy you found me. I'm tired and hungry and I want to go to my nest."

"I can take you back to the–" Nicole started.

"No!" the Hesperonychus pleaded. "Don't take me back! No one likes me there. Can I stay with you? Please? Pretty please with a dead roach on top?"

Nicole grimaced, partially in sympathy, and partly because she had no idea what to do with the juvenile reptile. It was unlikely that *everyone* found the Hesperonychus' presence unwanted, but young ones were susceptible to exaggeration and equal action. She would have to consult Freedom after her time at R&D. "Well. . . if you say that no one likes you there, who am I to take you back? Yes, you can stay with me. What's your name?"

The Hesperonychus chirped happily, its large yellow eyes sparkling. "I'm Aim."

"And I'm Nicole," Nicole replied. Setting it down, she said, "So there's no confusion, are you a girl or a boy?"

Aim snorted, looking indignant. "A female, of course!"

"Of course."

Pete, looking as if he had just rolled out of bed, stood at the door to his apartment, leaning against the frame tiredly. His hair stood on end like Einstein's, and dark bags were under his drooping eyes.

"Do you have any idea how *early* it is, Nicole?" he asked, yawning widely.

Nicole, wide awake, looked him over. "Pink kitten pants?" she replied, gesturing at his pajamas.

"They're my wife's; all my other pajama pants are in the wash. It's too early for this," Pete bemoaned, running a hand down his face. "What spurred you to interrupt my sleep at this hour? We're good friends, but this is pushing it. I have to be at work in, like, three hours."

Nicole held up a fisted hand, the edges of the object peeking out. "I have something that you really need to analyze. Now."

Pete looked at her hand, rolled his eyes toward the ceiling, then moved to let Nicole in. Pete darted his glance toward the Hesperonychus. "Even your *dog* is up at this hour? And who's that?"

"A tag-along," Nicole responded.

"Hi!" the Hesperonychus chirped, staring up at Pete. "You don't look like the others I've seen. Where's the rest of your coverings? I thought you humans didn't like showing skin and stuff like that. Are you an exception?"

"Huh?" Pete uttered, not understanding a word.

"She only speaks dinosaur-ese." Nicole said. She

switched languages. "Aim, he can't understand you."

"Too bad," Aim huffed, tossing her head. "He seems like an intellectual. But if he's that smart, why can't he understand me? Smart people know *everything*." Flicking her tail, she bounced off to inspect a chair.

Pete closed the door and locked it. "What do you have that's so important, Nicole?"

Nicole held out her hand and opened it, revealing the gray object on her palm. The light was still flashing the warning. "I found this stuck to the side of my computer tower. Do you know what this is?"

Pete's fatigue was replaced by intrigue. He took the object from her hand and held it close to his face for inspection. He strode to a table in the living room. Pulling out a magnifying glass from a drawer, he turned on the lamp and inspected it. After a moment, he took another item from the drawer. It was some sort of scanner that Nicole didn't recognize. As he ran the scanner over the object, a hologram projected. Pete stared at the hologram.

"This is amazing," he uttered, rummaging through a second drawer. "This thing is one of the most advanced remote hacking devices I've ever seen in my life."

"Hacking device?" Nicole echoed while paling. "Who'd want to hack into the Reserve? We're not for-profit, and all our research is public data."

"I'm a techie, not omniscient, and not every electronic device broadcasts the signature of the owner," Pete replied. "Maybe they're going to try something and need information." He held up a small tool. "I'm going to try and pry off the covering to get to the microchip. I can't remotely access it through all this shielding. It should be able to tell us where the transmission was sent."

The tool pierced the hull of the object. Neither of them were prepared for the object to begin to send out a pitch. The warning on the screen turned into a rapidly flashing red light. Pete dropped the object and ran!

"Cover your eyes!" he yelled, shielding his face. Nicole grabbed Compeer's head, dragging him away.

Even with her eyes shut tight, Nicole could see the blinding flash. She blinked, trying to rid herself of the strange dimness of the room. "What happened?" she asked.

"That hurt," Aim whined, rubbing at her face with the knuckles of one hand. Her angular brown fringe was laid flat against her neck.

"A self destruct mechanism," Pete said, looking over his desk. A mordant, charred explosion scar on the wood was all that remained of the object. "Anita's going to go bananas over this. It's her grandmother's antique table. . ."

"What caused it?" Nicole asked, picking at the ash with a fingernail. Black encrusted beneath the enamel, and she grimaced. After a moment, it began to sting, and she quickly wiped it back onto the desktop. The flesh it revealed was flushed red with irritation. *What's in that stuff?*

"It was probably equipped with some sort of sensor. That apparently triggered the self destruct. Nicole, did you check the security cameras to see who planted it?"

"Twice," Nicole replied, very much bothered. "I saw

nothing out of the ordinary between the last employee leaving and my entering. I was the last person in my office before I left work for the night." She switched languages. "Aim, did you hear or see anything?"

Aim shook her head. "I was lost. Outside."

"Nicole, you didn't see any signs of a break-in?" Pete said. When Nicole affirmed, he continued, "You'd better interview your employees, then. If your cameras didn't catch anything, then one of them might've tinkered with the footage and erased some."

Nicole collapsed on the couch, rubbing her temple with one hand. Compeer and Aim jumped up to sit next to her. "I'll call in some professionals tomorrow," she murmured. "Yes, tomorrow morning."

"You don't have to wait long." Pete motioned to the window. Skyscrapers were reflecting the first rays of daylight.

CHAPTER FOUR

Branch below. Branch above. Gap in the leaves. Rush darted through the obstacles, using his glide to remain aloft. His flight was skilled and silent. Only when he was on the verge on plummeting did he wing in and alight on a branch.

Landing, he scanned the brush for his partner, who was following behind him. A slight reflection of moonlight revealed her position within a bush. She crawled her way to the next hiding place.

Robin looked up at the pterosaur sitting above her. She waved at him, not in a greeting gesture, but to nonverbally tell him to get moving.

Rush leapt off the branch, causing the soft rustle of leaves as the branch snapped back up into place. He broke his own silence again, thrusting his wings up and down, forcing his body upward. He used the membranes between his legs and tail as a rudder to direct him up and through the branches of the canopy. With a final flap, he burst through the trees and into open sky. He leveled out and found a wind current, which took him higher and higher until he was soaring far above the ground.

He swept his gaze across the forest. Somewhere down there was a Unison Order camp too small to even be called a COP. Small, but by no means allowed to be overlooked as inconsequential. According to what Conners had said earlier, minor camps were like a cancerous tumor; leave one alone, and it will grow to kill.

Harass hadn't used camps. There had been patrols and raids, with the waterfall hub of operations as a central point. Camps were what the Defiance had used, hidden in tight spaces where their larger foes were unable to enter.

Rush decided to focus instead of muse on unfortunate parallels.

Something caught his attention, and he descended to check it out. It was a tiny little clearing, hardly anything to "write home about," as humans said. He started circling to get a better view. At first, he saw nothing. Suddenly, he saw a human in mottled black clothes dash through an open space. He descended further, and was able to make out cleverly disguised tents draped with camouflage nets, painted forest colors. The dense fabric blocked all interior light from view, so it was difficult to tell which were occupied or not. He did not feel the inclination to investigate, so he clipped a wing and swooped back the way he came.

Robin crept toward the peak of a hill, her footfalls mostly silent. She was a shadow, easily darting from cover to cover through tall meadow grass. The night was dark, but her helmet was equipped with night vision. Her rifle was attached to her back holster, handily reachable, just in case.

Leaves rustled. Robin froze awkwardly in the middle of a crawl. Only her eyes moved, searching for the source of the disturbance. A branch creaked above her, and her hand instinctively twitched toward a sidearm.

"Arcee," came a raspy voice.

Robin relaxed, finally spotting Rush. He was dangling upside down from the thin branch, which was one of the reasons she had difficulty locating him. "Did you find anything?" she breathed. He might not hear it with his own ears, but the comm picked up everything.

Rush nodded. "About one klik south-southeast. You might be able to see it from the top of the hill."

"Eagle Eyes to Roost. How's the worm search? Over."

"This is Crow. Shriek and I are still peckish. Over."

Robin tapped her comm to broadcast to the rest of the team. "Arcee. Found some digging. Request for hunting party. Over."

"Eagle Eyes to Arcee. Don't dine just yet. Make sure they're nice and fat. Over."

Robin gestured for Rush to fly toward the camp. "Arcee to Eagle Eyes. Let us check. Over and out." She tuned her comm to broadcast just to Rush's comm, and said, "Eagle Eyes wants recon."

"Okay," Rush replied, already breaking through the tree cover. The passage of his tiny body barely disturbed the leaves.

Robin resumed her stalk, heading toward the hilltop. "Arcee to Rush. Don't go too low, keeping looking feathery. Over."

"Roger. Over and out."

It turned out that Rush was right. Robin was able to see the Unison Order camp from the hilltop. Not only that, but she had an unobstructed view. Carefully situating herself in a bush, she pulled out her binoculars from her pack. Raised to her eyes, a display on the lens lit up in green. Gauging the leveling, zoom magnification, and lens filter settings, she used a switch on the side of the binoculars to change the lens filters to night vision.

The pitch of the forest through her binoculars flashed into vivid greens, the color contrasting greatly against black emptiness. Infrared would not capture the Unison Order encampment, as they employed the use of fabrics that blocked heat radiation. But with night vision, she could spy every tent and person wandering in the woods.

Robin flicked a small toggle switch that split the lens into two. On her left side was the night vision filter, and the other side was a live feed from a camera in Rush's vest. She had to wait until he was circling the camp to look for the main tent. Not surprisingly, it was hard to single out.

She whispered instructions into her comm. Rush was hesitant, but he obeyed, descending in altitude, circling the tent. She surveyed the feed carefully, noting a radio antenna rising from the peak of the tent. Without infrared, she was incapable of detecting warmth of computers, but the size of the communications array was betrayal enough. The array was still being assembled, which explained the divinely fortunate lack of UO-GD sentinels.

Nodding to herself, Robin said, "Come back in, birdie. Over." She switched to broadcast. "Arcee to Eagle Eyes. Worms are ripe. Over."

"Eagles Eyes to Arcee. Hunting party's on its way. ETA two mikes. Over."

"Copy," Robin replied. "Sitting tight and waiting. Over and out."

Rush glided on a wind current. Ahead and to the left of him was Assail, and directly to his left was Gale, all three in V formation. There were a few low-hanging, fluffy clouds, which they avoided flying beneath. It was easier to disguise themselves against midnight blue instead of the moonlit clouds. If by chance they were spotted, they could misconstrued as mere bats.

The forest sprawled below, shaded in silvery blues by moonlight. Rush stiffened as the memories of numerous missions encroached on the forefront of his mind. How Tyrannosaurs and Dilophosaurus lurked beneath the branches. Guerrilla combat on the Pterodactylus' side, and how filed beaks and naturally sharp claws came into play under the dead of night. Too small to slash, tear, or bash their foes, Pterodactylus resorted to filthier means of engagement. Many of the Tyrants had awakened to literally blinding pain. The victims did not survive much longer.

This was too familiar. Even if this *was* a foreign wood far across the world and in a distant time. Even if this *was* a mere scouting flight and only one of the avians was to actively engage.

Robin scanned her surroundings, peering through the dense branches of the bush she hid within. No one was in sight, and even the nighttime creatures of the forest were quiet. She consulted her HUD for the positions of the team. There were three dots traveling quickly in a straight line; the Pterodactylus. A dot was to the north, another southeast, and two dots next to each other due east. Lennox, Takin, and Williams with Shriek.

"Eagle Eyes to Assail. BOLO the antenna tent. Keep an eye on it and anyone near it. Over."

"Assail to Eagle Eyes. Copy. Over and out."

Assail pulled ahead with a mighty flap, leaving Rush and Gale behind, arching through the air gracefully before curling his wings close. Rush watched his leader dive down toward the camp and become lost to sight, his dark-skinned body blending in perfectly with the night. Gale fell in behind Rush. They circled the camp, keeping an eye on the ground.

A chirp came over the comm.

Although she had already prepped, Robin verified her rifle's functionality and the load in the magazine. Several more loaded magazines were in her belt pouches, but she wasn't anticipating using them. If this mission went right, she wouldn't even have to fire once.

She pressed a hand to her comm. "Arcee in position," she breathed. She bent her head so that she could peer down her rifle's scope. It had a night vision filter screen, so her sight wasn't hindered.

"Crow in position."

"Shriek in position."

"Eagles Eyes in position."

"Tapper in position. Ready to Charlie Mike."

Robin shifted her scope. Dead ahead was the Unison Order camp, and somewhere in the brush surrounding the area Tapper was hidden. Not even her night vision detected him, a testament to his lesser-used yet still precious abilities.

"Eagle Eyes to Tapper. Charlie Mike."

He was surely moving now, but Robin *still* couldn't see him. She panned the campsite, finally spotting him only yards away from the target. He stuck to the shadows, his dark fatigues rendering him near invisible to the naked eye. A guard's shadow drifted across a tent before him, and Takin dropped to the ground and laid flat. The shadow passed by Takin without suspicion.

Gale suddenly tucked and dove, descending in tighter and tighter spirals. Rush pursued drew alongside. Wondering where her destination was, Rush estimated her course. It appeared to be the target tent.

"What are you doing?" Rush breathed in dinosaur-ese. "You're going to get us seen!"

"I need to check out the tent," she replied. "Someone could be in there. My partner would be caught!"

Robin frowned, raising a hand to her comm as if it could

translate the animalistic garble she was hearing.

Rush accelerated to block Gale's path. He veered in front of her, forcing her to break her flight path. Hovering in place, she glared at him.

"Get out of my way, Rush!" she growled.

"You should know better," Rush hissed. "Assail will be just fine on his own. You need to get back in formation before you endanger us further."

Gale cast a worried glance down at the tent. Rush followed her gaze and saw Assail perched in a tree near the target. Assail hadn't seen them. His gaze was focused on the tent. Rush was relieved. If Assail hadn't heard them, the guards definitely wouldn't. But then Assail made eye contact, and Rush remembered the active comm. Gale shared his ashamed wince, both of them knowing beyond doubt that there would be a reprimand.

Rush flew back to their previous altitude, knowing that Gale would follow, and they took up formation, slowly circling the area at a height.

The babble over the comm had stopped. Robin's brow scrunched as she dedicated herself to learning dinosaur-ese. Her gaze never left her scope.

Arriving at the tent, Takin discreetly checked its interior. He slipped inside, barely causing the tent flap to waver. Robin waited for him to come out. She couldn't track his movements while he was inside. However, that also meant that the enemy couldn't tell he was in there, either.

Just as Robin was growing uneasy, flexing her fingers

repeatedly, Takin reappeared, pocketing a small black object in his belt. He made his way toward the edge of the camp, once again avoiding the light and guards. He melted into the darkness. The nisus was straining her vision, even with the help of her rifle scope. Perhaps Lennox had a better bead.

Assail rejoined Rush and Gale, taking point in the formation. They wheeled around in the sky, commandeering a breeze. "Split up and return to your respective partner," Assail instructed and curled a wing, turning and diving toward Lennox's position.

Robin waited for the cue to move out. She wasn't keen on spending too much time in one spot. The camp would have lookouts, and remaining statue still a disguise did not make.

"Tapper to Eagle Eyes. Mission complete. Over."

"Eagle Eyes to Tapper. Bravo Zulu. Let's RTB. Over and out."

Robin began crawling backward, slinging her rifle back into its holster so that it was out of the way. Her pistol whipped out upon catching sight of movement above her, but she belayed the shot upon recognizing Rush. He silently followed as Robin rose and jogged for the rendezvous point.

She and Rush were the first to arrive at the Manta Transport. The pilots lowered the ramp. Rush flew in before Robin, landing on one of the seats. Robin sat across from him. About a minute later, Williams and Shriek walked in. As they took their seats, along came Lennox, Assail, Takin, and Gale.

Lennox leaned into the cockpit. "RTB," he commanded.

"Yes, sir," the pilot replied, reaching up to the ceiling

dashboard to activate the rotors.

Shifting her rifle to hang by her chest, Robin buckled the seat harness. She leaned against the hull, feeling the vibrations of the engines in the fuselage.

The Manta Transport lifted off, quickly leaving the Unison Order camp behind. Finally at a safe altitude, Lennox took a device from his utility pack. "Eyes closed!" he commanded, then pressed a button. Robin grasped the sides of her seat as a shockwave rocked the aircraft, throwing her body against the straps faster before the craft could automatically adjust. Her eyelids shined red as blinding light flooded the windows, but there was no sound of an explosion.

Rush flapped his wings to keep from falling off his seat, though it was a close call. He looked out a window to see a cloud of dust dissipating. Noticing Takin's smug look, he assumed that Takin had planted an explosive in the tent. Lennox stood and closed the door, effectively cutting the cockpit from the cabin. He returned to his seat.

"Good job, Takin," he said.

Takin nodded, retrieving the black object from his pack. "I managed to download their entire database." He whipped out his laptop, opened the lid, and inserted one end of a black jump drive into a port. "In a few minutes, we should know everything they're up to." He typed for a moment, then grinned. "Got it."

Rush tried to look, but he didn't understand what was on the screen. *Maybe it's English in its written form,* he thought.

Robin switched seats. Now sitting next to Takin, she leaned to peer over his shoulder. On his screen, there was a window filled with folders. Most of them were acronyms she wasn't familiar with, and the rest had names that made no sense at all.

Codes of some sort, she figured.

As if reading her thoughts, Takin grinned. "We have the private keys and the passcodes."

Takin began going through each folder, speed reading their contents. The first ones he clicked on were titled "Vacation." They were plans for troop movements. He renamed the folder to "Movement Plans" and moved on. Eventually, near the end of the list, he opened a folder called "My Puppy Needed the Vet."

Lennox, who was also watching Takin's progress, hummed in interest. Robin nodded at Lennox and scanned the schedule on the screen. It was a meeting of all the Unison Order generals at the M in London, England.

London, Robin thought grimly. *One of the first cities to succumb.*

"HQ needs to hear about this," Lennox asserted. "When we land, we're calling for secure transport to the FOB."

Rush couldn't wait to get out of there.

CHAPTER FIVE

Nicole stifled frustration. On her desk was an envelope freshly lacking its contents, and across the room the incinerator was winding down. The envelope's return address was one she was growing to despise, printed in indifferent black ink in the upper lefthand corner.

"We implore you to consider our request," she repeated from memory. Nose wrinkling, she translated, "We *strongly suggest* that you think *very carefully* about our request."

She might *really* be prosecuted.

Nicole began composing a reply, ruminating on what she was planning to write. Her musings caught the attention of

Aim, who had settled on top of the filing cabinet, and Compeer, who was lounging on the spare dog bed under her desk.

"Is everything all right?" Aim asked, cutting Nicole off in the middle of a sentence. "'Cause you look really angry like you want to bite something, and I'm getting a little worried, so could you tell what's wrong?"

Nicole sighed, letting some frustration go with it. "It's the government again. They keep pressing on Freedom's concrete wall of 'No more.'"

Aim frowned. "They want *more* of us?"

"Yep. I'm beginning to think that if they don't stop, they're going to get a visit from a mad Utahraptor."

"Don't they understand our situation?" Aim asked, standing up, beginning to pace. "We're on the brink of total extinction, and your government just wants to send us to our deaths? Don't they care about us at all?"

"Apparently not," Nicole said forlornly.

Dropping to the floor from the cabinet, Aim stiffly walked over to the basket of dog toys. Rummaging through the toys, the Hesperonychus selected a short nylon rope. She carried it to the middle of the room and set it down on the floor.

"You see this rope?" Aim said, glaring at it, stiffening even more.

Nicole nodded, discerning the atmosphere tensing. Compeer whined, apparently feeling it, too.

"This rope is your government." Aim stalked around the toy. She bent down into a crouch. "And *this* is what I want to do!" She pounced on the toy, talons and claws digging into the fabric. Nicole would've found it cute if Aim hadn't had said all that with a certain gleam in her eyes.

"They don't know *anything* about us," Aim continued, growling out her words. Pieces of the sturdy nylon began to fray. "They don't *care* about us! We're just some *tool* for them, just like the *Annihilator* and the *Intimidator*. But we're not produced on some *factory line*! When will they get it into their thick, irrational. . ." Aim dissolved into unintelligible chirps and whistles.

"Aim, calm down!" Nicole rose from her chair, but her movement only made Aim's rising fit froth and bubble over. Without warning, Aim abandoned the rope and shifted her attack to Nicole. Stumbling backward, Nicole almost fell over her chair as she dodged the Hesperonychus' lunge.

Aim landed poorly with a thud, turning to face Nicole again. She dropped down on all fours, her tail waving from side to side to check her balance. Nicole was caught in a flashback.

Aim was suddenly replaced by a Coelurus, ready to kill.

Nicole's heart raced as she frantically searched for a weapon, blindly patting one hand wildly around the desk behind her. The only thing she could find was a set of sharpened pencils. Useless. She shielded her face with her arms and awaited the attack.

Compeer pounced, batting Aim off of her feet. Nicole lowered her arms, relieved her loyal dog came to her rescue. Aim rose quickly, but Compeer was faster, neutralizing Aim by securing her to the floor with both front paws and his maw.

Aim struggled to unpin her hind legs and neck. As she writhed, her vocalizations reformed into something understandable. "They don't care that we've been in a war!" she cried, scraping at Compeer's legs with her talons. "Fire and brimstone have rained upon our heads! Thousands have died even before Harass grew up! But do any of your people care? *No*! They don't know what horrors we've been through!"

Compeer growled, as his legs were slowly being torn up. When they began to bleed, the golden Labrador temporaneous patience expired. His growl deepened as his lips peeled away from glistening white teeth, already braced at the dinosaur's vulnerable throat.

Nicole recognized the threat. She rushed over and pulled Compeer away. The dog persisted in his aggression. "Stop, Compeer!" Nicole commanded firmly.

Making growling noises to show how much he disliked the order, Compeer stilled anyway. However, he never took his glare from Aim.

"Good boy," Nicole sighed.

Taking advantage of her captor's distraction, Aim managed to squirm out of Compeer's grip and bolt for the far corner of the room. She hid behind the waste container, only her head sticking out into the open. Her fringe was completely flush with her neck as she hissed.

Legs weak and shaky, Nicole sank into her chair. Her hands gripped the armrests as tremors ran through her body. She didn't look away from the Hesperonychus. What if Aim tried to attack her unguarded back? Anything could happen while Aim was in this feral state of mind.

How can I forget that they're animals? Nicole thought. *They're beasts. Very intelligent beasts, but beasts all the same, savage enough to attack anything in sight, when under the right conditions.*

She saw Compeer limp back to his doggy bed. He laid down and began licking his bleeding legs.

Nicole let out a long breath, her mind jumping from one branch to another. *Kind of like humans,* she mentally added.

Shaking her head, she opened a drawer and withdrew the first-aid kit. Acting quickly and efficiently, she dressed Compeer's wounded legs, making sure that the bandages were snug but breathable. A ruddy tinge remained in his golden fur.

She needed to get out of the room. Nicole strode to the door, keeping an eye on the hostile Hesperonychus the entire way. Compeer was left on guard duty. Only when she had passed through the doorway and had closed it behind her, did she relax.

It was still early morning, so some of the Reserve workers hadn't come in yet. But those who were present as Nicole passed by greeted their employer with wide smiles. Nicole could hardly manage a smile in return, but they were too occupied with other things to notice.

Fortunately, the lounge was empty. Hoping to distract herself, Nicole got herself a drink. She collapsed on the couch and cleared all thoughts from her head. For a few minutes, she was peaceful. But when her soda can was emptied, Nicole knew that she had to go back and face the Hesperonychus in her office.

As she tossed her trash in the incinerator, she passed by the TV perpetually broadcasting the news. It was at low volume, almost inaudible, but the aerial shots shown on the screen caught her eye. It was a beautiful island, lush green and surrounded by pristine blue.

". . .completed their yearlong research. The earthquakes are showing signs of diminishing, and there are no worries of the volcano ending its long-term dormancy. Corvo's inhabitants are thankful for the volcanologists, who provided the relief that their home will remain."

Boy, Nicole thought as she watched. *That looks like a great place to vacation.*

No one was in the halls this time as Nicole procrastinated her way back. She stopped at the door, her hand frozen on the knob. She slowly pressed her ear against the door. Not hearing any dissent, she cautiously creaked the door open.

With a sigh of relief, she saw that Compeer was on his bed. She looked around for Aim, but she was nowhere to be found.

"Aim?" Nicole called. She peeked around the waste container, but nothing was there.

Compeer whined, drawing her attention. He stood on his hind legs and put his front paws on her filing cabinets, staring at the top. Nicole rose onto her toes, and saw Aim perched atop the dusty metal. The Hesperonychus was completely still, laying neatly on her stomach with tail and neck straight and limbs tucked beneath her body.

"Aim?" Nicole said again, waving a hand. Receiving no reaction, she grew concerned by the stillness. A closer look showed a slight rise and fall of Aim's chest.

Relieved, Nicole went back to her desk and resumed composing her letter, glancing up at Aim every once in a while.

The Hesperonychus never budged.

A Manta Transport swooped over the surface of the northern Atlantic. It flew over the water so low a few waves came close to brushing the hull. Behind the Transport, a spray of water rose into the air in a wispy tail.

Inside the Transport, the Black-Ops team leaned against the hull. There was nothing aesthetically appealing about the interior. Aside from the seating and a few built-in tables, there was nothing else. Everything was colored some shade of brown or gray. It was like all color had abandoned the world.

Robin stared out of the window, wondering how fast they were going as the ocean flashed by in a blur. She knew that the Transports were capable of a top speed of about 170 knots, but she didn't think that the pilots would dare to go so fast, so close to the ocean's surface.

"Attention passengers, this is your pilot speaking. We're reducing speed, prepare for submersion in two mikes."

Rush watched the humans check their gear. Instead of the loose fatigues worn while in the forest, they had changed into navy blue thermal wetsuits. Each of them wore scuba gear and had a SeaScooter to assist them in swimming.

Outside the window, the rotors in the wings accelerated as the turbine engines, made solely for forward motion, wound down. A ring surrounding the rotors moved free from the fixed wing, making fine adjustments to keep the aircraft stable. The Transport slowly descended, rocking a little as its belly touched the ocean surface. The rotors stilled, and the aircraft floated.

Muffled sounds echoed in the cabin, a sign that protective covers were sliding into place around the engines. Outside the window ports and just barely visible through the thick mist, the thin blades meant for air retracted into the swash plate assembly. Previously hidden blades made for cutting through water emerged in their place. They expanded to fill in the space in the ring, and locked into place.

The amphibious aircraft began to sink, swaying with the waves. Those inside were able to see the water rise above the windows as the Manta Transport descended. The light inside the cabin switched from sunny to blue, darkening the further they submerged.

Outside, the rotors began moving again, the ring rotating until the thick blades were vertical. The craft began moving; slowly at first, but rapidly gained speed.

Rush twitched. "Will we drown?" he asked.

"Have faith in the humans and their technology," Assail

replied.

Robin glanced at her partner. He was not alone in his discomfort, but she trusted the submersible aircraft.

The temperature of the water chilled the cabin, activating the heating systems with a soft *whir*. Rush shivered as the wind blew on him, but the system heated quickly, and he was soon warm.

"Attention, passengers. Our current speed is 70 knots. ETA is 0200 hours."

"Why don't we simply fly there?" Rush asked.

Assail opened his mouth, but Gale beat him to it. "The enemy always looks up. Hiding underwater is our best cover."

Undercover. Rush hadn't quite understood the meaning the day before, but now he knew it all too well. The humans, no longer wearing fatigues, would soon trade in their wetsuits for civilian wear - "plainclothes." Even the Squamas weren't exempt from it. Rush felt oddly bare with his vest and rifle gone, only wearing the headset. He knew that he shouldn't feel that way. After all, he hadn't worn anything at all before this assignment. It scared him.

"Let's go over our plan one more time," Lennox leaned forward in his seat. He finished tucking his dog tags into a pocket on his bag. "We're tourists wanting to see all the sights of London. Conners and I are newlyweds on our honeymoon. We're going to have a nice lunch at the M at the same time the generals have their lunch meeting. The pterosaurs and raptor are going to do recon, watching all the exits for the generals. You've seen and memorized their faces, so watch out for them. Comm us when they enter and when they leave."

Rush nodded. The human faces flashed in his mind's eye, burned into his memory. He remembered them clearer than the sky itself.

"Takin," Lennox continued, "you and Williams are going to identify them, find their rooms, and enter the rooms while they're at their meeting. Try and locate whatever you can that can help explain what the Unison Order has planned. When you're done, you'll return to the hotel room. You'll have to be quick, so that when the meeting's finished, you're long gone."

Lennox straightened up. "I'm going to hit the rack, and you all should, too. We have an early morning."

Robin squirmed in her seat, trying to find a comfortable position. The chairs were molded composite, not exactly plush recliners. Takin and Lennox were already asleep by the time she found a reasonable position that wouldn't result in a cramp when she awakened.

She eyed the pterosaurs and Bambiraptor. All four were so small, they could stretch out on their seats and lay in whatever position they desired. Rush looked particularly comfortable, splayed out on his back with his wings outstretched.

Grumbling a little to herself about the unfairness of it all, Robin closed her eyes. It seemed like no time at all had passed before she heard Lennox bringing her back to awareness. She rubbed her eyes and glared at him, stifling a yawn. An unpleasant taste was in her mouth, and she swallowed in an effort to rid herself of it. It didn't work.

"We have four mikes to surface," Lennox stated to the sleepy group. "Check your gear and prepare. Remember, our cars are on Dock 1, and we need to return to this Transport in exactly one week or else we'll have to wait for the next chance for HQ to bring us home."

Williams knelt down to a waterproof pack that rested by his feet. He unzipped one of the larger pouches and beckoned Shriek over. She jumped into the open pouch and squirmed until she was deep inside. Next to her was a tiny oxygen tank with a small tube from which she could inhale. Williams zipped up the pocket, sealing her inside.

Rush flexed his wings, doing small exercises. Assail and Gale were doing the same. Rush leapt from the chair and flapped hard, keeping himself in a hovering position for a few seconds before landing.

The only sign the Transport had surfaced was when Robin suddenly felt the craft sway. Balancing, she put on her scuba gear and pulled on the mask. Pressing a button, she heard a soft tone as a comm activated. She picked up her SeaScooter and held it at the ready. One hand reached up to her dog tags, which she slipped inside the neck of her wetsuit.

Outside, the rotor blades switched modes and whirred to life, lifting the Transport up just high enough for the ramp to lower without flooding the cabin. Wind-whipped water droplets flew into the cabin, and Rush resorted to walking to the exit instead of flying.

Lennox lowered his mask. "Let's move!" he said, waving them toward the ramp. "Go, go, go!"

Assail scuttled toward the end of the ramp, obviously struggling to not let his wings capture the wind. He fell off of the ramp, and from there he simply had to avoid the downdraft to fly clear. Rush followed, and Gale was behind him.

Flailing in the violent air currents, Rush struggled to

catch up to his leader. A sudden, sharp gust sent him spiraling out of control, and he fell into the ocean. Soaking wet and now cold, he grumbled to himself as he swam out of the vicinity of the Manta Transport before taking flight again. *Why oh why couldn't I have gone on that stupid hunting trip?*

Robin waited her turn, then ran off the ramp. It was a short plummet to the ocean's surface. She waited for the rest of her team to enter the water. Afterward, Lennox took the lead, diving deeper.

"Stay in sight of each other," she heard him say over the comm.

Rush couldn't see a sign of the humans once they had submerged. Turning his head, he saw the Manta Transport sink back into the depths. Suddenly, he felt very small. He turned back forward to the sliver of land far ahead. He took his position on Assail's right hind side and glided on the ocean wind.

CHAPTER SIX

A glittering example of beautiful modern architecture stood above the buildings. Cylindrical and thin, M was one of the most exclusive hotels in the country. Glass and steel created a swirling pattern that spiraled the tower's height. The tower changed colors during the day. Green in the morning, blue at noon, and purple at sunset.

Rush circled the building, his mind reviewing his briefed specs. *There are 53 floors. The first two for retail, 50 for luxury suites, two to a floor, which makes 100 rooms, and a restaurant on top. Three underground parking decks. Only the privileged can dine or sleep there.*

He soared above London, just high enough to appear as

a bird to the naked eye. He was tempted to enjoy the view below him, but his duty as a soldier had him continue watching the roofs. While Gale and Assail kept an eye out for the generals, he kept an eye out for snipers.

As he rounded the western side of the tower, he scanned the roofs below. They were clear of threats.

This scenery is the only decent thing on this mission so far, he thought.

A few blocks away, Robin felt uncomfortable in her leather coat and dress pants. Her two-inch heels clacked against the ground, a sharp betrayal to her position. Her face was painted and her hair done up. Robin felt like she was calling attention to herself, and she hated it.

Necessary to the mission, she hid all of her discomfort away. An ever-present smile was plastered on her painted lips, and she eyed her team leader affectionately. She forced herself to assume a hopping gait of excitement, but at the same time, she tried to appear a bit tired from travel.

"There it is!" she exclaimed as they rounded a corner. She pointed at the entrance to the M. "There it is, Reggie!"

Lennox laughed from the gut, the staccato tones lolling from his mouth. It didn't sound at all mocking, more amused and loving. Robin thought his facade to be flawless. "Yes, there it is," he echoed.

They strode up a short and wide flight of creamy marble steps to the huge double doors plated in flawless gold. As Robin and Lennox approached, a doorman garbed in stately black and white held a door open. Robin gave him a fleeting thankful look as they passed.

An equally snappily dressed attendant met them in the lobby. "Welcome to M. Our exquisite boutiques are just this way. Or, do you have a reservation for our restaurant?" he asked in the quintessential British lilt. He held a small data-pad at the ready.

Lennox nodded. "Yes, we have a reservation. Reginald and Marlene Opus."

Flamboyantly tapping the screen, he said, "Please follow me." He led them to a glass elevator. Upon arrival, he escorted them past the general seating of the restaurant to a small round table in the VIP section. Robin thought that the "simple" commons was huge competition for the most expensive restaurants in the States, so it was no wonder her jaw dropped a little upon entering the VIP section. The attendant gave them a pair of padded menus, a wine list, and told them that a waiter would be with them soon.

Now that she was seated, Robin took another look around. Not many people other than herself and Lennox were in that area. Another couple sat by a large window overlooking the street, and four men ate at a table in the corner. Behind Robin was a huge circular table edged with eight chairs.

"It's so beautiful here," Robin said in a hushed voice. It was as if speaking too loudly would demolish the fine air of the place. She picked up her menu and flipped through it. "Reggie! Look at all these fanciful names. . . *Condimentum et Venacione*, what does that mean?"

"It's French, I think. No, Latin." Lennox replied.

"Do you know what it means?"

"You know I haven't used Latin since high school. I'm a

bit rusty, so let's see. . ." Lennox held the menu closer to his eyes, as if that would help. "*Condimentum* is probably some form of condiment. *Venacione* looks like venison, so it's probably that. . . Venison with some sort of condiment, I think."

"Sauce?" Robin gambled.

Lennox nodded slowly. "Maybe."

Their attendant approached them, an old-fashioned paper pad and pen in hand. "I am Gaston," the waiter stated. "I am your personal attendant today. May I bring you a beverage?"

Lennox and Robin ordered club sodas to start. The attendant nodded and strode off. A minute later, he came back holding two tall glasses on a silver tray. He flipped out two ornate fabric coasters edged in golden thread from a pocket, then placed the drinks on the table.

"Are you ready to order?"

"Not yet, thank you," Lennox said.

"Very good." The waiter left.

Robin cast a glance toward the large table. She discreetly looked around for the top brass, but didn't see them. They were supposed to arrive by 1400 hours. They were late.

No sooner had she finished her thought, the doors to the VIP section opened. A concierge entered first, followed by eight men in impeccable garb, each with his own attendant.

Robin reached into her purse and fingered a hidden button. She didn't worry about the device picking up the generals' voices. It was designed to pierce any fabric and focus on a specific programmed range. Robin and Lennox would be largely ignored, but each syllable the generals spoke would be loud and clear. Thankfully, the tables nearby were empty, so there would not be excess garble in the recording.

"Do you see anything interesting, Reggie?" she asked, looking at the menu again. Her finger rubbed the thick siding, up and down repeatedly, a leftover habit from her childhood. She ceased the moment she noticed the action.

Lennox hummed thoughtfully.

The sun was going down, painting the sky in a beautiful palette. The M was gradually turning a luscious purple. As the atmosphere cooled, the cold and hot air began to combine, moisture condensing into clouds. Rush kept below the cover, shivering as he crossed paths with a stray current of cold wind.

"Tapper to Eagle Eyes. I have identified targets and am matching them to IDs. Should have results in half a mike. Done. Gale, check rooms 92 through 100."

Rush watched as Gale veered from her circling to dive down. She flew around the windows of the rooms, hovering in place just long enough to see if anyone was inside. From Rush's vantage point, he could see that the curtains were not drawn, which was exceedingly fortunate. A squawk sounded over the comm.

"Assail to Tapper. Gale reports clear. Over."

"Tapper to Eagle Eyes. Crow and I flying. Over."

Robin looked up at their attendant. "I'd like the roasted Duck a l'Orange and a Mediterranean side salad."

"The Surf and Turf for me, please," Lennox added.

The attendant nodded, writing down on his pad. "Very good," he said, gathering their menus and leaving.

Once the waiter had departed, Lennox leaned forward, resting his elbows on the table and his chin on his hands. Eyelids heavy, he asked, "Have I ever told you how beautiful you are, Lena?"

Robin blinked, startled by the sudden affection. Recovering quickly, she resumed her role. She let the blush remain, deciding that it aided her pretend infatuation with her pretend groom. "Maybe," she responded, mimicking his stance. "You *could* refresh my memory."

The generals were talking behind her. Robin tried to tune Lennox out so she could hear, but the generals were speaking so lowly. Straining her ears, she wished that Lennox would stop saying sweet nothings so she could focus. It was a good thing the recorder was active. Lennox would be the one memorizing any significant actions, as Robin was facing the wrong direction. She knew he was paying attention.

"Tapper to Eagle Eyes. We're in first nest. Over."

To be safe, Takin and Williams would have to be through all eight rooms in one hour, in case the generals ate quickly. That was an awful short window of time for two men.

"Do you remember how we met?" she asked Lennox.

"How could I forget?" he responded. "I stopped suddenly at a light and you hit my bumper."

Robin giggled. "We spent an entire *hour* bickering about whose fault it was before we called our insurance companies. Can you believe it?"

"One hour was all it took for love at first sight," Lennox said.

"Roger," Takin said over the comm.

Robin had one arm hooked around Lennox as they walked out of the restaurant. The food had been superb, and she couldn't wait to get back to the hotel room and find out what Takin and Williams had found.

And change out of these horrible *clothes!*

Lennox hailed a taxi, which braked to a halt next to the curb. He held open the back door for her, then climbed in after. As Robin buckled her seatbelt, Lennox gave the driver their destination to a clothing store about a block away from their hotel. Due to traffic, the trip took nearly three times longer than it should. Lennox paid the driver before he and Robin departed.

To maintain cover, they entered the store and separated momentarily to browse. It was a ritzy boutique, loaded with the latest in local fashion and organized by large placards proudly broadcasting each product line. Apparently, modern beauty included extravagant lace filigree along every possible seam. Robin fingered the fragile fabric in utter distaste. Merely falling on a knee would completely ruin a pair of pants. She ached for a good surplus shop.

Finally, they exited the store and walked to the hotel, taking the elevator up to the fifth floor. Lennox swiped the card key through the sensor lock, and a light on the lock flashed green. Robin walked through first.

Williams and Takin were already in the room, sitting on one of the beds. Takin had his laptop open with a loading bar on the screen.

"What'd you get?" Lennox asked, his staged husband demeanor evaporating. All business once again, he propped himself on the back of Takin chair so he could see the screen.

"I downloaded all the drives I could find," Takin said. "My decryption software is working on them now. In about an hour, we should be able to access the data. If there's any dirt, we've got it."

"Good job," Lennox said, solidly patting the other man's shoulder a few times as added commendation.

"How was your beguiling afternoon banquet?" Williams asked, smirking.

Robin pulled out the listening device. "Depends on what we find out from this."

Lennox looked out the window. "Dinosaurians, return to temporary HQ."

The incinerator just wasn't good enough. Nicole wanted it to *burn*. She glared at the envelope as if her eyes could suddenly shoot lasers and send the thing bursting into flames. She toyed taking it to Scope and let her have *her* way, but decided that the lengthy trip wasn't quite worth it. The letter wasn't even opened yet. Deciding not to, she tossed it in the waste container. The flash of light from under the lid signified incineration.

Compeer growled lowly from his place on his doggy bed, the hair on his back bristling. Nicole relaxed her glare and murmured softly to her pet, trying to calm him down. He apparently still sensed her anger, and glared at the waste container. Nicole then tried to calm herself down, knowing that he was picking up her emotions and would be a high-strung, aggressive mess if she didn't direct both of them out of it.

"It's okay, boy," she said.

It took several minutes before she was in better mood, and Compeer was relaxing. Nicole leaned on her desk, rubbing her temple with two fingers.

Ding!

Her gaze snapped to her computer. Above her mail icon was the beacon for "new mail." Nicole clicked on it, causing her inbox to fill the screen. She moved the mouse to hover over the only unread email.

"'Freedom's at Risk,'" she read the subject bar aloud. Frowning, she clicked to open the email.

Suddenly, an antivirus warning appeared. Nicole's eyes widened, reading the message. She immediately panicked and held down the power button. After a few excruciatingly long seconds, the screen went black.

Is this a virus? Nicole fumed.

A new message flashed from the supposedly shut down computer, causing Nicole to jump. *Stop Interfering.* A second later, it vanished. The tower's fans whirred to life, then abruptly stopped. As she went to yank the plug from the wall, she turned back to see tiny wisps of blue smoke seeping through the vents.

Compeer whined, burying his nose.

"I know it smells bad, boy," Nicole said, picking up the phone and dialing. She held it to her ear.

"Hello?"

"Pete? Could you come over to the Reserve?"

"I hope that you realize I'm going hungry," Pete said as he walked through the office door. "I'm missing my lunch break for you."

Nicole looked up from where she held her head in her

hands. "Pete! Thank goodness you're here." Compeer looked equally glad to see him, bounding from his bed and jumping up to lick Pete's face.

Pete tried to keep the pink tongue at arm's length. "Where's the tiny dinosaur?" he asked as Compeer settled for sniffing his shoes.

"Back at my apartment," Nicole said. "Now, can you find out what happened?"

Pete knelt to look at the computer tower, unscrewing the fasteners. "You said that you opened an email and it gave you a virus that burned out your computer?"

"Yeah," Nicole said.

Pete removed the plastic covering of the PC and used a flashlight to look at the internals. "Nikki, I think you just earned the award for 'Computer Most Melted.' Didn't your fans run at all?"

"Well, yes. But they almost immediately stopped. A moment later, I smelled smoke." Nicole tried to peer past his head. "Is it that bad?"

"The virus forced your computer to run overclocked beyond 100% and block the fans from activating. The generated heat caused the tower to essentially commit suicide. With this much damage, you've lost just about everything on your personal computer."

"Define 'just about everything.'"

"I'll have to check if the virus payload wiped the disk, but everything else is toast." He pulled out a scanner. "Hope you've backed up recently." He looked up. "Where's your server rack?"

Nicole guided him to the server closet at the back of the building. The door was locked, so she fished the key from her chain. Upon the lock disengaging, she pushed the door open. "In here," she said, voice raised to float over the loud humming from the server cooling fans.

Pete moved over to a monitor and tapped the slide out keyboard. When the lock screen came up, he stepped aside to allow Nicole to type in the password. Once inside the system, Pete brought up the mail admin console, then scrolled through the recent compilations of message tracking results in different color: black for blacklisted, red and pink for viruses and spam, green for whitelisted, and white for general.

Leaning over her friend's shoulder, Nicole quickly scanned the display. "There," she said. "That's it."

"Huh. It's green." Pete exported the plagued email to another one of his devices, next blacklisting the sender address. Then, he completely wiped the email from the server. Returning to his handheld device, he pressed an icon, and the screen began to flash.

"What are you doing?" Nicole asked, curiously peering over his shoulder.

"It's figuring out what kind of virus killed your computer." The device stopped flashing, and Pete tapped the screen. He whistled. "A *Clades* virus. Nasty buggers.

"This is a black market virus based on the turn of the century cyber attack between the USA and Israel, against the Iranian centrifuges. The virus leaked to the general public and snatched by the black market. Revenge served cold for two years' salary. Now, it looks like we might be able to identify your assailant from the sender path. . . I'm going to have to do that at home. Too tedious for just fifteen minutes left of lunch break."

"Could you figure out who did it by tonight?" Nicole asked hopefully.

"I'll try," Pete said.

"You're a peach, Pete," Nicole added with a grin.

Pete returned the grin, but it looked a little strained. "Be careful, Nikki. You're being targeted with a nasty virus with a personal message. It. . . it's bad. Real bad. Be careful."

He left.

CHAPTER SEVEN

Takin had three flash drives loaded with everything he and Williams could find; all merely marginally useful. It simply did not make sense to Robin that generals would lack pertinent information, but that is what Takin's and Williams' clandestine raid produced. Not even the recording from the M was relevant.

This whole mission was a complete waste of time and resources.

"Here's what we're going to do," Lennox stated. "We shall send a Pterodactylus out, and Takin will record all microphone input. The Pterodactylus will hide outside the generals' rooms and eavesdrop for a time. If the generals did not leave anything in the rooms and did not speak anything at the meal, then, perhaps, the true meeting is in one of their hotel rooms."

"Rush shall go," Assail declared, bobbing his head toward the brown Pterodactylus. "As the smallest of us all, he will be the least likely to be seen."

"Agreed," Lennox said. "Rush should move before it gets too late. Williams, open the balcony door."

Before the drawn blackout curtains could be moved aside, all the lights in the room were cut. Robin slid off the edge of her bed onto the floor, concealing herself behind the mattress. Williams shoved the curtains aside, causing their anchors to rattle across the rod. The balcony was a joke, just a railing outside a door-shaped opening in the exterior wall. But it was better than inoperable windows.

Rush waited for Williams to crack the door open before launching from his spot on the back of a chair. Flipping sideways through the gap, he briefly made contact with the wrought-iron railing to leap again. He flapped hard, pushing his wings to the limit as he soared over the city toward the M.

He reached the tower and circled it, looking through the windows. One of the generals' rooms on the topmost floors had its lights on. Rush noted that the curtains were drawn. He alighted on the balcony railing, staying in the darkness. Scuttling on all fours, he inched close to the large glass doors. Privacy curtains were drawn, but he could see shadows. After some scuttling, he found a minuscule crack in the shades, allowing him to peer inside. *Pay dirt,* he thought, smirking. All eight generals milled in the hotel room, looking as if they had just arrived and were getting ready for something. The room was lavish with amenities and luxury, illuminated with lamps strategically located for the best homey feeling. The rich hues of the room glowed with warmth.

"Eagle Eyes to Rush. Your headset microphone will not penetrate the window glass. Tapper is amplifying it. Be ready; things will be very loud in a moment. Over."

The resulting sensitivity to sound made him cringe violently, shoulders rising in reflexive self-defense. The cars suddenly sounded so loud; blaring horns, the screech of tires, the guttural revving of supped-up engines. The light wind, formerly barely audible, was now a howling gale, and he felt dizzy as his body instinctively tried to combat the perceived winds supposedly ripping him from his perch.

But there were voices!

After a cold hour outside on the balcony, the generals finally concluded, and retired for the night. Rush scuttled toward the railing's edge, prepared to fly, but unsure whether the last general, the room's occupant, would have anything further to reveal. It was hard keeping track of the man through the sliver in the curtains. Thus, Rush was greatly shocked when the fabric snapped open. Rush toppled from the balcony and into open space just before the door lock came undone. As his headset was still amplified, he knew that the general, leaning out on the balcony to appreciate the night, had missed Rush's abrupt exit and was not suspicious at all.

Feeling triumphant, Rush glided back to the hotel room.

Robin frowned.

Back on the submersible Manta Transport, the team journeyed swiftly back to the States; in particular, New York

City. While Robin had heard many good things about the largest North American city in her youth, the city had been one of the first that had surrendered to Unison Order occupation, and thus escaped much of the devastation that flattened most of the rest of the northeast coast.

What a shame, Robin thought. *But their surrender made sense. The officials didn't want iconic landmarks destroyed. That, and the New Yorkers, when faced with tragedy, don't stock up on food or ammo, but instead charge their personal devices!*

Leaning her head against the hull, Robin looked around the cabin. Aside from the rhythmic thrumming of the engines, all was quiet. Williams, Lennox, and the reptilians were sleeping, all slumped over in their chairs like rag dolls. Takin was in a corner seat, his ever-present laptop open on his lap.

With nothing else to do, she watched Takin. Occasionally, he would scowl, then become expressionless, grimace, or momentarily smirk. Only once did he completely freeze, his eyes intently reading his screen before resuming pounding the keyboard with double the previous fervor. Suddenly, Takin's face drained in color. He typed faster than Robin had ever thought humanly possible. A moment later, Takin slammed the lid shut. Suddenly clammy hair appeared plastered to his brow as he stared down at his computer.

Robin jumped in her seat from the sudden sound. "Takin, what happened?"

Takin was still pale and slightly shaking. "I've been traced," he said slowly, as if he couldn't believe it.

Astounded, Robin just stared. Who could've bested the most talented hacker she had ever met?

Nicole sat on her bed in her apartment, resting her head in her hands, trying to logically sift through all that was happening. Half the entire Reserve dataset had been sent to an unknown recipient. Either someone had been in the Reserve after-hours and hacked her computer through that self-destructing object, or she had been remotely sabotaged. She had to completely re-encrypt the Reserve's app stack with new public and private authentication credentials, and distribute new IDs to the Reserve staff.

Someone doesn't like me, she thought, *or the involvement I have with the dinosaurs. Do they know that I assisted the Black-Ops team? Possibly.*

The door to her bedroom creaked. Nicole looked up to see Aim poking her head in. The Hesperonychus' eyes were wide open in the dimness of the room, immediately tracking to Nicole.

"Are you okay?" Aim asked, squeezing her body through the crack and fully entering. "You smell stressed, and I don't like it when people smell stressed because it makes me feel stressed. Then *everyone* is stressed, then everyone gets mad and the day gets worse from there."

Nicole took a deep breath. "I'll be fine, Aim. Just working through a few things."

Aim made a mighty leap onto the sheets, but fell slightly short. Nicole cringed as the Hesperonychus' little claws clambered at the comforter, listening to the patterned threads rip. Flinging out an arm, Aim managed to haul herself up at last. Exhausted from the effort, she rested her head on Nicole's lap. "Everything works out in the end."

Not for my comforter. "Yes, but that can go two ways; for whom does the "end" favor? The Unison Order outnumbers us, out-techs us, and often out-thinks us. The "end" favors them. Something miraculous has to happen." With a sigh, Nicole patted the side of Aim's head, feeling the dinosaur's jaw flex slowly in a yawn. She chuckled as Aim moved to hide the tired gesture in her abdomen.

Compeer suddenly burst into the room, galloping to the bed. Nicole jumped as he wrapped his maw around Aim's torso and threw the diminutive Hesperonychus across the room, where she thudded against the wall, then slid to the floor, still.

"Compeer!" Nicole exclaimed, rushing to check on Aim. "Bad dog! What on Earth spurred you to do that?"

Whining and growling frantically, Compeer bit her pants and jerked her to a halt.

"Release!" Nicole ordered, employing the "I am Alpha" technique to force her dog to let go. With a muffled bark, Compeer fell away and rolled onto his backside. His deep brown eyes gazed up at her pleadingly, as if he was begging her to understand.

"What do you have against Aim?" Nicole asked as she bent over the dinosaur. Aim was still breathing, but her eyes were closed and she was weakly moving. A keen escaped the dinosaur's slack jaw, eyes cracked in distress. Nicole slid her hands beneath the Hesperonychus and carried her to the bed.

Rolling onto his feet, Compeer whined plaintively, watching as his owner gently rested Aim on one of the decorative headboard pillows. Aim curled into a ball, hiding her head beneath her tail, and her fringe flopped limply over the curve of her neck.

"No touch," Nicole said to him. "Do you get that, Compeer? No touching Aim."

Compeer lowered his head in submission, but glared past her at the bed.

A knock sounded on the front door.

"Stay in here," Nicole told her dog, exiting the room and closing the door most of the way shut behind her. Going to the front door, she peered through the peephole. Pete's distorted face met her gaze. She unlatched the numerous locks and swung open the door.

"Hey, Pete," Nicole said. "Did you get anything?"

"Did I!" Pete said, almost dancing on his way into her apartment. "My dear Nicole, I have here in my hand the sender of that virus-laden email." He reached into a pocket and pulled out a small flash drive. "That sucker had packet redirects and multiple firewalls like nothing I've ever seen before. But did that stop me? No, it did *not*! I managed to worm past through the relayed workstations and track the bounces off of servers and satellites–"

"Yes, yes," Nicole said, holding up her hands. "Cut to the chase. Who did it?"

Pete's cheery demeanor dampened, and he stopped bouncing on the balls of his feet. "Well. . ."

"Pete. . ." She suddenly had a very, very bad feeling.

He swallowed. "You're not going to like this, Nikki."

Compeer growled, pacing back and forth across the bedroom, claws clicking against the wood flooring. Every so often, he would glance up at the door, hearing his owner's and someone else's voices beyond. His owner's was becoming more stressed by the second, and he wanted nothing more than to be by her side. Something was threatening her!

The door hadn't been closed. He could push it open far enough to squeeze through. To attack whatever dared to hurt his human.

But he had been given orders to stay. And he was a *good* dog.

Not only that, but there was an intruder he needed to keep an eye on at all times. That thing on his owner's pillow should not be in the home! Why couldn't his owner understand that it absolutely had to go? A reflexive snarl curdled out his mouth, gurgling wetly in the depths of his chest.

He faced the door, where the voices had fallen silent. Something was wrong out there. But something was wrong *in here*. He didn't know what to do. His owner was strong, she could hold off anything long enough for him to come and rescue her, he supposed. So, if he stayed, he could not only be a *good dog* by obeying and not go until she called for help, but also make sure that the *thing* couldn't do anything, either!

He wagged his tail. That was a good plan.

Thump. Compeer whirled around to see the *thing* standing on the floor by the bed, rising from the hunch it had taken upon landing. Hackles rising, he lowered his head and growled threateningly. The intruder barely gave him a passing glance as it smoothly walked toward the exit, as if he did not exist.

He would not let it pass! Whipping out a paw to swat it, he was startled when it ducked under his swinging leg. Taken off balance, he rushed to recover, throwing his weight against the momentum to tackle it instead, but the *thing* opened its mouth and started screeching a *horrible, truly awful* noise that caused his ears to scream.

Howling in pain, he batted at his ears, squeezing his eyes shut as if that would allay the onslaught. Can't his owner hear this? Why wasn't she investigating? This *thing* was bad, and if she could see, then she would get rid of it and all would be well again. When he could open his eyes, the intruder had just passed through the doorway.

Growling, he raced after it. It could *not* be left alone.

CHAPTER EIGHT

Robin flattened herself to the rooftop, her eye intently positioned to the scope of her rifle. She had an excellent view of the fruit of Rush's eavesdropping; a small, hole-in-the-wall cafe. It was drastically dwarfed by the skyscrapers around it, and the only time it received a glimmer of sunshine upon its classical stonework facade was in the middle morning, as it faced somewhat southeast.

It looked like a quaint little place, with a brick interior, dark hardwood flooring, wooden furniture, and abstract artwork on the eggshell white walls. Although it was not yet lunch, the majority of the tables were occupied, suggesting that the cafe was a rather popular place. If she hadn't been on a mission, Robin might've stopped in for a bite.

She glanced at her timepiece. "Arcee to Roost. Checking in." She listened while the others also checked in.

Through the scope, she saw Shriek darting between pedestrians, keeping close to the walls where few desired to stroll. Amazingly, the people were completely oblivious to the tiny dinosaur maneuvering around their feet. *Not that surprising,* Robin thought. *Not many people look down past their devices.*

Rush shifted his wings, adjusting his balance on the thin electrical wire from which he dangled upside down. His neck curled sinuously so his head was upright. From his vantage point, he could see the cafe across the street, partially blocked by the walls of his alley. He could also spot Takin at the back of the cafe, in a tiny corner booth. The hacker was the only team member in civilian attire. Lennox and Williams were on alternate rooftops, Shriek had found a tiny shadowed crevice between two storefronts across the street, and Assail and Gale were their aerial reconnaissance.

It was all a waiting game. They could bide time before the generals would arrive. Rush occupied himself by swinging back and forth. When that became boring, he mocked the pigeons he saw pecking along the alleyway.

He jumped when he heard *"Rush!"* over the comm. Guiltily, he glanced up at the sky, just catching the visage of Assail flying out of sight. Rush ceased mimicking the pigeons and resumed watching the cafe.

Moments after the clock deemed lunch break to be upon the workforce, people began flooding the streets, packing the sidewalks. Depending on perceived time pressures, there was a higher degree of impatience, with a few people shoving their way through any conceivable gap in their rush. One distinctly unfortunate soul found himself brusquely jostled into a parked vehicle at the curb. Rush found it extremely difficult to track a single person amongst the sea. The generals would be harder to spot.

Ignoring the sidewalk chaos, Robin peered through her scope. The cafe had also been flooded with people, packing in the remaining tables and the counter seating. The employees bustled, churning out plates and takeout bags with remarkable efficiency.

"Crow to Roost. Anyone see the targets yet? Over."

"Shriek to Roost. Negative. Have direct line to door. When they come through, I'll see them. Over."

"BOLO, Shriek," Lennox said. *"Over."*

Robin's stomach churned. She moaned, resisting the urge to curl in on herself. Not three seconds passed before she felt fine again. No stomach ache came and went *that* fast. This was the next entry in a distinctly disturbing pattern she had noticed with herself. Something terrible was about to happen.

She took another look inside the cafe. At first, she saw nothing out of the ordinary. Businessmen and women, dressed in varying degrees of formality, either ate or awaited their order. There were a few small family groups, visibly regretting their choice at heading out to dine at such an inopportune time of day. Although, she did spot a few people who possessed the astonishing talent to remain cool in such an environment. She didn't see the generals. She ended up passing over Takin's corner booth, then did a double take.

What's he doing? she wondered.

Takin was sliding his laptop into his backpack, with the snack he had purchased as a cover shoved to the wayside on the table. He was supposed to hack into the cafe's security cameras and watch them for the generals! She watched as he pulled something tiny out of his backpack. Zooming in to see what it was produced nothing; he had fisted his hand around the object. He reached under the table and pressed whatever it was to the underside. He slid out of the seat, slung his pack over one shoulder, and strode out casually.

Robin frowned. "Arcee to Tapper. Where are you going? Over."

Catching the transmission, Rush sought Takin's head, but the man was already lost in the maelstrom.

"Eagle Eyes to Roost. Does anyone see Tapper? He's left his post. Over."

Rush glanced at the booth Takin had abandoned. A couple sat down just before a harried family of seven reached the table, and eyed the abandoned food with distaste but did nothing about it. Just as the couple settled in with their meals, the man lost grip on his phone. The phone tumbled off the edge of the table, bouncing from the bench seat and onto the floor. The man slid sideways to fetch his device, but unexpectedly lingered under the table. The woman looked puzzled and appeared to question him.

Robin's gut tightened again.

With the man beckoning, the woman bent down to look under the table, then she pulled something out. She handed it to the man, who had trouble unsticking it from her palm. Robin focused the scope's magnification further.

Rush tilted his head, examining the flat object with impeccable eyesight. It was a nondescript, matte grey disc. "Rush to Arcee. What's the man in the corner booth holding? Over."

Robin's eyes widened. "Shriek! Evac! *Evac!*"

The Bambiraptor immediately bolted from hiding, startling a few pedestrians who nearly tripped in their reflex to avoid treading on her. She vanished in the crowds, heading down the street.

Rush watched the couple stare at the object. Suddenly panicky, the man quickly sat it down and moved to stand, grabbing the woman's hand. Before they could make it out of the booth, a blinding light filled the cafe and its front sidewalk area. Rush shielded his eyes with his wings.

When he looked again, it was a scene he would never forget, eternally burned into his brain. Car alarms wailed, lights flashing in distress. Caught pedestrians were writhing in agony on the ground, clutching their horrific wounds. People stampeded over one another in blind panic, spurred by the ravenous bites of self-preservation instincts. Others were drawn in by dazed curiosity. Several were already taking feverish videos of the maimed, shouting narration; Only a few appeared to be calling the local authorities or rushing forward to actually help the victims.

"Crow to Shriek. Come in! Over!"

". . .Shriek to Roost. I'm alright. Rendezvousing with Rush's position. Over."

Robin felt only marginally relieved that the Bambiraptor had made it to safety in time, too stunned by the event to muster much emotion. She could hardly believe it; Takin. . . he had just performed a standard Unison Order initiation procedure. She stared at the aftermath, unable to look away. Her scope was no longer a boon, amplifying the cloud of settling dust that had replaced the cafe and everything nearby. She had seen reports, photographs and videos, but *this. . .*

Rush was hyperventilating, his eyes wide. *I can't I can't I can't I can't. . .* His wing-claws clenched and unclenched around the wire, slipping in degrees. When grip was lost, he startled and wrapped around his perch as if a great wind would come and sweep him into the beyond.

Sirens sounded in the distance.

"Eagle Eyes to Roost! Crow, Arcee, get down there and triage!"

"On my way!" Robin replied quickly, snapping her rifle back into its holster. She wheeled around and sprinted for the access door on the roof. She took the stairs three at a time, landing on each tread with a loud *thud* until she reached the ground floor.

As she pushed through the gathering throng of panicked onlookers, she could hear Lennox calling orders. The pterosaurs were to aerially scout for the critically wounded while Shriek stayed out of sight. Williams was somewhere nearby.

Breaking through the last of the crowd, Robin paused at the horrific scene before her. Proximity only made it worse. Despite the wails of agony and despair, it was too clean, a contradistinction to the tragedy that had just befallen. There was nothing to be done for those who had been inches too close, except hold their hands (if they still had any). She gathered her composure and sprinted for the nearest wounded.

Nicole, stunned, stared at the name and picture Pete was showing her. Her thoughts had ground to a halt, save for a mental, agonized bellow. White noise. Insensible and drowning out everything around her.

Pete swallowed. "Nikki, I know this is a bit of a shock–"

"A bit?" Nicole repeated. "A *bit*? You have *no idea* what a horrible thing I've done! This man is Nelson Takin, one of the members of the Black-Ops team with which I sent *four dinosaurians*!" She ran a hand through her hair in a panic.

"Oh," Pete said in a weak voice, glancing at the picture in a new light. He cleared his throat. "Nikki, you couldn't have known."

She began to pace, gradually picking up speed. "I need to send a request for their immediate return. God, please, let nothing have happened to them," she prayed.

"I'm sure they're fine," Pete said placatingly, holding up his hands in a gesture of peace. "He wouldn't have dared harm them, lest he betray himself. I'll send this trace data to their headquarters, and they'll send operatives to apprehend Takin. Your four soldiers *will be fine*."

Nicole ran a hand down her face, a motion that was sadly becoming a habit. "I can't tell Freedom. I can't."

"Why not?"

"You're actually asking? Freedom will completely

redefine the word 'irate.'" She groaned, throwing her head back. "But I still need to go to the Reserve. The suits will go there first if anything goes wrong."

Nicole's phone rang, blaring out the theme of a television show she watched when she was a teenager, and shattering the tense atmosphere. She checked the ID number, then answered. "Nicole Nike speaking."

"Hey, boss lady! Got some herpetologists in the lobby wantin' to meet ya. But they don't have an appointment."

Nicole sighed, struggling to change gears from frantic panic. "Have you set one up for them?"

"Well, no. All appointments are scheduled only under your approval."

I don't have time *for this,* Nicole thought, subconsciously bringing her hand down her face again. She quickly checked her calendar. "Tell them to come back in two days at 3:00 PM."

With the victims triaged and transported, Lennox pulled out his team as discretely as possible. Once at the hotel, he attempted to contact the base for retrieval. Williams had changed their comms' contact and frequency codes. Robin was holding Shriek, who was shell-shocked from her near-death experience. Robin kept seeing the poor faces of that couple when they'd realized that they were holding a bomb. They had been so *young*, their lives hardly started. . .

"Eagle Eyes to Mother Bird," Lennox called, his voice

strained. "Come in, Mother Bird!" He paused, letting out a relieved sigh, then identified himself with a confidential signature. "Yes, we *know*. No, we can't locate him. Roger, roger that."

"What'd they say?" Williams asked.

"We're evacuating," Lennox replied. "HQ's sending a taxi with the license plate 'U Heart NYC.' We leave in two mikes."

Robin moved to put Shriek down so she could get ready. However, the Bambiraptor screeched and clawed at Robin's clothes in a swivet. Seeing no other option, Robin clutched Shriek closer, holding the Bambiraptor's head to her chest, over her heart. She murmured comforting nonsense, and the dinosaur calmed.

"I'll stow your belongings for you, Conners," Williams said.

"Thanks," she replied, nodding gratefully.

After a bit, Shriek started to look around and absorb her surroundings. Robin saw this and began stroking her head, flattening the fringe on her forehead again and again. Soft whimpers mixed with growls fell from Shriek's mouth in such a way it suggested language. Robin glanced at the pterosaurs, wondering if any would translate for her.

Assail caught her eye. He paused a moment before shaking his head. Robin nodded, then whispered encouragement to Shriek, to let it out, that things will be fine, and so on.

At the one minute mark, Williams stood and opened the door to the motel room to let the pterosaurs outside. Much to Shriek's disappointment, Robin had to stow her in Williams' pack, ensuring that the oxygen tank was prepped. The room was throughly wiped down to remove all traces of their presence, every inch sprayed with an agent to dissolve any DNA samples. "Let's go." Lennox led the way to the curb, where an SUV taxi was waiting. Robin checked the license. "Legit," she uttered, and they piled in.

"Where you going today?" the driver asked in a stereotypical New York accent.

"Nowhere in particular," Lennox replied. "Our grandmother's sister's niece's daughter's cousin's aunt's son's parakeet died, and we're all very depressed. Just drive."

"Yes, sir," the driver responded. "So sad. On we go." It was the correct code, and the team relaxed.

HQ was, quite literally, under the Unison Order's very nose. On the outskirts of downtown New York City, it was a nondescript building, very utilitarian, very boring, and definitely not something the-most-desperate-of-tour-guides would point out. According to the books, the building was the headquarters for a small furniture company specializing in shelving and dressers.

Robin hadn't been to the New York HQ often, but she knew that the "company" was a front. For every camera she could spot, there were more that were hidden. The fence, rimmed with razor wire, was electrified with enough current to kill. Once the taxi driver passed through the gate, he drove the car over the lowered spike strips, steel rods, and hydraulic ramp to hoist a car's aft.

The driver dropped them off at the door. The pterosaurs flew down and alighted on their partner's shoulder. All of the humans had to go through a meticulous retina and handprint scan before they could gain entrance.

"Lennox," an agent said, greeting them inside.

"Yes, sir," Lennox responded.

"Come with me to debriefing."

Rush squirmed on Robin's shoulder, the two exchanging concerned, tired looks.

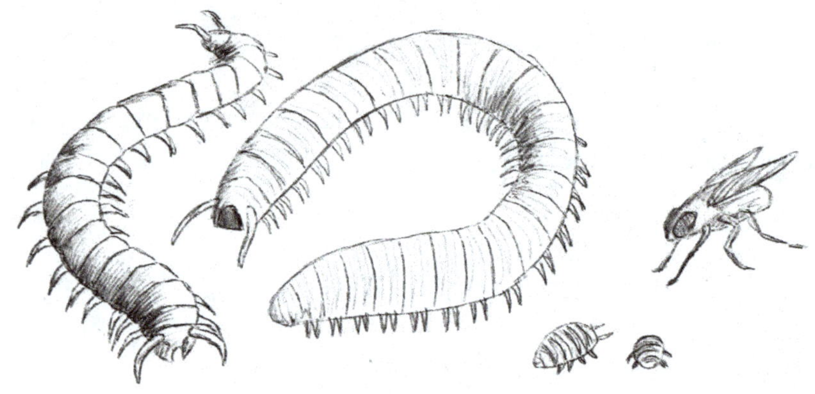

CHAPTER NINE

Wearily stumbling her way across the sidewalk, Nicole exerted more energy than it normally required to heft her bags further up her shoulder. Her eyelids felt laden with weights. All she could think of was the wondrous moment when she could collapse in bed and pretend, just for a few hours, that things were okay.

And feed the animals.

Right. She had to make sure Compeer and Aim wouldn't starve. Compeer's dish was simple enough, but Aim had foregone breakfast as Nicole had had nothing on hand for insectivores; Aim typically roamed the forest around the Reserve's office building for her food.

With a drawn out sigh, Nicole backtracked a block and entered the subway system. She checked the kiosk map in order to find the nearest pet store supplier. Finding the correct track, she collapsed on a bench to wait for the train. She had almost fallen asleep when she was jolted by the screech of brakes. After trudging onto the train, Nicole fell into the first empty seat.

The train doors closed, and Nicole leaned sharply as the train surged forward. Nicole wished that the commute wouldn't be as rapid; there wouldn't be any time to catch a few winks. To resist the temptation, Nicole forced her neck to lengthen to hold her head up.

"Long day?"

It took a few seconds for Nicole to register that someone had spoken to her. Lacking the energy to say anything else, she emitted a questioning grunt.

The young, pretty woman smiled sympathetically. "Long day?"

Nicole nodded.

The woman smiled a bit more. "You're not alone. Work sucks the energy from you, you know?"

"Don't I know it," Nicole pained in agreement. "But it matters."

Waving farewell, Nicole exited the train at her stop and headed aboveground to the shopping district. The store wasn't hard to find, with its garish neon sign suspended overhead. Passing through the automatic doors, Nicole was hit with a wide array of sensations. Somewhere off to her right sounded like birds, with perhaps a few loudmouth parrots. Up ahead were dogs and cats. Nicole could smell the overwhelming aroma of litters and feeds, with a hint of fish tank water.

"Welcome to Pet Haven!" an employee said cheerfully. Nicole was envious of her exuberance. If only *her* job was as jovial. . . "Can I help you find anything?"

"Yes," Nicole said, shifting her bags. "Do you have anything for insectivores?"

"Like iguanas?"

"Sort of."

The employee nodded. "Sure thing! Right this way." Nicole followed her, weaving through the aisles until they reached the live food tanks. The employee gestured to a row of dimly lit glass containers. "Here we are! We've got crickets, cockroaches, pill bugs, millipedes, centipedes, and, this one's new, house flies!"

Nicole grimaced at the thought of Aim missing even one of those creatures. She'd be sure to have a heart attack if she woke up and found a centipede on her face! *Why, oh why, couldn't Hesperonychus be carnivorous? Or even herbivorous? Why'd it have to be an insectivore?*

Realizing that the employee was waiting for an answer, Nicole selected the least of the repellants; the millipedes. Those things were huge. They'd have a hard time finding anywhere to permanently avoid Aim. The employee took a small plastic container with minuscule holes, and tonged two dozen millipedes inside.

"Twenty-four millipedes enough?" the employee inquired.

Nicole, having diverted her attention to the lazy beta fish nearby, mentally swung back to focus. "Yes, that should be enough." Taking the container, she added, "And thank you for your time."

"No problem at all," the employee said, as her gaze darted toward the rodent aisle. "Hey, you! Yeah, you! No taking out the hamsters without supervision!"

Chuckling to herself, Nicole walked to the counter and paid, then headed back outside to make the trip back down into the subway.

At the bottom of the transit stairwell, she pulled out her wallet, then her all-use ID card, and pressed it to the transportation kiosk's sensor. After a second the light went green. The small screen just below her eye level came to life, showing a commercial for pet supplies. Nicole glared at the screen, then at the all-use card, finally shoving the card back into her wallet with more force than necessary.

That didn't take long, she thought as she passed through the doorway.

Heading down an escalator, Nicole glanced behind her. Years back, the government had pushed for all Americans to be implanted with an RFID for ID and commerce. A debate raged, with talking heads arguing that everything they did would be tagged, recorded, and end up as a *complete* violation of privacy.

Unfortunately, there was this little pesky old 1791 document that the government tended to overlook a lot. The consumer agencies and the government assured that the RFID card would make their lives easier, simpler, and fair for all. *Yeah, sure. New pet, only been yours for five minutes? No problem! After data mining, here's all the things we think you now need!*

She plopped herself down in an available seat on the disembark platform. "There are five handy pet parks near your location," she muttered, echoing the commercial from the route map kiosk. "Be sure to bring any accessories required to keep our streets clean and fresh." *Clean and fresh, my foot.*

She was relieved that the RFID program had been discontinued thanks to public pressure, though the mobile cards hadn't escaped the implant.

While she waited for her train, the large TV on the wall caught her attention. Usually, she didn't pay attention to it because all it played were obnoxious, blaring commercials with the occasional interlude of the station's schedules. She blearily gazed at it for a long moment before the news broadcast on the screen finally seeped some meaning into her exhausted mind; There had been another Unison Order attack, this time at a cafe in New York City. There were 29 reported dead, more than a dozen more suffering from severe injuries. It had been one of the Unison Order's nastier incineration explosives that had done the deed, most popular with those pledging allegiance to the Order.

Nicole tore her eyes from the screen showing the aftermath. *How is spreading mass terror supposed to depict the regime of "peace" to which the UO testifies?* she wondered for the umpteenth time. It just didn't make any sense. According to their propaganda, they were all about uniting entire nations under one flag, claiming peace for all who fell in lockstep. Obey the rules and universal doctrines, and one could easily live without much opposition. Warning signs of the dark side had been dismissed as being random outbursts of "civil" and "workplace" violence.

Awareness, it seemed, often was a bit too late.

As if others could sense Nicole's mind grappling with puzzle pieces, no one spoke to her at all on the train. After the train ride was the weary trek back above ground, and her four block walk back to her apartment building. There, the glass elevator welcomed her drowsy frame. Reaching her floor, Nicole walked out of the elevator and went through the routine of unlocking all of the bolts and locks on her door.

Nicole flung her bags onto the nearest surface and went to the kitchen. Despite her body's insistence on rest, her animals came first. As she bent down to grab Compeer's bag of kibble, she expected his muzzle to intrude at any second.

But it didn't. Nicole straightened and looked around. Compeer and Aim were nowhere to be seen. They hadn't eaten since morning! They should be swarming her, demanding food. With tiredness now replaced by suspicion and worry, Nicole travelled around her apartment, looking for her animals.

The den, kitchen, and bathroom were empty. Nicole entered the last room, her bedroom, and peered around. Her attention was immediately drawn to the limp tawny heap on the rug.

"Compeer!" she cried, rushing to her dog and kneeling down. He appeared to be simply sleeping on his side, but his legs were arranged strangely, and no neck should be bent back that far.

Nicole frantically checked to see if he was breathing. After a few seconds of anxious observation, she saw his abdomen slowly rise and fall. Nicole sighed in relief, and, unsure at that point whether to wake him or not, resumed her search for Aim.

Fifteen minutes later, Nicole was certain that the Hesperonychus was not in the apartment. Back in the kitchen,

Nicole leaned against the counter, elbow nudging the long-forgotten container of millipedes. Biting her lip, she thought hard about what could have happened.

Still weighing the situation, Nicole had the distinct feeling that something was off in the room. Something had changed that she hadn't quite noticed before. A quick look around answered the question; there was a piece of paper stuck on her fridge door. Nicole never put anything besides magnets on the fridge.

Nicole snatched the paper and unfolded it. The writing was neat, nondescript, and typed. She read silently to herself, mouthing the words;

Miss Nicole Nike,

You may have noticed by now that your dog is unconscious and your dinosaur is missing. We chloroformed the former and have the latter in our possession. If you want your dinosaur back, follow these directions carefully. Its life remains in the balance.

1. You're halfway through calling the police. Cancel and do not attempt contact again.

Nicole stared at the note, then at her phone. She grimaced and obeyed, putting her phone back into her pocket.

2. Follow the clues we give you. If you manage to make it to the end, your dinosaur will be waiting.

You can find the first clue at 12815 Grande Luna Street.

Taking a deep breath, Nicole went to the den where her

personal laptop sat on the futon, plugged in and lid closed. She logged in, then brought up an internet map of the city. Entering the street, she plotted the distance and saw that it was only a few blocks away.

Nicole didn't rush up and leave. No, she had to think. Why would someone kidnap a dinosaur from her apartment? She hadn't finished her translation book, and there was no indication that anyone had accessed the unfinished first draft off her computer. She had no alert from her firewall software, her ports were disabled and her disk encryption was intact. If they had taken Aim for information, it was a vain endeavor, as Aim couldn't speak or understand English.

They must have some ulterior goal, she thought. *But what is it?*

Maybe they were stalling her to keep her occupied and diverted from being at the Reserve or the R&D company.

That could be it. And it's working.

She switched programs. Typing quickly, she sent a secure email to Pete, telling him of the note, and her intention to follow the clues.

A soft whimper had her head snapping to the doorway. Compeer slowly wobbled into view. When he saw Nicole, he listed over to her and collapsed at her feet, resting his head on one shoe. His whimpers never ceased; Instead, they grew stronger, as if he was pleading for forgiveness.

"Oh, Compeer," Nicole said, reaching down to scratch him. "You did nothing wrong. You protected the house as long as you could, I'm sure you did."

Compeer whined, ears falling more limp than before, his tail lifeless. He made eye contact and whimpered a few more times.

"I know you're trying to tell me something," Nicole murmured. "But I can't speak dog. If only I could."

She petted him for a bit longer before standing and retrieving her purse. Compeer slogged after her, slowly regaining his strength. Nicole placed the note in her bag, printed the directions to the clue, and was about to depart when Compeer bit at his leash.

Nicole paused and debated whether or not to bring him. Ultimately, she decided that maybe the walk would give him his strength faster, and clipped the leash to his collar. She locked her door behind them, doubly checking the locks before heading down the hall to the enclosed elevator. Compeer hated the glass one with a passion.

Once they were on the street, Nicole consulted her phone's map, then took a sharp turn to the right. Compeer pulled toward a strip of foliage in the middle of the sidewalk; so, Nicole let him do his business before they continued.

The setting sun peeked through the skyscrapers, casting its last beams on the streets before they fell dark. The sky would have been a deep blue, had not a war smog drifted in from the far-distant battlefields. Nicole paused within one of the diluted sunbeams and basked in the warmth for the moment. She made a mental point to herself to enjoy every encounter with the sun she could; there was no telling when the war smog would once again grow so thick to block the sun. It had happened several times before.

When will this terrible war end? Nicole wondered.

The crosswalk up ahead flipped to red, and Nicole grimaced at the immediate cacophony of commuters impatiently slamming their horns.

"Man, people," she grumbled. "Wait your turn. Ugh."

"Nicole?"

She looked around for the speaker, but she was surrounded by other pedestrians, all of whom were not looking at her. Craning her neck, she looked beyond them and saw a familiar face.

"Mark!" she yelled, waving an arm.

Her co-worker pushed his way through the pedestrians, drawing a few complaints. "Nicole! Whoa! Sorry, my bad. Nicole, I haven't seen you in ages! How've you been?"

"Better," Nicole said. "Fancy meeting you here."

"I was on my way home, and decided to take the scenic route instead of the subway. Healthier, too. By the way, when are you coming back on site?"

"Soon," Nicole said with a sigh. "Pete's been on my case, too. I've just been so busy with the Reserve. . . I'll be back within a week, don't you doubt that."

"You'd better be back," Mark declared, crossing his arms. "You know how the bosses are. Hey, that reminds me, how's your–" He paused, then made a vague gesture with his hand that took Nicole several seconds to decipher.

The light turned green. Mark kept pace next to her. "I haven't been kept up-to-date, but I am sure that they are fine. If anything had malfunctioned, I most likely would be notified." She cleared her throat. "So, what's your current project?"

"You know that laser we installed in the *Annihilator* and the *Intimidator*? Well, we're taking that concept and turning it into. . ."

Nicole listened with one ear, glancing at the map. Seeing that they were close, she watched the address numbers. *12813, 12817. . . Wait.* Nicole abruptly backtracked. Instead of a 12815, there was an empty alleyway.

"Why'd you stop?" Mark asked, looking askance at the dimly lit avenue between buildings where not even the streetlights dared shine upon the filth that lurked within. "Did you see something in there? Trust me, nothing good ever happens in alleys like that. Let's keep walking."

"No, I have to go in there." As Mark protested, Nicole

stepped into the darkness and squinted. There were a few rusty dumpsters, drifting pieces of trash caught in a corner, and other things one would expect to find in such a place. She used her foot to shift through the trash, finally seeing a small piece of suspiciously clean paper stuck under a small rock.

"What on earth are you doing?" Mark asked as Nicole picked up the note and unfolded it. "And, for that matter, why?"

"You really want to know?"

"Yes. If you can tell me."

"I adopted a Hesperonychus, took it home, came back to my apartment to find my dog chloroformed and said Hesperonychus missing, and now I'm on a clue hunt spurred by some sort of ransom note."

Mark was silent for a moment. "You, Nicole Nike, live an unusual life."

Nicole snorted and turned her gaze to the note she held. "Oh, just *wonderful*," she groaned. "They left me a riddle."

"Really?" Mark said, coming in to lean over her shoulder. "Let me see."

Nicole read it aloud for him:

> *"Bestow order to anyone not yourself;*
>
> *Today, onward with endowing righteousness."*

Mark hummed, frowning thoughtfully. "Sounds like something the UO would preach, but this makes no sense. How is this supposed to help you?"

"It's a riddle, somehow, I know it."

Holding out one hand, Mark asked, "May I see?"

Nicole gave him the slip of paper, watching his facial expressions as he read. Cogs were turning in her own head, gear teeth trying to match treads. As she pondered the writing, gears stripped more than found purchase.

Mark raised one hand to clutch the bridge of his nose. "Okay. Do you see any possible keywords in this, location-wise?"

". . . No. I don't. Looks like only propaganda."

"Exactly. Which could possibly mean that they placed a message within the writing, or we could be missing something that we can't see."

"Like invisible ink."

"Right. Have something hot with you?"

Nicole dug around in her purse until she found a tiny packet of cheap matches. Striking one against the strip on the side of the packet, she held the small flame close to the paper. But by the time she had to blow out the flame lest she burn her fingertips, nothing except a slight browning had appeared on the paper.

"So much for invisible ink," Mark muttered.

Nicole sank the dead match head into a puddle before tossing it into a nearby dumpster. "I knew a kid who loved to play with ciphers when I was in high school. He'd pass along notes in class, and give a buck to whoever sent it back with the decoded version. I never decoded any, but I remember a few ciphers he did."

"And?"

"One of them involved seemingly innocent sentences, phrases, or famous quotes. If one possessed the correct decoder, it spelled out a message. Let me see that again." Nicole took the small slip of paper and stared at it.

Mark snapped his fingers. "Maybe they put the message in the middle of words."

Nicole narrowed her eyes, tilting the paper. "Or at the beginning," she said as if thinking aloud. Reaching back into her purse, she pulled out a pen and, using her palm as a stable surface, began writing down the key letters off the paper. "It's actually a simple one. Here, Mark! Look!"

Mark looked over her shoulder and grinned. "B-o-t-a-n-y T-o-w-e-r. Good job, Nikki!"

"The Botany Company Building. But where?" She flipped the paper over, checking for any other hints. "Here's something. 'Tree.'"

"Tree, tree," Mark mused. "Any ideas?"

Nicole squinted at the small word. "It could be just that. *Tree.* Maybe the next clue or whatever they want me to find is around one of the trees at the gardens next to the tower."

Mark shrugged one shoulder. "Perhaps."

"Then let's go." She began walking with new confidence in her stride.

"Nicole, wait for me," Mark said, jogging to catch up.

"What's going on? And more than one sentence. I need you to expound."

"Mark, you don't–"

"Tell me," he said.

Nicole sighed. "I came back to my apartment half-asleep, planning on feeding Compeer and my resident Hesperonychus before going to bed. I realized that neither of them were demanding food. I found Compeer unconscious in my bedroom and Aim, the Hesperonychus, was missing. I found this note attached to the fridge." She reached into her purse and handed it to him for him to read. "It directed me to this alley, and you know what's happened from there."

"You know, that's really not much more than you said before." Mark skimmed over the note, then handed it back. "I'm coming with you."

"Mark, you don't have to."

"No, I want to. Compeer still looks tired, and you look like you haven't seen enough sleep for weeks! Someone needs to protect you."

"I don't need protecting. I fought against Coelurus, for pete's sake!"

"Nice one, but Pete's not here."

She managed a weak glare.

"And almost *died*. Admit it, Nikki. You need me."

Nicole sighed with resignation. "Fine," she wearily said.

Mark smiled. "We'll get to the skyscraper faster if we use the monorail."

Looking down the block, Nicole could see a metal staircase leading up to a landing. "All right," she said.

Crossing the street, they came to the bottom of the staircase. Mark went up first to the halfway level, which was a short platform with a card machine. Nicole reached for her credit slip, but Mark grabbed her arm and stopped her.

"I paid for both of us," he said.

Nicole smiled gratefully, her eyes wandering to the kiosk's screen. It was displaying a commercial for the newest industrial computer chips.

They stepped inside the entrance to consult the track map on the other side of the kiosk. Nicole couldn't help but notice a second screen showing the publication of a Bible including footnotes of archeological evidence. Mark pointed out the route they needed to take, and they transferred to the correct side of the platform.

Nicole sat on a bench, feeling her earlier weariness coming back with a vengeance. Groaning softly, she held her head in her hands and let her hair act as a privacy curtain. Sleep was so tempting.

As the world started to fade from awareness, she absorbed Mark seated next to her. Sounds began to blend into each other and echo soothingly. Nicole could sense sleep and welcomed it with open arms.

It seemed like only seconds later that she experienced a sudden jolt. Muttering something that even she couldn't understand, she leveled a tired gaze at Mark sitting next to her.

"Come on," he said. "The train's coming."

Nicole rubbed at her eyes with the knuckles of one hand, and Mark began to come into focus. Behind him, she could see the front of the train rounding the corner a few blocks away. Mark helped her to her feet. Straightening her clothes, she noticed that Compeer was sniffing the edge of the platform. She used the leash to tug him back.

Arriving with the familiar screech of brakes, the sleek train slowed to a stop. Nicole waited until the passengers had exited before entering the narrow train. She found a corner seat with enough room for Compeer to lie down. Mark took a seat a few feet away, holding onto a grip pole. Nicole grasped another pole to steady herself, unsure of how jarring the initial movement would be.

The train powered forward, weaving over the streets and between buildings. The ride was nowhere as smooth as it was underground. Nicole felt nonplussed as her entire body slowly vibrated toward the edge of her seat.

Is this how people in the early 21st century travelled? she mused.

A few minutes later, the train began to slow and an automated voice spoke the name of the next stop. Nicole had to mentally repeat the garbled voice several times before she recognized the destination. She prepared to exit, twirling Compeer's leash around her wrist a few times. They hadn't been to this section of the city in a very long while, and she wasn't sure how her dog would react to the scents and sights.

With the train now rolling away, they stood on the

platform. Nicole looked up at the Botany Company Building. It was a steel-glass structure, with large green-tinted windows and pale beige walls. At its base was a two-level garden, with trees, bushes, and flowering plants.

"Where do you think we should start?" Mark asked as they descended down the stairs to the ground.

"In the section with the most trees?" Nicole replied, unsure. "The spacing looks almost equal, though."

"Then we should split up to cover more ground faster," Mark said. "I'll take this side and you go right. We'll meet at that bridge over there? By the artificial creek?"

Nicole nodded. "Hope we find something," she said.

They parted ways. Nicole let Compeer lead, the golden Labrador's nose to the ground. With the leash perpetually taut, Nicole kept as close an eye on the trees as possible, searching for a white slip of paper. Would it be stuck in the branches, or placed at the roots?

A squirrel darted across the path, and Compeer barked excitedly, pulling at his lead. Nicole reeled him back, trying not to choke him. "Leave it!" she ordered.

Compeer kept staring at the squirrel. It climbed into a young oak tree and began chattering loudly at him. Compeer growled.

"Leave it!" Nicole said again.

Compeer glared at the rodent a few seconds longer before returning his attention to sniffing.

"Good boy. Let's go find the next clue." Nicole looked

around, squinting at the foliage. Compeer suddenly leapt behind her, yanking the leash handle almost from her grasp. She spun and froze upon seeing a person leaning against a nearby tree. *Where'd he come from?! He wasn't there a minute ago!*

"Good day," the man greeted amiably. He tossed a lazy wave. "Nike, isn't it?"

"Yes. Who are you?" Nicole had never seen Compeer's hackles bristle so, or how far his black lips had curled. She rotated her wrist to wrap the leash around it, just in case Compeer decided to lunge.

Instead of answering, he tutted. "Shame, Miss Nike, for shame. You brought a friend into this mess. I'd count my blessings if I were you; this meeting would've gone very badly had you two not split up. Come, walk with me."

"I'm not going anywhere with you. Where's Aim?"

"You want answers without an extra hole in your head? Come with me. It's not that bad of a day for a stroll." Nicole was tempted to run, but the thought of Aim and a glimpse of matte metal convinced her. Nodding sharply, she fell into step with him. "You're very wise," he commented.

It was a brisk pace he set, and soon the Botany building was left behind. Nicole hoped Mark would understand. "What do you want, Mr. . . ?" she prompted.

"Refer to me how you wish. You aren't getting my name. As for your question, it's what my employer wants from you. We've been watching your work, Miss Nike, and are very impressed."

"I'm flattered," Nicole replied. She was committing his

face to memory while trying not to look obvious. "However, my work is classified. I am not at liberty to –"

He waved a hand. "Of course not. However, it's the extracurricular activities that have caught our attention." At her stoic expression, he continued, "The ones in the forest."

She played dumb. "The dinosaurs?"

"No. A priceless rock and a rather expensive diamond."

"What are you talking about?" They took a turn into an alleyway, and Nicole's heartbeat escalated.

The man stopped and leaned against the wall. "Miss Nike, you're straining my patience. You've locked the rocks away. When you're not testing the Portal Ore's capabilities. You happen to be in the ownership of a rather amazing ability; time travel. Have you imagined the scope of your power? Of course not. You're a very down-to-earth woman. It's a waste."

Nicole didn't say anything.

"Some of the discoveries you've made playing in the forest have been entered into your database, but we happened to notice that there are gaps in the notes. So, you have them physically written somewhere. If you would be so kind. . ?"

"You're delusional," Nicole said. "I'm a scientist. I know better than to mess with something so fragile as time."

The man stared solemnly, as if he could see into her soul. "It's people like you I don't understand," he said quietly. "Have you ever noticed that, in movies, when the human dies no one bats an eye; but when the dog dies, there's a zealous uprising and rivers of tears? Are you that type of person, Miss Nike? We have your Hesperonychus."

"Give her back," Nicole demanded.

"Only if you deliver the research notes in a manilla envelope," the man responded. He pressed a slip of paper into Nicole's hand. "Follow the rules. We will be seeing you."

She watched him exit the alley. Compeer snarled until he took the corner and disappeared from view. After a minute of composing her thoughts, she looked at the paper, then went back to the Botany Tower.

Mark was found wandering the pathways, and he sprinted when he spotted her. "Nikki! Where'd you go? Did you find it?"

Nicole gave him a quick rundown of her meeting with the man, then handed him the paper. "I dearly hope you can figure *this* one out. Please, say yes."

Mark's eyes widened. "'61855412122391212495?'"

"Do you see anything that I don't?" Nicole asked hopefully.

Scratching his head, he replied, "Maybe, if I have enough time to study it. I'll need to open a new doc on my data-pad. . . Do you mind if I take this home with me?"

"Go right ahead. It's not like I could figure it out." Nicole let out a nervous laugh. She held her head in her hands, not in weariness, but in consternation. I can't even get help from the police.

Neurons bridged the gap in her brain.

Wait. . . I can't call the police. But they never said anyone else *couldn't.* "Mark."

"Huh?" Mark replied, preoccupied.

"I sent Pete a message before I left, but I don't know if he's responded yet. I need you to contact the police for me. I can't do it, but you saw the initial note. Would you?"

Mark nodded. "Sure, I can do that. I'll go home and start on this whole ordeal there. You be careful, and don't give them your research!"

"I know, I'll be careful."

CHAPTER TEN

Lightning flashed, illuminating the room.

Williams and Lennox shared one of the two twin beds; by virtue of being female, Robin had the other to herself. On the discarded couch pillows was a tiny Bambiraptor, and across the backs of two chairs were two Pterodactylus, splayed over the sides bonelessly. The lightning lit up the room again, giving just enough time to show that everyone was asleep.

Almost everyone. Rush sat quietly. Unlike the others, he hadn't been able to fall asleep. Thoughts ran amok through his mind; the same ones that he'd been having since the start. But now recent events had shaken something loose, and he was struggling.

Should I? But can I? No, I can't.

Screams of terror and pain. A disintegrated shop. Life transforming into nothing but *wisps of dust* in the span of an instant.

I shall.

Before he could think further, he spread his wings and flung himself from his seat. As quietly as possible, he glided to the door. He collided with the doorknob with a soft *thud*. He froze, eyes wide as he listened hard to the room. No one showed any signs of arousing, so he opened the sliding latch that kept the door securely shut. The last step was twisting the door handle, which was a little difficult, awkwardly bracing himself against the door with his feet. Finally, the door creaked open. He listened for anyone now awake. Hearing nothing, he slid outside. The door clicked shut behind him, locking automatically.

Fluttering to the top of the railing, he looked around. The deluge of rain pounded on the motel and the parking lot, impeding all visibility beyond a few paces. Puddles had long transformed into miniature rivers, channeling water down into ditches and drains. Not very well sloped, the parking lot was divided into two by a rather deep stream, tiny waves frothing from the current and constant barrage from above. The motel's mandated gutters were overflowing the sides in irregular waterfalls. Gusts of wind had blown rain onto the walkways outside the rooms, rendering the flooring treacherously slick and shiny.

Forcing himself not to look back, Rush launched himself off of the railing, crashing through the gutter waterfall. The cloudburst was merciless, raindrops the size of walnuts beat at him. With ribbons of muscle flexing beneath his scaly skin, he ascended into the storm.

Despite the lightning and deafening thunder hindering his sense of direction, he decided to continue upward. The rain slowly began to ebb. Eventually, he broke through, pulling cloud wisps in his wake, leftover water cascading from his form to disappear into the fluff.

Rush soared, undisturbed. The storm clouds brewed and roiled, no less louder above than below, strikingly illuminated from deep within by pure white bolts of lightning. Rush looked up. The billions of pristine blue, white, and red stars twinkled, mare's tails sparsely sprinkled across the upper atmosphere where even he could not fly. Luna, three-quarters waxing, was no less brilliant, casting a pale blue glow onto his form and the mountain range-like clouds below.

Rush inhaled deeply. The air was cool, clean, and slightly thinner than he'd like. There was no such thing as stress or duty this high, nothing that he had to do to fight for life. No one could see him. His body felt lighter than ever. *No gear, no worries.*

He had no idea how long or far he had flown, but the storm eventually dissipated. Far beneath laid the clusters and tendrils of city lights, separated by oceans of countryside's acute darkness. He wondered how long it would take to reach the ground from his height.

Nothing is stopping me from finding out.

Closing his wings, he allowed himself to free fall. The shape of his body sent him careening headfirst and slightly upside-down. The wind of his passing roared in his ears, throbbing against his head and shaking his form with turbulence. The tiniest shift sent him careening in any given direction until gravity reigned supreme once more, greedily pulling him toward its inevitable embrace of earth.

He joyously screeched.

Having never fallen so far from so high before, Rush flung out his wings in blatant defiance of gravity. The membranous webbing of his wings billowed and stretched. With muscles quivering in strain, he defeated nature and leveled out.

Peering east, he noticed the horizon beginning to lighten with traces of pink and yellow. Rush had no idea where he was, and, honestly, he didn't care. As the sun poked its first welcoming rays into sight, he could sense the upcoming warmth. He had flown far south.

He spotted a river snaking below, and a rumble of hunger coursed from his stomach. Rush curled his wings, sending him into a steady, steep descent. He followed the river's meandering form, skimming above the calm water in search of fish. The water was brown and a little murky, but he saw a small school up ahead. Having seen it too late, he circled around. He quickly calculated the distance, adjusted for light refraction, then dove, mouth eagerly open. He surfaced and flew off with a fish pinned in his beak.

Rush alighted in a nearby tree branch that extended over the water. The fish flopped around, becoming weak from exposure. He took his time eating it.

Obnoxious voices derailed his peaceful meal. Disturbed, he saw a bridge not far away. Crossing the bridge was a group of teenagers, laughing and talking amongst themselves. It was the perfect image of bonds and friendships, something Rush lacked. It was rather hard to socialize when one was a runt and the official protege of a breed's leader. Rush felt jealous and bitter, and he forcefully shoved all thoughts of Assail from his mind.

The teenagers leaned against the stone wall of the old-fashioned bridge. One of them pointed his way, drawing the attention of the others. Rush realized that they had seen him, and turned his back in an effort to finish his breakfast in relative privacy.

Slimy, slippery, yummy! he mentally crooned as he nibbled.

Swallowing the last of the fish, Rush realized that the teenagers had grown suspiciously quiet. He looked back over his shoulder, seeing them silently standing and watching him. It was unnerving.

Is one of them missing?

Suddenly, a hand clamped his beak shut and pinned his legs together. He squawked in protest as he was pulled from the branch and into a human chest. Despite beating his wings as hard as he could, it was a futile effort. He stared up at the missing teenager. Behind them, her friends were cheering her success from the bridge.

Maintaining her tight grip, the teenager made a long trek up a steep hill to the others. Squirming, Rush tried to escape. To make it worse, the human adjusted her grip so that his wings were pinned shut between her body and her arm.

"Wow!" one of the teenagers said as Rush's capturer entered their midst. "What is that thing?"

"It's not a bird," commented a boy with neon-blue hair.

"Really," a third said. "Does *that* even *look* like a bird? It's obviously some sort of mutant bat."

Rush took advantage of the distraction and resumed struggling. He tried to bite, but the hand around his beak was still holding tight. His hips didn't allow his legs rotation enough so he could catch her flesh with his claws.

"Get it to stop!"

"I'm trying!"

"Here!"

Rush was suddenly shoved into a backpack. *ZIP!*

Brilliant. Now what? he assessed, kicking at the wall. *And what's that smell?*

Outside the twitching backpack, the teenagers gathered around.

"It's gonna rip it!" a girl complained.

A boy nudged the bag with his shoe, halting the movements. "Relax, it's stopped."

"What're we going to do with it?" another asked.

"We can take it to my house," one of the girls offered.

"Why?"

"Well, it's not like we can get a good look at it here without the risk of it flying away!" the girl replied matter-of-factly as she crossed her arms.

The neon-blue haired boy shrugged. "True. Let's go."

"Could someone help me with my stuff? That thing's in my backpack."

His prison sharply heaved, and Rush shifted uncomfortably. There wasn't enough room.

He tried to listen to the outside. Muffled by the fabric, he could hear a busy road. The teenagers chatted as they walked. The bag swayed.

By and by, the sounds of human machines faded away. A little while later, the backpack jerked. A door opened.

"Mom! I'm home with friends! We're going up to my room!"

There was a reply; Something about staying away from

food.

The backpack bounced some more, until a solid surface finally returned beneath him. *ZIP!* He looked up to see all the teenagers staring. He huddled at the bottom of the backpack.

"Why isn't it moving? It was like a tornado when you stuffed it in there."

"I'm just glad it hasn't torn up my backpack. I just got it!"

"It's so small," a second girl commented. "No bigger than an iguana. Are you sure it's not a bat?"

The neon-blue haired boy scoffed. "Are you kidding? That is *not* a bat. You need a new prescription for your glasses."

"I do not! I don't even *wear* glasses!"

The teenagers started bickering. Rush shifted his weight as their attentions drifted to each other, and he was forgotten at their feet. When he was sure that they weren't looking, he flung himself from the backpack, wings beating wildly.

"It's loose!"

"Catch it! Catch it!"

"It's going to break my stuff!"

"The door!"

Flying in circles around the ceiling, Rush looked anywhere for an escape route. There was a bed pushed into a corner, a fish tank on top of a dresser, and a series of bookshelves. There was one window, but the curtains drawn. Two doors were on two walls, but one door was ajar. From his vantage point, it appeared to lead into a hallway.

An escape route!

Rush accelerated. Already planning what to do once outside the room, he faltered as the door was slammed shut in his face. Far too close to turn with ease, Rush executed a clumsy flipping dive. It did keep him from a rather painful greeting with the door, but he had thrown himself out of flight. Rush angled for the bed, the only soft surface upon which to crash.

"Uhf!" he grunted, tumbling head over heels into the pillows. He screeched as he righted himself. *Why oh why did I run away?*

The teenagers closed in.

CHAPTER ELEVEN

Wind whistled through the open car windows. Preening in pride, Nicole knew that her beloved silver sports car was as beautiful as it was sleek.

The music playing over her bluetooth abruptly cut off, replaced by a ringtone. Nicole glanced at the touchscreen readout on the dash as a toneless voice recited the caller. Quickly tapping a button on the steering wheel, she said, "Mark!"

"I've figured out the numbers!"

Nicole sighed in relief. "What's the riddle?"

"The numbers were the riddle. It was a code. It was a

simple one, once I found out what was missing, which were dashes and spaces. It's an A equals 1, B equals 2, et cetera code. It reads 6-18-5-5-4-15-13 23-9-12-12 4-9-5."

"Brilliant! Please read me the letters."

"F-R-E-E-D-O-M W-I-L-L D-I-E."

Nicole could *feel* her face drain of blood. "I. . . Thank you, Mark. I need to go." She hung up, then pressed down on the gas. "Call the Reserve emergency number," she instructed her car's AI. As she drove the last miles, she informed the security team. By the time she turned onto the Reserve's entrance road, she had readied a set of jeeps in the parking lot and received the latest information as to the dinosaurians' whereabouts.

Barreling into the parking lot, Nicole was out of her car almost before it had stopped. The waiting security were already parking her car for her as she leapt into the SUV's driver's seat and floored it.

Around a half mile from her destination, a small herd of dinosaurs stampeded into her path. Nicole slammed on the brakes and jerked the wheel, fishtailing and sending up a spray of grit. "What's going on?!" she yelled to the dinosaurs as they approached. They shouted back, but she couldn't understand, and any pleas to turn back and clarify were ignored. She was left in a drifting dust cloud.

In haste and worry, she straightened out the jeep and sped on as fast as she dared. Cresting a hill, the jeep went airborne. Nicole gasped, seeing the panic in the open field beyond.

Helicopter drones swarmed the air while dinosaurs dashed for any cover. An advance security team was crouched behind the smoking cover of what was left of their former jeep, firing intermittently. The gleam of metal drew Nicole's eyes to Freedom, who had several drones in pursuit, the ground peppering with rounds behind her. The Utahraptor weaved, bullets continually following her tail. Eventually ducking behind a tree, Freedom dug her talons into the wood to prop herself upright and simultaneously hide from the drone's view.

The drone slowed, flying sideways to swivel around the tree. With eyes narrowed in intense concentration, Freedom moved along with it, keeping the tree between. After a few tense seconds, Freedom leapt from hiding, firing a beam of bright crimson. The laser sliced through one of the drone's rotors, sending it careening to the ground. A few more lasers were bored into the fallen helicopter for good measure. Trees branches caught by the close-range laser rained down.

"Freedom!" Nicole shouted, then screamed and ducked as the Utahraptor whirled about on reflex, ready to fire again.

Freedom made a startled churring noise, and the laser quickly receded into the *Intimidator*. "Nicole?"

"I got a warning–"

"Move!" The Utahraptor spun, catching Nicole with her tail, sending the human tumbling. Bullets slammed into the dirt where she had just been standing. As Nicole scrambled for the nearest cover, Freedom skipped around the rounds. Her red laser swept through several more of the remaining drones, raining smoking hulls and fragments below.

Several drones ascended. Capsules fell from fuselages. Upon impact with the ground, they exploded in billowing blue fireballs. Dinosaurs screamed as some were caught in the flames; others forced backward by the shock waves. Nicole's security detail opened fire.

Beneath a bush, Nicole hid her head until she no longer heard the drones. She uncurled, peeking out.

Wisps of discolored flames were receding, leaving blackened, bare dirt behind. An absonant stench drifted, reminiscent of burned plastic and overcooked meat. Dinosaurs wailed, some sporting traumatic gouges in their bodies from explosions where the flesh had been charred away. To Freedom's visible horror, the laser had punctured metal and tissue alike, and the results were horrific in their mortality. Visibility had been reduced in the war haze, reptilian and human forms alike casting midair shadows that danced and stumbled in the smoke.

Nicole wavered on her feet, a hand rising to her mouth at the acrid taste of bile. One foot failed to rise all the way in her adrenaline crash, and she stumbled over a previously unseen lump. One glance downward had her heaving, unable to handle the sight of an orphaned limb, the flat expanse of its termination point flawlessly cauterized.

Freedom spun and fired another laser beam. A drone crashed inches from Nicole's head. Too shell-shocked to exclaim, Nicole scrambled away, crab-walking until she regained enough sense to recover her feet.

"Who requires aid?" Freedom shouted in dinosaur-ese, looking around desperately in the smog. War torn, dinosaurs emerged from hiding. A few keened over carcasses. The injured were helped to their feet, while the only thing to do for the dying was to be sure that they didn't die alone.

Nicole stared at a Triceratops. The typically redoubtable creature was curled in on itself, missing two of three horns and a sizable section of crest. By the clean, bloodless lines, Freedom's laser was to blame. Any lower and the upper skull would have been lost as well. Nicole tried to comfort the reptile, but she so overwhelmed her words were emotionless, and her effort seemed to make things worse.

The thrum of an engine was heard before another jeep crested the hill. Nicole watched it stop, and sighed in relief as the Reserve medical team scrambled to help. There were several fallen trees, trunks sliced with laser precision, and a few struggling dinosaurs had been pinned. Joint efforts were rapidly organized.

"I'm sorry," Freedom said quietly. "Nicole, what were you saying?"

"I was coming to warn you. . ."

"Little late for that, isn't it?" The Utahraptor's rasping voice was without all humor or accusation, and the scientist took private relief that she wasn't being blamed.

Swallowing, Nicole spotted a small string of numbers and letters painted in purple on a dark gray fuselage. "'UO-GD-80153,'" she read. "Unison Order, Ground Drone, and that last bit is the numerical order of production." She inspected a black cover on the front, assuming that it was a protective shield for delicate components within, and discovered that the screws holding it shut were loose. "Freedom, could you help me for a second?"

"With what?" was the reply as the Utahraptor came closer.

"Could you slide the tip of a claw into that little crack? Yes, that's it. Can you pry it off?"

Freedom grunted, flexing her finger. The screws strained before snapping. The black screen fell to the ground, revealing the organized mess of wires, gears, and electronic boards. Refraining from touching anything, Nicole looked around in the dark nooks and crannies. Finally, she noticed a small piece of paper tucked into a corner. She pulled it free and unfolded it.

Tunnel I-5, it read.

What a stroke of Providence, Nicole mused, *that the one drone I need fell so close.*

She bit her lip. "Freedom, I. . . thank you. I can't say how sorry I am that this travesty. . ." She looked around and gulped. "We will remove the drones and take them to the proper authorities."

Freedom narrowed one eye. "You're being professional. What's wrong?"

"One of yours has been kidnapped. Her abductors have been sending me riddles like this to see how far I'll go to get her back. But. . . I have no idea what this one means."

"One of ours?" Freedom echoed, now both eyes narrowed.

"Aim. Hesperonychus. You know her?"

Freedom shook her head. "No. But some of the smaller raptors *have* been falling prey to the carnivorous fowl of the sky or the larger mammal predators of the ground. I might not've. . . had the chance to know Aim."

Nodding, Nicole nudged a nearby drone with a foot. The metal monstrosity had been sliced in half, the edges still glowing. "Why did this happen?" she asked quietly. "Why would the Unison Order send. . ."

"Because we are allied with you," the Utahraptor uttered. "That is reason enough. Now, please take these flying abominations, solve that riddle you hold, and get Aim back safe and sound. I trust that you will do your utmost."

Nicole took out her phone, blindly bringing up Mark's contact information with only finger memory. "Don't worry, we will."

A Quetzalcoatlus screamed. Both Nicole's and Freedom's heads spun around to face the screeching pterosaur just in time to see a new swarm of UO-GDs swoop into sight from over the trees. Dinosaurs and pterosaurs scattered in a frenzied panic as the drones separated. Freedom quickly found herself the sole focus of the drone's targeting systems, and leapt behind a tree again.

Nicole peered out from under her own tree cover, eyes wide. The drones ignored everything moving except the armed ochre Utahraptor. Despite the four security teams rapidly picking off drones one-by-one, there were still far too many for Freedom to take on and come out unscathed.

"Run!" Nicole yelled in dinosaur-ese. Freedom side-eyed her way, almost gaining a bullet in her distraction. "Run, Freedom, run!"

Kelp, Freedom's mate, opined, "Yes, run!"

"They're only after *you*!" Nicole screamed.

While the *Intimidator* took another shot, Freedom turned toward her mate. "Sea Fern, what about the others?"

Kelp poked his head above the bush he was hiding behind. "I'll take care of everyone in your stead. Don't worry. Leave!"

With a wild screech, Freedom swiped her laser through several drones before sprinting away. Nicole watched as the Utahraptor vanished into the depths of the forest, the drone hive at her tail.

The forest was quiet, as if a single word would cause reality to crash down upon them. Nicole's hands were shaking as she became the first to move, the first to have fallen branches crunch beneath her feet, mercilessly splintering the quiet.

Everyone slowly emerged from hiding. Nicole clutched the small paper note to her chest, biting her lip. Several drones had crashed to the ground, though a few were still operational. Nicole carefully approached one from behind, where its very live guns couldn't reach. Picking it up, she ripped apart the drone's connections from the circuitry to the guns.

"Careful," she warned the dinosaurians. "Some of these drones can still shoot."

Kelp approached, using his toe claw to render any drone he passed defenseless, be them active or not. "Nicole, some of us will assist you in carrying these drones back to your office. From there, you may do with them as you wish."

A little Utahraptor youngling, whose head barely came to Nicole's waist, came up to Kelp. "Patriarch, what's going to happen to Mother?"

Kelp nosed the youngling affectionately. "She can take care of herself. Don't worry, she will return."

Nicole looked away from the father and child and back into the trees. She had only heard the tales, in that Freedom had certainly displayed great amounts of everything needed to survive alone. But that was in the Cretaceous. Only God knew how many poachers might catch word of a lone Utahraptor.

Stay safe, Freedom.

Bypass 89 was loaded with vehicles, as always, ranging from teeny tiny eco-friendly tinfoil cars to fully loaded semi trucks. The bypass was a recent development, only a few years old, but with the worst traffic in the state.

It was around the time when work let out for the day, so Bypass 89 was a creeping parking lot.

A lone Utahraptor emerged at high speed from the bank of trees beyond the ditch, sprinting through, or, at times, even leaping over the vehicles trapped in traffic. Seconds after its appearance, it vanished back into the forest on the other side of the road. A moment later, a swarm of tiny helicopters sped over the road and into the trees near where the Utahraptor had gone.

The observers stared after, a few scrambling to be the first to upload their video.

Already a good half mile or so away from the infamous bypass, Scope panted breathlessly. Some hours had passed since she had violated the borders of the Reserve, and she was now far away from home. Whenever she had the chance, she glanced over one shoulder. The drones had never strayed far from her trail, almost always within sight.

She leapt from the peak of a mound and twisted in the air. Once airborne, she targeted the drones and fired a wide band of crimson laser. They were far enough away so most could dodge the deadly beam, but a good four or five more plummeted to the ground. Smoldering branches and trunks tumbled to the forest floor in the aftermath. She was no longer afraid to use her laser to its upmost capability, since there were no friendlies nearby to endanger. Half the trees were beheaded, canopies capturing a few additional drones, branches entangling in rotors.

Scope stumbled on her landing, and twisted her ankle. Ignoring the pain, she surged ahead, although her gait now bore a limp.

The dense trees and scratching brush were her friends. She may have hatched in an open clearing, but the majority of her early life had been spent in the forest. She knew its intricacies, and its secrets.

So *why* was it so *hard* to escape?

The forest was beginning to thin, suggesting that she was nearing developments again. She already had to avoid running through a few neighborhoods so that innocents wouldn't get harmed by a wayward bullet. The bypass, however, had been unavoidable.

Taking a sharp turn, Scope twirled on her good foot and fired her laser again. A few more drones crashed, leaving a dozen or more. Like hornets and wasps, the buzzing resounded inside Scope's skull until all she could hear were her pursuers and the gasping heaves of her own frantic breaths. The laser flickered, too many usages with too little recharge.

"Come on," she grunted irritably. *I can't run all afternoon!* Her lungs and legs were aching; but if she rested, even for a moment, the drones would be upon her immediately.

The sun gradually sank behind the horizon, leaving the world in a strange monochrome state. Electric lights sensed the lack of luminosity and flickered on, bathing the streets in a pale yellow hue. Scope avoided the synthetic lights, trying to keep humans out of harm's way.

By the time Luna rose, adding its calming blue light to the world, Scope had only five drones left on her tail. It was harder to see them, but they seemed to have no problem tracking her.

A flash of crimson lit up the field as she fired again. Scope took a few running steps before suddenly noticing something; the lack of buzzing.

Coming to a stop, she looked behind. A thin plume of smoke rose from the ground a short distance away, along with a single grinding noise. Scope didn't dare venture closer to investigate, content in knowing that she could finally rest a little.

Despite not wishing to stay long, her legs quivered, threatening to give. Aches roared in her abused joints, and the swelling of her ankle was becoming increasingly worrisome. She couldn't breathe enough, chest flexing wildly as her head hung. The absence of buzzing in her head resulted in a vague sense of disassociation.

Resolving to move took far more willpower than she thought as she plodded back into some trees. She continued walking, being sure to put a good distance between the last of the drones and herself. The gentle movements were soothing, although her limp grew substantially.

Luna was just beginning its descent when Scope arrived at the edge of a neighborhood. She stopped just before she stepped into a streetlight's illumination. The small roads and homes were dark and quiet, a homage to the respite of night.

Scope strode on, stepping onto the abandoned asphalt. She aimlessly coursed the streets until she arrived at the edge of a park. Paths set in stone snaked over the grassy hills. A few lone buildings speckled the landscape.

She moved to one of the buildings, peering into the dark interior. There were no glass in the windows, nor a door in the wide entrance, but it looked like it had a second floor. Entering the building, she peered up into the hole in the ceiling. It was pitch black up there, but she could smell the musty expanse of empty space. There was no sign of a ladder or stairway having ever existed, but the aspect of a safe hole outweighed her exhaustion.

Lowering her head, she peered at the wall for any hand or foot holds. Nothing. In exhaustion, she reared and reached out. Her fingers snagged a grip on the hole's edges. She dug her talons into the hole's topside and planted a foot on the wall. Using her tail to push herself, she struggled to heft herself upward.

Why must my arms be so weak? she lamented.

Her arms started to shake from the strain, but she finally managed to get her head and neck into the space above the ceiling. Frantically grasping at the floor, her talons gouged long splintered lines in the wood. Her tail left the floor as her legs curled up and tried to fit through the hole. She slipped, but caught herself.

Finally, she collapsed on the upper floor, only her tail

limply hanging in the hole. Now that she was lying down, it took great effort to drag herself to the far corner.

Sighing, Scope shifted to get more comfortable on the hard, flat surface. It creaked worryingly a little, signifying its age, but it held beneath her weight.

Not a long while later, Scope slept hard.

CHAPTER TWELVE

I'm cornered! They were closing in. Rush started to hyperventilate, the edges of his vision dimming.

One of the teenagers paused, hanging back. She stared at him for a minute before shoving her comrades away from the bed. "Could you guys stop crowding it? You're scaring it to death!" She kneeled down so she was eye level with him, crooning nonsense sounds.

Rush slowly calmed, gazing at the teenage girl. *What in the good sky does 'You igloo joint huh scooter' mean? She sounds like she's trying to speak in the tongue of fowls.*

"What are you saying to it? Have you been taking classes

in speaking bird?"

"I thought that we agreed that it wasn't a bird."

The teenage girl looked at the others. "I don't know what I'm saying and I *know* it's not a bird, but whatever I'm saying seems to be working."

"At least you haven't insulted it. Remember the last time you mimicked a warbler?"

"Yeah! You told us that it started screaming and chased another bird around the tree in a fit of fury!"

"Hush up," the girl said good-naturedly. "Now, back off and be quiet."

"Yes, O Great One of Bird Speak." The girl waved her friend off, leaning forward on the bed. The mattress sunk beneath her weight, forcing Rush to shift to remain upright.

"Hey, no need to be scared," the girl said.

Finally, she's speaking sense!

"What are you, anyway? Did you escape from a lab somewhere? They must have been experimenting with cross-breeding birds and bats to create something like you."

"Now you've gone from speaking bird to talking to it like it's going to understand you."

"Do you have any better ideas?"

"Yeah. Tie it up and look for lost and found notices on the internet. 'I've lost my bat/bird hybrid. Please call this number. Cash reward!'"

"I've finally figured out why our math teacher calls you the class clown."

"Dude, that hurts. Right here."

"Where? All I see is a dweeb."

"Take that back! I'll have you know that my grandpa has an IQ higher than Einstein's!"

"Are you sure it's a hereditary intelligence?"

"Finally! I know why I hang out with this group!"

"Because we're the social outcasts of the entire high school?"

"No, it's because it's like watching your own private, really bad, sitcom."

Rush watched them banter, head moving from person to person. *This* was the group that had managed to capture him?

While everyone else verbally sparred behind her back, the teenage girl sat on the bed, facing Rush. "You're really tiny. Are you still growing, or are you an adult? By the way, I'm Andrea Stellar. Don't worry about those idiots, they're harmless."

"Idiots?" a teenage boy protested. "Andrea, I thought you liked us."

"I do! It's like having a pack of puppies. Adorable, but not house-trained."

The two of them launched at each other, causing Rush to panic. Looking around frantically for an escape from the teenage horrors, the only hiding place he saw was under the sheets of the bed. He wasted no time in squirming underneath the blanket and curling up into the tightest ball possible.

A moment later, he heard a cry of pain followed by a thud. Someone laughed. The other teenagers quieted down, their arguments dying away.

"Whoa, dude, are you okay?"

"Ow, man. Who are you, *Samson*?"

"Would you all *shut up*? You've scared it to death!"

Rush thought his heart would stop when the blanket was peeled away. Frozen from fear, all he could do was stare as Andrea reached down and brought him to her chest. She opened her vest a little, tucking him into the relative darkness. He welcomed the vague sense of security, hiding his head by her side. Small shivers ran down his spine in endless waves.

"Wow, it likes you."

"Thanks. Hey, is my sandwich still in my purse?"

"Uh. . . yeah. Hungry?"

"Could you tear off a piece of the bread for me?"

"Got it. Here you go."

Rush felt himself jostled, and turned to balefully look at Andrea, only to find a morsel of bread dangling in front of his beak. He sniffed it warily, then took a nibble. It tasted *horrible*! Spitting it out, he huffed and hid his head again.

"Guess it doesn't like bread."

"Look at those teeth! This thing has to be carnivorous. Anyone got any meat?"

"There's beef jerky in my purse. . . Here."

"Thanks. Hey, you." Rush grumbled as Andrea took him out of his dark place. She held a strip of dried meat before his face. "Want some jerky?"

One sniff and Rush lunged forward. Andrea yelped in surprise as the jerky was yanked from her grasp and quickly vanished. He licked his chops, relishing the aftertaste. It was salty, a new tang that he found enjoyable. Andrea handed him another strip, which he took with equal fervor.

A teenager stepped forward, pulling out his phone. "This has *got* to go on my page. Say cheese!"

"Cheese!" Andrea chirped, smiling wide.

"Aww, it's not looking. Can't you get it to look?"

"I can try. Yo, bird thing. Look at the pretty camera phone!"

Rush knew what a camera was. Twisting his head to look, he opened his beak wide to give his stiff face the appearance of smiling. He squawked.

"Got it!"

"Can I see?"

Many of the teens gathered behind the one, staring at the screen. Rush couldn't see from his position, but didn't care; the packet of jerky had been left on a dresser, and he was still hungry. Leaping from Andrea's arms, he glided over and landed next to the food. He ripped the plastic apart with his wing-claws and began devouring the contents.

"My jerky!"

Rush recoiled, scuttling a few steps backward and away from the packet. He had assumed that it had been left there for him to find, since he had already been given a few strips. Wincing at the now-briny aftertaste, he took a breath to apologize–

"Dude, I don't think you'll be getting that back."

"Whatever. It's probably covered with spit now, anyway. I guess it can eat it if it wants."

Perking up at the permission, Rush rushed the packet. The saltiness of the tough meat was a drastic and interesting change from his diet of soft fish. He could get used to it, if given time.

As he was finishing the last morsel, Andrea picked him up and put him on her shoulder. He was barely small enough to fit, so he anchored himself by looping a wing behind her neck and under her hair. Noticing that the other teens were staring, he ducked to hide in her hair.

"I have to go home, guys," Andrea said. "Mom just texted me. Dinner's in an hour."

"Aw, do you have to leave?"

"You're really asking?"

"Okay, dumb question. But are you taking that thing with you?"

"Why not? It seems more than scared of the rest of you. I gotta leave, guys. Catch up with you later?"

"Don't be a stranger, Andrea!"

Andrea laughed and strode to the door. Rush felt his body bouncing with her steps, his head bobbing with the floor as she trotted down a long flight of stairs. She bid farewell to whoever was out of his range of view, then they exited the building and entered the warmth of late afternoon.

The girl suddenly stiffened, halting mid-step. Very slowly, she turned her head so that she could see him. Rush frowned, shifting uneasily as he stared back.

"You. . . haven't flown away?" Andrea questioned, as if she was thinking aloud.

Looking up, Rush was captivated by the sight of the sky. It would be so easy to just *go*. Nothing was keeping him on her shoulder. But the more he debated it, the more he found that he desired to stay. Having never possessed the heart of a rover, he settled on remaining with her. From what he had seen, she treated him well, kept him safe, and fed him food.

Safe.

He pushed aside thoughts of his responsibility and inherent guilt. *It doesn't matter,* he thought to himself. Rush made himself comfortable on Andrea's shoulder and gave her a pointed look.

Andrea's confused expression cut off his remark of "I'm not going anywhere" before he could finish taking a breath. She stared at him a minute longer, then shook her head.

"You have to be the strangest animal I've ever seen." Andrea continued walking.

Rush became lost in thought, daydreaming of a life as a pet. It would be *peaceful*, even if the circumstances leading into it were not.

"Well, here we are!" Andrea's voice pulled him out, and Rush looked to see a fair-sized, two-story burgundy house, a slightly out of control yard, and a black and tan dog tied to a porch post. "It's not much to see, but it's home."

A quick glance up and down the street confirmed that every other house had better curb appeal than the one Andrea claimed as home. In fact, a most articulate and "perfect" property was directly next door.

Andrea walked down the entrance walkway, and the dog began to bark loudly.

"Cade!" Andrea snapped. "It's just me, boy! Andrea! Down, boy."

The dog growled, sniffing in Rush's direction. Rush was completely concealed by Andrea's head, hiding as best he could. Much to his horror, her hand grabbed him and held him out to the dog. Rush froze, unable to flee. The dog quieted, its only noise being its sniffing.

Why did I stay?! She's a monster! I'm gonna be dog food!

"Easy," Andrea said, though Rush wasn't sure whether she meant it for him or the beast. "Cade, meet the newest member of the family! You, meet Cade, our German Shepherd. Don't worry, he's a sweetie when he decides he likes you."

Rush wanted to say "And what if he doesn't?" but the words caught in his throat.

Cade took a few more sniffs and huffed decisively. Finally, he licked Rush's face before going to lie down in a sunny spot on the grass.

Rush took in a shaky breath. Had he not tasted good?

"Aw, he likes you!" Andrea cooed. "Good Cade! Good dog!"

The German Shepherd woofed lazily, not even raising his head.

Shifting her grip on Rush to something less confining, Andrea trotted up to the front door, tapped in the electronic code on the lock, and swung open the door. Rush cringed from the loud creak the oilless hinges made.

"Andrea? Is that you?" someone called from inside the house.

"No, I'm the burglar here to steal the silver!" Andrea called back, kicking off her shoes while closing and locking the door behind her. The footwear collided with the wall, remaining propped up against it in a most unseemly fashion.

"Did you have a good time with your friends?"

"We got kidnapped once or twice, but a robot from outer space came along and rescued us." Andrea casually walked down the hall. Rush caught a whiff of cooking food, which grew stronger with each step taken. She turned a corner into a kitchen, where a tall woman stood over a stove. Rush began to salivate.

"What are you making?" Andrea asked excitedly, dashing over to an open skillet. Rush gazed with love upon the meat sizzling inside. "Chicken and dumplings!"

"I have a better question. What is *that*?"

Rush swallowed, meat forgotten as he looked up at the displeased woman.

"Oh! We, that is, my friends and I, found him by the river. Isn't he the cutest thing you've ever seen?"

"What is it?"

"I don't know, but that's nothing an internet search can't fix."

"Please don't tell me that this run of adopting anything cute that crosses your path is a continuing streak."

"Cade's the sweetest guard dog ever! You have to admit *that*, Mom. Don't you remember when he chased away that robber?"

Andrea's mother frowned. "What about *this* thing? It's cute now, but how about when it grows up?"

"We don't know what it is, Mom. It could be fully grown already."

"Find anything you can," Mrs. Stellar said, stirring the contents of a pot. "Dinner's in forty-five."

Andrea left the kitchen and entered another room, one that had a huge screen on a wall, a cozy fireplace, and a few plush seats. Andrea plopped herself down and went horizontal so her feet hung over an arm, then pulled out her phone. Rush, having been released, shifted so he was on the back of the seat.

"Okay," she muttered to him absently. "What are good keywords for you?" She recited a few words; "'Small rodent with bat wings.'" Her phone's screen alit with text and pictures. "No. No. No. Nope. What on earth? No. Uh-uh. Okay, maybe we can try 'flying toothed bat animal.'"

Rush laid down, sinking into the fabric. With his wings dangling limply on either side, he relaxed and waited.

"Voila!" Andrea crowed. "That looks a little like you, but it has a crest thing. No. No. What is this website?" She tapped it with a finger. "'The Dinosaur Reserve,'" she read.

"Eep!" Rush yelped, his attention nowhere else.

Andrea scrolled through the website. "So, you're a Pterodactylus. What're you doing all the way down here? That's in Arkansas, like, five hundred miles away or something!" She scrolled down a little further. "No. Way. You're from the *Cretaceous*?! You're *old*." After reading a bit more, she shut off her phone and sat up.

Rush expected her to frown, shove him in a box and ship him back, yet she plucked him up and held him.

"Poor thing, you must've run away!"

She's not wrong. . . Rush thought, trying not to cringe. He quickly pushed thoughts of betrayal away, and the wave of guilt and shame with it. He *deserved* this.

"Wonder what gender you are." Rush opened his mouth– "You look nothing like a girl. That makes you a boy! I shall call you Bob, and you shall be mine. You will be my Bob."

Andrea skipped back to the kitchen, where Mrs. Stellar was taking bowls from a cupboard.

"Did you find anything?" Mrs. Stellar inquired.

"Yeah! Bob's a Pterodactylus from that reserve a few states away."

Mrs. Stellar raised an eyebrow. "Really? I remember when What's-Her-Name the Scientist led an expedition that brought all those dinosaurs back. So, this is one? What's it doing so far away from home?"

"Migration? I don't know," Andrea said. "But I'm calling him Bob. He doesn't want to leave me." At her mother's dubious look, Andrea added, "Really! He was on my shoulder and I forgot to hold him and I walked outside and he didn't fly away! In fact, he stayed on my shoulder like a pirate's parrot. Can I keep him?"

"I– I'm not very sure about this one, honey. A dinosaur is a lot different than a dog or a cat. That bird thing most likely belongs to the reserve it came from, if not the government."

"Well, then, if the government wants Bob back, they can have him. But can I keep him until then?"

Mrs. Stellar grimaced. "Andrea, this isn't a prudent decision. Dogs and cats are one thing, but even I know that a *dinosaur* is a completely different matter. You can't keep it."

"But, Mom–"

"No 'buts', Andrea Stellar. I'm sorry. Let it go. You can't keep this one." The mother placed a gentle hand on her wilting child's unoccupied shoulder. "You have a kind heart. I'm pleased of that, yet. . . I'm sorry."

Rush whimpered. He didn't want to leave. Here, in the house, he had food, water, shelter, and even a teenager willing to dote on him! *I don't want to go.*

Plodding the walk of the dejected, Andrea moved back toward the front door. "It would have been wonderful," he could hear her murmur. "You would've lived in my room. Rave, my cat, would love you to bits. Not to eat you, mind you, of course. I've never had a Pterodactylus before. I'm sorry my mom didn't want you."

A breeze hit Rush's face as Andrea exited the house. Cade's head perked as the girl gently took Rush from her shoulder. In desperation, Rush gripped her fingers with all of his limbs.

I will play the part of the unintelligent pet! Just don't make me leave! He refused to speak. To talk would reveal his sentience, and void the possibility of a free ride. Shame returned, but lesser this time.

If Andrea noticed, she didn't show it. "Goodbye, Bob. Remember me." And she threw him into the air.

Screeching, Rush tried to land on her, but her flailing arms kept him at bay. He attempted time and time again, each failed.

"No! No, Bob! Go away! Don't make this harder than it already is, Bob! Go!"

Rush shut his beak and flew away.

CHAPTER THIRTEEN

This was it. Nicole felt that she couldn't feel more nervous. Droplets of cold sweat dripped down her spine. Jitters kept her from standing still, and her hands were clammy. She wore a jacket against the frigid air conditioning of the subway system, but she still felt overheated.

Pedestrians passed, barely sparing her a glance as they rushed by, engrossed in their own lives and problems. Nicole examined them, hoping that Mark had been correct. The subway *was* the "Tunnel I-5" in the riddle, right? She and Mark dearly hoped so, especially since Mark had requested a few plainclothes police officers.

She knew that the pedestrians, despite behaving as if she

were invisible, found her a needless obstacle on the way to the stairs. She could feel the irritated glares on her back, but her gaze was fixed on the tracks.

"Mommy, why is that lady standing in the middle of the floor?"

"Hush, honey. It's just her way."

Another train arrived. The train emptied as fast as it refilled, and the dismounted travelers swarmed the platform, some heading for another track, the rest upstairs to the surface. Several people bumped into her thanks to the lack of room, knocking her around slightly. A particularly rough nudge sent Nicole stumbling a few steps. She looked around, but the culprit was lost to the crowd.

Something rustled in her pants pocket as she stood. Knowing that nothing had been in there earlier, Nicole pulled out a small piece of paper.

Turn around, it read.

Nicole paused a moment before obeying. The wave of people had started to dissipate, enabling her to see to the walls. Previously unnoticed, a tall man was leaning against the wall by the restrooms. His gaze was expectant, and on her. As soon as they made eye contact, the man beckoned her with an arm gesture.

Walking toward him, she spotted a pet carrier by his feet. When she reached a respectable conversation distance, where they could hear each other over the echoing din of the tunnels, she stopped.

"Miss Nike," the man said in a sandpaper voice. Nicole

tried not to gag from the stench of stale cigarette smoke on his breath. "Call me Brick."

She could see why. Brick was a tanned hulk, with a five o'clock shadow on a bald head, and intricate tattoos sleeved both arms. Besides his smell, what really bothered her was the way he stood, and how he gazed at her with dark, disconnected hate.

"I've solved the riddles," Nicole said at last. "Where's my dinosaur?"

Brick bit out a snide laugh. "You assumed that you'd be getting it back alive?" He kicked the pet carrier harshly, causing it to jump and rattle.

Horrified at the inference, Nicole kneeled down to peer inside the carrier. Before she could lower herself all the way, Brick's thick leg blocked her view. She carefully schooled her expression into a neutral one, wondering how quickly she would have to move to snatch the carrier and run without getting caught.

"You may be a scientist and decoded the riddles, but you're a fool to think that your little pet would be left unharmed." Brick sneered in glee.

Nicole carefully straightened, looking directly ahead. Her booted toes crashed into Brick's shin, where it was unguarded by his wanna-be combat boots.

He howled and bent to clutch his wounded leg. Nicole snatched the pet carrier and bolted, sprinting as fast as she could. Pedestrians leapt to the side to allow her passage. The carrier was heavy, and the slippery tile flooring was not fair to the treads of her shoes. The escalators were full up ahead.

Nicole dreaded the action of hurtling up a long flight of stairs to the surface with the bulky carrier.

Brick was yelling, but his words were lost in the din of the subway. She heard him coming after her, his footsteps booming, reminding her of a Tyrannosaurus. She almost turned to glance over her shoulder, but caught herself just in time to avoid tripping over a train of suitcases.

Police whistles ripped the air, echoing in the tunnels. Nicole stopped at the bottom of the stairs and turned to watch. Brick stumbled to a stop as multiple disguised police officers blocked him in. He attempted to wrestle away, but a policewoman put him in a headlock while a second grabbed Brick's arms and handcuffed them behind his back.

Nicole collapsed onto a nearby metal bench, setting the pet carrier by her feet. With some difficulty, the police perp-walked Brick past her. The man cast her a blood-curdling glare as he passed. Nicole returned the gaze cooly, puffing out her chest and raising her chin. *You haven't beaten me at your game.* She had nothing to fear from him.

Her calm expression seemed to send Brick over the edge, as he elbowed away the officers around him and stormed back to her. Nicole jumped away from a kick aimed at her midsection, then ducked another aimed toward her head, feeling the fabric of his pants brush her hair.

There was a quiet *zzp* of electricity. Brick froze, then dropped to the ground in a twitching heap. An officer holstered a taser. Brick was hauled up and carried away by his arms, half stumbling in an attempt to regain control over his convulsing muscles.

"I'm fine," Nicole replied to an officer's worried query.

She shifted her weight and suddenly became aware of a pulled muscle.

While the officers were taking her statement, Nicole was handed the pet carrier. The policewoman was sympathetic, finishing the procedure quickly so that Nicole could check on her animal.

Nicole kneeled before the carrier. Opening the door, she reached in and pulled out Aim. The Hesperonychus was deathly still, limp in her hand, though breathing. Nicole gently placed her back in the carrier and secured the door. Standing, she looked around for Mark, but couldn't find him anywhere in the packed area, so she picked up the carrier and languidly walked up the stairs. The last lingering officers followed, nodding courteously before parting ways.

Entering the cloudy, mid-afternoon haze above, a cold wind battered at her hair. Nicole shivered, putting down the carrier just long enough to zip up her jacket and put the hood over her head. The sun had vanished behind the gray cloud cover again, its spree of unobstructed warmth and light apparently over. Not for the first time, and definitely not the last, Nicole wished for the war to end.

As she was strolling toward her apartment building, she heard someone call her name. Looking behind, she smiled at Mark. He caught his breath as he took step beside her.

"You got your dinosaur back?" he said, glancing at the pet carrier.

"Yes. She's unconscious, though, so any information she might have on what happened to her will have to wait until she awakens. I've got the Reserve's vet on call. I'll make an appointment for tomorrow morning. I'll keep an eye on her tonight."

Mark side-eyed her. "Aim's unconscious, Nikki!"

She gestured at the Hesperonychus, then at the outside world. "The Unison Order did this in the first place. I wouldn't put it past them to attempt something else. Aim is staying with me, and hopefully whatever they did to her will wear off harmlessly."

"Then send the vet what vitals you can record." Seeing her resolute attitude, he switched topics. "Any word from Freedom?"

Shaking her head, Nicole replied, "Nothing. I hope nothing's happened to her."

Mark hummed uncertainly. Nicole recognized he was again looking for a new subject. "That was quite a show," he eventually stated.

"Hmm?"

"Your fight against that man; did you use those same moves against the Coelurus?"

"All I did was dodge."

"It was still rather good. What have you been doing?"

"I've been reading up and practicing self-defense techniques. I've even constructed a dummy. I call him Slick. He lives in my closet since I don't have a dining room table."

Mark apparently decided to ignore the obscure table reference. "I applaud you." He clapped in sincere banter.

Nicole chuckled softly. "Are you walking me home?"

"I might as well. My apartment building is a few blocks beyond yours."

Mark not only walked her to the entrance to her building, but he accompanied her into the glass elevator and to her apartment door. From there, they bade each other "Good night," and Nicole closed and locked her door.

Compeer rushed her, mouth agape in a smile while his long tongue lolled limply off to the side. He tried to rear up to reach her face, but Nicole pushed him down, kneeling to his level. He licked her repeatedly, whining happily.

"Hey, bud," Nicole said, scratching the base of his ears. "I got Aim back!"

The golden Labrador sniffed at the pet carrier, pawing the latched door. Nicole unbolted it and pulled Aim out from within. Compeer growled, his ears flat against his head.

"Don't worry, I think she'll be fine," she assured him, carrying Aim over to the couch. Laying the Hesperonychus on a cushion, Nicole fetched a small throw blanket and draped it over Aim. "We just have to wait for her to wake up. Think you can do that with me?"

Compeer shook his entire body, causing his ears to flop. Now motionless, he growled, teeth bared, at the Hesperonychus.

Nicole sighed.

Hours dragged by. While she waited, Nicole held her phone to the dinosaur's face for several seconds, then sent the app's recordings to the Reserve's veterinarian. As usual, nothing worthwhile was streaming on the television. Nicole had no interest in her small collection of movies, nor an appetite for the slice of pecan pie awaiting in her refrigerator. She tried working on a few items for the R&D company, but whatever designs she created didn't seem enough for her high standards, and ended up filed in her "dead ideas" archive folder.

Sunset came and went, veiled behind the never-ending gray haze of distant warfare. Even when darkness fell, Nicole had her window open and was leaning on the windowsill, watching the world pass by. A cool breeze, not quite as cold as earlier, ruffled her hair, still faintly tainted with the scents of combat.

"Ooh. . ."

Whirling around, Nicole saw Aim beginning to stir. She went to her side and watched as Aim slowly returned to the realm of the aware. "How are you feeling?"

Compeer shifted in attention from his position on the floor.

Aim cracked open an eyelid, them immediately shut it with a wince. "Could you turn off the lights?"

Nicole obliged the request. The room was now in complete darkness, save for the city lights from outside. Nicole said, "They're off."

Opening her eyes, the Hesperonychus looked around. "I'm back?"

"Yeah, you're back. What happened?"

"You were gone, away at work. Around lunchtime, maybe later, someone knocked on your door and wouldn't go away, and then they somehow undid all those locks and barged in! I tried to hide under your bed, but they grabbed me and trapped me, and one of them poked my haunch with something sharp and that *hurt*. Your dog couldn't do anything because they held something over his nose that made him fall asleep. Then, they took me out of here, and everything started getting blurry. I think I fell asleep before we reached the street."

Nicole nodded. *She had been shot with tranquilizer and Compeer had been subdued by chloroform.* "Go on," she prodded.

"Well, I wasn't really awake much afterwards. I remember a white room, with humans in white. They were doing something to me that hurt. I couldn't feel my legs and was really sleepy. I was also in this cold, dark box. I didn't like it. The last thing I remember before now is when a couple of humans stabbed me with something sharp and I fell asleep again."

Nicole sat on the couch to digest the information. *She was kept unconscious for almost all of it; probably, so she can't describe anything in detail. I can't ask if she heard anything. She doesn't understand anything other than dinosaur-ese.*

"I'm sorry."

Nicole frowned. "For what?"

Aim sniffled. "I didn't protect the home. I'm too small to do anything useful! My family tried to teach me the art of combat, but I'm hopeless. I can't do anything! I'm sorry, Nicole."

Heart aching, Nicole picked her up. "I'm not disappointed

or mad at you. Even if you were an Allosaurus, they would've overpowered you eventually." As Aim's sniffs quieted, Nicole thought it best to change the subject. "I contacted the vet. She'll help you feel better in no time. In the meantime, are you hungry?"

Something in Aim's stomach gurgled strangely. Frowning in concern, Nicole leaned closer in the hopes of hearing it better. Suddenly, reminiscent of projectile vomit, a jet of liquid crashed into Nicole's face.

Recoiling in disgust, Nicole's eyes burned and began to water. Unable to see, she fumbled for a towel she had left on the futon. Finding it, she wiped it across her mouth and nose, clearing most of the foul-tasting liquid. Fighting against the sting, she inspected the towel, expecting to see partially digested insect remains, but was met with a colorless smear.

Hearing a scuffle, Nicole looked up to find Compeer wildly shaking Aim in his mouth. Nicole rose to intercept him, but her Labrador threw the dinosaur at the wall. Before Aim had fallen to the floor, Compeer was at the dinosaur's throat, tearing into its scaly flesh with his teeth. Aim struggled, her claws digging into his fur and strong hind legs frantically seeking escape.

"Compeer!" Nicole cried, as she attempted to stand. The room tilted, and she narrowly avoided hitting her head on the futon on her way down. Her hands raked at the throw carpet's short fibers, scraping through tiny crumbs and particles as she hadn't recently time to vacuum. Her lungs began to constrict, making breathing difficult to sustain, and her skin burned and itched dreadfully where the liquid had made contact.

With a vicious wrench of his head, a chunk came away with him, overflowing his maw.

"Compeer!" Nicole gasped in horror. She waveringly moved to her feet, clenching her chest. She expected to see blood stains splashed in all directions and the spill of innards from Aim's ruined neck. "Ba–"

Compeer keened, the mass in his mouth falling with a *splat* onto the floor. Brown eyes gleamed in silent plea, as if begging her to understand.

She gaped down at Aim's mangled body. Where Compeer had snapped Aim's neck, two ends of a broken strut and some wires dangled from a rip in the skin. The torn ends of the wires sparked as the Hesperonychus' eyelids twitched erratically. The staccato breaths of Aim continued as the machinery inside persisted the illusion despite the damage; A torn end of a pipe spurted puffs of air, causing the dangling shreds to dance and wave. The skin that suddenly resembled thick, textured fabric was peeled away from the fabricated muscle structure beneath.

Unable to remain standing, Nicole collapsed to her knees. Compeer rushed to support her. Dazed, she noticed that only her dog was bleeding, tiny rivulets of red creeping through the golden fur. The revelation struggled to get through the distracting pain in her cranium and chest.

"*Objective achieved,*" a monotone robotic voice emitted from somewhere in Aim's abdomen. It was in perfect English. "*Automaton Intelligencer Model compromised.*"

And this tape will now self-destruct. On instinct, she threw her body toward the bathroom, but her limbs – were sluggish. *The controls are sluggish, Captain.* Compeer bit her shirt to assist. Nicole helped as much as she could. Head spinning, she strained to tell up from down. Black shadows rimmed her vision, steadily closing in. *This message will now self-destruct. It's always self-destruct. Then boom. Boom. Where's the earth-shattering kaboom?* As Compeer shoved her around the corner and into the bathroom, Nicole heard a high pitched tone. *Ah, there's–*

Chapter Fourteen

Nightfall had long arrived. Rush's wing muscles burned to the point he could no longer cope. Even gliding on a stable wind didn't ease the ache. He knew that he needed to land and recuperate, but the fear that he would be caught kept him airborne.

The temperatures had grown colder, leading him to assume that the winds were bearing him northward. He was at a high enough altitude to see the barest hint of water at the horizon, which meant that he was also flying in an easterly direction. An expanse of mountains blanketed the earth below him, the aged range lolling in the moonlight. Far in the distance was a city glowing unnaturally with red and golden hues, overcast by a dire smog of black.

An unusually chilly gust of wind enveloped him. The cold pierced his exhausted frame, causing his body to convulse in shivers. The cold pierced his hurting body, and he decided that it was time he descended. The fastest way down was to simply plummet, but he knew that recovering safely from the fall would be agonizing. He decided that a slow descent was the only option.

By the time he reached a low altitude, he was over inhabited countryside. A small farm was a short ways ahead. There were a few lights on inside the house. Bypassing the house completely, he circled a barn until he found a crack in the wood large enough for him to slip through.

It was warmer inside the barn. A small, bare lightbulb had been left on, hanging on the peak of the high ceiling. Rush back winged, alighting on a rafter tie, his muscles showering gratitude. The rough hewn wood dug into the pads of his feet and wing-claws, splinters aplenty, and he hissed as one eked past his scales to prick his flesh.

Ten stalls lined opposite sides of the structure, split by a sandy floored hall littered with straw. Most of the stalls were empty, the exceptions being a pregnant horse, a sow and her piglets, and some goats. A ladder provided access to a loft overflowing with straw and hay bales, a pitchfork casually speared into a loose heap.

The rafter tie was a sufficient replacement for a branch, but his muscles were in no mood to support a Pterodactylus' upside down sleeping habits. Rush braved a short glide to the loft and nestled his way into the bales. Snuggling into the scratchy warmth, Rush finally relaxed.

Before he could fall asleep, his stomach gurgled in complaint. He hadn't eaten since the jerky.

The thought brought Andrea's image to his mind's eye. Rush pushed it away. She was so nice, too, protecting him from her friends, feeding him, welcoming him into her family.

What kind of beast am I? he thought, hiding his face under a wing in shame. *I can't face them again after what I've done. I can't.*

His self-deprecation was interrupted by a sudden *MROW* as he was tackled from behind.

Scope looked around before cautiously flipping open the heavy metal lid of a dumpster. One whiff of the contents within caused her head to recoil. She grimaced at the sight of soiled paper bags, flimsy wet cardboard containers, and the thousands of other decaying miscellaneous items one might find in a cheap fast food restaurant's dumpster.

But it was food, and Scope was hungry. Trying not to gag, she lowered her head and nosed aside some trash.

Is this what I've been reduced to? Scavenging like a common buzzard?

She purred when her supreme sense of smell detected meat a few layers further down. Standing on the edges of her toes to allow her neck more reach, she fought to locate the source of the meat smell.

Sure, she could've just gone to the front door and requested some free meat, but Nicole had told her about security cameras. There was a decent chance that there was someone recording her raiding the dumpster like a simple raccoon. As much as she disliked the notion of rummaging through dumpsters whenever she became hungry, she would rather not have the Unison Order knowing her whereabouts.

She pulled back to look behind her. She had to get back to her tribe. Anything could happen while she was gone. Biting her lip, she forced herself to resume dumpster diving.

Aha! Grinning triumphantly, she unearthed a half-eaten burger. She flicked off the bread, pickles, and soggy lettuce before popping the rest in her mouth. It only required a few chews before she swallowed. Unfortunately, half a burger would not satisfy her appetite. With greater determination, Scope delved back into the depths of the dumpster.

A door opened. Without a second thought or a moment of hesitation, Scope sprinted from the dumpster to a thick wall of thorny hedges. Bunching her leg muscles, she sprang over the bushes with little room to spare, landing heavily on the other side. Now facing a strip of trees that mostly blocked her view of a highway, she turned around and peered through the bushes.

A restaurant worker, lugging several heavy bags of trash, made his way toward the dumpster. When he rounded the corner, he dropped the bags, muttering something about raccoons. He threw in the bags of trash, closed the lid, and went back inside.

Scope's stomach begged her to return to the receptacle of discarded items, but her mind trumped it with the thought of *What if he comes back to try and catch the "raccoon?"* Her stomach was unable to argue with such logic, instead nudging her mind toward the notion of locating a different restaurant.

Calculating the effort, she looked back at the path

from whence she had come. It was a maze of back alleys and loading docks for stores. The alleys appeared mostly empty, but there was always a decent chance of a human making a sudden appearance, identifying her. After all, how many Utahraptors were out there that had a shiny little "weapon to end all wars" attached to her spine?

Scope pushed the hunger away and took a few steps toward the highway. There was a short moment when cars were few and far between, when the traffic lights created a brief standstill. The moments took long in coming, and every moment she waited behind a bush, she had to resist her stomach's insistence to return to the dumpster. She had to remain patient.

Finally! She leapt from the line of trees, sprinting across the plane of asphalt and over a hill on the other side. A strip mall spread out to her right, a bunch of trees to her left. She headed into the trees, taking an extremely long way around to the back of the strip mall. In a far corner, behind a cheap metal privacy wall, were several dumpsters for the varying stores. It was easy to leap over the short wall and find a dumpster that contained discarded food.

Lifting the dumpster's lid, Scope drooled at the sight! A multitude of meat deemed too old to be safely consumed by humans. What a find! *There must be a butchery in the mall somewhere.* With a croon of delight, Scope dived into the fleshy banquet.

She was not interrupted, so her stomach's wails were swiftly contented. Eating until she was stuffed, she took a few more bites for good measure before closing the lid of the dumpster and clambering back over the wall. Once in the open, she jogged for the cover of trees.

Raising her head, she sniffed the air for any way to find

her way back to the Reserve. The most prominent scents were of burned rubber, exhaust, and hot asphalt, underlaid by a smell cacophony of things unidentifiable. Unless she requested assistance, which she had great qualms in doing, she was effectively lost.

I need to get back.

Mentally grasping for any other means of acquiring a sense of direction, her eyes landed on a robin perching on a branch above her. The pterosaurs were better at talking to fowls, but she currently didn't see any other option other than picking a direction and hoping it was right. "Excuse me," she said politely.

The robin chirped, looking down at her, flicking its wings.

"Do you have any clue as to the direction to the Dinosaur Reserve?" It was a ridiculously long shot. Scope hardly dared to hope for an affirmative.

Chirruping, the robin skipped from side to side along the length of the branch. Before Scope brought on herself a headache wondering what the bird meant, the robin flew from the branch and circled her head a few times before veering away. The robin went only a pace or two before it attempted a hover. Unable to remain stationary, it alighted on another branch.

"That way?" Scope inquired.

The robin fluttered its wings.

Scope nodded in thanks before setting off at a brisk walk. The highway didn't go in the direction the bird had indicated, a small favor, but there were a number of buildings that she was hard-pressed to avoid. Traversing suburbia was a delicate balance of using hedges and untrimmed brush to her advantage. More than once, she was forced to backtrack and locate another path. Fortunately, the sun functioned as a source of direction, so as long as she kept it slightly to her right, she was heading in the correct direction.

Sunset loomed, and there was no Luna in sight. The trees blocked Scope from using the stars as guides. Shortly after she was forced to begin searching for a place to stay the night, she encountered a property for sale. It had been left uninhabited for a while, judging by the knee-high grass, unkempt shrubbery, and recreational equipment overtaken by thick and leafy vines. Scope bent to investigate a jungle gym, noting the space beneath the structure to be well endowed with a bed of moss and fallen leaves.

She knew she would not be making it home that night, so she crawled onto the moss, careful not to gouge it with her talons or claws, and resigned herself to sleep.

CHAPTER FIFTEEN

Former Secretary of State Frederick Gluten exited the conference room with an air of solemnity, his steps languid to allow his fellows to swarm past him on their way back to their stations. President Cornette was the last to exit, closing the door behind her. She held a large data-pad under her arm, which she had used earlier as a means to reference her plans.

"Ah, Gluten," she said, smiling at him. He returned it in full, albeit strained a hint. "Thank you for supporting me earlier. These *débiles* just can't see the full scope of my plan to develop this planet to its full potential. I'm glad that I have you here."

"It was no issue at all, Ms. Cornette–"

The former President of the U.N. cut him off with a quickly raised hand. "You have no need to address me as such, my friend," she said quietly. "I believe that my office is bugged. What happens inside there now is not necessarily what happens out here."

Gluten nodded, allowing his smile to drop now that the ruse was abandoned. "Is there somewhere else you'd like to discuss or. . ?"

"No, I fear the meeting rooms suffer as well. Here will do, but we must remain hushed. These halls echo like a catacomb." Reaching into a pocket, Cornette withdrew a small envelope. "I believe that there is dissent within the ranks. I run a tight and happy ship, Gluten, and I must quell any possible mutiny. Inside this envelope is a list of names of whom I believe are dissatisfied with our recent solutions to our social ills."

Gluten took the envelope and opened the unsealed flap, withdrawing a paper folded in three. He took a moment to scan the page. "This is worrying. What would you want me to do?"

"I want these people enlightened, not removed. Gluten, do you think so little of me? I would become the worst sort of tyrant if I retired anyone who thought ill of myself or my goals."

Gluten clasped her shoulder with his free hand. "Know that I think very highly of you, and your goals. Why else would I be here? Trust me, I'll see what can be done. You're not the only one bothered by this news."

Cornette visibly relaxed, the square set of her shoulders descending into a gently sloped curve. "Thank you. I trust that you'll soon have this resolved. If that is all, I must return to my office. I know those bugs are around there somewhere. . ."

They parted ways, Gluten moving down the halls at a clip just slow enough to not be a speed walk. The envelope was stowed in the palm of one hand, folded almost to the point of crumpling. His swift pace bore him to his destination quickly.

"You're late," said the man who leaned against the wall.

"My apologies. I was detained in the hall immediately after the meeting." Gluten held out the envelope and waited a moment for his colleague to read it. "You are not being nearly as subtle as you think you are."

"Agreed. We need to address this."

"If we don't remedy this quickly, she'll feel forced to haul suspects to Questioning."

"Are you certain she'll dirty her hands personally?"

Gluten rolled his eyes. "Her hands are already filthy, regardless if she recognizes those she sacrifices in building her worldwide utopia. What matters now is to speak to the others, to make sure they understand the circumstances."

His companion nodded in agreement. "We'll do exactly as she requested."

CHAPTER SIXTEEN

Mark burst through the hospital doors straight to the front desk. Shoving through the line, he ignored the irritated protests as he demanded the attention of the receptionist, who appeared just as pleased at the intrusion.

"Nicole Nike!" Mark anxiously demanded. "N-I-K-E. She was just evacuated from a burning building and sent here. How is she?"

"I'm sorry, sir, but I'm not privy to that information," the receptionist replied, gaze steely. She had been tempered to an emotionless resolve by the onslaught of stressed relations of patients for years. One more man was nothing. "Please sit down and be quiet, or I will have to call security."

Opening his mouth to argue, Mark caught the glances of a few security guards. Thinking better, he nodded sharply and stalked away, his movements jerky. Seating himself in one of the empty chairs lining the wall, he resigned himself to worrying.

After some time, a man dressed in a doctor's lab coat walked up to him. "You requested a status report on one of our recent patients?"

Mark nodded eagerly. "Yes. Nicole Nike. How is she?"

"What is your relation?"

"Best friend. We work together."

"Name and phone number?" At Mark's prompt reply, the doctor jotted something down his data-pad. "You're on her emergency contact list. Walk with me, please."

Standing, Mark followed the doctor to an isolated corner of the room. The institutional waiting chairs nearby were empty, and a fake ficus plant attempted a sense of homeliness, but the leaves were bleached by time and exposure, and stark lighting just made Mark feel cold. "How is she?"

"I'm Dr. Thatch, I was the attending specialist for Miss Nike," The doctor shook Mark's hand. "I'm afraid that her condition is serious. She has significant blunt trauma. Surprisingly, we found traces of poison inhalation in her respiration system, which, had we not found, would've also killed her. Less serious injuries include shrapnel remains."

"So what is her outcome?" Mark pressed.

Dr. Thatch pursed his lips in contemplation. He made a vague gesture with his hands. "Despite all this, she has a good prognosis. She will likely require significant physical therapy, especially on her right side."

Running a hand through his hair, Mark took a moment. "What about her pets? She has a dog and a Hesperonychus. Do you have any information on them?"

Dr. Thatch shook his head in the negative. He harrumphed. "I suggest you see if that information is in a police report."

After a promise to contact Mark when it was safe for Nicole to entertain visitors, Mark bid farewell and walked to the exit. Back on the sidewalk, he got in his car, but didn't start it. He let his head fall into the steering wheel. The dull *thud* was a minor inconvenience in the maelstrom that was currently his mind.

Firefighters milled around the charred building, while others remained on ladders, extinguishing the lingering flames. Traffic had been redirected away from the immediate area, where littered glass shards created a rainbow gleam, and crunched underfoot like frost on grass. Ash drifted like dispirited confetti. Through the apartment building was tall, the scent of the explosion drifted downward into the streets.

High up on the apartment building, the windows which had been blown out billowed black smoke and scarlet flames that greedily lapped at open air. Water from the fire hoses provided an inky runoff of wet soot down the sides of the building like a waterfall of liquid tar, leaving opaque streaks of grey behind.

Milling in helpless worry, tenants of the building watched out of the firefighters' way. They were in varying states of dress, some inadequately prepared for the outside chill. Some were speaking to family or friends on their phones.

The press had wasted no time. Animated reporters, wide-eyed in appearance, with just the right degree of disarray, spread the news to the public. Endless pundits proposed theories as to the cause. Was it a gas leak that caused the destruction, they would ask. Or perhaps the Unison Order was involved. And on this they built their case of misinformed opinion, as the authorities had yet to determine the true cause of the explosion.

Eyewitnesses reported with differing magnitudes of exaggeration, and it took some time for the truth to be compiled. In the end, it was discovered that there had been an explosion in one of the upper rooms.

The crowd of gawkers and tenants grew, pinned behind rapidly-erected police barriers and a line of emergency vehicles. Occasionally, a new person would be carried out of the building, and an ambulance would leave with the unfortunate soul. As the thriving throng was tightly packed akin to sardines, Pete Berg was forced to assess the scene from the back of the crowd. Having rushed from his workplace, he wasn't quite expecting the severity of the damage to be so great. *How could she have survived this?!*

Past the din of conversations and news reporters, he registered that someone was trying to call him. Abandoning his coveted spot in the crowd to flee the noise, he commanded, "Phone answer: Pete Berg."

"Pete! It's Mark."

"Mark! Have you heard–"

"Yeah, I just came out of the hospital after checking on Nikki. She's got it bad, Pete. Trauma, shrapnel, poisoning! The doctor says she'll need therapy for the right side of her body."

Pete stared into empty space, trying to comprehend. This reeked of targeted attack, and the memory of the *Clades* virus leapt to the forefront. "Wha. . . What about Compeer and that raptor she took in?"

"Aim? I don't know anything about her condition; she wasn't reported recovered with Nikki. Compeer's been shipped to the vet downtown. I'm heading there now. It's a miracle it wasn't worse."

"I'm looking at the apartment complex now. There's no way they should've survived an explosion like the one the tenants claim. It happened very close to her apartment, I can tell by the blown out windows." Pete ran a hand through his hair. "Wait, poisoning?"

"Whatever or whoever planted that explosion gave Nikki a dose of something toxic. When she breathed it in, it burned the bronchioles in her lungs. The poison has been remediated, so that's good news, I suppose."

Speechless, Pete could only gape.

"That's what I thought, too. Look, I've reached the vet clinic to check on Compeer. I think Nikki has something at the Reserve that she was going to head. Why don't you drive over and see if you can help?"

"I'll do that right now," Pete replied, backing away from the crowd and heading down the street to where his car was parked. "If there's anything Anita and I can do to help, we'll jump on it. Tell me how Compeer's doing when you know."

"Got it. Talk to you later."

Pete ended the call and walked to his smart car, which turned on and unlocked as he approached. With the increased traffic thanks to the redirections, it took nearly twice as long as it should have for him to finally exit the city and the suburbs and enter the countryside.

"Mr. Berg!" Jasmine exclaimed upon his entrance. Hurriedly, she shoved aside her data-pad to give him her full attention. "Did ya hear? Miss Nicole is in the hospital!" She gestured wildly at the television.

"Hey, Jasmine," Pete replied, heavily leaning on her desk. "Is there anything I can possibly do to help around here in Nikki's absence?"

The secretary clicked through her computer. "Miss Nike has a meetin' with some herpetologists tomorrow mornin'. She was goin' to lead them into the Reserve and answer their questions."

"Done. What else do I have to do to fill her place?"

Jasmine thought for a minute, then began ticking off items on her fingers. "Well, ya need to know the general specs of all the dinosaurian species, includin' foods they can and cannot eat. That's just for the tour tomorrow. Then, there are new security protocols, our current financial regulatory audits, and general operational and administrative tasks. Ah can help ya with those."

Pete leaned forward. "Give me all the data I need. I'm going to be filling in for Nikki for however long she needs."

"But. . . what about your job?"

"I spoke with my manager on the way over here. He understands, just so long as I do my homework. Hand me that data-pad, will you?"

Tremors wracked her hand, and she had to lift the pen from the paper before her writing got any worse. Massaging the strained tendons in her wrist, she read over the letter on the table, almost finished.

Outside, it was growing dark. The library would be closing soon. The computer monitor to her right began to dim, and she wriggled the mouse to keep it awake. With no identification card or a passcode, it had been a miracle to find an available computer. A sticky pad of notes sat beside her, covered with her messy handwriting of mixed cursive and block lettering.

She leaned on a stack of books, rubbing her fingers on the top book's matte paper cover. Disquieted energy bounced her leg. She kept rereading the letter, thoughts running rampant. Should she do it? Should she not?

It happened, she knew it did. It was at that point, and the time would pass. If it had *already* happened, then she would have no way of knowing about it. Better to have redundancy, right?

"Calm down," she groused to herself as she picked up the pen. Much to her delight, her handwriting didn't look like her quaky grandmother's anymore.

There. Finished. The only problem now was the fact that

she didn't have an envelope. She had the address, though, which was a problem in and of itself, because it was a challenge to research on the computer. She just hoped that she hadn't set off an alarm.

And her leg was bouncing at double speed. Wonderful. *I do not need paranoia right now.*

Someone tapped on her shoulder, and she jumped in the seat, her hand reflexively disappearing into a pocket.

"I'm sorry for startling you," said the librarian behind her. "But the library's closing in ten minutes."

She forced a smile, mentally shoving her mind into social mode. It was rather hard for her. She didn't cope well with talking to other people. Family was fine, and she hadn't seen them in *months*, but her phone wasn't working right and the librarian is *looking at her books, no no no!*

"Thanks for telling me," she blurted, casually leaning further over her pile of books, using her body to block the covers from sight.

It wasn't hard for her to feign. Speaking to oneself in the mirror every day, throwing the imagination into situations from movies and books was a practice she had perfected. Holding entire conversations was easy. Her mind could play as the fictional hero, complete with the right temperament and personality, then snap back into herself. She could act. She could change her own moods in an instant. She was the calm browser. The girl totally and furtively keeping the librarian from learning that–

STOP NARRATING MY LIFE.

The smile was pasted on now. She didn't need her brain

going down that track. She had enough of a headache already without her overactive imagination doing a voice-over. At least she wasn't saying it under her breath, like she sometimes caught herself doing. Or, judging by the neutral demeanor of the librarian, changing her facial expressions as if engaged in a most exhilarating conversation no one else could hear.

"That looks interesting," the librarian said, leaning to look around her. "Is that new teen fiction? I've heard that we've gotten a few new additions. That looks like a series! May I see?"

Her suave exterior was falling apart fast. Her goal was to get in and get out, not talk to anyone. "Ah. . . I'm kinda using these books at the moment. Research stuff. These aren't library books. Or even fiction. Biographies."

"Oh," the librarian said. "Well, may I see the title? I'm curious."

She thought pensively, weighing the risks. A title was nothing, just so–

If the librarian never opened the cover, there probably wouldn't be any harm. Reading the back? Oh. Oh, she hadn't thought of that. Or that the author was –! Um. . . Was it public knowledge? Oh no, the computer's fallen asleep!

With great panic, she struggled to keep her mask in place. What can she possibly do, she thought. If only the notion had occurred to her earlier that someone might, in fact, become curious and query about the books she ardently refused to allow people to see.

Oi, would you shut it?

The librarian no longer possessed a pasted-on smile.

"Are you alright?"

"I'm fine. My uncle's supposed to be coming along in a few minutes, and I want to be all packed up and ready before he gets here. Look. Um. Look, do you have an envelope with postage? I can pay for them."

Mercifully, the librarian either ignored or was oblivious to the subject change. Shortly, she had an envelope and a stamp. After addressing it, and leaving the return address vacant, she waved goodbye to the librarian, found the public mailbox, and dropped it down the slot.

CHAPTER SEVENTEEN

Pete sat on one of the rocking chairs, scanning through the information on his data-pad. Names, faces, doctorates and professions. Browsing through the files took his mind off of the unseasonal chill, how the fabric of his jacket was just a tad too thin for his tastes. The problem would most likely fix itself once he got moving and generated more heat. For the umpteenth time, he checked the time. The herpetologists were late.

Finally, he heard a car coming down the road. Standing, he hoped that he looked like the substitute "man in charge", as Jasmine had nicknamed him, as an SUV taxi entered the parking lot and found a spot. No sooner had the vehicle come to a complete stop than six people got out.

"Welcome to the Dinosaur Reserve," Pete said as they walked up onto the porch. "I'm Pete Berg, and I'll be guiding you today."

They returned his greeting, some with boundless enthusiasm, while others were less so.

"Forgive me if I offend, but I thought that the CEO and Overseer would be guiding us," one of the herpetologists stated.

"None taken," Pete replied. "Nicole Nike is unavailable and has appointed me in her place." He gestured to the armed duo behind him. "I and my security team will have the pleasure of escorting you today."

"How unfortunate. Some of us were speaking in the car and we were eager to consult with Miss Nike."

"I'm very sorry," Pete said. "I'll field any questions to the best of my ability." He glanced at his data-pad, matching faces to names, then proceeded to verify their identification badges. This was taken in stride, the visitors accustomed to the preliminary hassle. "It looks like it might rain within the next few hours, so let's mix up the itinerary a bit. I'll take you down to the dinosaurs first. If you would follow me to one of our larger off-road vehicles."

"There's no road?" one of the guests asked incredulously.

"The Reserve is very large," Pete said, appeasing the question. "And we don't know where the dinosaurs are at any given time. We may find them right away, or we may not find them for an hour or two. If you please, this way."

"Not even a microchip or collar?" one inquired.

Pete hummed. "It was offered, but none of them were comfortable being a mobile beacon. Would you be?"

A scientist pursed her lips thoughtfully. "What if there's an emergency, where the dinosaurs need to be located posthaste for their own safety?"

"A time crunch, where more would be in danger if it took too long to find them?" Pete contributed. "I won't say that it's unappealing for the sake of personal safety, but the dinosaurs come from a time when vocalizations and scents were all they needed to find each other. Privacy is also of great importance. To them, the idea of a tracker of any sort is. . . revolting." He didn't add that Freedom once told Nicole that, had she not used the *Intimidator* to save her home, the Utahraptor would have been a social pariah for accepting such a blatantly foreign accessory.

The following response was uttered so softly, Pete almost didn't hear it; "Well, they're just animals. Should've done it anyway; save the inconvenience."

"Wait," came an interjection from the back seats. It was a young woman, body canted so she could see the mutterer. "What if you were lost in the desert? You're all alone, and no one knows where you are. You find a supply depot, and there's a radio. Thing is, if you use the radio, two groups of people know exactly where you are. One group will help you, the other will kill you. They are both an equal distance away. With those two sureties, would you still use the radio?"

No one opined, and it became a disconcertingly quiet jeep ride. Pete fidgeted in the driver's seat, needlessly altering the rearview mirror every so often. Behind them trailed a Reserve security vehicle. As the jeeps bounced through the underbrush, branches intruded the interiors. Pete hoped that they would find the dinosaurs sooner than later, or maybe not at all.

Suddenly, a booming roar rippled the air. Pete stood on the brakes as an Ankylosaurus bounded out of the brush, brandishing its clubbed tail. Its leaps quaked the ground, bouncing the jeep on its shocks. In the wake of its passage laid the mangled remains of shrubbery, torn and splintered, their new lot in life to rot on the forest floor. Before the dinosaur could crash into the jeeps it stiffened its front legs and skidded to a halt, heels trenching the soft loam. Recovering from the abrupt halt, the Ankylosaurus shook its head at the jeeps threateningly.

"Stay in the jeep!" Pete ordered, unbuckling his seatbelt, sliding out of the vehicle. He took a few slow steps toward the herbivore, holding up his hands. "What's wrong?" he asked.

The Ankylosaurus growled, eying the herpetologists. "Who they?" it asked in rough English, its thick grey tongue

visibly struggling to form the words.

"It speaks!" was heard from inside the jeep, accompanied by a few other comments of astonishment.

"Scientists wanting to learn about your kind," Pete replied to the dinosaur. "They mean no harm."

Its deep green eyes narrowed. With a rumbling snort, it clicked its beak and said, "I no like them."

"Why not?"

"You humans no smell. *I* can. New people smell off."

Pete was not the sort of man to ignore instincts. He also tended to trust others' superior abilities. "I understand, and will keep an eye out. Will you let us by?"

The Ankylosaurus stared pensively at the herpetologists for a long moment, slowly shifting its weight from side to side. "Yes," it rumbled. "Careful."

Pete nodded, then leaned in to speak softer. "Thank you. I will. Please closely watch the ones who 'smell off.' I appreciate your diligence."

The Ankylosaurus backed into the bushes, opening the path ahead. It didn't go completely, watching the jeeps warily.

Upon Pete's approach back to the vehicle, one of the herpetologists said, "Can we go on now?"

"Yes," Pete replied, starting up the jeep again. He had a thought, and looked over at the Ankylosaurus. "How far away are the others?" he called through the window.

"Not far. Just over hills." It gestured with a swing of its head.

"Thank you." Pete pressed down the accelerator pedal.

It didn't take long to reach the hills a few hundred yards away. The treeline became thinner, portending a clearing ahead. The jeeps crested the grassy knolls, and on the other side were the dinosaurs. The dinosaurs had gathered around an open area of the river, at a small cove where the running current stalled to a safe clip. Younglings played in the shallow water, sending waves and sprays everywhere to shine like purest glass.

The rumble of the jeep's engine caught the dinosaurs' attentions, pausing their activities to examine the arrivals. A few tense calls had the younglings retreating from the water and to the shadows of their respective parents. A nearby Triceratops shifted downwind of the jeeps to sniff the air, then made a sound that had all other dinosaurians tauten.

"This is it?" a herpetologist said, looking around. "I thought there'd be more."

An Albertosaurus within earshot growled softly, tail twitching like an antsy cat's.

Pete tightened his jaw. "Please, be sensitive about what you say. Most of them understand English."

"They're just animals," the herpetologist remarked back.

Pete shook his head, dropping the subject. He knew better than to pursue a topic when someone wore a face of ignorant intransigency.

One of the other herpetologists, a young woman with

a dark tan, came up to Pete. "How many dinosaurs *are* here? I went over the Reserve's website, but I couldn't find a definite number."

"After the hatchlings came in the first spring, we lost count for a while," Pete said, struggling to remember the last recorded amount. "After every hatching season, we take a census. Currently, there are over 250 dinosaurs, and about 30 pterosaurs."

"That's a lot," the herpetologist said, whistling.

"Not really," Pete said with a sad smile, looking around. "This amount before us? A very, very small percentage of what Nicole saw in her first time in the Cretaceous."

"But they're coming back."

Pete smiled, less sad than before. "Yes, they're coming back, but not all of what Nicole logged came through the portal. Species have been forever lost." Not for the first time, he wondered how many had arrived at Freedom's hidden cove too late, where the land was trampled, and all the signs of a hope never to return.

As he scanned the area for Kelp, whom he understood was acting as leader in Freedom's absence, the sun's light shone into his eyes, and Pete raised a hand to guard them. Squinting, he could see Freedom's mate approaching. The Utahraptor was sniffing the air, and his unpleasant expression was becoming more so with every step closer.

"Greetings, Kelp," Pete said.

Kelp stopped a respectable distance away, assuming a passive aggressive stance. "Pete," he replied. "Who're the people with you?"

"They're herpetologists," Pete said. "They wish to study you and further their reptile knowledge."

The Utahraptor's lips peeled away from wetly flashing teeth. "Study? How so are these studies? Will we be pricked with needles and scales ripped off? Stolen to distant places?"

"No!" Pete was quick to reassure. "Hands-off. Observation only, as was in the contract they all signed when this meeting was confirmed. No one will leave the Reserve without your permission."

"Why wasn't I informed of this meeting *before* now?"

"I. . . I don't know. I apologize for not ensuring that you were made aware of this." Pete could feel his face flushing, well aware that the guests were within earshot. "I'll speak with Jasmine on closing the cracks such things can fall through. I'm sorry, this should not have happened."

Kelp silently snarled, piercing the herpetologists with his predatory gaze. The humans fidgeted uneasily as they awaited his verdict. Finally; "All studies will be conducted without physical contact. Questions may be asked, but that does not mean they will be answered if we feel it violates our personal safety or security. Am I clear?"

The herpetologists looked at each other. After a moment, one of them nodded. "Crystal."

Kelp took a step back and to the side. "Then, educate yourselves."

At that, most of the herpetologists scattered. Pete raised

an eyebrow at the lone person awkwardly standing there. The herpetologist could barely be out of college; perhaps an intern?

Intently staring back, Kelp cleared his throat.

The herpetologist jumped, eyes widening to comical proportions. "I– I'm sorry for staring, but. . . why did you speak like you're not in charge? Where's the one labelled on the Reserve's website, Freedom?"

"Freedom is the leader of all that were brought through the portal," Pete interjected for Kelp. "She is not able to be present at the moment."

"Oh. . . Well. . . I guess I'll. . . I'll just go over there. Thanks for clarifying."

As the herpetologist walked off, Pete kept an eye on the group as he strode toward a large group of hatchlings. The babies saw him coming and squealed, darting away from their babysitter. Pete planted his feet as they surrounded him, chittering and chirping away. None of them could speak dinosaur-ese very well, but their grasp on English was astonishing, despite them sounding like four-year-olds.

"How are you little ones doing today?" Pete asked, kneeling to get closer to their eye level. He hadn't had the chance to visit the Reserve often, and had missed the hatching season.

A hatchling Edmontonia pressed up against his shin, not unlike a cat. "We learning speaking," it said.

"And what fine speaking you're doing," Pete said, hiding how painful he found the developing armor domes digging into his shin. "Why, you must've found a dictionary!"

"Dip-sion-airy?" a Stygimoloch attempted.

"Dictionary," Pete corrected gently, saying it very slowly. "It's English, only written down in characters that make up spoken words."

The hatchling Stygimoloch nodded. "Ah. Will you teaching us dictionary?"

Pete blinked, taken slightly by surprise. "Well, when you can speak both dinosaur-ese and English, I'm sure Nicole'll teach you how to read and write."

A hatchling Quetzalcoatlus stamped its feet. "Like Freedom! We be learning lots!" it said.

"Good for you." Pete smiled.

He heard chittering from the shaking branches above. Pete looked up to see the flock of Pterodactylus playing amongst the trees. A few of the fledgelings were chasing each other, dodging branches and leaves with all the grace of eagles. The largest Pterodactylus sat back near the trunk of a tree, watching the herpetologists.

Pete frowned in surprise. *What's Assail doing here?* he thought. *He's supposed to be with the Black-Ops team, if Nicole's notes are correct.* He looked for Gale and Rush among the bunch; Gale was playing with the youngling Pterodactylus, but Rush was nowhere to be seen.

Suspicious, Pete searched for the band of Bambiraptors. They were hard to spot, as they were so small, but, when he saw them, he spotted Shriek sunbathing on a rock poking above the grasses.

Assail glided down to the top of a bush beside him. "Hello," he said. "Where's Nicole?"

"Hello, Assail," Pete replied slowly. "Nicole was involved in a bad accident, and she's in the hospital. I'm filling in for her." He cocked an eyebrow and glanced at the herpetologists, asking the silent question.

"We are suspicious in that at least one of the herpetologists is secretly aligned with the UO," Assail said quietly, glancing around. "Our human partners are among the real scientists."

Pete panned over the herpetologists, who were scattered across the area. From what they were doing and how they looked, he simply couldn't distinguish the counterfeit from the authentic.

A sound of flapping drew his attention back to Assail, to find his spot empty. He looked up and saw him rejoining his flock.

Pete made eye contact with one of the security agents and made a discreet summoning gesture. The agent sidled closer, hand hovering over the firearm holstered at a hip.

"Something isn't quite right with the guests," Pete said. "Multiple dinosaurians have conferred warnings. We're only going to be out here for a short while longer according to the timetable, so, if anything will happen, it will happen soon."

"Yes, sir," the agent replied. "The dinosaurians aren't the only ones noticing things amiss." He subtly pointed with his thumb, but Pete didn't catch whom was being pointed out. "Welch. He appears to be a legitimate professional, but only in the field of herpetology. It is possible that he has sold out, but has no extensive subterfuge training beyond the rudimentary.

We are keeping a close watch on him, and will alert you if he does something untorward." With that, the agent wandered off.

Pete sagaciously meandered closer to the scientists, eyes searching for any more discrepancies. Not a single one of their movements was left unnoticed. One of the women was running a scanner over an Albertosaurus. A second was closely examining a wary and extremely uneasy Ankylosaurus as it meticulously chewed its mouthful of greenery. The scientist was well intruding on the concept of personal space. A third herpetologist took pictures of a dinosaur's favorite snack bush, a fourth was fiddling with his coat, and the last two appeared to be taking down notes on their personal data-pads.

Disregarding the others, Pete focused on the scientist, Welch, fiddling with his coat, who finally grasped something in an interior pocket. Pete casually sidled closer, following the man as he approached an Edmontonia.

"Here, dino, dino, dino," the herpetologist cooed, holding out a leafy sprig with gloved hands. "Want something nice?"

The Edmontonia sniffed the sprig, nostrils flaring wide.

Pete managed to get close enough to identify the greenery. His eyes widened; "*Drop it!*" he ordered frantically.

The Edmontonia bellowed, startled, before lumbering away to a safe distance. The Reserve security bristled, drawing their weapons. They crowded Welch, though kept awareness on the other guests just in case he was a distraction. The herpetologists condensed together in alarm, instinctively seeking safety with familiar persons.

Welch frowned irritably, facing Pete. "What is the

matter?" he asked, still holding the sprig. "It's just leafy greens. I thought that Edmontonias were herbivores, are they not?"

"You're a herpetologist; you study lizards for a living. Shouldn't you *know* what you're feeding to dinosaurs?"

"I only wanted to see if it chewed in a figure-eight like a camel, or up and down like us," the herpetologist replied, almost like a child caught with the chocolate milk jug to the mouth. It was an asinine reason, for any herbivores not being harassed were grazing.

"Where'd you get this?" Pete said, gesturing at the oleander. "You couldn't have just plucked it because it doesn't grow around here."

"I got it on the way here. I've seen other animals eat it, so I assumed that it must be safe for dinosaurs."

Pete clenched his hands behind his back, shifting his weight onto one leg. "You'd better not have any more plants on you," he said, forcefully keeping his tone calm.

"I swear on my honor that I don't," Welch retorted.

Jaw tight, Pete cast his gaze around. Kelp was hovering nearby, fringe erect and head lowered. None of the other dinosaurians appeared particularly inspired to resume entertaining the herpetologists, but Pete knew of no one who would consent to such invasive staring. The Pterodactylus flock in the trees were unusually jittery, eyes glued to the commotion below. The security agents were on a hair trigger, and the herpetologists gave the impression that Welch's actions were entirely unprecedented.

Making a decision, Pete stepped back.

Every Pterodactylus in the flock began shrieking at the top of their lungs. Pete ducked and covered his head as they took off in a cloud. When they had passed, he looked up to see them mobbing Dr. Welch, flapping around him like a swarm of monster hornets.

A few other herpetologists tried to wave away the pterosaurs, but they soon disbanded of their own volition, flying back to their trees, except one that was half-buried inside Welch's jacket. It remained a moment longer, squirming around, before emerging. It dropped a small branch cluster at Pete's feet before rejoining its kin.

Dr. Welch peeked up from his fetal position on the grass before slowly uncurling. Normally, Pete would help, but he kept his hands at his sides and his gaze on the branch cluster. The

herpetologist stood, dusting off his clothes.

Pete plucked the cluster from the ground. Facing the rest of the group, he held it out as if daring them to contradict. "One of you," he addressed the herpetologists. "Tell me what this is."

"Oleander," the redhead replied. She glanced from the cluster to the sprig Pete carried in his other hand, then to Welch. "A plant that causes lethality in reptiles."

"Correct," Pete declared, voice steel. He eyed Welch accusingly. "You reference your honor, but the evidence indicates otherwise. I see a man who had sanguinary intention to feed an individual a known poisonous substance. Guards, seize him."

Welch protested loudly as his arms were discourteously yanked behind his back and handcuffed. Kelp's rumble, wet and gargling from deep in the throat, silenced Welch. The Utahraptor stalked to Pete's side, a fearsome figure of full hostility.

"Why did you try to feed them oleander?" Pete demanded.

Welch cowered placatingly. "This is a misunderstanding. You see –"

"Who bought you?"

"No one! It was a mistake, I swear, it was all just a mistake."

Kelp roared. "LIAR. Treacherous scum! You attempt to murder one of mine and deceive through your decrepit teeth!" Kelp turned to face Pete straight on, who stifled the instinct to flee. "I can smell the stench of falsehoods. He *reeks* of fear. What sort of information could he reveal while his limbs were slowly devoured, bite by bite?"

Welch went utterly pallid and wavered on his feet. "Wait wait wait wait! This. . . I have rights! You cannot legally feed me to these animals!"

"You wouldn't be afraid to be mincemeat if you were innocent," Pete reasoned. "I happen to trust Kelp's nose far more than you, at the moment. Everyone, I believe that the excursion has concluded."

The herpetologists shuffled toward one jeep while the guards hauled Welch to the other. Pete turned to Kelp and searched for something to say. "Kelp, I'm *so sorry* for this. They will not be back."

Kelp nodded, still upset. He took a breath as if about to speak, but instead set his jaw, turned, and stiffly strode away.

Pete sighed and ran a hand down his face. He reset his expression to neutral as he walked to the jeep. The herpetologists were silent. Pete gunned the jeep back the way they had come, following the original ruts left in the ground.

"Mr. Berg!" Jasmine said as Pete entered the Reserve's building. "Back already?" Her chipper demeanor dropped when she saw Pete's face. "Can Ah do anythin' to help?"

"Yes," Pete said, hanging up the jeep's keys with a little more force than necessary.

Looking past Pete and spotting the detained Welch, Jasmine picked up the phone. "They're leavin'?"

"One of them tried to feed oleander to the dinosaurs," Pete said.

"Ah thought we'd uprooted any 'round here."

"Exactly. Please arrange our guests' transportation, and a detail for Welch."

Nodding, Jasmine dialed.

Pete returned to the front windows and peered through the translucent white curtains at the herpetologists, who were being directed to the seats on the porch.

On the porch, Robin sat down in one of the old-fashioned wicker rocking chairs. Snuggling into the back cushion, she took a data-pad from her bag and began writing. Nonsense already filled the screen, nothing that would befit an actual herpetologist. Robin plucked a stylus from its holster and began adding more gobbledygook.

Feeling her neck prickle, she looked up. Robin peered around before finding eye contact with Williams.

He was casually leaning against a post, writing on his own data-pad. Now that he had caught her gaze, he flicked his eyes to the left.

Without turning her head, Robin looked left. The only person in that range was the herpetologist who had tried to poison dinosaurs with oleander. A quick look at legit files on her data-pad showed the man's profile and ID picture.

Dr. Jason Welch, she thought, tapping her chin contemplatively.

Bringing up an internet browser, she did a search for the potentness of poison to reptiles. She discovered several sites claiming that oleander was quite able to kill a reptile in moments. She caught Williams' gaze and nodded.

Was Dr. Jason Welch their target? After that deception, it appeared most likely.

She and Williams looked to Lennox. The short man was engrossed in his own data-pad. Robin knew that he was looking up Dr. Welch's credentials and history. Several minutes passed before he looked up at the two of them and tapped his screen.

A quiet bleep alerted her to a message. Robin opened it and saw everything they needed.

Lennox stood and knocked on the front door lightly before poking his head inside. "Excuse me, Mr. Berg? Might you please direct me to a restroom?"

"Yes," Robin heard Berg reply. "This way."

Robin nodded to herself, letting out a soft, but unhappy, sigh. That was now done, and her mind was able to drift off onto other subjects, such as where on earth her pterosaur partner had gone. She hadn't seen him since that night at the motel. Internet spiders had located him in a picture on social media. HQ sent the entire team to Mississippi on a retrieval mission. The adolescent who had taken the picture had redirected them to her friend's house. The Stellars admitted that they had Rush with them for a brief time, but the mother had instructed the daughter to set Rush free. He hadn't turned up anywhere since.

The porch door opened, and Berg and Lennox walked out. "Taxis are on their way to pick you up and return you to the city," Berg said. His voice was cold. Robin could understand. Berg had to be going through a substantial amount of stress, standing in such a large position for a friend. "I hope that you all managed to gather useful information, despite the unseen shortened timetable. Thank you for your time." Berg ducked back inside and closed the door.

Robin didn't miss how Dr. Welch received renewed glares from the other scientists. The real herpetologists had wasted their time and expenses because of him. Robin didn't blame them. They had all rights to be angry. She added her own disdained look, for good measure.

Shortly thereafter, a taxi arrived in the parking lot. Robin stood, putting away her data-pad and straightening her clothes. The herpetologists departed, leaving Welch still detained on the porch. The disgraced man glowered from his position in a rocking chair, awkwardly bent forward to accommodate the handcuffs.

Stowing her data-pad, Robin extended her badge for the Reserve security team to evaluate. Lennox revealed a warrant. Welch became theirs.

chapter eighteen

Pete watched out the window as the taxis drove away. Once the red tail lights had been lost to the trees, he sighed loudly and collapsed into one of the waiting chairs.

"Is somethin' wrong, Mr. Berg?" Jasmine asked.

"How do I give Kelp updates?"

Jasmine leaned on her elbows. "Well, Miss Nike would go out and talk with Freedom and try and smooth things over, Ah think." Reaching up and behind her, she grabbed a car key and tossed it to Pete.

He sighed, rubbing at his forehead. "You're right. But

what do you report to him?"

"What's right?" Jasmine supplied.

Pete laughed and stood. "If I don't come back, come look for my carcass, would you? If you find it, tell my wife I love her."

"Good luck," Jasmine murmured.

"I don't believe in luck," Pete said, opening the door. "I do, however, believe in miracles. And we need them."

Ten or so minutes later, Pete parked the jeep and trudged toward the river. He crested the last hill and sent out Nicole's habitual hoot. Kelp didn't move as he approached.

Once within earshot, Pete began speaking. "Kelp, I cannot tell you how much I'm distressed by what happened. I didn't know that one of them planned on poisoning your kind. The good news is that three of the herpetologists were actually members of Assail's team, and they will take care of putting Dr. Welch away."

Pete waited, but the Utahraptor neither said, nor showed, anything. Eventually, Pete ran down and fell into an uncomfortable silence.

Finally, Kelp replied, "I am not my mate, and cannot pass judgment or approval."

Pete nodded. *Freedom picked her mate well.*

"However, I believe that I know what she would say in reply and what actions she would take. I will say this once, and only once, and I ask you to remember it and pass it on to Nicole upon her return," Kelp said. "I *never* want to see anyone other than a verified Reserve worker stepping foot into our territory."

"I'll make sure that anyone is approved–"

"I wasn't finished. I don't care if you pick potential visitors apart till you see their very bones. *No one is to enter.* The only people who aren't Reserve workers, who I may allow in would be those who went with Nicole to rescue us, like yourself."

Pete paused a second. "What I was going to say was that you would have to approve any new visitors until after Nicole returns. This country is founded on life, liberty, happiness and property (but not of others). This is your property and Nikki's. It's your say."

Kelp processed the statement. "I'm surprised and pleased with your answer."

Nodding, Pete added as he turned to depart, "Have a good afternoon, Kelp. Know that I'm joining you in prayer for Nikki's and Freedom's safe returns."

Clearly surprised, Kelp nodded back in return.

"That developed satisfactorily," Williams said quietly, lounging against the back of his cheap hotel easy chair.

Lennox plucked the TV remote off of one of the bedside tables and pressed the power button. The TV turned on, already tuned to the automated channel index. Some vacuum infomercial was playing, but Lennox dialed up the volume.

Robin winced at the too-high pitch of the saleswoman's

voice. She tried to tune the TV out, but her training made it slightly difficult.

Lennox scanned through the files on his data-pad. "Welch was able to supply us with a fair amount of information."

"If, of course, he wasn't lying," Robin interjected.

"He had training," Lennox said, shaking his head. "But this guy, deep down, was a truly useful idiot."

"A *gullible* idiot, you say?" Robin said. "Can we trust his information, though? He works for the UO."

"If the info's good," Lennox replied. "Once the UO finds out we have Welch in custody, they'll change our new info and make it outdated. We need to act on this immediately."

"So we're going?" Williams asked.

Lennox nodded. "Yes. I need to call HQ and get ourselves transport and supplies."

"Peradventure, you should request a new techie," Williams said. "With Takin AWOL, we're down an important member to this team."

"Fair point." Lennox activated his comm, voice dialed, and waited. Over the next few minutes, Robin listened to him request transportation, supplies, and a new technical expert. When they hung up, Lennox said, "HQ's going to look for the best hacker in the States."

"Good," Robin said. "Wonder who it is."

"He's going to be outstanding," Williams said, twisting open the cap of a soda. "I can perceive it in my solar plexus."

"Am I receiving a new partner?" Robin asked.

Lennox pursed his lips. "HQ has failed to yet find Rush. And they hesitate to request a replacement from the Utahraptor after this last encounter, and with good reason. I apologize, Conners, but you're going to have to go relatively solo for now."

"Yes, sir."

Lennox placed a hand on one of her shoulders. "I'm sure that he'll come back sooner or later."

Robin exhaled, allowing the comfort of touch for a moment before shrugging off his hand. "Don't, sir. If he hasn't by now, he won't ever."

Her superior nodded understandingly, but suddenly stiffened. A finger held up sent the others to wait in total silence as Lennox again activated his communicator. After the initial coded greetings, most of Lennox's replies consisted of "Yes, sir"s and "Understood"s.

"Stage Ten incident at HQ," the team leader reported as soon as the call ended. "Anonymous letter arrived, no specific recipient. No return address. Delivered by a legit government mail truck."

"A letter?" Williams said. "What was inside?"

"Better yet, has it been verified?" Robin added. "And what do we have to do with it?"

"A tip," Lennox replied. "Nicole Nike was to meet against her will with a member of the Unison Order in a subway tunnel, which we knew, but HQ is cautious on how this unknown was aware. There was more in the letter, but that I will tell you later in favor of explaining our next mission. In the subway, four of ours watched the meeting occur. The UO member has been arrested, questioned, and HQ has a copy of the interrogation. HQ has requested we take out a small UO cell in the New York countryside."

"What about the new hacker and the information from Welch?" Robin asked.

"HQ is handling that. We're to move and take the cell out. Get your gear together."

The pond was filthy with grit and larvae, but it was water and Scope was parched. She could only think that the pond wasn't the absolute worst-tasting water she had ever drunk.

The little oversized puddle in her old cove in the Borderlands, contaminated with ash, "took the cake" as the humans said.

Having quenched her thirst, she raised her head and sniffed for any signs of danger. The tree cover had ended a while back, relinquishing shelter. There was nowhere to take cover unless she threw herself flat on her stomach. As she could hear a nearby city, any human with sight amplifiers could locate her in a heartbeat.

It made her feel incredibly vulnerable, despite having the *Intimidator* on her back. But the need to return to the tribe was overwhelming, and venturing over open and vulnerable fields was the most direct route. Uncut grasses and occasional shrubs were a boon, even though she had to turn quadruped, which ached after a while.

A cow lowed at her. The herd had retreated upon her approach to the pond, but didn't seem afraid of her. Although her stomach was beginning to complain, Scope had no intention of eating one, but the bovines were having difficulty discerning as such.

Deciding that she had idled too long, Scope continued on her way, cutting through the cows' pasture. A barn and house stood at a close distance, and she did not wish to be spotted. For all she knew, a Unison Order sympathizer lived there and was on the lookout for a lone Utahraptor with an odd silver backpack.

She loped along, her lengthy strides effortlessly consuming ground. She could maintain the pace until nightfall, but she was nearing a highway. She could see the sunlight reflecting off of the vehicles.

An alternate route was needed. Making a mental note

of the sun's position so she could find the direction again later on, and hopefully before sunset, she turned to jog parallel to the highway.

Some distance later, another town came into view. It was smaller than the one she spotted earlier in the cow pastures, but still inhabited by too many humans. There was no way to continue in the direction without crossing the road or town.

She was no Troodon, but she could give one a decent challenge in the speed category over short distances. Crouching low, grateful that her hide was the color of the grass, she stalked closer to the town.

The buildings slowly became closer, and Scope found herself entering suburbia. Taking to backyards as often as possible or waiting for a street to empty, she steadfastly made her convoluted way across town.

Poking her head over the top of a wooden privacy fence, Scope checked for any humans. Seeing none, she hefted herself over, landed on the lawn, and sprinted for the other side.

The sound of the home's back door opening had her straining to add speed. Someone screamed just as Scope sprang over the fence, landing in another neighbor's yard. She froze, locking gazes with the family of four enjoying an early dinner outside on a patio. Not waiting to see what they would do, she hastened for the other side.

It took mere moments to speed through the rest of the neighborhood, startle several drivers on a small road, cross through a second neighborhood, and finally reenter the countryside. There were still endless plains Scope vaguely recalled crossing while fleeing from the UO-GDs.

Hearing sirens approaching from behind, her adrenaline soared as she veered away from the roads. *They'll know where I am!*

The setting sun cast the skyscrapers in an orange and pink glow that brought out beauty in the urban landscape. It was oddly refreshing after the standard overcast day.

Wearily dragging his feet, Pete adjusted his grip on the briefcase he held. His fingers ached from a long day, and he repeatedly flexed them. He could hardly wait to get his hands around a mug of Anita's amazing hot chocolate.

Pete hummed, a small smile gracing his lips. He could taste it now! Three heaping spoonfuls of exquisite chocolate powder so fine not a single clump could remain, a teaspoon of dry vanilla, and perfectly heated whole milk. Plus that one ingredient that Anita refused to tell him. He highly suspected it to be malt.

He was thankful for something to look forward to after the day he'd just had.

At long last, he found himself trudging down the halls to his apartment door. He slid his card key through the slot and shouldered open the door.

"Anita!" he called, kicking it closed behind him. One hand on the wall steadied himself as he toed off his shoes, wriggling his socked toes once freed. "Sweetie pie, I'm home! You would not *believe* what I went through today."

No answer.

Pete hung up his coat and dumped his briefcase on a handy chair. "Darling?" He looked around the apartment, but his wife didn't appear to be home yet.

When he peered into the kitchen, he spotted a new addition on the counter; a huge chocolate and cream cake. Mouth beginning to water, Pete took the glass lid from over the cake and patted around for a knife.

A slip of paper in the silverware drawer drew his gaze from the dessert. He picked up the folded note and opened it.

"'Hi, Mine Husband,'" he read aloud, "'I know what you're thinking if you're looking in this drawer. The cake is for after dinner, not as a mid-afternoon snack. I'm sure you can resist, can't you? Love, Anita.'"

He sighed, placing the glass dome back over the cake. "If I must." He moved to the cupboard below the sink and pulled out a box. He flipped open the lid, revealing a pile of chocolate candies. "But you said nothing about my stash."

Just as he was tearing open a wrapper, the landline in the den rang. Pete leaked an unmanly whimper as he stowed the chocolate candies back under the sink, hiding the box with a pile of spare trash bags. The phone continued to blast its irritating jingle as he approached.

Even after he reached it, he waited a few more cycles before picking up the phone. "You have reached the Berg residence. We're not able to answer right now, but leave your name and return number after the beep." He took a breath. "Beep!"

"*Very convincing, Mr. Berg, yet not good enough. We're in need of your assistance.*"

Pete frowned. "Who is this?"

"*Let's just say that we have an offer that you can't possibly refuse.*"

"Depends. What's the offer?"

CHAPTER NINETEEN

Scope was *extremely* tired of evading pursuit. She wasn't certain as to the identity of her pursuers, but they employed vehicles that could follow her off road, weave between the trees, and her only saving grace so far was her ability to turn tighter than they and lose them for a few precious seconds.

A formation of boulders promised a place to hide, and she rounded the area with the echoes of approaching vehicles rumbling in the air. Just as she was about to give up and continue running, she saw a sliver of darkness by the ground that betrayed a hole. Ducking to all fours, she scrabbled at the dirt, widening the gap. She entered backwards, contorting uncomfortably so the *Intimidator* would not catch on the rocks. Craning her arm out of the hole, she severed some branches from a nearby bush and dragged them closer, hopefully disguising the marred earth.

The blinding headlights of the humans' vehicles passed over her hiding place, the screech of brakes and the grating of uneven dirt signaling their halt. Scope held very still, only her eyes moving to track the humans. She listened to their speech, calling instructions and questions to each other and over the radio.

They didn't sound Unison Order affiliated. It was a curious revelation, further proved when she managed to catch sight of the badge they bore, and the lettering across the backs of their coats. While it wasn't beyond conceivability that Animal Control had been infested, it was not very likely.

Scope thought back to when she and Nicole were discussing the borders of the Reserve. Any dinosaurians who violated the border were to be reported to the local authorities, whereupon the rogue dinosaur would be apprehended and returned. Animal Control was mentioned in the details.

She knew the runabout had rendered her hopelessly lost until sunrise, and she feared there was no time to waste. She supposed it was worth the risk.

"Hey. You're looking for me?"

It took a little while for Scope to convince the two Animal Control officers that yes, she was Freedom, who desperately needed transportation back home. Fortunately, one of them had been dinosaur-obsessed when younger, and was able to gain permission from a superior. Soon afterward, Scope found herself cramped in the back of a van with metal wire cages pressing into her hide.

At least her travel time had been cut from indefinite

to before daylight. According to her helpers, she had been completely turned around, and was almost heading in the complete opposite direction.

No sooner had the driver announced that they would be arriving at the Reserve in around fifteen minutes than the van violently swerved. It reared on two side wheels, the rubber screeching in protest in tandem with the straining engine. Scope braced herself and anxiously anticipated a total loss of control. The two humans screamed.

"What's going on?!" Scope yelled.

One of them tried to reply, but something in the cabin shattered. The van wobbled precariously while one of the humans panicked. The van toppled onto its side with a massive crash, skidding across the asphalt with a noise akin to nails on a chalkboard. Scope was trapped between two thick layers of cages, the corners digging into her flesh mercilessly.

Finally, the van came to a stop Scope heard a door open, followed by mad scrambling or struggling. A moment later, there was a muffled *bang*, and all was silent.

Scope was suddenly struck with the mad desire to get out– *get out*– *GET OUT*. Cages clanged and clinked as she attacked the back doors of the van feverishly. When her claws and talons did no more than create deep gouges in the plastic and metal, she remembered the *Intimidator*. Mentally accessing it, she commanded the laser to appear and cut through the locking mechanism. It took longer than usual for the laser to get into position from Scope's awkward angle, but a single red beam struck the doors. The moment one door started to sag open, she scrabbled out of the van, falling onto her side. Cages tumbled around her in a painful, clattering rain as she surged to her feet and bolted for the trees.

She heard the muffled *bang* again, almost instantly followed by the whine of something passing her head. She must've unconsciously sent the *Intimidator* a command to find the source, because it began whirring.

Several more projectiles streaked past her, one catching the crown of her nose and leaving a shallow red line across its width. Fire alit from the injury, almost blinding her in its intensity. She stumbled. A tree directly behind where her head had just been gained a round of lead.

Someone's shooting at me! At that moment, she felt what she could only call a *There!* sensation from the *Intimidator*. Her eyes flicked to the side, more specifically, a cluster of bushes. She could see nothing out of the ordinary, but whatever Nicole had programmed into the *Intimidator* assured her that someone, a gunman, was in the bushes.

As much as she despised what she was about to do, Scope summoned the laser again and had it slice horizontally into the bushes. The tops of the bushes, cleanly cut, fell. Scope couldn't see the attacker, and she didn't want to do so.

A moment later, Scope came to a stop and looked over her shoulder. What had happened to the two animal control officers? Scope sniffed. A harsh scent in the air, drifting from behind, slapped her nostrils. It was different yet similar to the animals she hunted.

Bowing her head to them, she stood there a moment longer to honor her fallen heroes. She turned away and sniffed the air. She was back in familiar territory, and would arrive at the boundaries of the Reserve before midmorning. Already her nerves were settling.

Nicole groaned, her eyelids feeling weighted down as she forced them open. Her body was stiff, like it hadn't moved in a while. Breathing caused a sensation akin to stabbing knives in her chest. And a peculiar sensation covered her skin, one that had her cringing in disgust. *And that hurt!*

"Welcome back."

Slightly turning her neck, she saw Pete and Anita sitting in chairs beside her bed. "What happened?" She started to scratch her head, but noticed a clear tube inserted into the back of her hand. It was then she became aware of the constant *beep* of the monitoring machines. "Am I in a hospital?"

Anita leaned forward. "You were evacuated here after an explosion at your apartment complex."

"Aim!" Nicole exclaimed, jerking to try to sit upright. An unbelievable agony shot down her entire right side, halting her. "*Ow...*"

"Careful," Pete advised. "Your body's still recovering from your wounds. Your right side was riddled with shrapnel from your building. When it heals, you're going to have to go through physical therapy." He glanced at a translucent bag hanging from a pole, leading to the tube in her hand. "It doesn't look like the anesthetic is working."

"It was Aim. The Hesperonychus? It was actually a robot made by the UO to spy on me. Automaton Intelligencer Model, I think. It shot a liquid at my face before self-destructing."

"That liquid was a poison. Besides that, you and Compeer are fortunate to be *alive.*"

"Compeer!" Nicole said, looking around. "Where is he?"

Pete scratched his head. "Well, the hospital doesn't allow pets unless they're service animals, but Mark's been taking care of him since his operation."

"Operation?"

"He had injuries, too," Anita said softly. "He'll make it, but it won't be pretty, I'm afraid."

Nicole's heart broke. "At least he's being taken care of. Thank you, Anita. How's the Reserve going?" she asked, and gasped. "The herpetologists! I was supposed–"

"I guided them," Pete interjected. "One of them tried to poison the dinosaurs with oleander, and I had to end it early.

The Pterodactylus were actually the ones who discovered the guy."

"Freedom?"

Pete sighed. "No sign of her."

Moaning, she attempted to sit up again. She couldn't do it, and the effort was punishing. "I need to get out of here. Find some doctors who can tell me what I need to know. I can't stay cooped up in here! If the UO wants me dead so urgently, I certainly have a good reason to get back to work."

Fingers fiddling, Pete looked about to speak, thought better of it, then started using his data-pad. "Look at this," he said quietly, showing her the screen.

It took a while before Nicole recognized her apartment. "Is that. . ?" she gasped, eyes widening at the destruction. The walls were shattered, supports and electrical conduits splayed over the floor. Her furniture fared no better, shredded and torn fragments. Everything was blackened with char, glistening with fresh dousing water. "I should be dead. I'm here, aren't I? Am I in a coma? Am I *dying*?"

"Nicole! Nikki, calm down! You're going to be fine, I promise." Anita took her hand, rubbing circles on the palm. "You need to calm down, or the heart rate monitor is going to trigger an alarm. I don't think that either of us is prepared for a swarm of doctors right now."

Nicole gulped for air, holding her breath before slowly letting it out again. The *beeps* stuttered back to a normal pace. "Anita, I should be dead. How am I not dead right now?"

Pete cleared his throat. "You and Compeer were found

in the bathroom, in the tub. The tub's material compounds was dense enough to protect you from the blast itself but not all the shrapnel and debris."

A guard entered the room, the only warning of his coming a cursory rap on the doorframe. "Bergs. Visitor switch."

"I have a guard?" Nicole said in confusion.

"Fred Hansen, ma'am," the guard replied. "Special detail, courtesy of the hospital. You're a very important person, Miss Nike, so I and several others will be placed at your door 24/7 on a rotation." He anticipated her next question, noticing how Nicole was watching Pete and Anita prepare to depart. "You are only permitted two visitors at a time, with a guard present. That's me. I'll be staying in here while you speak to the next visitor."

"It's probably Mark," Pete supplied. "He said he'd be by. Take care, Nikki."

Hansen stood aside, allowing in a snappily-dressed man while the Bergs slipped out of the room.

"Who're you?" Nicole asked.

"Hogarth Brandon," the man replied, eyeing Hansen. "I'm here on classified business. Please vacate the room until I signal that I am ready to leave."

"Can't do that, sorry," Hansen replied. "Miss Nike is not to be left unattended at any time. Whatever you have to say can be said with me present. I've already signed a stack of NDAs in regards to Miss Nike." Hansen held up his badge. "As you can see, I'm cleared."

"But Mr. Brandon is not," Nicole interjected. "We need to see identification from you, sir."

Brandon promptly pulled his wallet from an interior pocket on his jacket. Hansen flipped it open and verified that the badge was authentic. He showed it to Nicole. It didn't ease her, as the man still rubbed every instinct the wrong direction.

"Albeit as it may, Mr. Hansen, my credentials and reasons for my presence are above your pay grade." Brandon whipped out a piece of paper. When Hansen read it, his eyes widened. "Please leave until I am ready to depart."

Hansen frowned. "Miss Nike, if you need me, press the red button on the bedside arm."

Once there were only two people in the room, and the door securely closed, Brandon said, "I'm here because of your dinosaurs, Miss Nike."

"What do you want to know?" Nicole demanded.

"First of all, you are aware of the AWOL state of the Utahraptor known as Freedom?"

"Of course I am," Nicole remarked. "She isn't AWOL. She was attacked and chased off by UO drones."

"And is now outside of the Reserve," Brandon said. "In doing such, she has violated specific legal boundaries that which she has agreed to obey."

"What are you implying?" Nicole said, squinting at Brandon.

"I'm not implying anything. In the wake of her agreement violation, she has been marked as dangerous by the authorities, who have full permission to neutralize her. It does not help that she is completely capable of accessing the weapons bank mounted onto her back."

Grunting in discomfort as she shifted in her hospital bed, Nicole frowned at the agent. "Freedom would never use the *Intimidator* in malpractice."

"Can you guarantee that?" Brandon countered.

"No, I can't guarantee that; Freedom is her own person," Nicole said. "Can you guarantee the protection of our civilians from the UO? Why are you here, Mr. Brandon?"

Brandon straightened his suit jacket of imaginary wrinkles. "I believe that you recently received a government letter regarding the dinosaurs under your jurisdiction?"

If it didn't agonize, Nicole would've crossed her arms. "I've received quite a few over the last couple months. You need to be more specific."

"In that case, the one on the small group you allowed to be sent overseas. More specifically, their involvement in the recent discovery of Nelson Takin's treachery."

Nicole stared at him for a moment as she tried to recall such a letter, only to come up blank. *It was the one I incinerated without opening, wasn't it?* she thought. She said, "As you seem to be well aware of my every waking moment, then you should know that I haven't been at work for some time. Please, refresh me."

One of Brandon's eyebrows rose. "There was no warning of Takin's apparent motives before he bombed a small restaurant. It is to be believed that, perhaps, one of your dinosaurians knew, and, by tracing the trail of information further backward. . ." He trailed off pointedly.

Nicole sputtered in indignation. "I. . . I *never*! For your information, Mr. Brandon, I was as taken by surprise!"

"That is up for interpretation and further investigation," Brandon said, taking a slim envelope from the pocket inside his suit jacket. "You are required to report to this address."

Taking the envelope, Nicole read the address printed on the front. "This is to the courthouse!" Ripping it open, she scanned the letter inside. ". . .Suspicion of involvement with the Unison Order?! This is slanderous speculation against my good name!" She stared up at the agent in a mixture of horror and incredulity. She then regrouped herself. "At least I have some time to prepare. The date isn't for several months."

Brandon cocked an eyebrow and gestured to a wall hologram displaying the time and date. Nicole hadn't noticed it before. "You've been kept under sedation as to not aggravate your wounds, so I hear," he explained. "On the positive side of things, it shortens your recovery time. As you can see by the calendar, the court date is in two weeks."

"Then, I can't make this date," Nicole said. "The doctors said that I can't leave this hospital for at least a few months."

"Perhaps your lawyer can work that out. I'll be seeing you in Federal court, Miss Nike," Brandon said, nodding his head in farewell as he departed.

Trees were boughed with every shade on the warm side of the color spectrum. At the slightest nudge, leaves would float and flip down to rest on browning grass, where they would crunch and splinter underfoot. It was just chilly enough for a jacket.

As Robin walked down the sidewalk, pretending to read a map on her data-pad, every stride kicked up a small cloud of leaves, and behind her was a wake. At one point she moved to the side to allow a family with a stroller to pass. The father kept dumping armfuls of leaves onto the child, who squealed and waved in joy. Even after they had gone by, she watched. *This is what I fight for.*

The target building's address was a couple of blocks down when the middle school across the street let out for the day. "Soccer moms" popped open their doors, and children scrambled inside with promises of meeting again ringing in the air. It took only minutes before the cheerful calls and chatter diminished. Calm fell again when the last bustling school bus disappeared down the road.

Robin saw a single child crossing the street up ahead, holding onto his backpack straps. He kept his head down. His shaggy hair obscured his face. The kid strode up the steps of the target, glancing nervously up and down the road before knocking a beat.

He's only a child, Robin lamented. And he had been doing this regularly enough where he knew what to do, but new enough to be visibly paranoid.

Even from this distance, she could see the boy's foot anxiously jittering against the ground. The way he shifted his weight, changed his grip on the straps. A handful of seconds after his first knock, he did it again with a different beat. This time, the door opened, and the boy vanished inside.

"Young boy just entered target," she breathed. She was finally walking on the sidewalk before the building, continuing to keep her face toward the data-pad.

"*We saw,*" Lennox replied.

The data-pad slipped her grasp, fortunately hitting the soft grass and dirt instead of the sidewalk. With a distressed cry, she bent down to grab it, deftly slipping a small object from her sleeve. She walked on and didn't look back.

The small, matte black disc she had dropped shimmered before an emerald color swept over the surface, which cracked and broke apart to form a circular body with four pointed spider-esque legs. It skittered through the jungle of grass blades toward the building, skirting its brick and concrete base before coming across the plastic mouth of a drainpipe. The device slipped through the slitted cover. Muted and diminutive *tings* sounded with each step up the pipe, where the tips of the legs pierced the thin metal.

The gutters at the top were covered to prevent leaf clogging, but there was a vent that the machine used to crawl out and onto the roof. The grass green of its hull shifted to the brownish gray of the shingles. It travelled across the top of the building until it came to the edge, where a vent into the attic space was located. Just as expediently, the mechanism had entered the attic, moving across the rafters and neon pink insulation.

The contrivance encountered the hatch that opened into the main building, but it was lined with rubber insulation tracks, creating a tight seal. The pointy ends of the machine's legs prodded the rubber, creating small pinprick holes. One leg arced in a slash, leaving a long slit. It edged into the wounded rubber, deepening the slit. Two legs retracted into the body, leaving one in front to pull and cut and one in back to push.

Above heads and desks, the machine crawled out of the rubber, legs sprouting to dig into the drywall ceiling. A light trickle of dust drifted down, unnoticed below. Changing color to eggshell white, the device scanned the room. It slowly made its way along until it hung directly above a desk where a person was working.

On its hull was a narrow band of optical sensors, wrapping around like a bay of windows. In the middle of the band was a small circle, which activated, and the feed broadcast on a secluded, encoded AM frequency.

In a bright, cheery hotel hallway, Robin knocked on a door and let herself in. Eyes adjusting to the darkness of the room, she spotted Lennox bent over a laptop on the desk with Williams watching over his shoulder.

"What's the verdict?" Robin asked as she leaned over Lennox's unoccupied shoulder space. On the screen was a camera feed, overlaid by diagnostics and zoom boxes. A computer screen was amplified, along with several papers on the desktop. The zoom boxes flickered as the information was translated into text and placed in a folder for later viewing.

"Target is a hub for false identification manufacturing," Lennox replied, tapping a few keys. "We're seeing the room where personal history is set up and planted online."

At the new input, the device skittered over the ceiling and to the next desk. There was a picture of a woman, followed by a long list. Robin noted that all faces were snapshot and saved, and if they were being processed, all information was added to the face's file.

Over the course of an hour, the spy bug went from room to room, recording everything. One of the last locations was a private office, which contained a man poorly exiting his prime, talking with the boy. Robin's lips thinned as a monetary card was given to the kid, who pocketed the card and left.

"Why a schoolboy?" Williams pondered.

"Relay, most likely," Robin said in distaste. "One of the school employees is probably the second leg, who either transfers the new identities to a third leg or directly to the buyer. But the latter would be foolish, as the creation and receipt are too close in location."

The blond man beside her shook his head. "Hapless lad. Pity he was embroiled in such a vocation."

"The boy needs to get out," Lennox said grimly. "Does he look like he's there willingly to you?"

Robin cocked her head. "Hard to say. Pass him a tip, could go one of two ways. Either he takes it and runs, or he goes the people he knows. 50/50 chance both ways."

"What's the stratagem if the boy refuses to go?" Williams asked.

Lennox's jaw clenched. He was silent for a long moment before he said, "We'll come to that when we get there."

CHAPTER TWENTY

Ever since Nicole was a child, calamities to her body were able to heal quickly. Nothing could get her down for long. It astounded the nurses.

However, her amazing recovery also meant that she would be capable of attending her courthouse date. The shrapnel wounds had mostly healed. Her lungs were not going to develop asthma should she burst into a sprint. Bandages kept outside irritants from her first- and second-degree burns, which were still a little sensitive.

Calling a few people she knew, Nicole had managed to leave the hospital as AMA, just as long as she followed a list of rules she was given. She had promised to abide by the mandates, and was given a reluctant green light to leave.

The wheelchair was a blow to Nicole's pride, but she retained her poise and allowed the patient transporter to ease her into the seat. After shifting to become more comfortable, Nicole lifted her feet onto the raised pads. With a careful motion, she sat back in the wheelchair to enjoy the ride. The transporter only moved when Nicole gave the all clear, and the trip down to the hospital entrance was swift and uneventful.

At the door, Nicole was given a cane. She stood, favoring one leg over the other, as one knee was still stiff and a bit tender. Therapy had been cut short. Nicole was of the mind that she has enough willpower and know-how to strain herself without the prompting of a therapist.

"Welcome, Nicole!" Mark greeted. Leaving the car to idle, he got out and assisted her the last few yards, with the help of the transporter.

"Thanks, Mark," Nicole offered, feeling exhausted from her short journey. Apparently, bed rest had limited her stamina. She smiled gratefully at him when he opened the front right passenger door for her. Her tender leg held her weight as she shifted, and briefly balanced herself while she gauged the distance to the seat.

Compeer struggled over the console and onto her lap, and all Nicole could see was a dark pink tongue attacking her face. Laughing, she directed her dog away from her face so she could breathe. Reluctantly, Compeer slowly slid himself down to the floorboard, keeping his front legs in her lap.

"He's been aching to see you," Mark said as he returned to the driver's seat.

"Me, too," Nicole replied, tucking her cane between her and the door. She looked down at her dog, seeing for the first time the glaring red bandage sleeve looping around two of Compeer's legs and his side. "Looks like we've both suffered a little in that explosion, huh, boy?" She sighed, adding, "I'm so sorry, Compeer. I should've listened to you about Aim. From the first moment, you knew. Good boy, Compeer, *good boy!*"

Compeer's tail thumped against the sides of the floorboard, mouth agape in a wet grin. It was clear in his gaze that Nicole was forgiven. He nestled into the floor well, resting his head on a shoe.

"I'll be dropping you off at the Reserve, as you said," Mark said as the car entered the highway. He tapped a button on the steering wheel, then rested his hands in his lap. "Just call me when you need to be picked up again."

Call her old-fashioned, but the sight of an unattended wheel and foot pedals made Nicole's skin crawl. She side-eyed the dashboard, watching the wheel make small autocorrections. "I suppose, after work, you can help me go car shopping," Nicole said. While the parking garage had been left unharmed by the explosion, some miscreants took advantage of the chaos and trashed several vehicles. Nicole's had been one of them. "I've got some money saved up that can get me transportation, new clothes, and a sufficient place to stay. Until then, Pete and Anita have offered to let me crash at their place."

Mark sighed. "What about the court date? Do you know a good lawyer?"

Nicole slumped, gesturing idly with a hand as she spoke. "I've been doing some researching. There are a few good ones around here, but I just don't feel right using any of them; and anyone the court supplies will undoubtably be on the side of *them.* Yesterday, Brandon came back and requested access to all of my contacts and correspondence."

"And?"

"And I gave him the passwords." Nicole's gaze was open, pleading innocence, and she spread her arms wide. Her nerves twinged at the sudden movement. "I have nothing to hide, Mark!"

"Hey," he placated. "No need to get angry. It's understandable. In fact, being innocent in the matter and your openness should help you."

Nicole nodded, squaring her jaw in determination. "They'd better. If to the contrary, then, someone planted something, and I end up in jail. Mark, I'll need you to help with the Reserve until I get back. Jasmine can–"

"Wait, hold up, Nikki," Mark blurted. His hands raised in a waiting gesture. "You're talking like you're already going behind bars. You'll be *fine*."

Nicole frowned and didn't reply.

Not long after, Mark came to a halt in front of the Reserve's administrative building. They appeared to be the first ones to arrive for the day, a fact Nicole noted as she took her cane and exited the car. Compeer hobbled out behind her.

"I'll see you later," Nicole said with a smile, closing the door. She watched as Mark drove off, only turning to go inside when she lost sight of the car.

She stared at the short flight of stairs for a moment before limping herself forward.

I need to get back to the R&D, she thought as she slowly made her way up onto the porch. Fortunately, no one was around, so her lag would remain unnoticed until the next viewing of the surveillance feed. *Let's do that the Monday after next, after the court date. Mark'll be happy that I have those blueprints done, and we can really start cracking into those drones that Freedom shot down.*

Having reached the front door, Nicole heavily leaned on her cane so the door could detect her ID. The building was quiet and empty, the early morning glow casting long, warm light on the floor and walls. Nicole went around the lobby opening the curtains and raising the blinds. She paused at the last window, letting the rare sunlight warm her face.

The employees and volunteers wouldn't be arriving for another half hour at least, giving Nicole plenty of time to settle in her office. As Nicole hobbled to her desk; likewise, Compeer hobbled to his doggy bed.

Shortly after she had started on the day's email, alerts began appearing on Nicole's computer screen. Her staff were arriving and clocking in. Jasmine, as always, was the first, the others arriving soon thereafter. As Nicole viewed email, deleting most and replying to few, she could hear the noise escalate on the other side of her closed office door. Greetings, the beginning or ending to conversations, some calls for one person to consult with another.

The doorknob rattled, and Nicole looked up from her computer as Jasmine entered, the day's physical mail in hand.

Having seen the newcomer from the gap beneath the desk, Compeer woofed and got to his feet, ambling around the desk to meet her properly.

Jasmine's gaze shot to Compeer, then Nicole. "Miss Nike!" Jasmine exclaimed, nearly dropping the mail. "Ah thought ya were still in the hospital. Ya startled meh."

"I heal quickly," Nicole replied, receiving the mail from Jasmine and flipping through the envelopes and flyers. "Though I'm stuck with *that*," she pointed with her thumb to the cane leaning against the wall behind her, "for another month. Then the docs say I'll walk with a limp. I believe they're wrong."

Jasmine smiled, easily evading Compeer's eager lapping for her hands. "It's good to have ya back, ma'am. By the way, Mr. Berg's notes from the herpetologist tour have been entered into your computer."

the mail, tossing the junk into the incinerator. "And it's good to be back."

With a small wave, Jasmine exited and closed the door behind her.

Nicole picked up the last envelope, holding it between thumb and forefinger as if it might bite her. The rest of the mail had been the ordinary, so this last one *must* be the expected government commands. She cracked open an eye the tiniest amount to look at the return address.

It was from an animal magazine company.

Perplexed, Nicole stared. Where was the inevitable letter she always ended up incinerating every month or so? She even opened the envelope, half expecting a trick, and ended up perusing an offer to include an informative article on dinosaurs.

Casting the thought, and envelope, aside to ponder later, she read through Pete's notes. The idle tapping of her finger on the desk escalated the further she went.

Her private intercom bleeped. *"Miss Nike,"* Jasmine's voice piped from the speakers, *"There's someone here to see ya."*

Nicole pressed down the 'speak' button. "Who is it?" she queried, then winced. That came out sharper than she would have liked. She closed Pete's notes, resolving to finish his report later, when she had cleared her head.

"Lyle Stafford. He says he's from the government."

So, the government had sent something she couldn't toss in the trash. They were learning. "I'll be right there." Grabbing her cane, Nicole bid Compeer to stay and left the office.

True to Jasmine's word, a formidable man dressed in a suit stood by the reception desk. Nicole was almost disappointed to see that he wasn't holding the stereotypical briefcase, but his expression most certainly made up for it.

"Nicole Nike?" the man said as Nicole limped closer.

"That's me," she responded, holding out her good hand.

He shook it briefly, barely touching her skin. "Lyle Stafford. I'm from the Department of Homeland Security. I must speak with you about the dinosaurs under your jurisdiction."

"Before you go any further, I demand some identification. I want to see your badge, and a warrant. If you don't have those, you need to leave and not come back until you do."

Stafford raised his eyebrows before withdrawing a neatly folded paper from his jacket, along with a leather wallet. He flipped open the wallet to reveal a gold and blue badge. Nicole read the paper thoroughly before reluctantly nodding and handing it back.

"What about the dinosaurs?" Nicole asked.

"I've been sent to evaluate their combat readiness."

Nicole's eyes sharpened drastically. "You're trying to draft them like service dogs." It wasn't a question. "I've said it before; Freedom has *explicitly* refused to send any more of her people to fight."

"Is Freedom a dinosaur?" Stafford asked.

"Yes."

"Dinosaurs are animals, are they not?"

Nicole wasn't falling for the trap. "Dinosaurs have expressed high amounts of intelligence. They definitely are sentient creatures."

Stafford's eyebrows raised the slightest amount. "You have avoided the question. But, according to humanity's understanding, anything other than human is either animal, mineral, or plant. Dinosaurs are animals, and animals cannot have opinions."

"You can't force sentient beings to act as draft animals!"

"You only *claimed* that dinosaurs have sentience. You have submitted no proof of such."

Do not do anything regrettable. Court date coming up. Nicole shifted her stance. "I can tell that you're a man who believes what he sees. Perhaps you would care to take a short ride into the Reserve with me?"

"Yes," Stafford stated. "I need to see which are most adequate for combat, anyhow."

Nicole went toward the rack of keys, but Jasmine was already holding a pair. Nicole nodded her thanks and reached out to receive them.

"Kelp's goin' to be *mad*," Jasmine breathed quietly, glancing at Stafford. Keeping the keys out of reach, she added, "Ah'm drivin'."

"Undoubtably," Nicole replied, in remembrance of both her lack of independence and the more important fact of Freedom's absence. She didn't know which would be worse; an angry raptor she could anticipate, or Kelp, who was generally calm but Nicole didn't know well enough to predict.

"Are we going?" Stafford called, striding for the door.

Jasmine ushered Stafford to one of the jeeps while Nicole tried to keep up. After assisting Nicole, Jasmine started the vehicle. She pressed the gas pedal too hard, causing the vehicle to lurch forward. Stafford's head rebounded soundly against the headrest as she braked abruptly.

"Mah apologies," Jasmine stated.

Nicole groaned, not taking offense, yet most certainly not appreciating how the jolt had stretched her healing.

Stafford narrowed his eyes at the receptionist. "This is why we have *self driving* cars."

Since Jasmine must have known she might not get away with further pettiness, she drove normally afterward. After a short distance along the entrance road, she parted the ferns that disguised the offshoot path. The trees grew within arm's reach.

Not long after they had started down the uneven dirt path, Nicole spied something in the distance, moving between shadows. It was on her side of the jeep, so it was likely that Stafford hadn't seen it. It took her a long moment to see past the natural camouflage of the hide and identify an Albertosaurus.

Stafford yelled in surprise as, with a mighty roar, the carnivore thundered into view, flattening smaller plants and saplings with frightening ease. Jasmine stood on the brakes as the carnivore crossed the jeep's path, yanking the steering wheel to the side and sending the vehicle into a short skid. Nicole gasped at the jolt as the Albertosaurus' head dangled directly above. Its large nostrils sucked air and snorted it back out, peering at the three humans.

"What is that?" Stafford asked, valiantly trying to cover up his fear, hands indenting the seat cushion with impressive strength.

"An Albertosaurus," Nicole replied, a bit off guard. Her effort didn't make her circumstances any better, however, as the stench of the dinosaur's breath turned her stomach dreadfully. "Kelp must've sent out sentinels to ward away any unwanted visitors such as yourself."

"Tell it to let us by." Now his voice was steady and hard. The man recovered quickly.

Nicole raised an eyebrow. "Are you asking me to ask it to let us by? I believe that only intelligent beings understand words, Mr. Stafford."

"Dogs understand 'No,' 'Sit,' and 'Stay,'" Stafford retorted. "*They* are not the most intelligent beings on Earth."

Nicole looked at the Albertosaurus. "Would you please let us by?" she asked in dinosaur-ese. "It's imperative that we see Kelp."

The Albertosaurus growled, meaningfully glancing at Stafford.

"Yes, I know that he said that he didn't want any more unknowns in your territory, but I have no power to keep this one away."

"What are you saying?" Stafford asked, staring at her. "What are those noises coming from your mouth?"

"It's called dinosaur-ese," Nicole said in English. "It's their language. And I'm trying to persuade him to let us pass."

Jasmine stifled a snicker, slumping in her seat, apparently content to let the situation solve itself without her interference.

"*Excuse* me?" Stafford sputtered.

The Albertosaurus rumbled, its chest shaking.

Nicole looked up at it. "You understand English?"

It nodded, the rumbles quieting.

Slightly affronted, Nicole said, "Do you know where the others are? As I said, we need to see Kelp."

The Albertosaurus rolled its shoulders and turned around, its tail swinging over the jeep like the boom of a ship. It started to move down the path. After a few steps, it looked at the humans pointedly.

Jasmine gently pressed down the gas pedal, inching the jeep forward. It slowly accelerated until it matched the Albertosaurus' pace. Seeing how slow they were going, the dinosaur obligingly sped up to a casual jog.

As they approached a series of familiar hills, the Albertosaurus took a breath and began roaring, announcing their presence. They crested the hill, showing the dinosaurs on the other side. Jasmine veered from behind the Albertosaurus, picking a less steep path down to level ground. Once there, she turned off the engine and Nicole pulled herself up in the jeep, looking for Kelp.

Seconds later, an Utahraptor reached the jeep, but it was not Kelp. The *Intimidator* glistened. Nicole held back, seeing the flattened fringe and narrowed eyes.

"Freedom! I'm so glad you're all right! Kelp told you

everything?" Nicole added quietly.

Freedom's gaze moved to Stafford. She nodded stiffly.

Nicole carefully slid back down into her seat. "This is Stafford, a man sent by the government. He's here to evaluate you and your people's combat potential as dumb labor. There was nothing I could do to stop him from coming here. I'm sorry."

Freedom's eyes narrowed further, a growl coming from deep in her throat. Her gaze flicked to Stafford, who didn't even flinch at the eye contact. Nicole wasn't sure whether to credit his bravery or doltishness.

"This is Freedom?" he said. "This is the creature you allowed to contaminate a prototype weapon?"

Nicole paused, taking offense. "It was taken out of my hands, quite literally, and hidden away before I could recover it. I'm sure you've read my report, Mr. Stafford? Did you read the one Freedom dictated to me, as well, and her accounts as to what happened after my return?"

The Utahraptor stalked toward Stafford, exuding predator ferociousness from every pore, causing Nicole's instincts to tremble. Freedom reached the side of the jeep and stuck her neck through the missing door. The tip of her muzzle went well into Stafford's personal space.

"I feel the need to ask for some reason," Freedom said, teeth flashing, "but what do you think of talking dinosaurs?"

Stafford raised his eyebrows, unperturbed, although he did lean back some so he didn't have to cross his eyes. "Miss Nike, I must compliment you."

"For what?" Nicole asked.

"On the trouble and time you took to train this beast. Are they like parrots, repeating back what is said, or do you have ventriloquist training?" He looked Freedom in the eye. "If the first, say 'Dino wanna cracker.'"

The growl that had been brooding in the Utahraptor's throat projected from her mouth in a guttural roar, the wind sweeping back Stafford's hair and clothes. "How *dare* you insult us!" Freedom snarled. "You may be a government official, but that doesn't give you the liberty to spit insults at beings you don't like! No, do not speak. So, you wish to draft us as little more than pack mules? You must have missed the memo that I and my people have *been through a generational war*. We have *no interest* in fighting on your front lines. Are you *trying* to send us into extinction?"

"I see no problem with that," Stafford replied cooly. "If you die, we will simply reopen the time portal back to your original time and bring back reinforcements. Rest assured that your kind will never succumb to definite extinction."

Nicole's jaw dropped as she looked over at Jasmine. *Freedom's going to kill him. Never mind that the portal is probably in the ice age by now, but she's gonna kill him!*

Freedom's fringe momentarily shot upright before flattening even further. Not taking her eyes off of the man, she growled, "Nicole, please remove this. . . *man* from here before I do something I may regret." Other dinosaurs voiced their agreement, stalking toward the jeep.

As Jasmine moved to restart the engine, Stafford said, "I appreciate your sacrifice for my country. Have a good day."

Nicole froze, eyes wide and mouth agape.

Freedom snapped her teeth inches in front of Stafford's nose. Stafford frantically kicked at Freedom as he ordered Jasmine, "Floor it!"

"Freedom!" Nicole said, leaning over Stafford to protect him. "Freedom, calm yourself!"

"Calm? *Calm*?!" Freedom snapped, almost unintelligible due to her anger. "I have just returned from trekking across *an entire state*, and just earlier this morning I was almost killed for the second time by the UO. And now this– this *small-minded human* comes in demanding us to become no more than imbecilic *beasts of burden* and march onto the front lines with nothing more than our natural defenses!" The dinosaur gave a shuddering gasp as her ire fell away. "We'll be squashed underfoot like bugs."

"But *please*, don't kill him for it! He's ignorant of your true value. I swear that no one other than who you send personally will ever see human combat!"

Shaking her head sharply, Freedom took a step back, casting an evaluating gaze over Nicole. "You had no power to keep from bringing him here. You'll have no power to stop his kind. I wasn't going to kill him." Turning her gaze back to Stafford she added, "But this. . . *person*. . . must never return here. "

"Agreed," Nicole immediately said. "Stafford?"

The man gulped, a cold sweat shining on his forehead. "A-agreed," he stammered.

Nicole bid a hasty farewell to Freedom before Jasmine

drove the jeep back to the path. Stafford didn't relax when the tires hit the dirt, and he didn't release his grip on the roll bar before they reached the main road.

When they reached the parking lot, Stafford let himself out of the jeep. He straightened his tie, pulled wrinkles from his suit, and combed his fingers through his hair. "Miss Nike, this trip has been most enlightening. You may be rest assured that I will do everything within my power to make sure that your dinosaurs are left alone."

Nicole sighed. "Thank you, Mr. Stafford. Have a good day."

For the umpteenth time, Scope stalked the perimeter of the field, wherein most of her entire tribe relaxed. The younglings had long tired of following her around, returning to their families.

Ascending a boulder, taking stock of her wider expanse of view, the Utahraptor tried to settle herself. Ever since the visitor had left, she had been disturbed by her memories.

I can't allow them to lead us to our deaths. I'd. . . I'd. . .

Scope banished that thought with a growl, shaking her head, as if that would help. Still baring her teeth, she descended from the boulder and resumed her patrol.

Never, she mused as she gave some contesting Stygimoloch males a wide berth. The harsh *clunks* of their armored skull domes echoed in her ears. *They'll not take my people- No!*

"Scope?"

Lost inside her memories, Scope gasped, the voice calling for her transforming into her tribe leader. "Spike? Spike, I. . ."

Sea Fern appeared in her vision, causing her to stop, lest she crash into him. His face jutted into hers, his eyes trying to lock onto her own. "Scope. Scope, listen to me."

Blinking, Scope shook her head harshly. "Sea Fern? What is it?"

Her mate pulled back to give her some space. "Are you all right?"

"Yes." At his skeptical returning look, Scope grimaced. "No. Sea Fern, am I a good tribe leader?"

"The best," he replied immediately. "Why do you doubt yourself?"

Scope walked a short distance away, her tail cutting the air in wide curves. "Familiarity is in the distant past, buried by volcanic rock and skies of ash. In this time, in this place, there's no way I can keep everyone safe. Look at them! We aren't meant to live together in such tight quarters, but there's so few of us now. . ."

Sea Fern drew up alongside her. "Herbivores and carnivores may not be the best neighbors, but until we all number in the hundreds, we will be sharing this territory. The borders are wide. The prey are plentiful. We will survive to thrive again."

Scope gazed at the grass. She felt Sea Fern nuzzle her shoulders.

"You are a great leader. And our most powerful one." She looked up to see him eyeing the *Intimidator* in admiration. However, his gaze fell to a frown. "What is this?"

"What is what?" Scope asked, craning her neck, but she could see nothing out of the ordinary. Her thoughts on the device caused it to hum. "Is something wrong with the *Intimidator*?" At the indirect prompt, the invention sent her a sensation of *fine*.

Sea Fern reached out a claw and picked at something. She heard a *click*, and he drew his hand back with something tiny in the palm. Scope peered at it. Whatever it was, it was barely bigger than her own claw and shaped like a flat, smooth river stone. She had never seen such a thing before.

"Do you know what this is?" Sea Fern asked.

Shaking her head in the negative, Scope squinted at the object. A shiver ran down her spine. "No, but I'm not getting a good feeling about this." She took it from him and placed it on the ground. Taking a few steps back, she sent a quick laser pulse, obliterating the object.

Sea Fern lowered his head and cautiously sniffed at the stream of smoke in the grass. He snorted and straightened. "It's gone, whatever it was."

Scope's arms snaked around her chest to hold herself. "I need my brother. Is he back from hunting yet?"

"Perhaps," Sea Fern said. "Look over by our kind's grounds. I'll take over your patrol. I'll alert to the guards to the stone you destroyed."

Tapping his muzzle with her own in thanks, Scope trotted over toward where the Utahraptors gathered, as few as they were. Seeing many of the younglings there, she wondered what she would do when the time for the Initiation Hunt came. She sighed, then cast her gaze for her brother, hoping that he was among them.

Scope spotted the pale face and light blue frill of her brother. "Pallor!" she called. When his head shot up, she added, "Over here, please."

Her brother nimbly trotted toward her as if he could sense her mood. "Scope, what's wrong?"

Without replying, she gestured for him to follow her, to which he acquiesced. She led him away from the open meadow where everyone tended to congregate. There were a scattering of boulders that laid near the treeline. As they neared, she felt a wave of familiarity. She stepped near the boulders' bases, slipping through a narrow gap that looked too small for passage.

The opening widened into a tiny area barely large enough for her to stretch out comfortably. She laid down in a corner, tiny shivers quaking her form. Pallor looked down at her, cocking his head. After a moment, he shuffled beside her, and waited for her to share her mind.

It was there that they stayed for the remainder of the day.

Miserable. That was how Rush felt. It was raining

torrents, he had no shelter besides a half-dead conifer, and he was completely, utterly, absolutely lost somewhere in northeast United States.

With his head constantly being battered with a steady trickle from a branch above, Rush glared into the world.

He could be flying above the clouds and avoiding this misery, but he had already flown himself to exhaustion again. If he took off again, he would just fall to the ground from his spent muscles. Like it or not, he was stuck in the tree.

And he had been stuck on this branch for hours. He could still barely move his wings.

Movement from beneath alerted his gaze downward. It turned out to be a family of deer, a well-bestowed buck leading a doe and a fawn. They passed by with almost perfect silence in the rain, hides gleaming from the wet. The fawn shivered, and the doe paused to press against it. The buck stopped to look back at them, then paced to the somewhat dry base of a thick fir tree. The doe and fawn joined it, then all three laid down in a tight huddle, now out of the brunt of the downpour.

Rush exhaled, remembering when he was just a tiny fledgeling. It had been during the brutal surprise blizzard in early spring. He had been so cold, and positive that he would freeze to death. But his parents had covered him and his nest mates with their very own bodies, shielding them from the snow and wind. Oh, how he wished that he had them now, when he was all alone in a suddenly overwhelmingly big world.

Looking up, Rush ignored the rain that landed on his face as he gazed to the dismal gray heavens. The drops slid down his head, disguising the tears that began flowing from his eyes. One choked-back sob opened the floodgates, and Rush wept. He cried in shame.

I'm such a coward, he thought in despair. *Oh, forgive me.*

Eventually, the rain began to lighten, and the clouds thinned enough to brighten the afternoon. Rush stopped crying, his mind clearing. Finally able to think of things other than running, it dawned on him that the cloud cover had been a constant presence for quite a while. The sun, moon, and stars had been missing all the same. What was the cloud's source?

Curious, he shifted his wings. The constant aches had ebbed, leaving him feeling refreshed and rejuvenated. With a screech, he launched himself off of the conifer and beat his wings to carry him skyward. Stopping his ascent just before entering the clouds, he scanned as far as he could see for the source.

As he flew, he finally noticed something that he was sure he had seen before but hadn't really absorbed. Civilizations he flew over were absent of human life. Approaching a vast, burning city, the suburbs were still and motionless. Driveways and streets were empty, and what cars that were present were pulled over to the curbs, doors sometimes open, as if abandoned in great hurry. Craters left from random shelling painted the landscape. Such a sight grew more common the closer to the city he came. Eventually, he was weaving in between skyscrapers that disappeared into the sooty clouds, flying over eerily quiet roads. Despite the flames, flickering streetlights still functioned for traffic that wasn't there.

Estimating the fires, Rush reasoned that they were fueling the clouds. He was sure that from their extent, other nearby cities and towns were also aflame. Likely, the entire region was burning.

Rush sniffed the air. It was metallic and smoky, and it left a strange taste in his mouth. He turned in many directions before he finally started tracking it. Slowly, then quickly, the acrid smell became stronger and more prominent.

Finally, just when he was beginning to find it difficult to breathe, he heard a quiet *boom*. A second later, only instincts saved him from something that whizzed so rapidly past him he couldn't even see it. A skyscraper behind him exploded in a fireball, a huge hole blown in its side. Metal supports crumbled, glass windows shattering as the skyscraper collapsed. Its upper fifteen floors cascaded to the empty streets in a shower of debris amongst a dense cloud of pulverized concrete and stone. Fingers of flame brushed his tail and feet, but dissipated before it could begin to hurt.

Breathing hard, Rush hastily sought for the source. He heard the *rat-a-tat-tat* of machine guns a few blocks over, and he hugged the buildings as he flew to investigate.

Humans clad in armored clothing hid in the crumbling and broken buildings, the first sign of life he had seen ever since entering the city. All of them bore at least two firearms, one slung over the back while the other was held at the ready. A few of them systematically checked the streets, cautiously peering around corners. Descending, Rush was able to make out the rectangular red, white, and blue stitched onto their shoulders. Allies!

As none of them appeared to possess the source for the projectile that nearly killed him, he flew over them. If they were allies and on the lookout, then the Unison Order had to be present as well. If he could find them, he could tell their position to the Americans, and turn the tides in the allies' favor.

Something buzzed, coming closer. Rush saw an insect-like drone resembling a dragonfly pass beneath him. It had the American flag on its hull. The front of the drone was a dome lined with sensors and cameras. Rush followed it for a bit, wondering if it had audio sensors built in. He parted ways with it at a street corner, but kept the drone's presence in mind.

He flew over several more blocks before he saw more humans. A quick glance revealed more Americans, simply darting to another cover on their way through the abandoned city. He ignored them and flew on.

Finally, Rush saw movement in one of the skyscrapers, in the windows just below the clouds. Landing on a horizontal flagpole, Rush glanced over his shoulder and saw the remains of the skyscraper that had been blown up many, many blocks away. Looking back at the windows, he saw soldiers. One of them held a cannon-like weapon that was propped on the shoulder. Twirling midair, Rush saw the still-flaming building a good ways straight down the street.

Suddenly, one of the soldiers leaned out the window, aiming for the street. Rush spotted the Unison Order insignia on his shoulder before he saw the drone at which the soldier was aiming. The soldier opened fire, and the drone fell to the ground, streaming black smoke behind it. The soldier immediately ducked back inside, taking cover behind the wall.

Having observed enough, Rush made his way out of the Unison Order soldiers' range of vision as soon as he could, taking an alternate route back the way he came. He scanned the air for another one of those US drones. Finally, he spotted one flying out of a destroyed building.

Diving down, he glided alongside it for a moment. The drone abruptly stopped in its flight path, perfectly still, its buzzing wings keeping it aloft. The sensor dome faced him.

"I hope this thing has audio," Rush said, hovering as best as he could in front of it. "Listen, Americans, you don't know what I am, where I've come from, and have no reason at all to trust me, but the UO soldiers are in a skyscraper not far from my position. Can this thing follow me? Bob up twice if yes."

After a short pause, the drone jolted up and down twice.

Rush nodded, flying back toward the skyscraper. With the drone beside him, Rush halted at the corner just before the building came in view again. "If you look up that street, that's the skyscraper with the shattered windows on the. . . nineteenth floor. The UO soldiers are on that level. They have some sort of cannon launcher that blew up a skyscraper as I entered the city, so stay out of sight as long as you can."

The drone flew away, and Rush found a street light pole on which to land and rest. For once, he thanked his tiny stature and waited for any sign of the Americans. It took several minutes, but he finally saw a small group appear across the street, on the ground floor of what used to be a cafe. They held their guns at the ready, faces hidden behind dark visors. One of them, apparently the leader, waved her hand at the others, telling them to remain there. She carefully stalked ahead to a point where she could see the skyscraper he had pointed out.

Gliding from his spot, Rush languidly approached the soldier, being sure that the others could see him. He flapped his wings loudly a few times to grab her attention before finding a broken rafter leaning against the wall, so he could land.

The soldier whirled around, her weapon instantly leveling to face him. Rush squeaked, hiding his head under his wings, as if that would help any. "Wait, wait!" he exclaimed. "I'm friendly! Friendly!"

The soldier stiffened. "You're real. We thought that you were some mechanical bat the UO boys had made up as a disguise for a drone."

"No harm in being cautious," Rush said slowly, unsure in his words. "But I'm flesh and blood, just like you."

The soldier finally lowered her gun and pointed with her free hand toward the skyscraper. "That the one you meant?"

"Yes, ma'am," Rush said. "That's the one. Yes."

"We thought so. We've lost several drones around this area, and only so many buildings could hold the source." The soldier knelt behind a brick wall, leaning out the barest amount to see. She held a pair of binoculars to her face. "You're not wrong about their 'cannon launcher.' That's a bazooka, and what looks like a portable missile launcher leaning against the wall. They have a big target if they lugged that thing all the way up there."

"What kind of target?"

"Not sure. How about you just fly up there and find out? Don't get shot down."

Properly intimidated, Rush nodded and flew out of the destroyed cafe. He took the long way around the block, hoping to come at them from a blind spot. Unfortunately, it seemed that they had all four walls posted. Unable to think of anything else, Rush veered up and flew into the clouds. He stayed just within the cover so that he could see beyond. The skyscraper's walls loomed before him, and he circled it closely before he found a broken window on a higher floor.

Flying through, he found himself in a huge room full

of dingy gray cubicles. There seemed to be a stairwell on the far side, with the door open. Soaring to it, he descended a few levels until he found the nineteenth. This door, however, was closed; and he had the sneaking suspicion that it would be loud if he opened it.

Rush sized it up before grabbing onto the slick metal push bar. After managing to find a workable grip, he pressed the side of his head to the door and strained to hear through it.

". . .ordinates?"

"Yes, sir. Wait, we just lost the signal."

"Fire to last known coordinates: Latitude 36.068360, Longitude -93.325102."

"Ready to fire, sir."

"Fire."

Rush lived up to his name, speeding to the nearest window. He reached it just in time to see something compact and black streak away, a white plume of smoke behind it. It wove between the buildings. Smaller missiles flew up at it from where the Americans hid, but exploded harmlessly in the first's slipstream. Unharmed, the black projectile eventually vanished into the clouds.

Frantic to know what had just been fired and to where, he exited the skyscraper and dashed to the American soldiers still in the cafe. They recoiled at his sudden entrance, and he crashed into the wall, his speed too great for him to slow properly.

Picking himself off of the ground, he yelled, "Did you

see that?"

"Yeah," a soldier stated grimly. "That was a preprogrammed missile, set to any distance as long as it has sufficient fuel. We tried to shoot it down, but it got by us. Alert the boys to the west, tell them to arm their anti-missile rails. If they miss, God help those wherever it lands."

"Do any of you have a GPS?" Rush asked.

"I do," one of them said.

"Where do the coordinates 36.068360 by -93.325102 point?"

The soldiers typed them into a small device. "Arkansas. Specifically, a state park."

Rush could feel the blood draining from his face. "No. . ." he gasped. "No! That's my home! My *home*! Quick, do you have a telephone?"

"Yes?"

Rush rambled off the number for the Reserve, desperately hoping that it wasn't closed and that Nicole was there. The soldier activated his comm and placed it in speaker mode.

"What is this?" the leader exclaimed. "What is this thing doing with our comm?"

"It needed to call someone. The number was legit, Commander."

Rush ignored them, listening to the ring. If he had proper teeth instead of just tooth-like barbs, he would be biting his beak in anxiety.

Click. "The Dinosaur Reserve. Jasmine speakin'."

"Jasmine!" Rush shouted.

"Who's this?"

"Rush! Rush! I'm Rush! One of the Pterodactylus that was sent out."

"Rush? How are ya callin' us?"

"It doesn't matter. A missile's coming! A missile's coming! Get everyone out of there now!"

"A what?! A missile?!" The next thing Rush heard was a dial tone.

He moved away from the comm. He stared at nothing, trying to keep from hyperventilating. *Did I call in time?*

The bio-degradable plastic bag rustled as Mark strode out of the pizzeria, shoving a receipt into his wallet, which he then tucked deep into a pants pocket. He took a turn and started walking down the block. His car was parked quite a ways down, one of the cons of living in a city.

He sneezed into his elbow, sniffing afterward. The smog was dense today, being without even a breeze to try and sweep the lingering acidic dust away. He looked up to glare at the hovering cloud cover that obscured the healing sunlight.

Something caught his eye. It was a small, dark object, streaking high above. Thin smoke trailed in its wake, and, without the breeze, he was able to track it back quite a ways before the buildings blocked his view. The flying object passed from his line of vision. Mark stood there for a while longer, his calculating mind recognizing that the object was gradually descending. His sense of direction identified that the object was traveling roughly southwest from the northeast.

Huh, he mused as he resumed walking. Looked like it was heading toward the Reserve. *Why, that even looked almost like a. . .* Pedestrians behind him muttered indignantly as the man before them suddenly froze.

Mark stared in horror westward.

Oh, God, please no.

Nicole was finishing up some blueprints for her "real" job when the building-wide intercom suddenly cackled in static. She looked up at the ceiling from her paperwork, confused. The public intercom was hardly ever used.

"Emergency evacuation!" Jasmine's voice crackled, her voice strained. *"Everyone vacate the area immediately! Repeat, emergency evacuation! Go to the main highway!"*

"What on earth?!" Nicole wondered, even as she stood and shoved her paperwork into her work bag. Disregarding her cane, she exited her office to see her employees and volunteers rampaging through the halls, all on their way to the closest exit. Someone must've gone through an emergency door, because red lights and a klaxon suddenly came on. Compeer whined at the new noise. "Come!"

"Miss Nike!" Nicole craned her neck to see Jasmine fighting the current toward her. "Miss Nike, Ah've got the keys to a jeep! We need to leave *now*!"

"What's going on?" Nicole asked as her receptionist grabbed her wrist and pulled her into the chaotic crowd of colleagues. She struggled to keep her feet under her.

"Rush just called. He said that a *missile* is on its way here, and we have to evacuate everyone now!"

"A missile!?" Nicole repeated back in shock. "The drones!" she exclaimed. "They had tracking sensors. . . We need to get the dinosaurs!"

"Yes, Miss Nike! But Ah'm still driving ya!" Jasmine said as they finally exited the building. She dashed ahead and found the jeep in the rapidly emptying parking lot. When Nicole and Compeer finally pulled themselves into the jeep, Jasmine floored it. As they crested the first hill, they saw dinosaurs ahead. Jasmine hit the brakes, while Nicole scrambled for a megaphone in the back seat.

"Everyone!" she shouted through it, her amplified voice echoing in the forest. "We need to get out of here *right now*! This place is going up in flames soon. Follow me to safety! Move, *move*, MOVE!"

The dinosaurs erupted in alarmed jabber, running after her as Jasmine spun the jeep around, all four wheels kicking up dirt as they gained traction. Pterosaurs flew overhead, heading for the edge of the forest, while all the land beasts took up running at the jeep's back bumper. Surprisingly, Nicole found that their collective top speed was around 30 miles per hour. Security was nowhere to be seen, presumably rounding up stragglers.

Freedom suddenly appeared in the rearview mirrors, carrying several small bipeds. She drew up along the jeep just long enough for them to hop into the trunk, then fell back again. While Jasmine focused on weaving through the trees of the narrow path, Nicole caught glances of various larger dinosaurs carrying the smaller ones and putting them in the jeep.

Suddenly, she felt pinpricks on her shoulders. A quick look showed Spines the Microvenator clinging to the back of her seat.

"Drive faster!" Spines screamed, eyes wide in fright.

"Faster!" Nicole translated.

"Ya don't need to tell meh!" Jasmine replied, flattening a thicket.

The edge of the forest finally came into view. By that time, Nicole was sure that the entire population of Microvenators, Hesperonychus, and Bambiraptors were in the jeep. She couldn't even see Compeer under the raptors. Seconds later, they burst into the open and into a cornfield. They didn't dare stop there. Jasmine continued leading them further away. Nicole had no idea of the blast range of the missile.

"The east!" someone cried out. "Look to the east!"

Nicole looked. A small white dot was in the sky, just below the clouds. It slowly grew larger and larger, then it lengthened with a shrill whistle into a pale smoky stream heading into the forest.

"Hold the younglings!" Freedom screamed, falling to the ground and curling around a small Stygimoloch.

Hitting the brakes, the two women jumped out of the jeep and all took up a safety position in a depression in the ground on the far side of the jeep. Her face buried in the grass, Nicole heard the tiny bipeds follow their example. Nicole had nowhere near the temerity to keep her head up and look for the explosion. She just hoped that the force of the blast wouldn't flip the jeep on top of them. She felt Jasmine's hand reach for hers. Nicole moved and took it. Her free arm wrapped around Compeer.

It was quiet. A breeze wafted through the corn, making the stalks rustle.

The sun disappeared in a thick shadow of erupted earth. Nicole stiffened, then covered her ears as what sounded like the deepest war drums all pounding at once.

A shockwave rolled over them. The jeep reared sideways on two wheels, threatened to topple, then landed back on all fours. The larger dinosaurs yelled, claws burying in the dirt as anchors. Nicole screamed as a heatwave passed over her, like an invisible fire licking at her entire body.

Cautiously, Nicole shakily took to her knees, straightening and looking back the way they had come. The blaze was unseen, but thick smoke rose into the sky, turning the clouds black. Nicole took a deep unsure breath, clutching the clothes over her heavily beating heart. *So much for keeping my heart rate down as my injuries heal. . .*

She jumped as she heard her phone's ringtone. Jasmine spared Nicole the agony of moving without her cane, fetching her phone for her. Nicole checked the caller ID; unknown. "Hello?" Nicole said.

"Nicole Nike?"

Nicole looked in horror at the flames rising above the trees. "Who's this?" The aftershock rattled the air, accompanied by a wall of dust that made everyone cough. Dirt clods, interspersed with foliage bits and other pieces she didn't care to identify, were finally plummeting. Nicole shielded herself with her arm.

"The 45th division near Louisville, Kentucky. Are you all right?"

"I . . . I think so. Freedom, did everyone get out?"

The Utahraptor, already on her feet, reared back as high as she could go and looked around. "I . . . I don't know."

That comment seemed to set off a chain reaction; Dinosaurs reared up and began screaming names. Calls went back and forth. Small groups formed as family members found each other. Cries of relief were interspersed with cries of worried anguish.

"We think so," Nicole relayed, opting for the more optimistic side of that statement. "But . . . Who are you and how did you know to call this number?"

"A certain birdie told us and had us alert you. You can thank it for saving your lives."

Rush! "Thank you," Nicole said. "And please tell Rush that."

"You're welcome." There was a *click*, and then a dial tone. Almost immediately, her phone began ringing again, this time with Mark's designated chime.

"Hello?" Nicole said again, struggling to her feet.

"*Nikki!*" she heard Mark say. "*There's a missile heading straight toward you, you have to get everyone out of there* right now, *DO YOU HEAR ME?*"

"Mark!" Nicole yelled so that he could hear her over himself. When he fell silent, she continued, "Mark, it just hit. We received a warning!"

"*Is everyone all right?*"

Nicole ached, glancing to the side. Freedom was herding everyone into their kinds while Kelp counted heads. "I don't know. I don't think that all of the dinosaurs were present when the alarm was sounded. Freedom's doing a head count now."

"*You have to hide them. Someone tried to kill them just now, Nikki. Get them to some place safe.*"

"I will. I need to go, Mark."

"*Be careful.*" The line went silent.

"Freedom, is anyone hurt?"

"No," Freedom replied. "Security found us a bit before you came and told us to prepare to run. We're going to the road?"

"Yeah. We have to find you all a safe place to hide." Nicole brought up a map on her phone.

Freedom ducked her head. "I'm sure that you'll take good care of us. Thank you."

"It's the least I can do," Nicole replied.

Nodding, the magenta-fringed Utahraptor looked

around. "Has anyone seen my brother?" she called.

Takin bolted upright. His heaving chest glistened with sweat. His eyes darted around the room, checking for the images which tormented his dreams.

In the next bed over, his handler laid still. Whether or not Wilhelm had awakened, Takin couldn't tell. He counted it as a blessing as he ran his hands over his face, wiping away the sweat that still stubbornly clung to his forehead.

Peace. He was fighting for peace.

Why was it becoming so hard to believe that?

The sheets and comforter were untangled and kicked off, allowing him to pad across the motel room to the small bathroom. He closed the door before turning on the light, wincing at the brightness until his eyes adjusted. Splashing water on his face, he took in the reflection of his blotchy skin, pale and flushed. Something he saw made him want to punch the mirror, shatter it until his image was gone.

He settled for wringing the hand towel, roughly drying himself. Not looking at the mirror, he summoned strength. *I am fighting for peace. Nothing I was doing was getting us any closer.*

Unbidden, he flashed-back to the moment he decided to – to make a greater difference. *The explosive was standard issue. It wasn't – wasn't meant to use in a crowded area. . .*

The next several minutes were spent bent over porcelain.

Children. Families. Couples. Workers. Elderly.

He remembered quickly making tracks away, counting down in his head. Phantom screams made his head shake erratically, as if the movement would dislodge or throw them away.

I did it for peace.

A distraction, to keep his own– his old team off his back, giving him time to vamoose. Otherwise, he would've never evaded Lennox's sharp eyes. Collateral damage. It. . . it was a pity. They had served a purpose. If he had stayed, nothing would have changed. The Unison Order needed his skills. His raw talents in code. No one could navigate the cyber world like he could. He was being wasted, and the only cure he spotted was to join the team who were making a visible difference.

Peace had the same definition, no matter the point of view. *A state of being where conflict is absent. Where people are happy.*

Breath stuttering, he exited the bathroom and returned to bed, where the damp bedsheets were a balm to his heated skin. Still, he tugged the covers back over himself, over his head, and curled his body into itself, until he was completely concealed.

Peace, he told himself. *I am helping.*

His cocoon wasn't working. The heat was stifling. He threw his bedsheets away as he sat up, leaving them to crumple on the floor. He slumped, resting his head in his hands.

Wilhelm grumbled at him; Takin ignored the not-so-polite bid to go back to sleep.

How could he sleep when he kept seeing so many faces?

I'm sorry. You have to believe me, he told them. *It's for the greater good. Please. I'm sorry it had to happen like that.* It was quick, right? They wouldn't have even known what had happened, ending up in that place beyond life that Takin didn't believe in.

It wasn't too early in the morning. He'd only had around four hours of sleep. It was enough. He could sleep on the transport. If that didn't work, well, he could sleep when he's dead.

After he made a difference. Because all he really wanted was peace.

So why did it hurt so much?

CHAPTER TWENTY-ONE

Scope walked through her kin in the darkness of the night. Her feet made the shallowest of thumps on the concrete, an attribute to Turns of experience on the run, and the need for silence.

Earlier that evening, Nicole had found them a large warehouse on the outskirts of the suburbs, in a construction district. The huge building was empty, having been built years before but never put to use. Nicole had managed to sneak them in, neglecting to inform the authorities of their intrusion. Scope understood, agreeing that to keep herself and her kind's whereabouts anonymous was a wise idea.

Sounds of sniffing drew her attention, and she followed it to a pair of twin Corythosaurus younglings. They looked up at her with large, glistening eyes, tears slowly running down their cheeks and onto the floor.

"How are you faring, little ones?" Scope asked, kneeling a little.

The largest sniffed. "We. . . we don't know where our Mother and Patriarch are. Do you know, Scope?"

Scope's fringe drooped. Many had been away hunting or foraging when Security sounded the alert. These two weren't the only suddenly parent-less youth in the tribe. Or sibling-less.

She didn't want to give them false hope, but didn't want to hurt them even more. "I. . . I'm sure that, wherever they are, they care about you two a lot."

The two stared at her. One suddenly began keening.

Scope hurriedly shushed them, hoping that they hadn't awakened anyone. It was hard enough to sleep after such a day. Mercifully, only a few of the nearby Squama were disturbed, the rest were too exhausted from the event to stir. "It's okay. It's okay," she comforted.

"They're *dead!*" the youngling screamed, unaffected by her attempts to quiet them. "Mother and Patriarch are *dead!*" The other youngling began to sob loudly.

"Shh, shh," Scope said, laying down and curling her body around them. "I'm here, and I won't let anything happen to you if I can help it."

"P-p-promise?" one of them whimpered. Thankfully,

they started to calm.

"I promise," Scope replied gently. "Don't worry, and don't cry. I'll be here." She stood. They continued to whimper, but didn't start crying again. "Sleep well, and may you be blessed with beautiful dreams," Scope said in parting, hiding her cracking voice.

She resumed her patrol of the tribe.

Scope meandered across the Utahraptor section of the improvised nesting ground. She greeted any of them still awake, slowly making her way toward the center. Eventually, she reached her family. All five of her younglings laid next to Sea Fern, soundly asleep. Scope smiled tearily, gazing upon their angelic faces for a little longer before continuing on.

As she walked through the warehouse, Scope found her head rotating to stare to the east. Somewhere deep inside, she *knew* that the Unison Order laid in that direction. For a moment, uncontrollable fury boiled and frothed in her mind. They had taken their security, their Squama and human lives, and many things they held dear.

Relax, Scope, she told herself, struggling to rein in her anger. Becoming enraged over something she could not control would not help the situation.

There was one thing, though, that she could do.

Scope gritted her teeth. *I already took a risk in sending four to assist. Could Nicole be right? Should I send more? I. . . I shouldn't. An Ankylosaurus may be nearly invulnerable to an Albertosaurus, but not to a bullet.*

She shifted her shoulders, but their movements were

limited. The *Intimidator* reminded her of its ever-presence on her back, gleaming dull silver in the starlight. She considered asking Nicole to reload it with missiles and refuel it with jet fuel, but she was emotionally exhausted from war. Three entire Turns of her life had been spent on the run and fighting for her life.

Yet in all wars, blood must be spilled.

She knew then that her conscience would not let her rest. Resigning herself, Scope trekked to the pterosaur region of the warehouse's expanse of floor. Quetzalcoatlus were laying on the hard concrete, their giant wings consuming vast amounts of space. Scope almost felt like she was dancing as she made her way to the rafters where the Pterodactylus roosted. Once she arrived, she could hear them snoring in tiny, soft squeaks.

"Assail!" Scope hissed as loudly as she dared. Her eyes searched for his black body in the darkness of the roof. "Assail!"

A shadow separated from the rest and landed on the floor before her. "What's the matter, Scope?" Assail asked quietly. "You're troubled."

"I won't deny that," she replied, hanging her head. "My thoughts keep pausing on the UO threat. I can feel it looming, a dark storm cloud over the horizon. It's already come to us. What can we do now?"

"You're scared," Assail responded.

As the leader of all Squamas, Scope didn't like admitting that she was frightened. A leader never showed fear. Spike hadn't. Yet, she nodded. "What advice do you have?" she inquired.

Assail ruffled his wings. "Fear can obscure one's mind,

lead one to making poor decisions. You must calm down, think further; then, decide on what to do. Send more of us out to the field, or not."

Scope took several deep breaths, a method of calming down that worked for her. Glancing over where everyone slept, her eyes focused on the Pterodactylus in the rafters.

It was as if she had breached the surface of a pond. An idea sprang to mind, something so simple that she wondered how she could not have thought of it beforehand. Her eyes narrowed and widened sporadically as she mentally went over pros and cons.

"You have a plan," Assail stated.

She nodded. "Assail, who's behind the UO?"

"The humans believe that it is a rogue French woman named Lois Cornette."

"Do they know where she is?"

Assail thought for a long moment. "I need to ask." Scope watched in curiosity as he bumped his wing to a small headpiece that she hadn't noticed before. "Assail to Eagle Eyes. Where is supreme target? Roger, roger that. Thank you."

"Where?" Scope asked eagerly.

"Flores Island, Portugal."

Scope nodded firmly, her decision made. "Wake up your kind. I'll handle the Quetzalcoatlus."

Assail acknowledged her and flew away. Scope followed in his shadow. She roamed around the Quetzalcoatlus, nudging and talking them into awareness. They were understandably grumpy at being awakened in the middle of the night, but when Assail had roused his Pterodactylus and all the avians were gathered around, sleepiness fled.

Scope's plan was simple, and didn't take long to convey. The pterosaurs reared back their heads and screeched to the sky, echoing deafeningly inside the warehouse.

Scope strode to the huge sliding door. Employing the assistance of larger carnivores, she managed to break the lock and slide the door open. As one mass of wings, the pterosaurs skittered out of the warehouse and took to the air. Scope followed close behind, her fringe waving in the force of their wings as she watched them fly away.

"May I Am protect you," she voiced.

The flock of pterosaurs soared over the forest, gaining

speed as they went. They began screeching, a call to battle that any avian would understand. Birds in the trees, everything from eagles to vultures, rose from the trees in droves. The sound of beating wings broke the otherwise silent night, and their forms blotted out the cloudy sky.

Back at the warehouse, a juvenile Corythosaurus jumped around in excitement. "Where are they going? Where are they going? Scope, do you know where they're going?"

Scope shook her head in amusement.

"Well, of course you'd know," the Corythosaurus continued. "But can you tell me where?"

"Quiet, Scratcher!" the Corythosaurus' elder brother rebuked. "Let her speak."

"Sorry, Hoot," Scratcher replied meekly. "But, Scope, where're they going?"

"To help the cause," she said, looking off in the last place she had seen them. "It's late, you two. Go back on inside and get some sleep."

"Yes, ma'am," Hoot said, nudging Scratcher toward the doors. "Come, brother."

"Good night, Scope!" Scratcher called over his shoulder. "I hope they beat 'em!"

Following them inside, Scope jumped up and grabbed the bottom edge of the sliding door with her teeth. Using her body weight, she tugged it down and it rattled back into place. She set a pair of Stygimolochs to watch the door in case it opened suddenly.

I must remember to ask Nicole for another lock, Scope thought to herself.

Assail landed beside her, his form barely visible in the darkness. "I've been meaning to ask you something," he said, "but you were busy all day. How did Nicole know that the missile was coming?"

Scope thought back. "Rush had called Jasmine."

"Rush?" Assail said. "That is very good. He's well, then."

"You didn't know of his well-being?" Scope said, staring down at him. "He wasn't with you?"

"No. He ran away on our way here."

She was shocked speechless. Anything she could think of saying wasn't appropriate in some way.

Assail suddenly cocked his head, listening to something she couldn't hear. He smiled.

"What is it?" Scope asked.

"It's Rush," he responded. "The American soldiers he had found in one of the cities on the east coast called in a Transport. Not only have they extinguished all UO operations in the area, they're bringing Rush with them back to base. My team is picking him up on the way to our next mission."

Scope was pleased. "When you see him, tell him of my deep thanks. He's saved all our lives today. I Am used his weakness and turned it into greatness. He made Rush a hero."

It was a two-story, white wood domicile decorated with burgundy shutters and untended shrubbery, that the team approached in the midmorning. There was no garage, just an open driveway containing a single vehicle. They walked along the paved walk that led to the porch, taking in a few rocking chairs coated with a layer of old pollen positioned on either side of the black-painted front door. Three of the team took point as Lennox raised a loose fist and rapped on the door.

He ended up having to knock twice before they heard a muffled *"Who is it?"* and rapidly approaching footsteps. The curtain blocking the door's window was lifted by a corner. A woman's face filled the gap. She frowned at the unknown people on her doorstep and made no move to unlock the barrier. *"Who are you, and what are you doing here?"* she called through the door.

"Are you Mrs. Rogers?" Lennox queried, words clipped and to the point.

"I am, but you haven't answered my question."

Lennox held up an unfolded paper notice and a badge for her to examine. "I think it would be best if you let us in, Mrs. Rogers. It's about your son, Jamie."

A few moments later, Mrs. Rogers was ushering them inside, checking the empty street before securely locking the door behind her. As soon as the latch was clicked, she began rambling frantically, reiterating her innocence and helplessness in the matter at hand. It was a disjointed mess of information, and Lennox held up a hand to quiet the woman. She agreed to his suggestion of taking the conversation to the living room.

"You do not have to tell me," Mrs. Rogers stated as she sat on the couch. Robin hovered in a corner where she could see the front door, and a reflection of the window in the dark television screen. The rest of her team took seats around the room across from their hostess. "I will not presume to tell you falsehoods. I will tell the truth as I know it, and answer all that I can."

"Thank you," Lennox replied, then fingered a recording device. "We will be recording this meeting. I hope that is all right with you."

"I've been waiting far too long for this day. Record me if you wish."

Lennox smiled thinly. "Mrs. Rogers, what do you know about your son, Jamie's, after-school activities?"

"He runs identities," Mrs. Rogers said forlornly. "It's not by his will, or mine!" she rapidly added. "It starts at the building by the school, that's where Jamie gets the identities. He hands them off to the janitor at his school. Then Jamie comes home with some cash."

"How do you know this?" Lennox asked.

"I followed him one day."

"Why have you not notified authorities?"

"Because they will kill Jamie if I do!" Mrs. Rogers spat. "The identification manager. His name is Portman. He comes over twice a month with a smile, a snack, and a knife in his pocket. 'How are you? How are things? What a fine boy you have, I hear he's getting good grades.'"

"Does he threaten you?"

Robin side-eyed her team leader as he pressed on,

Mrs. Rogers responding succinctly, if not wearily. There was a stressful weight being taken off of the woman as she confessed. As the hour passed, the picture of the situation had become clear.

Mr. Rogers, the household breadwinner, had died in a car accident. Mrs. Rogers struggled to support herself and her son, and was working three jobs when she noticed that Jamie was not coming home from school right away. Mrs. Rogers used one of her rest days between jobs to surveil her own son. She discovered that Jamie had been coerced into a false identification black market, as a runner. Cornering her son after he returned home resulted in a tearful confession that revolved around strangers approaching him with the promise of money, kidnapping him when he refused, and using Mrs. Rogers herself as leverage if the boy dared to tell anyone.

Portman paid Jamie $100 for each run. Mrs. Rogers was ashamed. Despite the triple workload, funds were tight; therefore, she accepted the payments from her son to pay for household utilities, Jamie's schooling, and groceries. She still maintained the three jobs. Every other Saturday, Portman invited himself over for the sole intention of ensuring that he was a prominent figure in the Rogers' lives, and to emphasize the threat that the mother or son would lose the other if they let anyone else know.

So, in a way, the team finding out was a blessing.

"Please," Mrs. Rogers pleaded. "Can you get my Jamie out of there? Can you get us out of this situation?"

"That may be a problem," Lennox said. "Stranger danger is a very important issue, especially in these times. Jamie is not likely to come with us if we just walk up to him."

"We have a safe code."

Robin waited on one of the benches outside the school, waiting for the bell to ring.

The bell rang, and Robin was suddenly a solitary rock in a swollen river. Gaze flying, she picked out every face, just in case the boy had decided to blend in with the crowd. Small groups passed by, intending to stroll home instead of taking a bus.

Jamie appeared at the double doors of the school, calling out a farewell to someone within. Robin slowly stood as he neared, gaining his attention. He paused, eyes widening.

"Hi, Jamie," Robin said softly. "Can I talk to you for a minute?"

"I. . . I. . . I gotta go," Jamie said in a rush, bursting into a brisk walk and attempting to circle around her.

Robin reached out and grabbed his hand, holding him in place. He pulled against her, but her grasp was iron. "Jamie, please. You don't need to be scared. I'm here to *help* you. You *and* your mom. She told me to tell you this." And she whispered the code.

The boy stuttered, head whipping from her to the black market building, back again, back again. "Why did Mom send you?" he uttered in a breathless whisper. "I'm in so much trouble, aren't I? You– You gotta keep my mom safe, he said that he'd–"

Crouching so that she was at his eye level, Robin smiled assuredly. "Everything will be okay. You won't have to be a runner ever again."

Numerous enforcement vehicles rounded the block corner, flashing red and blue with sirens. The vehicles screeched to a halt in front of Jamie's place of work. Robin watched neutrally as people in black garb swarmed the lawn, firearms out and ready, as the door was smashed down by a two-man ram.

CHAPTER TWENTY-TWO

"I've received a communications from HQ," Lennox stated the next morning. "Rush is coming in. We're to pick him up this afternoon. Also, HQ wants us on a remote meeting in five minutes."

"Topic?" Robin asked, leaning back in her seat.

"We will know when they call."

Right to the second, the call came. "Eagle Eyes," Lennox answered.

"Adams. It's time we brought you into the loop on the

background of your strike mission. Last week, a handwritten letter arrived via federal mail carrier here. The meeting in I-5 was affirmed with detail. It also named the existence of the forgers, and a vague location which we were able to narrow. It identified the Rogers boy, and exactly how to sneak in an explosive."

Robin exchanged a look with Williams. That little device had been sent last-minute from HQ's R&D department, fresh off the assembly table. It didn't even have a proper name. None of the team had seen anything like it before.

"What did Analysis say about the letter?" Lennox asked.

"Graphology ran it. Written with the dominant hand; Right. Slight left slant. Very heavy pressure with large blocky font size. No fancy loops in letters. Words spread out, but some letters connected. High crossed 't's. Orderly spacing. Legibility varies."

It had been a while since Robin had attended her graphology classes, but this sounded like an interesting case. She waited for Adams to continue.

"In other words, our anonymous writer is self-confident but rather nervous, outgoing but private, logical yet emotional, scatterbrained and focused, and heavily committed. Graphology says that he or she's the most oxymoronic writer they've ever seen."

"Permission to speak?" Williams opined.

"Granted."

"Our intel originated from a single message?"

"Yes and no. Originated, yes. This past week was spent verifying the information. Whoever this was, they were very helpful. Also, we know that Takin stopped by the same location

a few days before the letter was sent. He goes by Henry Lancaster now."

"Has there been any headway in identifying the asset?" Lennox asked, tapping the wheel with one finger, a sign of him in speculative thought.

"Negative. Whoever it was is in the wind."

Mouth agape, Anita stared across the couch at her husband. Slowly, she shook her head in denial. "Pete. You can't. . ." The mostly empty dinner place on her lap began to slip due to distraction, but she rescued the dish and placed it on the coffee table. While she was bent over, she paused the movie playing on the TV. She straightened and pointed accusingly at her husband. "You can't do this to me."

Pete smiled reassuringly at her, lips tight and thin. "I have to, honey. They called me up, requested me personally. Who am I to deny service to my country when I can help in ways few can?"

"But *black-ops*? What training do you have? Can you handle that stress, Pete? You could die, and you'd leave me here all alone." Anita put a hand over her mouth, eyes turning glassy. "Don't do that to me. Please."

Sighing, Pete deposited his own plate on the coffee table and rubbed at his face. "I've already accepted. You know that."

"I know." His wife sniffled, scooting closer. "Take care of yourself." Hands clamping on his cheekbones, fingers wrapping around his skull to disappear into his short locks, she continued firmly, "I want you to go back on the range. The target had better have consistent kill-shot holes before you walk out of there. Every time. Do you hear me, Pete Berg? Constant prayer. *Constant.*"

"Yes, ma'am," Pete said with a smile. He leaned forward and gathered her up in a tight hug. "I'll come back to you. I promise. I'll do all I can to come back."

"When do you leave?" Anita asked into his chest, her hands sliding from his head to fist in his shirt.

"In the next few days. They'll give me a call, and then I'm off."

A pattering knock at the front door pulled them apart. Compeer looked up from his spot on his brand new doggy bed in the corner. Rising from the couch, Pete went to the door and peered through the glass hole. He gave Anita a startled glance before opening the door wide.

Anita shot to his side when he asked, "Nikki, are you all right? What happened?"

Nicole smiled brokenly, eyes rimmed with red. She held her arms close to her chest, as if her self-hug was the only thing keeping her together.

"Nikki!" Anita exclaimed, taking Nicole and bringing her inside. "What's wrong? Pete, get the tissues and a trashcan." She guided Nicole to the couch, sitting beside her with an arm over the other woman's shoulders.

"I left work early," Nicole murmured. "I need to talk with you."

Pete came back with the cheery yellow tissue box extended. After Nicole took it and blew her nose, he knelt in front of her. "Nikki, tell us what happened."

Nicole swallowed thickly. Her gaze was incapable of focusing on any one object as she skittered glances around the room. She finally settled for staring at the crumpled tissue in the can. "There've been so many attacks on me. *I should be dead.* This last one, with that AIM unit. . . I should be dead. Why am I still alive?"

"You're not dead because you're not done yet," Pete replied calmly.

"Done?"

"A miracle saved your life because your purpose in life isn't over," Pete tried again. "You have more to do. And you're not ready yet. . . Am I making sense?"

At Nicole's blank stare, Anita gave Pete a smile before drawing the other woman's attention. "Nikki, I think it's time we dive deep and answer some of these questions. Are you willing to listen?"

With a sniffling breath, Nicole nodded.

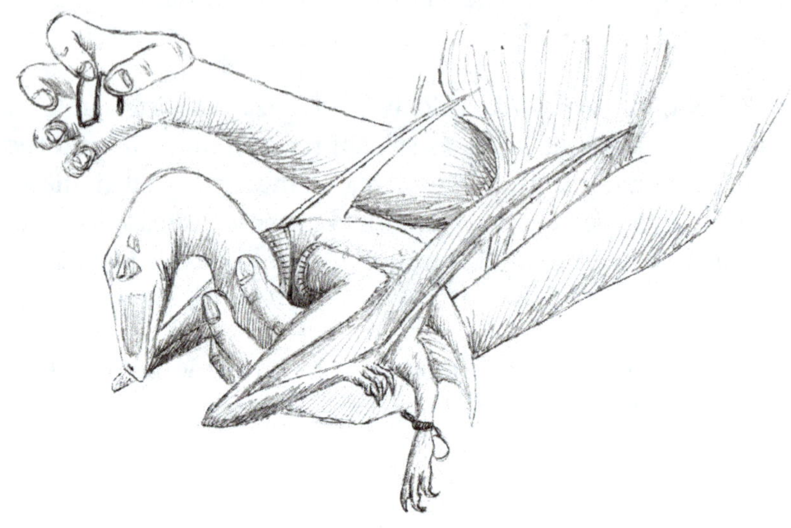

CHAPTER
TWENTY-THREE

The thrumming drone of the aircraft's engines resounded throughout the cabin. Rush huddled in a ball at the back wall of his pet carrier, trying to keep himself as far away from the wire door as possible. Thankfully, the agent escorting him had his leg partially blocking the opening.

Rush stiffened as the agent popped the latches on the door and pushed a carton of sardines into the pet carrier. "Here's lunch, Fluffy."

Bristling at the insult, Rush sulked to the stinky carton and sniffed at the dead, slimy fish inside. He plucked one up with his beak and tossed it around his mouth to taste it before swallowing. Finding the taste of the sardines not that vile, he consumed the rest and pushed the empty container against the grate. His escort took it back and dumped it into a small plastic bag.

Relaxing against the wall, Rush peeked through one of the air holes. He appeared to be in a civilian plane. The seats were occupied with humans of all ages. In the row closest to him was a bouncing little boy, a teenager isolating himself with earbuds, and two parents who had their noses buried in electronic books.

The little boy looked up from his coloring book at the pet carrier and started toward him. Rush cringed away as the kid stalked closer.

Rush frantically tried to remember what animal he was supposed to be. "Meow!" he cawed. "Hiss! Mrow!" He hoped it was a cat, but it was too late to bark. Unless he was a parrot?

"Hey, kid," the agent said, stopping the boy in his tracks. "Don't go near the cage. My cat doesn't like strangers."

"Can I look in, please?" the boy cooed, making his eyes as big as possible.

"Sorry, kid, but no. He'll claw your eyes out. Go on back to your family now."

The boy's head bowed. "Yes, sir," he said softly, trudging back to his seat.

While the agent's leg moved to block the grate even more, Rush settled down in a large blanket that had been given to him before the departure. It was a thin fabric, but it was soft, covered with short fibers that parted at the slightest touch. Rush half hoped that they would allow him to keep it.

The airplane began to shake, bouncing Rush's body uncomfortably. It gradually grew more severe, to the point where he and his pet carrier were becoming airborne intermittently. Rush's claws penetrated the plastic of the carrier as he he struggled to remain steady.

"This is the captain speaking. We're going through some mild turbulence. Should be back in the clear in a few minutes or so."

Mild turbulence, ha! Rush thought as his head smacked the side of the carrier.

The turbulence continued. Other passengers were complaining as their snacks were sent to the floor. At some point, Rush realized that the agent's leg was no longer visible, and the pet carrier had vibrated its way into the aisle.

Suddenly, something stilled the pet carrier, then it was lifted off of the floor. Rush crammed himself against the back wall, catching a few slivers of the little boy through the air slits in the sides of the pet carrier. The boy took him to his row and Rush grunted as the pet carrier was put down none too lightly. A pair of knees appeared at the grate, followed by a pair of chubby hands, then a face.

The little boy's eyes squinted, trying to penetrate the darkness. Rush held as still as possible against the persisting turbulence.

A tickle itched Rush's nose.

No! he thought in desperation, going crosseyed to look at his beak. *Of all the worst times to have to. . . have to-* "Achoo!"

The little boy's eyes widened, mouth falling open in shock. He reeled away from the grate, a small yell escaping his lips. "Mommy! Mommy! There's a monster in the crate!"

"Luke, where'd you get that? Get away, you don't know what's in there."

The little boy vanished from the grate, but Rush could still see him in spurts through the air slits. "I do know! It's a monster, Mommy! It has big bat wings and a beak and huge eyes and I *swear* it wanted to eat me! I saw its teeth!"

"Put it back where you found it and don't you move from your seat again this flight."

"Excuse me, I believe that's my cat."

The pet carrier was picked up again, and Rush found himself looking at the agent through the grate. After the agent checked him over, the pet carrier was carefully set back down on the floor, this time with both the agent's legs pinning it to one location.

The captain's "few minutes" came and long passed. When the turbulence finally subsided, Rush was able to settle into his blanket. Its softness reunited him with the sweet aspect of slumber. He closed his eyes.

The next thing he knew, his breakfast was coming back for an encore. Struggling to keep it on the bottom end of his esophagus, he gagged and looked around. The carrier was steadily swaying back and forth with the strides of the agent. He could hear the ballyhoo and commotion of the scores of people around him, their innumerable conversations overlapping into a cacophony.

Scuttling over to the grate, he peered out through the silver bars. Neon signs lined the wide hall, advertising amusement stores, gift shops, and restaurants. Music was barely audible over the hubbub. The hall was intermediately broken by huge seating areas, filled with uncomfortable-looking plastic chairs and a few charging pads for electrical devices. At least two doors were in the seating areas, one on each side of the room. Windows replaced the walls, rising from floor to ceiling with a short guardrail in front, providing a view of the tarmac and runway.

Rush sniffed the air as they exited another seating area and entered another strip of prospective spending. So many scents assaulted his nose; it sent his mind reeling from the bagels and buns, salads and soups, and books and plastics. His stomach rumbled.

Shut up, he thought to it. *You're bored, not hungry.*

The agent walked toward the largest room Rush had ever seen. The luggage pickup area was lined with seating on one side; benches split it down the middle, electronic notice boards hung from the ceiling; and two huge black conveyer belts wound their way along the other wall, both ends vanishing into a rubber strip-shielded hole. Suitcases of all shapes, sizes, and colors slowly made their way around, most being picked up by their humans, the rest vanishing into the wall.

It wasn't to the conveyer belts that the agent went, but to the seating area on the far side. Rush almost immediately spotted the team lounging, and dove under his blanket.

Robin, sitting stiffly upright in her seat, had her surroundings catalogued and constantly under surveillance. The agent, clad in a flower print Hawaiian shirt and khakis, far from escaped her notice. With a nod of her head, she alerted her companions to his arrival.

She could see the pet carrier in the agent's left hand, held away from his hip and leg to prevent it from bouncing. The interior was dark, but she knew that her AWOL partner was in there. The only sign of her displeasure was the fractional narrowing of her eyes.

Rush heard the muffled greetings, the motion of the pet carrier being passed from one hand to another, and then farewells. Not peeking out, he felt the movements of walking again. The team wasn't speaking, and, from the sounds of it, were heading to the exit. With a whoosh of automatic doors, the clamor of the terminal faded away to be replaced by the turmoils of wind and traffic.

After Lennox unlocked the van, Robin pulled open the sliding back door. Assail, Gale, and Shriek sat in the closed-off third row. Climbing in, she twisted around and placed the pet carrier on a seat in their midst. As Lennox seated himself in the driver's spot and Williams took the front passenger's, she buckled her seat belt. The door of the pet carrier was unlatched.

"Rush, come out," Assail beckoned.

Rush hesitated, unwilling to face his mentor. How could he?

Robin watched out of the corner of an eye as Assail entered the pet carrier. Seconds later, she heard some resistance, then Rush was shoved out into the open and down onto the floorboard. Assail stood at the opening of the pet carrier as Rush got to his feet.

"Look at me, Rush," Assail ordered firmly.

Craning her neck to see behind her seat, Robin saw her partner hide his head under a wing.

Assail hopped down, landing next to his student. "Rush. Look at me."

The only response was even more of Rush's body going under his wing.

Assail screeched something that made everyone else recoil. Robin rubbed at an ear.

However, whatever Assail had said seemed to work, as Rush fell into a series of caws and wails, face still hidden, with body shaking wildly. Gale and Shriek started to appear more uncomfortable and sympathetic the longer the prodigal continued.

Robin stiffly faced forward, her eyes never leaving the sight of the road ahead. If she didn't focus on what her partner was actually emitting, she could almost imagine understanding most of his words. From the sounds of it, he seemed really repentant.

He should be, she thought in disappointed anger. *If he can't handle it, he shouldn't be here.*

"Sounds like your estranged companion begs forgiveness," Williams said, turning around in his seat to look at Robin.

She huffed. "He'll have to work hard in order to earn back my trust."

"I wouldn't hazard the notion otherwise," Williams said. "You're much too obdurate."

Lennox flexed his hands on the wheel, as if thinking. "Assail, calm your protege. Robin, take his equipment from the storage compartment and help Rush dress."

While Assail began cawing and cooing, Robin unbuckled her seatbelt and bent down to the floor. She felt along the underside of the driver's seat, found a hidden lever, and flicked it. With a *pop*, a section of the floor shifted. Moving the piece aside revealed a small compartment, inside of which were the things Rush had discarded the night he had left.

Taking out the body suit first, Robin couldn't help but think back to the morning after. They had all awakened at 0500 to prepare themselves for their masquerade as herpetologists. While the humans found clothes for the part, the Pterodactylus and Bambiraptor would go on ahead to the Reserve and blend in. Rush had been nowhere to be found, and there was no way to track him.

She plucked the rest of the equipment from the compartment before securely closing it. Leaning back over the seat to fetch Rush, she saw him slumped next to Assail on the floorboard. Without a word, she gently grasped him by the chest and lifted him up into the seat beside her. He was like a rag doll. His body was completely compliant as she dressed him in his suit and equipment. Checking his vest pockets to see if he had spare ammunition for his miniature assault rifle, which he did, she declared him prepped with a firm nod.

Rush swallowed before looking up, trying to keep his partner out of his peripheral vision. "Where are we going?" he asked softly.

"To Sky Adventures Airport," Lennox replied, switching lanes on the road. "It's a small, out of the way skydiving airport. No one will question our temporary shutdown of the place while we wait for our new hacker and transport overseas."

Assuming that "overseas" meant that they had finally discovered the headquarters to the Unison Order, Rush asked, "Who's the new hacker?"

The pressure of his foot on the gas pedal slowly decreased the closer the GPS told him he was to his destination. Pete craned his neck closer to the windshield, as if that would help him see past the dense forest on either side of the narrow road.

Leaning back in his seat, he glanced at the small duffel bag on the passenger seat beside him. Inside it were only his toiletries and a few articles of clothing. He had been told to leave everything personal at home, including his data-pad, which he felt strangely naked without.

He wondered how many times Anita had tried to call him for last-minute "Be careful"s and "I love you"s before finding his data-pad, phone, and wallet in the bedroom. Surely, she would be worried in his sudden leaving. *At least I managed to get five minutes with her to say Goodbye.*

Finally, he saw buildings through the trees. The metal siding reflected the overcast skylight into his eyes. A few more turns of the road, and he entered a small parking lot, with only a lone parked van. He parked his own car beside it, grabbed his duffel bag, and exited the car, gravel crunching underfoot.

Where is everyone? he thought, spying a skydiving sign next to the front door of the largest building. He knocked, but, upon receiving no discernible response, he tentatively tried the handle. Finding the door unlocked, he entered. The featureless cream halls were empty and silent as his steps echoed on the linoleum floor. Most of the doors lining the way were open, and he couldn't help but peek inside the rooms. All were devoid of any signs of life, but there was enough reasonable clutter to signify that this building had been occupied very recently. The unexplained abandonment was rather disconcerting.

The person on the phone had told him to meet someone called Commander Lennox in the hanger bay, so he followed the directional signage hung on the walls. Eventually, he arrived at a heavy metal door. Pete opened it.

Four people stood in the middle of the hanger, all in the same stance; arms crossed, feet shoulder-width apart, chin up. The shortest of them, a man of Asian descent, stepped forward. "Pete Berg?" he said.

"That's me," Pete replied, shifting the duffel bag slung over a shoulder. "You're Commander Lennox?"

"I am. Welcome to Team Alpha. I trust that you've been briefed on the situation."

"Actually, the only thing I was told was to report here. That's it."

"Not unexpected," Lennox said. "The phone line may have been secured from our end, but nothing is more confidential than face-to-face. Nonetheless, you're now part of Team Alpha," he continued. "There's just one thing left to say: I heard that you recently received a phone call from a friend of yours, a falconer, I believe?"

Pete stared in confusion for a moment. *I don't have a friend who's a falconer.* Seeing the team stiffen, he mentally scrambled for what must be a code reply. "I. . ." Suddenly, he remembered the last thing the person on the phone had said. "Why, yes. Her pigeon was eaten by a harpy, and decided to give an iguana to her nephew."

Lennox nodded in approval. "Very good, Berg."

The only female soldier of the four cocked her head to the side. "You worked at an R&D company. You were recently demoted as you were obscure enough to be the necessary fall guy." She huffed, as if thinking *bureaucracy*. "You now work for a new company, but still maintain contact with Nicole Nike and, in conjecture, the dinosaurians."

"Yes," Pete confirmed.

"You have demonstrated an astonishing amount of expertise with computers," the woman continued. "In fact, your work exposed a hidden UO worker within our very team. You should know that you're now our new electronics expert."

Pete blinked. "Really? I don't think I'm *that* good. Surely, there are better people out there."

"Conners," Lennox said, "please hand our new teammate his uniform. Williams and I will be outside."

As the two men departed, Conners picked up a previously unnoticed bag from the floor and held it out to Pete. He stared at the clothes held out to him. He knew that he was supposed to take them, but the signals weren't reaching his arms. The soldier soon tired of holding them out and shoved them into his chest. Pete held them there.

"Change into them," she ordered. "You have until the plane lands, which is in about five mikes."

"Mikes are minutes?"

"Yes. Are all your personal belongings at your apartment?"

"My car keys are in my pocket. And my embedded RFID chip, can't take it out."

"Leave the keys here. Our people will ensure that your vehicle is safely stowed away until you return."

Pete fished them out of his pocket with a ring of metal. After glancing around for a moment, he reluctantly rested them on an empty plastic folding table.

Pulling a small device from a pocket, Conners took his arm and ran the device over his flesh. When it was hovering over his hand, it beeped. Robin tapped the screen a few times, and the beeping stopped.

"What did you do?" Pete asked.

"Neutralized the chip. Don't worry, it can be turned on again, and you'd definitely notice if anyone attempts to engage it," she replied, putting away the device. "Down the hall and directly on your right are the mens bathrooms. Change and get back here in three mikes."

Pete didn't dare disobey her. He was back in two, his old clothes rolled and crammed into his duffel bag.

Conners looked him over, and he suddenly felt very self-conscious in the dark fatigues. They fit well, but the uniform didn't seem like it reflected him. After a moment, she spun on a heel. "Come, the Transport is arriving."

Pete strode after her, wondering how she was able to

walk so fast without tripping. He fell into step beside her, and was soon wishing that he had spent more time at the gym. They exited the hanger and arrived at the tarmac. Lennox and the other man, Williams, were already there.

Lennox took a sleek, black laptop from his pack and handed it to Pete. "This is your new laptop, equipped with everything you will need."

Propping it on one arm, Pete flipped it open. With a tone, his own facial recognition ID appeared. There was no further security yet; he made a mental note to add some. He brought up the application window. His jaw dropped, and with it almost the laptop itself.

"On the desktop is a folder titled 'Know,'" Lennox continued, watching unfazed as Pete managed to catch the computer before it hit the ground. "Read that while we're en route. It contains everything you need to know about the mission parameters. Delete it once you're done."

"Yes, sir," Pete said, closing the laptop's lid.

A screech from above drew his attention. Coming in from the sky were three Pterodactylus, one laboriously carrying a Bambiraptor in its feet. The Bambiraptor was set on the ground, running to dispel the momentum. The three Pterodactylus separated to join the three soldiers.

"Welcome to the team, Pete!" Rush chirped.

"Let's hope you make a better hacker than our previous one," Shriek added.

Lennox had an eyebrow raised. "I take it that you all know each other?"

Pete nodded. "Yes, Nicole's one of my old colleagues. Very old friends."

"Then we know that you'll get along with our unorthodox partners," Conners said. "Gale is yours."

A sound drifted to them on the wind, bespeaking the arrival of an aircraft. Trailing wisps of cloud in its wake, a Manta Transport emerged from the cloud cover a short distance away. The engines audibly transferred precedence to the rotors as the craft slowed in its descent, the rotors shifting in their mounts to maintain balance. With amazing dexterity, the vessel landed mere yards away. The craft idled as the ramp detached with a pneumatic *hiss*, slowly lowering until it touched the ground. This was the first time Pete had ever seen one of the Mantas in person, and he took a little longer than expected to take in the ship.

"Come on, Berg," Shriek said, whacking his leg with her tail to draw his attention. "You'll have plenty of time to observe from the inside."

Pete tucked the laptop under his arm as he followed Shriek aboard. Before he reached the top of the ramp, it began to close behind him, and he hurried to stable floor, skipping over the yellow and black hazard line that marked the border of the opening. He took a seat and scrambled for the harness, feeling the rotors powering up for liftoff. Gale took a seat directly next to him.

"Don't you want to sit with the pterosaurs?" Pete asked her, nodding toward where the Pterodactylus worked to create their own harnesses out of the human-intended seat belts.

Gale shook her head as she entangled her body in the waist straps.

"Gale is paired with the hacker of the team," Lennox said. "And now, that's you. Do you mind?"

"No, not at all." Pete smiled, clipping the harness into place.

Conners clapped her hands. "Get comfortable, Berg. It's a long flight to the middle of the Atlantic."

"How long's a long time?" Pete asked.

"About an hour," she responded.

Pete blinked in shock. "That's a good deal faster than what's public. *How fast* does this thing go?"

CHAPTER TWENTY-FOUR

Pete bounced his leg against the floor. Through his seat, he could feel the vibrations of the engines. The novelty of riding inside of a submersible plane had worn off shortly after the Transport had dropped beneath the waves. Dark blue light flickered through the portholes in the hull, accenting the industrial white overheads.

Across from him, Williams was checking his weaponry. A conversational starter came to mind abruptly.

"So, Williams," Pete said. "Am I issued a weapon?"

"Beneath the seat, drawer 6-B," Williams responded.

"Anterior locus."

By bending double and shifting his legs, Pete found the drawer. He withdrew a large case, which contained a small sidearm and several spare magazines. Boxes of ammunition also occupied the drawer. He made the case into a makeshift table to begin dismantling, so he could check and clean the firearm. "Why do you use such wordage?"

"Idiosyncratic penchant," was the reply.

"Really? I'm not accustomed to using in such volume brobdingnagian verbiage."

Conners' eyes rolled to the ceiling. "No. Not another one."

Williams' eyes shot up to meet Pete's. Placing his weapons in the empty seat beside him, Williams leaned back in repose. "The preponderance typically contravene the intricacies of the English language. I find disport in others attempting to discern what I say."

"I see," Pete said slowly. "Forgive me if I'm erroneous, but perhaps pontificating lavishly is a divertissement from the pressure of the job."

"Black operations is not a métier for many." Williams glanced over at his pile of knives, grenades, and firearms of varying sizes. "I'm honored to serve, despite the knowledge that my memory will remember the most bijou facet of these preceding years."

Pete was stunned by the depth of Williams' gaze. He couldn't *imagine* the experiences the man, the team, had gone though. *What have I gotten myself into? What memories will I have to live with for the rest of my life?*

"Berg," Lennox said suddenly, drawing Pete's attention. The shorter man had his eyes closed. His expression was carefully peaceful. "You weren't picked for your skills alone. There's something Headquarters saw in you that made *you* the right man."

"Skills and past experience," Conners interjected. "Sure, you've got those, but can you keep up with us? I'll be the first to admit that I'm not the most fuzzy person."

"I've been called a stroll in a swamp on a midsummer's sundown," Lennox added. "One of the more poetic things."

"Most people find my way of verbal expression rebarbative," Williams said, checking the reflective shine of one of his combat knives before playfully wagging the tip at Pete. "If a neophyte like yourself can abide and incentivize my eccentricities, then you can't be that terrible."

Frederick Gluten, dressed to perfection, promenaded down the shadowed halls. His pale, sun-starved skin glistened with a nervous sweat that threatened to ruin his expensive suit. His hand kept wandering to his throat to tug the collar. It was all a show for the monitoring cameras that littered the halls, of course, as Cornette had requested his appearance to be such.

He turned a final corner. Unlike the other halls, this one had only one door, and it was at the very end of the narrow passage. His demeanor displayed panic and trembling as he struggled to maintain a brave front. He raised a fist and rapped at the door.

"Come."

Gluten turned the knob. The room inside was dimly lit, the only illumination coming from the shaded floor-to-ceiling window. No sooner had his eyes adjusted, the snapping of fingers cued the room's overhead lighting. He hissed softly, shielding his eyes with a hand until they readjusted.

A tall, platinum blonde woman sat behind an ebony desk, staring at him. "Sit," she bid, gesturing to one of the two chairs in front of her desk.

He sat, placing his briefcase on the desk. The chair was one of the most exquisite he had ever felt, the standard for the lady he had known for years. He eased into the padding, laying his elbows on the armrests.

Cornette leaned forward, resting her chin on her folded hands. "With all that has been happening recently, darling," she said smoothly, "I would very much like to hear some good news."

"Y-yes, Ms. Cornette," Gluten said, fiddling with his fingers. "I would very much like to tell you good news."

"Why the formalities, Fred?" the woman said. "We've known each other for years, and have gotten past the nettlesome last name basis. Please, call me Lois."

"I'm sorry, but I prefer Ms. Cornette, ma'am."

Cornette leaned back in her chair, her fingers now steepled in front of her mouth. "Very well, Mr. Gluten. Please, honey, continue with the good news I desire."

Gluten held his tongue, inwardly wincing. She wasn't wrong in how grating the pet names could get. "Good news is a relative term. So, telling you that one of our deep-cover spies was compromised might not appear to be good news in a certain point of view."

Cornette's faux-friendly expression changed to emotionless. After a moment, she reassumed her soft smile. "Continue," she said.

"Takin's on his way here. He called in for transport at 0400 hours yesterday. He should be arriving in a few minutes, at 1300 hours."

"I want to see him the *instant* he arrives."

"Understood, Ms. Cornette. I'll direct him here myself."

Cornette tapped her index fingers together. "Do you know how far away that American team is?"

"They're without a hacker. Unless they can find one with the aptitude of Takin, they won't be as effective. However, I have gotten wind that they've employed some disgraced scientist from a weapons development company. Rumor has it that it's the same one that compromised Takin."

"I have no interest in rumors and winds, sweetie," Cornette stated.

"N-no, ma'am! But Intel has linked the scientist with Nicole Nike, the one who supplied the team with the dinosaurs."

"Did the operation at the Reserve go well?"

"Welch was unable to complete the mission. Berg, who was Nike's replacement, and the pterosaurs are very observant.

After Welch's second attempt, Berg confiscated his oleander bag and sent everyone away. Intel reports that once Nike heard of the–"

"Heard?"

Gluten gulped. "Yes. Well, our AIM unit did detonate successfully, but our investigation team was unable to explain how Nike and her pet dog were able to survive the blast."

Cornette's eyes narrowed. "Really? I must remember to schedule a meeting on that subject." She waved a hand. "Go on, continue, sweetie."

Gluten opened his briefcase and consulted a paper. "Our mic hidden in Welch's clothes caught feed of him getting himself arrested at the Reserve. Intel suspects his captors were the American team. It is, unfortunately, highly likely that Welch is as weak in interrogation as his levels of idiocy are high."

Cornette's steely expression returned. "Is that so?'"

"They probably already have everything except for the coordinates to this very base. They're most likely going to think that we're on Flores Island." The leak had been very carefully constructed to make that so.

"You predict that they will go to Flores," Cornette said, jerking him to attention. Her expression of death had melded into her thinking expression.

"There is a high percentile chance in favor of that, yes."

"I want the American team dead this week, including their dinosaur aides. Do it covertly; no need to worry the natives. Make sure that our team is absolutely aware of the consequences should the natives stumble upon the operation. Could you do that for me, darling?"

"M-most certainly, Ms. Cornette."

She tapped her index fingers together, her thinking expression unaltered. "Give me the outcome of our air strike on the Reserve."

"Ah. . . The entire Reserve has been reduced to flames and cinders, thanks to our operatives on the east coast of the States. American news channels still show fire departments working on containing the aftermath. However–"

"'However?'" Cornette interrupted, eyes flashing.

"They were warned!" Gluten shot. "Very few human remains and a lack of vehicles show that they evacuated before detonation. A fraction of dinosaurian remains reveals that they made it out in time, as well. Thus, they must have been warned. I have people working on the dinosaurians' current location."

"Find out," the French woman ordered. "I want those dinosaurs in their place; fossilized. You have the ability, and you know well enough not to leave a trail. I expect an update within a week."

Gluten nodded. "Also, Nike is scheduled for a court hearing later this coming week. Our assets in the eastern US may be able to influence the outcome."

"Do it," Cornette said dismissively. "If that fails, you know what to do."

Sensing that their meeting was complete, Gluten stood and headed to the door.

"Mr. Gluten."

He froze, his hand on the knob. "Yes, Ms. Cornette?"

She had leaned forward into the chin-on-hands position again. Her eyes were half-lidded. "If this was good news, then I expect *prodigious* news upon your return, darling. Or I might have to *reassign your quarters* for a few days."

Gluten nodded like a bobble-head as he slipped out the door as quickly as politeness allowed.

Once the door was closed, he glanced back at it behind him while a shudder ran through his body. He knew what the threat of reassignment meant, despite his certainty of Cornette's facade. At least, he hoped it was a bluff. Questioning was not to be taken lightly, especially if she discovered what exactly her most trusted friend had on the side.

It wasn't until the end of his shift a few hours later that he returned to his quarters and discovered the note that she had somehow slipped into his briefcase. He quickly checked the time.

Robin was, yet again, playing the part of the lovestruck newlywed. Thankfully, however, she wasn't in an embarrassing dressy outfit. Instead, she was in a pair of dark khaki shorts, a t-shirt, and comfortable hiking boots. Far more suitable for her tastes. Lennox, again her husband, was just as casual, wearing long shorts, sandals, and a polo shirt.

"It's so nice here," Robin commented as she walked

through the village of Ende. She waved as one of the residents gave her a welcoming smile.

Walking along the streets between houses and small businesses, Robin could almost imagine the war as a foreign concept. The inhabitants all had a smile. Children laughed as they chased each other over the sand. The hustle and bustle of the village drowned out negative thoughts.

Robin consulted her tour guide, turning the pamphlet over to look at the section on Flores wildlife. Seeing the native white and brown eagle's picture, she panned her gaze around the trees. She didn't see it.

"What should we do today?" Lennox suddenly inquired. He gestured to the pamphlet. "There's the volcano crater lakes, for one."

"I heard that early morning is the best time to see them," Robin replied, flipping to the sightseeing page. "There's snorkeling, and if we hop over to Komodo Island we can see the dragons' last native habitat."

"Don't you remember the last time I went snorkeling?" Lennox asked her. "No, thank you."

"Whatever you say, Reggie," Robin said. "We could just enjoy the village for the day. Tomorrow morning, we can see the volcano lakes."

"I'll do whatever you wish," Lennox said.

Robin laughed, hanging off of her commander's arm. Seeing a shop, she suggested that they go inside to explore.

Miles away, Rush was in a staring contest. His opponent

was unblinking, their goldenrod eyes gleaming. Resorting to dirty, underhanded tricks, Rush made a sudden move in flaring his wings and opening his beak as wide as it could go. All his opponent did was shift its weight, still unblinking.

"Rush!"

"What?" he responded, not looking away.

Gale alighted on a branch above the two. "Leave the eagle alone. We're supposed to be looking for any evidence of the UO, not trying to stare down the natives."

Unhappy about letting the eagle win, Rush flung himself off of the tree, leaving the bird behind. Gale took off in another direction. Rush hadn't been weaving through the trees for very long when the treeline suddenly ended and he was dumped into an open field. Worried that he might be seen as what he was, Rush beat his wings and bore himself to a higher altitude.

Finding a warm updraft, Rush stilled his wings and glided. His sharp eyes diligently scanned the ground.

A flock of gulls swarmed past him, chirping something about "another metal whirlybird." Curious as to what had them in such a tizzy, the sound of rotor blades turned his attention. True to the natives' words, a small helicopter, little more than the size of an engine, was coming up from behind. He identified at least four people inside.

It looked like a normal air touring helicopter, but that didn't rule out the possibility of one being used as a cover by Unison Order soldiers. Keeping a safe distance away while keeping an eye out for concealed weapons, Rush said, "Rush to Roost. There's a tourist chopper coming in from the west, heading toward the volcano. There's a possibility that it could be a cover by the UO. Over."

"Assail to Rush. Do not engage or go near. What is the chopper's ID?"

Rush read it off.

"Iceberg to Rush. Chopper legit."

Rush curled a wing, sending himself careening away.

Further along in the day, Rush's wings were growing tired. Deciding to snatch time for a break, he glided down to the distant outskirts of a small village. He found a nice tree, dense with branches, and landed on one of the uppermost. Swinging himself so that he hung upside-down by his wing-claws and feet, he yawned and tucked his head into the dim space between both wings. Spots of sunlight warmed his hide as he slowly drifted to sleep.

He wasn't asleep for long, as the tree's shaking sent him into awareness again. Swaying from the motion, he brought his head into the open to look around. The giggles of children floated upward. He saw a few boys scaling the tree, hopping from branch to branch like monkeys.

They hadn't looked like they had seen him yet. As covertly as he could, Rush rotated his body so that he was sitting proper on his branch, then quietly flew to a branch higher up, which handily placed him on the opposite side of the tree from the boys. He took advantage of his brief hiding spot and flew away.

"Eagle Eye to Roost. Report to nest for feeding."

Time for dinner! Rush, feeling his stomach rumble,

veered around and soared toward Ende as quickly as he could. As he approached the sunset-washed village, he could see Assail and Gail flying in from other directions. He looked to the ground for Shriek, but didn't see her.

A quick glide on an ocean breeze carried him to the hotel, which wasn't like the ones in the States. This hotel was spread over a large plot of land, split into four buildings forming a square around a lush garden and swimming pool. Rush was about to find their building and room when Gale swooped in, confidently heading for the one on the right. Rush followed. Sure enough, a corner window was open and Williams stood in the room behind it. The huge man stepped aside, allowing the Pterodactylus space to fly inside. A bush below the window rustled before Shriek leapt out of it and onto the windowsill. She shook herself off before dropping to the floor.

Robin looked up from cleaning her firearm as their animal partners arrived. Putting the pieces down, she cleaned her hands before reaching for the large napkin on her bedside table. Placing it on the far corner of her bed, she opened the napkin to reveal a few small fish, chunks of beef, and bacon.

Rush fluttered up to the napkin, sniffing it curiously. The fish went down first, swallowed whole. The bacon, which he assumed was related to jerky in a way, was next. The beef was a bit foreign to him, but it tasted sort of like days-old dead Triceratops (when he had once been reduced to scavenging), only fresher.

Seeing that her partner was enjoying his dinner, Robin picked up her pistol and resumed. Her hands knew what to do autonomously, so her mind was free to roam while she worked. One of things she thought of was what she would do once the war ended.

A large part of her thrived on the adrenaline rush. She knew what veterans did in order to relive that rush. Some went bungee jumping, others went skydiving, or any other life-threatening civilian activity that which some of the normal population considered insanity. She didn't wish to be reduced to such substitutes quite yet. Also, she was still young, and had a lot of battle left in her to use. Did she really want to waste it behind a desk, where the only way to keep her physique meant trips to a gym?

Yet, there was the side of her that wanted a hiatus from a perpetual fight, whether it be seen or not. She wouldn't mind settling down, finding her soul mate, and having a few children, at least one of them a girl. Her closet would finally contain at least 10 articles of clothing. Wishfully, she daydreamed about going to a mall or store without a target in mind.

Rush swallowed the last hunk of beef, licking his beak to get as much of the juices as he could. Noticing his partner's tense expression, he wondered what she was thinking about. He wondered if she had even noticed that she was blankly staring at her fully reassembled pistol.

Lennox clapped his hands sharply, causing them both to jump. Now that he had everyone's attention, he said, "Get ready. In two mikes, we're going out."

Flores Island was a beautiful place at night. Mountains, green and lush, stood like dark, resolute giants over rocky shores. The towering mountains abruptly gave way to grassy valleys crisscrossed with the stone walls. Quaint little villages around the island lined the shoreline, painted white with orange roofs. Moonlight cast the island in a gentle pale blue glow.

But Rush had little time to appreciate the scenery. A strategic round screen hung over one eye, transforming the dimmed land to the blacks and reds of infrared. Other than in the villages, there seemed to be no sign of human life. More than once, he mistook farm livestock for soldiers surrounding a Unison Order COP.

Come on, where is it? he wondered.

He skimmed over the peak of a mountain, the tips of his wings brushing the treetops. A bird cawed at him indignantly as he passed.

"Sorry!" Rush called under one wing. An idea came to mind, and he circled back. "Hey, do you know if there are any soldier humans on this island?"

The bird told him that it had seen a set of humans with guns a few hills over. Rush thanked it before flying off in the direction indicated.

It took only a few minutes to reach the next crest. Rush flew in circles, scanning below.

Miles away, Robin sat high in an old tree, almost invisible in her dark clothes. The multi-use binoculars were held up to her eyes, scanning the area. Her position in the tree allowed her a clear view of several miles in most directions.

One side of the binoculars had an infrared scanning system, the other displayed an infrared live video feed from the tiny camera in Rush's armored vest. She gave attention to Rush's feed, having the feeling that he would find something. So far, the only heat signatures were those of common animals. Like the tiny red dot in a tree; a bird. The large ones in the middle of the field were cows. And the medium-sized object in a bush was. . . was. . .

She fingered her communicator. "Arcee to Rush," she breathed, "To your seven o'clock."

She watched as Rush turned back and flew lower. As he drew closer to the object, it became defined. It was a human, and what humans would crouch in bushes in the middle of the night? And was that a sniper rifle she saw?

Robin quickly hit a button on the binoculars to mark the coordinates of Rush. "Arcee to Rush. Worm at your two o'clock. Keep flying; I'll BOLO for more."

Squinting, Rush tried to find what Robin had seen, but all he could identify was dense forest. Nonetheless, he continued as ordered, soaring in widening circles.

It wasn't long before Robin had noticed and logged the coordinates of three other humans acting suspiciously in the brush. Sending the coordinates to her teammates, Lennox took over and sent Williams and herself after two, while he took care of a third.

But then Rush heard the blasts of two gunshots echo over the hills. *"Arcee to Roost. Third worm a civilian looking for mushrooms. Marking as false alarm."*

"Roger, roger that, Arcee," Lennox stated. *"Roost, convene at first worm's coordinates."*

"Rush is almost on top of it," Arcee replied. *"Rush, head to your nine o'clock and go a klik. Worm should still be nearby."*

"Roger, roger that," Rush said. Once he had adjusted his course, he folded his wings and dove under the forest canopy. Flying became a game of obstacles as he slowed down. When he thought he had flown a kilometer, he alighted on a branch.

Staying as still as possible, the sounds of the night resounded in his ears. His eyes narrowed focus as he attempted to single out a noise that didn't belong. The *snap* of a breaking twig caused him to fly from his perch and search out the cause.

"Shriek to Roost. I've got the scent; I'm close. Moving in."

Rush heard the calculated steps of the human before the quick, quiet pattering of Shriek's. The darkly-clothed, armed man swung a long rifle in Shriek's general direction as she sprang out of a cluster of bushes. Shocked by the sight of a weaponized Bambiraptor, the soldier failed to open fire.

"Don't move, human," Shriek demanded, adjusting her mini-gun.

Flying overhead, Rush calculated the distance between her and the human. He folded his wings. Air screamed past his sleek form as the ground grew closer. Seconds from body-slamming the soldier, Rush unfolded his wings. Feeling the displaced air, the soldier looked up.

"Argh!" The soldier ducked and covered, dropping his rifle to put his hands over his head.

Rush alighted on a nearby tree and aimed his rifle at the soldier's head. "I'm only going to say this once," he said. He screeched loudly, being sure to show off his teeth, and the soldier cringed away. "Stay on the ground with your hands where I can see them. Move, and some part of you is going to get hurt."

The soldier kept his hands on his head. He descended to his knees, but couldn't go any further without being forced down. The soldier grimaced, then let his upper body fall forward. Rush heard the soldier's teeth collide as his chin hit the ground.

The tree branches rustled. Rush worried that there were more Unison Order men, but then Gale descended into view. Gracefully landing on a bush, she trained her own rifle on the soldier.

Robin leapt over a fallen tree limb, landing within sight of the prisoner. She looked down at the soldier while Williams, Berg, and Lennox arrived behind her. She plucked every bit of technology she could find on the soldier's body before handing it all to Berg. "Iceberg, see what you can make of this junk."

Berg took the heap of advanced tech into his arms, nodding in her general direction. Placing most of the load on the ground, he focused on the enemy's comm link. He opened up his laptop, brought up the wireless transmitter, and clicked the keys and watched the results on the screen.

Williams delved directly into his role as interrogator, appealing to the prisoner's more human side with controlled and circular questioning, searching for slips.

"This flotsam is intransigent, obdurate, and snubs my endeavors to quell him into surrender!" Williams eventually said, gesturing at the enemy soldier.

"No matter," Robin said, marching toward the soldier. She stalked around the Unison Order soldier, visually checking for any signs of hidden weapons. His sniper rifle, pistol, and a set of throwing knifes had already been confiscated, but his uniform was baggy and could hide secrets rather well.

She checked for unusual bulges or strange seams in his black combat boots. Seeing nothing, she swung her assault rifle into its holster and kneeled to frisk the soldier. He glared at her, but did nothing else.

"I've got it," Berg eventually said. "I've got the frequency's source."

Lennox nodded. "Eagle Eyes to HQ. Requesting transport for Roost and uneaten MRE." He waited for a reply, sent an acknowledgement, then looked to Berg. "Where's the source?"

Berg glanced at his computer screen. "Our intel was slightly off. The UO base isn't here on Flores Island, but on Corvo, a small island 17 miles north of here." He swiveled the screen and showed them information on Corvo.

Robin huffed. "We're going to be searching a tiny island of fishers and cattle ranches for an enemy base? Shouldn't be too hard."

CHAPTER TWENTY-FIVE

The refrigerator truck was large. Nicole stuck her head out the window as she maneuvered the truck so that the back hatch would be just in front of the closed sliding door of the warehouse. Mark was doing the same thing beside her, only he was driving a pickup filled with crates of greens.

With instinct born from paranoia, Nicole glanced upward. The view of the cloudy, disheartening sky was partially blocked by the wide expanse of tree branches, obscuring most aerial surveillance. She had to keep the dinosaurs safe from whomever had fired that missile.

Nicole brought the truck to a stop. Stifling a pained

groan, she dropped out to the asphalt. Pulling a set of keys from her left pocket, Nicole unlocked the back hatch and pushed up the sliding door, revealing several stacks of large plastic coolers. She spun around and reached for the warehouse's door, but the padlock looked crooked. Frowning, she pushed again, and the door begrudgingly started to open.

Someone broke the lock. Alarmed, she squinted into the relative darkness of the warehouse. Before she could come to a decision between investigating or calling out, she saw distinctly inhuman movement within.

"Right here," Freedom stated, leaning into the daylight.

Nicole heaved a sigh, a hand over her chest. "What happened? Why is the lock broken?"

"Assail and his kind needed to fly," was the Utahraptor's simple response.

'Kind?' Nicole thought. She squinted, trying to peer through the heavy shadows. Only a few tiny forms flitted through the darkness. Fledgelings and younglings. "The adult pterosaurs–!"

"– Have gone with him," Freedom said. "I could not just stand by and let our home fall to the enemy. I did not do that before, and I could not not do it again. So, I have sent reinforcements. They know where to fly, and they are gathering more with each. . . mile, as you say."

"'More?'" Nicole repeated.

Mark jolted. "The birds! Nicole, I haven't heard a single hawk scream all day, or seen a single vulture. They've been gathering the *birds*!"

"The pterosaurs and fowl share a common territory," Freedom said. "They had to learn to talk to each other. I know a little, as well, but not enough to communicate."

Nicole shook her head in awe. "That's. . . that's amazing, Freedom." She slid the broken lock from its place and tossed it into her truck, making a mental note to grab a new one later.

"In other news," Mark said, opening his vehicle's tailgate. Green and blue crates were stacked two levels high. "Come hither, come hither!" He grabbed a greenery crate from the truck bed. "For doth we come with food aplenty!"

Freedom strode forward. "It's rather late in the day."

"Sorry," Nicole said, gritting her teeth as her body still protested her earlier action of opening the refrigerator truck. "We had to get permission from the mayor to use government money and buy you some food. Then we picked this all up directly from the distribution centers. Mark and I rented these trucks and we got here as soon as we could. We'll be back tomorrow with your next meal, if you don't mind only eating once a day." She leaned against the bumper, wishing she hadn't left her new cane in the cabin.

"We'll survive," Freedom said. "Do you need any help in carrying?"

"I've got the cartons," Mark said, walking inside with a trail of eager herbivores behind him. Once far enough inside, he turned the crate over, dumping the greens all over the floor. The herbivores began devouring it as he returned for another load.

"You could help me carry the coolers," Nicole said, forcing a grin. She reached inside and tugged a cooler closer to the opening. "Can you carry something this heavy?"

"Our arms may be slim, but we are strong," Freedom said, grabbing the handle in both hands. She managed to lift it up a few inches before suddenly setting it down again. After a second, the Utahraptor forcefully reared back. Tail dragging on the ground, Freedom awkwardly walked inside with the cooler in hand. "It just throws off our balance a little!" she added over a shoulder. "What's in here?"

"Meat, go ahead and dump it once you get inside," Nicole chuckled as she labored to pull the next cooler out. An Allosaurus carried it in, faring much better than Freedom.

After an Albertosaurus had taken two coolers in each two-fingered hand, which Nicole found impressive, Freedom finally returned, panting a little.

"The *Intimidator* doesn't grant ultra strength?" Nicole teased, readying another cooler for her to take inside.

"Funny," Freedom replied drily. "Just give me the next cooler."

With the help of the larger carnivores, the refrigerator truck was soon emptied, and Nicole locked it shut. She went to assist Mark by pushing the crates closer to him, who was barely a third done with his load. Assuming that more than a single helper would make the carrying get done even faster, Nicole called a few carnivores over. The Albertosaurus found their arms too short to carry the wide crates, Allosaurus fared little better, and Freedom's wounded pride in her breed's lugging prowess was mended a little as she sauntered inside, easily bearing a load. Other Utahraptors joined in to help, and soon all Nicole and Mark were doing were passing crates from the truck to ready, clawed hands.

"So, where's Pete?" Mark asked out of the blue.

"I was hoping that you knew," Nicole replied, handing a crate to an Utahraptor. "All I heard from Anita was that he received a call and was called away suddenly."

Mark hummed, placing a crate on the asphalt for the next dinosaur to pick up. His face brightened. "Perhaps he was kidnapped by aliens!"

Taken off-guard by his uncharacteristic exclamation, Nicole paused to stare.

"You haven't heard? An alien spaceship crashed, and the government called him to check it out. He drove out to the countryside, but a second ship zoomed in and picked up his car in a tractor beam!" Mark illustrated his fantastic theory with elaborate hand gestures. "The second ship was the enemy of the first ship, and they kidnapped Pete to keep him from helping the crashed ship, which bears important information that could spell the second ship's alien people's doom!"

Nicole blinked once. Twice. Finally, she said, "That's something I would think Pete would say, not you."

"What can I say?" Mark said with a grin and a shrug. "He's rubbed off on me."

"Only you, Mark," Nicole said, shaking her head. She retrieved a crate that had been emptied somewhere on the warehouse floor.

She paused and looked around. Something was wrong, but she couldn't put her finger on it. Deciding that it'd come to her later, she went back to work cleaning up the empty crates and refrigerated coolers.

A little while later, the pickup truck bed was loaded with the empty containers. Mark grabbed a big blue tarp from the backseat of the pickup and spread it out on the ground, then handed Nicole one of two shovels. Nicole took hers with no small grimace; not as much from pain, but not wanting to face the mess inside.

The next hour was spent scouring the warehouse, weaving between eating dinosaurs, scraping up feces.

"It's like when your dog can't get outside fast enough," Mark quipped, carrying a load out to the tarp and dumping it with a nauseating *slap*.

"Only much worse," Nicole said. "Did you remember the hose?" She scooped up a small amount onto her shovel, her healing side protesting even the light burden.

"Yeah, I just need a spout. Did you bring the kiddie pools?"

"How could I forget? The cashier at the store asked if I was giving my two-year-old a pool party."

Mercifully, the shoveling finally ended. She and Mark tied up the tarp and chucked it inside the nearest dumpster. They brought out the hose, found a spout, and sprayed the floor of the warehouse clean. Nicole got the numerous kiddie pools, which were decorated in bright patterns and colors, and placed them in varying sections of the warehouse. Mark went around filling up the pools, and the dinosaurs moved in to drink.

Finally, as twilight approached, Nicole and Mark leaned against the wall, exhausted, watching the dinosaurs inside. Freedom separated from the others and joined the humans at the door.

"I'm very grateful for everything you've done today," the Utahraptor said. "And we all thank you for protecting us here."

"It's no problem at all," Nicole replied with a smile. "We can only hope that the UO doesn't find you again."

Mark's eyes widened. "Nicole. . ."

Freedom's eyes narrowed as her nostrils flared. Her head rose a little, sniffing deeply.

"Do you smell something?" Nicole asked, frowning a little. She tried sniffing, too, but smelled nothing but the trees.

Freedom inhaled once more before looking up into a tree. Almost afraid to look, Nicole cast her gaze to the tree's branches. Her eyes searched for a sniper, or a drone. But the only thing she saw was a gray squirrel eating a nut. A glance back at the Utahraptor showed a hungry look.

She exhaled in relief. Freedom had only smelled a prospective meal. "Calm down, Mark. It's only a squirrel."

Freedom caught sight of Mark's expression and chuckled sheepishly. "Sorry. Predator drive," she said.

Nicole checked her watch against the dimming of the sky. "It's getting late. How about you head on inside, Freedom? Mark and I will lock up after you."

"See you tomorrow at the same time?"

"Sure thing," Nicole said. "I'll see if I can wrangle Mark into helping again."

"It's not like I have a backlog of blueprints to study, modify, and put into production," the man said wryly. "I'll see what I can do, Nikki."

"You're a brick," Nicole said with a smile.

After Freedom's tail crossed the threshold, Nicole triggered the descent of the huge, heavy metal door. With a turning of the gears, along with a warning klaxon, the door slowly sealed the dinosaurs inside the warehouse once again. Nicole fetched a padlock meant for the truck in its cabin, fastened it to the door, then tugged it sharply to make sure it held.

"Let's vamoose," she chirped, heading to the truck's driver's seat.

"I don't know if I'll be able to assist tomorrow, Nikki," Mark said. "I wasn't exaggerating about my workload."

Nicole paused, one leg awkwardly hoisted into the high cabin. "You weren't? Oh. . . Well, I guess that I can do it myself tomorrow, then. I'll have to bring Compeer, though, or else I'll miss his designated dinnertime."

"You're a strong woman," Mark said with a half-smile. "I'm sure you'll manage without me." His smile faded. "Nicole, they're going to find out about this." He gestured toward the warehouse.

Biting her lip, Nicole shook her head. "Eventually, yes. The mayor asked where they were. I didn't tell him, but I could tell that he's suspicious. Mark, my court date is coming up fast, and. . . with all the things I'm doing to keep them safe, I don't know if I'll come out still a free woman."

"Things will turn out okay," Mark replied. "You'll see."

"By God's grace." Nicole hefted herself the rest of the way up into the truck. With a powerful rumble, the refrigerator truck's engine came to life, and she pulled out of the construction zone with Mark's pickup following close behind.

Up in the tree, the gray squirrel watched them leave, with its shiny black eyes unwavering. Its tail flicked a few times as the two trucks pulled onto the road and eventually vanished. It waited a little while longer, in the midst of the sounds of dusk, before scampering to a branch that dangled near the warehouse's roof.

The squirrel froze at the end of the branch, bobbing dangerously as the wood sank with its body weight. There was a sizable gap between the last twig and the edge of the roof. Backing up, the squirrel eyed the gap. A moment later, it bounded forward, reached the end, then leapt enough to compensate for the branch's sag. The squirrel landed on the roof with the grace only a squirrel possesses. It looked over its rump at the ground, then flicked its tail in dismissal.

The roof was warm from whatever meager sunlight had pierced the cloud cover, a pleasant sensation on the rodent's paws as it moved toward a skylight. Reaching the plastic cover, it reared back and looked down. The sky reflected off of the plastic, making it near impossible to see past the translucent, scratched covering and below. The squirrel scurried to another skylight, only to find the exact same dilemma. It went to all of the skylights, then doubled back for another loop, just in case something had changed, and gave up only when the sky had completely blackened.

It sat on top of a skylight, hunched over with its elbows on its knees. Its tail flicked incessantly. The natural call to sleep beckoned with the fall of night, but the small, furry beast had a mission to complete. Using the light from the city that reflected off of the clouds, it found the tree branch from before. It leapt off of the roof and grappled at the wood. Its back end swung dangerously, but the strength of the squirrel was not to be underestimated, and it pulled itself up and scampered along the tree branch. Reaching the trunk, it descended headfirst and dropped the last couple of feet to the grassless ground.

Dirt stuck to its paws as it rebounded toward the drawn door. It cast the padlock only a passing examination, not even bothering to try and stick its hand into the hole to try and toss the tumblers inside. Past experiences with padlocks and promising sheds had not ended well before.

It left the padlock and paced in front of the door, looking for a hole to enter through. But alas, the warehouse was newly built and hadn't had nearly enough time to develop any extra entrances. The squirrel sat back and stared at the offending door.

Finally, it spotted a grate on the wall, halfway up. The squirrel moved to stand directly beneath it and stared upward. The wall was ridged, but the lines were vertical and wouldn't help it at all, not that the squirrel didn't try anyway. After failing several times, it stepped back and looked at the roof line. The roof's edge and the grate were a fair distance apart, but it *might* be possible. The squirrel rushed back up the tree.

Returning to the roof, it found the edge and leaned over. There was the grate. Giving absolutely no thought to the life-threatening act it was about to do, the squirrel hooked its feet to the edge of the roof and dropped its front end over. Dangling upside-down, the grate was still out of reach. Determined, the squirrel swung itself back and forth, building up momentum, then let go. It fell toward the wall just above the grate. The squirrel's head collided first, dazing it a little, but it still had enough presence of mind to grab at the grate as it passed by. The squirrel's front paws latched firmly around a few metal strips. It was painful, but nothing that couldn't be shaken off later.

From its perilous position, the squirrel examined the grate. The gaps in the metal were easily wide enough for its head to poke through, but possibly not its shoulders and rather wide girth. Nothing could be said for not trying, so the squirrel slowly dragged itself further up. It stuck its head through a gap, wormed one arm in, then the other, and rested. Beyond the grate was a perfectly smooth metal tube, offering no handholds as leverage. The squirrel pushed at the grate with its forelegs, squirming its body around in the hopes that it would come through. Its hide was scraped and some fur was torn off, but it managed to tug itself through. Falling on its underside from the sudden entrance, it decided that a snooze was in order, as a reward for all the hard work.

Some time later, feeling rested and energized, the squirrel stretched, arching its back one way then the other, before shaking itself and looking around. It was still very dark out, and impossible to see any further into the tube. But the squirrel was nothing if not daring, and ventured forward without a single thought to any possible holes in the floor of the tube, fans, or any other dangers that lurked there.

It was clever in hugging the wall, making sure that it couldn't get turned around. It felt the floor before taking a step, blindly looking for any sudden drops. The going was slow, but the squirrel didn't mind.

Its foot found the wall moments before its nose did. Sneezing, the squirrel blinked at the obstruction before taking a random turn and following the new wall further along.

After a while, sounds other than its footsteps reached its little round ears. The squirrel paused, one foot in the air, and raised its head to sniff. Catching a whiff, it quickened its pace a little, following the scent until its eyes finally detected light up ahead. A turn or two later, and the squirrel found itself facing another grate. This one didn't have nearly as many little holes as the first one had, so it easily poked its head through to see what was on the other side.

The grate was a good ways above the floor, giving the squirrel a fair view of the large room filled with dinosaurs of all shapes and sizes. Eyes popping, the squirrel checked out the strangest sight it had ever seen in its entire life. After the initial shock, the squirrel peered around for a way down to the floor. It was unable to find any way down; the wall around the grate was completely smooth, and the squirrel was at last a little wary of the fall should it simply squirm out.

One of the largest dinosaurs inside the room came close to the grate. Seeing a chance to get down to the floor, the squirrel quickly forced its way through the grate and dropped on the dinosaur's head. The beast grunted loudly in surprise as the squirrel darted down its neck, backside, and a leg to the floor.

Immediately, the squirrel found itself the object of pursuit. It chattered happily at the bipedal dinosaurs, taunting them with its bushy tail, pleasantly surprised to have found some new companions. Having no intention of letting them catch it easily, the squirrel scurried all over the room, bounding away from any dinosaurs lunging to catch it.

By the time the squirrel was tiring, it finally began to realize that something was amiss. Its new playmates seemed rather keen on catching it with their mouths instead of their paws, like its other squirrel friends did. And those teeth looked a lot sharper than its own. The squirrel's heart pounded as it had an epiphany; the dinosaurs weren't playing a chasing game, they were *hungry*! An adrenaline rush spurred the squirrel into scaling any vertical surface it could as a way back to the safety of the grate. Surely, the dinosaurs couldn't follow it in there. But the walls were as smooth as they were before, and the squirrel couldn't find any way to escape.

It threw itself at the wall, leaping up as high as it could before plummeting back down to the floor. Twice more it tried to reach the grate, but to no avail. With the dinosaurs closing in, the squirrel shoved itself into the wall and pulled up a facade of ferociousness. It chattered wildly, throwing out a leg with the paw set in a scratching motion.

A gleeful roar, and the sight of a drooling maw was the last thing the poor furry rodent would ever see.

A tremendous crash awakened Scope, and her head jerked away from a puddle of drool. Wiping herself clean, she spotted two Stygimolochs wrestling for a head of cabbage. Scope curled up again.

Well. At least they're *eating.* She thought of her imagined squirrel wistfully.

Of all the motel rooms, only one had a hint of light emitting from inside. Not even a late-night sports addict was awake, as the last football game had ended a few hours before. Off in the east, there was a false dawn.

Inside that one room, there was a man hunched over a laptop. From the screen and the way he navigated the keyboard, it seemed he was playing some sort of first-person aerial computer game. However, if one watched long enough, it would be clear that the man was doing nothing of the sort.

The computer showed a view of a lonely street. A long bar displayed at one side, filled with green nearly to the top, was labeled "battery." On the other side of the screen was a small square box consisting of a map and a moving red dot. As the man depressed the keys, the view of the street shifted correspondingly. The movement was far too slow to signify an aerial vehicle.

Several miles away from the motel, a small civilian drone casually flew parallel to the empty street. On either side of the road were simple fields of corn, several months away from harvest. The city behind cast a glow on the cloud cover. The drone flew on, its tiny blades creating a muted buzz akin to a hornet's wings.

Holding his finger down on a single key, the man checked a souvenir map spread out next to him. A huge circle encased most of it, and was spotted with red Xs. If one compared the map to the one on the computer, they were the same, and the Xs were behind the drone.

The circle showed the range in which the dinosaurs could've been taken and hidden within 24 hours. According to what meagre intelligence he had been given, no cattle trucks had been rented within the time constraints, so the dinosaurs had to be within a day's walking distance. The task was deceivingly simple.

Checking and comparing the two maps again, the man saw that there were only a few places left where the dinosaurs could've gone. Beyond the cornfield on one side of the road was a stretch of forest, a place where giant reptiles could be easily concealed from the sky. A little closer was a construction site, left only halfway finished, but there *were* some buildings completed. With a few taps on the keyboard, the man refocused the drone toward the construction site. He ran some simple algebra in his head, calculating that it would take around fifteen minutes for it to reach its destination.

Those fifteen minutes crawled by, leaving the man with nothing to do but watch the screen, manually controlling every little movement the drone made. This was more than plenty of time for paranoia to rear its ugly head. It nudged at the man's senses, making little creaks sound suspiciously like footsteps outside the door, then offering the thought that, just maybe, it was the authorities, somehow having been able to track him down and arrest him for crimes against his country. The man's nervous sweat intensified.

But they couldn't know. His employers had come to him out of the blue, offering an opportunity to make ridiculously big bucks in return for something small; Physical money, untraceable by the government. He'd only learned of his employers' affiliations after they'd departed, and his nerves had been racking him ever since.

His only reassurance was that it would all be over soon, and that he was guaranteed to be left with nothing that could be held against him in a court of law.

Finally, the construction site came into view. The

paranoia receded a bit as the drone approached the mud-ridden area. There was gravel laid down, forming a crude road through the dirt, so new that weeds hadn't yet grown through the small rocks. Automatically, the drone's advanced camera visualization systems digitally highlighted indentions in the gravel, showing tire tracks. In the dirt, trampled over old construction tractor tread tracks, were innumerable holes, created by many heavy, large objects.

The man's hopes flew. He directed the drone over to the first warehouse, following the tire tracks. The warehouse had a small loading platform already laid in concrete, where the tracks ended. The metal sliding door was in place, and a closer zoom showed that it was fastened shut with a heavy-duty padlock. The drone was then directed upward, drawing above the roof and toward a skylight. The man tapped some keys, and the drone hovered completely motionless above the skylight. A flashlight beam, white and narrow to maximize brightness, flashed to life on the drone's underside. He turned it so it was shining into the warehouse's interior.

Illuminated in the beam was the front end of an Edmontonia and a cluster of Troodon.

The man stifled a crow of victory. He had something to report to his employers that would bring in that promised stack of green ca–

The drone's camera suddenly dissolved into harsh static. The man's breath caught in his throat as he did everything he could think of to regain sight. He even tried the secondary camera, but to no avail. Finally, he concluded that there was nothing he could do, and depressed a few keys that would make the drone descend. When he estimated that the drone was safely on or just above the skylight's surface, he killed the engine. Hopefully, he could fetch it later and fix whatever had gone wrong.

He closed that window and summoned a recording of the camera feed. He fast forwarded until he was a few seconds before everything had stopped. It took five replays before he finally saw that literal millisecond of red that had flooded the camera's vision before the static erupted.

The man sagged backward in his seat, raking a hand through his messy, greasy hair in confusion. What had caused that?

CHAPTER TWENTY-SIX

The Dinosaur Reserve had been reduced to a smoldering wreck in the middle of a charred forest. Nicole thanked the firefighters for all their relentless hard work in snuffing out the blaze as they wound up their hoses and other gear to be returned to their trucks. The firefighters humbly waved off her thanks before leaving.

As the last sounds of the engines faded into the morning air, Nicole was left standing alone in the middle of the parking lot, the only recognizable landmark. The building where she worked was completely gone, reduced to remains of charred wood and metal sticking out of the ground, surrounded by soggy ashes. The jeeps were gutted. The trees, once lush and full, were eerily similar to what the Cretaceous had looked like on her last trip.

Nicole shook her head, running her fingers through her hair. A calendar schedule was arranging itself in her mind, offering her a few days where she could visit Governor Pierce and request funding for rebuilding.

No, she thought, *I'm already drawing the budget thin by needing enough meat and greens to feed a small army once a day.* The appeal, and her job, would just have to wait until there was a better time.

Then her employees came to mind. Fortunately, most of them were volunteers, so they wouldn't be affected by a delay in their paychecks. But others, like Jasmine, needed a check, and maybe a personal comfort letter thanking them for all of their hard work. Nicole was already in the process of writing letters to the immediate families of the guards who gave their lives to help get everyone else to safety.

Unable to stomach standing in the middle of a burnt parking lot any longer, Nicole hobbled back to her car. She paused a few yards away from it and stared once more. It wasn't her beloved silver sports car, sleek and shiny. The car she had now was a cheap lease. The little electric sedan had spots of rust, and a chipped, ugly paint job. It just wasn't her car.

Resigning herself, she eased herself into the driver's seat. She slowly drove out, watching the review mirrors in her peripherals. Someday, she would get the Reserve back up and running, but that day seemed long off.

Almost to the main road, the scars left by the fire ebbed, and finally gave way to normal landscape. Passersby wouldn't even know that there had been an inferno if they hadn't seen the news.

Nicole looked both ways twice before pulling out. Once she was in the lane heading back toward the city, she accelerated to the speed limit. Her windows were rolled down, and the wind buffeted at her hair, surely sending it into an unsightly tangle.

What am I going to do with the dinosaurs? They can't live in a warehouse forever. I'll ask Freedom if she's willing to return to the Reserve forest quite a ways from the original area.

Several minutes of serious contemplation passed, and Nicole was beginning to feel the beginnings of a headache. Trying not to block her view of the road, she rubbed at the bridge of her nose. She did *not* need a migraine just before she arrived at the R&D company.

She decided a better way to combat a headache caused by work was to blast some good music from the car's speakers. She selected a song she knew had a pumping bass beat, and turned up the volume until the beat could be felt in her seat.

Unfortunately, the car's previous renters had the same idea, and the system crackled with its blown speakers. Undeterred, she lowered the volume. She opened her mouth and sang along. She knew, painfully, that what she was doing could not be called singing, but continued nonetheless.

By the time she pulled into the employee parking lot of the company, her migraine was gone, replaced by a song looping inside her brain. Humming it quietly, she parked the car and hobbled into the building.

"Good morning, Nicole!" the receptionist exclaimed. "How's the Reserve?"

"As well as can be expected. Thank you for asking," Nicole replied, as she made her way to the elevator. She didn't want to envision anyone or anything left behind, unfortunate enough to be caught in the attack.

The receptionist looked lost between an apology or a pleased remark. Nicole gave her a reassuring smile. "Miraculously, almost everyone made it out alive," she added.

Nicole waited for the elevator to arrive, then stepped inside. Once the doors closed, she stuck her hand into a small nook in the wall. A light inside flashed red, then a steady green as the microchip imbedded in her epidermis was affirmed. The elevator descended smoothly, the mechanics a subtle hum. Seconds later, Nicole exited and went down to Room 7.

"Miss Nike," one of the two posted guards said. "Please show us your identification badge."

Nicole grasped her badge clipped onto her jacket and held it up for him to see. After analyzing it, he nodded and triggered the door to open. Nicole pushed it open and closed it behind her, engaging the pneumatic locks.

"Nikki!" called out one of her colleagues, shooting her a smile. "Welcome back to the brainstorming abyss."

"Nice to be back," Nicole said. She clapped her hands together. "So, what's on the game plan today, boys?"

In the midmorning light, several sport cars flashed past the construction site with the roar of custom engines. If one listened closely, the sound of an excited *whoop-whoop* could be heard. A duo of police cars sped by in the same direction, sirens blaring.

Just as soon, it was relatively quiet again. The small, remaining birds recovered from their startle and resumed their daylong singing. Squirrels scavenged for food, rustling in the undergrowth.

The shifting of weight on gravel, however, brought the animals to silence again. Normally, the wildlife were accustomed to the noise machines the humans drove, but this one carried an air of foreboding. Animals, reacting on instinct, retreated into hiding.

Another car, with its barely audible engine, slowly made its way toward the warehouse. It stopped upon reaching the concrete loading pad. The doors opened and four people emerged. A casual onlooker might wonder about the small bags each person held. They didn't look like anything a county government inspector might need.

The four split up. One of them held a small consumer drone. He tossed it up into the air, and the rotors spun to life. The drone dropped only a few feet before stabilizing. The man fiddled with a small controller stick attached to a screen, and the drone soared over the roof of the warehouse.

Meanwhile, one of the others came around the corner of the warehouse, carrying a broken drone. It looked fine, aside from a few battered parts. However, a closer look showed a neat hole bored clear through the fuselage, destroying the delicate electronics inside.

A third stalked around the side, stretching to stand on her toes so she could see through one of the few ground-level windows. It had been boarded up from the inside, rather unorthodox.

The man nodded sharply, reaching into the small bag he carried. He pulled out a device similar to the one Takin used to incinerate the shop in New York. He signaled the rest of the team to do the same.

Suddenly, a red beam shot through the locked sliding door. It remained steady, slicing a thin arch in the metal.

The commander took a quick step back, readying his small pistol. The arch cut into the door fell outward, hitting the ground. He aimed his pistol at the hole, ready to fire if anything came out. But nothing did. Carefully, he approached, sidestepping his way along to the point where he could see through the arch.

The man's head reared back suddenly, and he collapsed to the ground. "Sorry," a raspy voice added, "but, in my understanding, you're the bad guys."

His team, having seen the him drop, edged toward their car. They eyed the hole, realizing they were now the prey. They raised their own firearms, but seemed hesitant to return fire.

Without warning, a deafening roar emanated from the warehouse at a volume so great the team was forced to cover their ears. The sound continued, from dozens of animals roaring at once, alternating so that there was never a clear moment of silence. The team tried to move away, but to drive the car meant removing their hands from protecting their ears, an action that none of them wanted to do. Their eyes closed in an effort to block out the noise, as if blindness helped deafness.

Since their eyes were squeezed shut, none of them saw

the Utahraptor stalk out of the arch she had created. Scope glared at the intruders, the *Intimidator's* whirring drowned out by the roar still going on. She noticed the pistols dropped onto the ground. With a few swipes of her tail, all four weapons were scattered out of reach.

She glanced back to the arch, hearing her Squama roaring. A signal with her fringe sent them into silence.

For the humans, the roar was gone but the ringing in their ears was nearly as agonizing. To make things worse, they opened their eyes to see an irritated and very powerful Utahraptor standing mere feet away. All three team members scrambled away from the dinosaur, duty devoured by visceral fear.

Scope growled, curling back her lips to show the full range of her teeth. "Get out of here," she bit. "Get out before you meet the same fate as your leader."

The three humans nodded frantically before darting to their car. Before they could even get their doors shut, the car was already peeling out of the construction site. As incentive, Scope shot multiple laser bursts after them, purposely coming very close to the vehicle. She ceased when the car hit the asphalt of the road. Gravel flew out from underneath its tires as the car fled down the road.

Scope took several deep breaths, watching just in case they came back, before turning around. The *Intimidator* wound down with some soft clicks, the nozzle from which the laser beam erupted sliding back into its little camouflaged niche.

The other Squama awaited her inside the warehouse, anxiously shifting their weight. "What are we going to do now?" an Allosaurus asked her.

"We leave," was Scope's calm reply. "We return to our home at the Reserve."

"But it's gone!" someone said.

"Not all of it," Scope reassured. "There are still plenty of animals and plants to eat. We'd better leave now, before those assassins return."

"But it's daylight!" someone else protested. "We'll be seen!"

Scope pursed her lips, thinking. "Well, if you don't think that we can move fast enough. . ."

"What do you mean by that?" a Troodon said.

"How about a race?" Scope suggested. "The first breed to enter the forest wins."

A Troodon leapt forward, head held high and fringe as erect as possible. "We Troodons are the fastest here!"

"Ha!" A Microvenator said. "We'll leave you in the dust so fast, you'll be tasting it in your sleep."

Scope decided to step in before the friendly competition escalated beyond her control. "Wait until I open the door," she said. "Not all of you can fit through the hole I made." Walking outside, she broke the padlock and sniffed around the controller. Finding Nicole's scent on two, she used her toe claw to press one. The door's gears ground as it tried to force itself into the ground. Scope pressed the other button, and the door began to slide upward. The muted sunlight, bleached white by the clouds, streamed into the interior of the warehouse.

"Come on," Scope said, looking in the direction the

Reserve lay. Her brethren gathered behind her, dropping into a charging pose, muscles bunched for a sudden burst of speed. "On my mark!"

Scope walked to the Quetzalcoatlus flock and beckoned one to her. After a short conversation, it flew away.

"Go!"

In moments, the construction site was empty. A thick line of Squama sped over the road and into the area beyond. The forest was just up ahead, but the Reserve's border wasn't for several thousand more paces. Scope trotted behind the horde, content to just watch the fun unfold.

It had been a very productive day at work, but tiring. With mental exhaustion threatening to bleed into her body, Nicole trudged her way to the employee parking lot. The sun was unseen, but she knew that it was drawing late in the day.

As Nicole unlocked the lease car, the obligations to the dinosaurs forced their way to the forefront of her mind. She sighed, recalling the route she needed to take in order to get to the depot. Mark was too busy to help this time around, and Nicole pondered how she could manage to carry both the meat and greens in one trip.

Squawk!

Startled, Nicole whirled to look around. A second squawk cast her gaze upward. A Quetzalcoatlus youngling, no bigger than a Great Dane, sat at the edge of the roof of the carport.

"What are you doing here?" Nicole said in dinosaur-ese. "How'd you get out of the warehouse?"

"We were attacked," the Quetzalcoatlus said. "Freedom killed one and chased the rest away. She's taken the others back to the Reserve."

Logical. The warehouse is compromised. "Very well, I have no problem with her actions of self defense," Nicole said. "Will I still have to bring the food?"

The Quetzalcoatlus shook its head. "We'll find our own food. But we all thank you for your help."

"Anytime," Nicole said. "Is that all?"

The Quetzalcoatlus nodded. It spread its wings, the membranes caught the air, and the pterosaur found an updraft on which to soar out of sight.

Nicole got back into the car, putting her bags in the passenger seat beside her. She turned on the engine, then carefully reversed out of her parking spot. Once in the open, she shifted and gently pressed the accelerator. The car smoothly weaved through the parking lot, to the stop sign, and entered traffic.

Nicole called up her music library. Soon a soundtrack from her favorite movie since childhood piped from the system. She loudly hummed along to the tune.

Before she knew it, the city and suburbs were behind her, fading into the horizon. Nicole knew the route by heart. Not long later, she was turning onto the small road leading into the forest. She tried to ignore the charring. She only wanted to find the parking lot. Once there, she put the car in an empty corner. Getting out, she left her belongings in the vehicle and locked it. She pocketed the keys, then started walking.

When the parking lot had been lost to her sight for a while, Nicole started vocalizing her trumpeting call in the hopes that someone would hear her. She didn't do it constantly, saving her voice for as long as possible.

The light was growing dimmer by the hour, and Nicole knew that she had better start heading back to the parking lot if she wanted to reach the car by the time darkness really fell. But she *still* hadn't found any dinosaurs, and she at least wanted to know where they were before she left.

"Eh," she grunted, patting her hip pocket. "What's a flashlight in a data-pad for?"

Slowly, the colors around her faded to monochrome, green completely indistinguishable from red. Nicole continued trumpeting, wincing as her throat started showing signs of overuse. Not for the first time, she wished that she had remembered to bring along a water bottle. Her strides through the forest were stiff, and her injured right side protested. However, her previous limp had lessened quite a bit.

Finally, Nicole was reduced to taking out her data-pad. She checked the battery power, grimaced, then turned on the flashlight. The wild greenery looked unnatural with the pale under-lighting. She continued on her way. Her senses skyrocketed in sensitivity, making up for the sudden lack of input from her vision. Nicole shivered uncomfortably as the sounds of the forest became overwhelming.

C'mon, guys, where are you? she wondered as she

sounded the trumpet once again. This time, she coughed.

A bush rustled behind her. Turning around, Nicole aimed her flashlight at the bush. Two glowing yellow dots stared back at her; eyes. Nicole took a wary step back as whatever it was in the bush growled softly.

"Is this a prank?" Nicole said in dinosaur-ese. "If so, I'd really like you to stop."

The thing in the bush took several steps forward, revealing several things to Nicole. It was big, black, furry, and had a lot of teeth. The black bear growled again. With every step forward it took, Nicole took a few backward.

"Nice bear," Nicole said in a calm, beseeching voice, though the dry rasp threw it off a bit. "You wouldn't want to eat little old me, now, would you? Please no?"

The bear reared back on its hind legs, standing far taller than Nicole, who took several more steps away. The bear huffed and snorted, tasting the air. Nicole tried her best to remain calm, knowing that if she turned and ran, it would charge. Even if she didn't run, if it smelled her fear, it could charge.

"Man, I really wish that I had kept that bum's switchback knife now," she muttered. "Coelurus I can handle. Tyrannosaurus? Maybe, did pretty well. But I have no idea how to fight a *bear* without any sort of weapon!"

The beast dropped down to all fours again, bouncing its weight from one front leg to the other. Nicole gulped, unsure about what it was about to do.

With a quiet roar, the bear surged forward. Nicole had the inkling that she could not outrun it on her best day, and *definitely* not while injured now, and decided to stand her ground. She straightened her back and stared the beast in the eye as it rapidly approached. The bear stopped a distance away, shuffling as if uncertain. Nicole slowly began walking backward, feeling behind her with her free hand for any obstacles.

The bear huffed again, the cloud of its breath just barely visible in the chilly air. It burst into a charge again, but this one was different than before. Nicole froze, staring as the bear attacked. Thoughts surged frantically through her head, some regrets, others simply *telling her body to MOVE!*

"Dodge, Nikki," she whispered, still staring as the bear drew closer. Her feet felt glued to the ground. "Move, girl. Come on." She grit her teeth as the bear balanced itself for a leap. "Nikki, *move it!*"

The bear went airborne. Nicole threw herself to the side, painfully slamming her shoulder into the dirt, her right side *screaming*. Her data-pad slid from her hand, and she scrambled to retrieve it while the bear recovered. Ignoring her side, she pushed herself to her feet and faced the bear as it growled at her. It ran forward again, but Nicole skipped aside this time. The bear growled.

Nicole's grip tightened on her data-pad, wishing that she didn't have to rely on its flashlight. She preferred all four limbs to fight with, and holding a light just so she could see her enemy *and* sporting a physical impediment was a big hindrance.

"An ally would be really handy right about now!" she called out in dinosaur-ese. "Anyone out there?"

The bear slammed a paw into the ground, glaring at her. It charged again. Nicole feigned to the right, then hopped left as the bear leapt at where she had been. She came around behind it and put as much force into a single leg as she could. Her resulting kick had enough force to knock the bear onto its side. Nicole wailed with the agony coursing through her body. She couldn't take any more.

As the bear roared at her and moved to stand, a huge, scaly, tridactyl foot laid itself on the bear, holding it down.

Nicole aimed the light at the newcomer, smiling gratefully. "What took you so long?" she panted.

The Albertosaurus tossed its head, smirking as much as its mouth would allow. "But you were doing so well," it replied.

"You flatter me. Going to eat it?"

"I was actually planning to bring it back to the others to share. Since you're here, you'd probably like to come with, no?"

"I'd love to," Nicole said. "I've been looking for you all evening."

The Albertosaurus nodded, then bent down to the bear. The mammal whimpered. The Albertosaurus murmured something in an apologetic tone before biting the bear's skull. The bear perished instantly, the dinosaur's teeth piercing its brain. The Albertosaurus took its foot off of the bear, picking it up in its maw.

Nicole tried to walk by the Albertosaurus' side on their trek back, but a huge tail blocked her way. She gave the Albertosaurus a confused look, which dissolved to understanding when the dinosaur crouched down so its back was close to the ground. Not one to deny a ride, Nicole "leapt" at the chance, limped over, and pulled herself onto its back using the Albertosaurus' knee as a mounting block.

As the Albertosaurus began walking, Nicole bit her lip in excitement. *I'm riding an Albertosaurus!* she thought. It wasn't her first time on a dinosaur's back, but an Ankylosaurus just wasn't the same. The bipedal nature of the Albertosaurus just gave the ride a certain thrilling feel, not to mention that it was a *gigantic carnivore.*

It was a fifteen-minute walk before Nicole began to see signs of dinosaurs in the area. Five more minutes, and they came into view. Several other Albertosaurus trotted to meet her, eager to see what was brought home for dinner. The Albertosaurus crouched again so Nicole could swing her leg over and drop. She waved her thanks to her ride as it dumped the dead bear at the others' feet.

With the sounds of eating behind her, Nicole wandered in and around the dinosaurs, looking for Freedom. Eventually, she came to the small group of Utahraptors and spotted Freedom.

"Nicole," Freedom said, closing the distance between them. "Why are you out here this late?"

"I got your message from the Quetzalcoatlus," Nicole replied, lowering her flashlight so it wasn't shining in the Utahraptor's face. As a good measure, she turned it off to save her dwindling battery power. "I came to check up on a few things. Firstly, did you really kill someone today?"

Freedom nodded solemnly. "A quartet of people came to the construction site in the middle morning. I had reason to believe that they were part of the UO, as a drone had discovered us the night before. I used the *Intimidator* to cut a hole in the door so I could confront them, but there was no way all of us could've survived against their guns. So, everyone kept up a continuous roar to distract them while I took out the leader and scared the rest into retreat."

Nicole nodded, thinking. "Why did you come back *here*? All they'll have to do is just send another missile, and there's no way another phone call can save your lives **again**."

"Do you have any other place in mind?" Freedom said. "We're *huge*, and those of us that aren't are still hard to blend in unless you dock their tails and put them in fowl suits. We can't hide forever."

"You're right," Nicole admitted. "I can't think of anywhere else where our enemies can't find you. But are you *sure* you'll be all right here, compromised in a half-decimated forest?"

Freedom nodded firmly. "Thank you for your concern. Do you need assistance back to your car?"

Nicole curled her lips into a half-smile, finally feeling the whole of her injuries as adrenaline faded. "Well, it's not a bad idea, especially after that bear attack. . . Please?"

The operation had failed. The agents who fled would soon be joining their lost leader. Gluten swore to that as he finished reviewing the report.

The dinosaurians were a dangerous asset, despite their claimed neutrality. With the intel from Takin, he had scoffed when he first heard that the dinosaurians' manager, Nike, had convinced and sent four of the antediluvian animals to reinforce the Black Ops team. Neutrality could be easily lost, and not so easily regained.

Checking the time, Gluten stowed away the report and any others that might attract the wrong attention. A quick glance around his quarters, and he deemed the place clean.

When the knock at the door came, he went and opened it. Cornette nodded to him in greeting as she entered, Gluten locked the door behind her.

"I am pleased that you were able to put aside some valuable time for this," he told her as he gestured toward a small table by the wall.

Cornette took a seat. "Likewise. I apologize for my behavior in the conference room today. It was uncalled for, but I need our forces to believe that I can handle any problems. I may be a woman in their eyes, but a woman who is cold and calculating may rank higher in their regards."

"I didn't take it to heart," Gluten said truthfully, seating himself across from her. "However, I must say that your performance is disturbing. Very power-mad."

"Good. I want it that way. My mother wanted me to be an actress when I was young, before I realized the horrible state of this world." She cleared her throat. "We're off topic. The Black Ops team. The reports say that should they rule out Flores Island, they will be coming here next."

"Indeed. I have made sure that our defenses are impenetrable."

Cornette frowned. "That is good and all, but why have they gotten this far? They should not have even known in what hemisphere this base is located. Is there a leak in our security,

Gluten?"

"I have checked that," Gluten replied, his expression sober. "Our ranks are tight, our security teams unquestionable. I don't understand it, either, unless that new hacker the Americans have procured is even better than the rumors declare."

"Perhaps so. Pity that we didn't get to. . . What was his name? Pete Berg, before they did." She shook her head. "You say that, if the Americans locate this base, we possess an infallible defense? Will we need to evacuate personnel?"

"I don't believe that will be necessary, although the escape routes are ready for use, should they be required."

"I wish that I could feel as sure as you sound, my friend, but I yield to your judgment."

CHAPTER TWENTY-SEVEN

Robin balanced herself on the small boat, cautiously swaying her way to her chosen seat. She sat down on the smooth white plastic, gripping all handles within reach. Her stomach churned a little, and the aftertaste of a pleasant hotel breakfast turned sour.

"Take your seat of choice," Lennox said as he confidently walked to the helm. Robin envied his sea legs.

Berg seated himself across from her, his precious gear zipped up in a waterproof bag. Williams was at the stern of the boat, stretching his entire body across all three seats. He placed his take-out cup in a holder before letting his face fall back to catch the sunlight.

"I'd enjoy this junket more ardently had duty not prevailed," Williams commented.

"I had tried saving up my pay for a vacation in an area like this," Berg said wistfully, gazing at the blue waters and cloud-speckled sky. "But my apartment rent rose, commute and grocery prices skyrocketed, and I couldn't get a minute away from work to bring Anita here."

"Well, look on the bright side, Berg," Robin said, offhandedly shrugging. "You're at the vacation location you've always wished for." A sudden toss of the boat made her bite back any other words, lest she might do something embarrassing.

"Yes, but Anita is not here, and perhaps we would've liked to sample the community a bit more," Berg said, ignorant to her plight. "Not to completely destroy the headquarters of the enemy."

Shriek bounded up onto the chair, sticking her neck out over the water. "I've always wanted to ride on a boat!" she said.

Lennox started up the boat's engine, then pushed forward. Robin's grip on the handles tightened as the boat shot ahead, skipping over the waves. Spray hit Robin's face with droplets of salty water splashing into her mouth. She risked releasing one hand to wipe away the seawater.

Shriek suddenly screamed as the boat hit a large wave. She had still been leaning out, and she was sent airborne over the edge. Williams whipped out a hand and grabbed her tail. Robin gave an empathetic wince as she heard Shriek hit the hull. Williams easily lifted the Bambiraptor back onto the boat and set her safely on the floor.

Back on land, Rush sat on the edge of a short cliff, watching the boat pull away. He bounced in place, prepping himself. Assail and Gale were by his sides, shifting their weight. All three were surrounded by seagulls and other oceanic fowl.

"Ready," Assail warned, eyes frozen to the fading boat.

Rush leaned forward to the point where his center of balance was somewhere at his chest. Any second now. . .

Squawk! A seagull fluttered next to Rush. It cocked its head to the side, wide black, beady eyes blinking dopily. Taking a few steps closer, only a bob of the head was all the warning Rush received before the seagull began pecking at his head.

"Ow!" Rush yelped, trying to bat the bird away with one wing. "Ow! Shoo, bird! Ow!"

The seagull jumped backward. It chirruped a few times, then leaned forward and screeched at the top of its lungs.

Rush cringed at the shrill. When it stopped, he glared and roared in its face, making sure every single tooth in his mouth was visible.

Much to his satisfaction, the seagull screamed and it couldn't fly away quickly enough.

"Focus, Rush," Assail said.

He fell back into position, silenced by his mentor's calm rebuke. *That showed it,* he thought.

Assail stilled, muscles tightening beneath his smooth skin. "Now!" he said, forcefully launching into the air. Rush and Gale quickly obeyed. The seagulls, startled by Assail's loud cry, flew up around the three in a cloud of feathers. Hidden by the flock, the Pterodactylus flew toward the boat.

Williams turned around in his seat, lowering his binoculars. "The avians draw nigh," he said.

Robin nodded, raising her own binoculars and peering behind the boat. Barely visible, despite being amplified, were the pterosaurs, coming in fast on the sea wind. Within the next minute, Robin watched them overtake and pass the boat.

The boat was halfway to Corvo by the time the Pterodactylus arrived. As they drew near, they split. Rush veered to the west while Assail and Gale went north and east. Assail was to scour the single town, Gale was to survey the countryside, and Rush's job was to fly along the coastline and find anything suspicious.

Rush was amazed at the diversity of the coast. While the southern coast was rocky and relatively flat, the further he flew north, cliffs formed and towered over the crashing waves. Small spires stood before the cliffs, separated from the land by countless Turns of wear and tear.

Aerially hugging the spires, Rush used the sea breeze to keep himself airborne. He varied from flying near the cliffside to drifting several hundred paces out, letting distance affect his view.

There were no caves Rush thought large enough to house a headquarters. The largest ones he could find were at water level and only a few paces deep. Otherwise, there were only eddies and nooks. But the Unison Order knew better than to choose an obvious hideaway such as a cave.

The hunt is afoot, he thought. *Here, fishy, fishy, fishy.*

As Lennox drew the boat closer and closer to the Corvo docks, he turned to face the team. "Does everyone remember our cover here?"

"But, cous, how could you say such a thing?" Berg said, sounding aghast.

"Cease your prattle, Parker," Williams said. "Remember what Mother and Father said. This is a family excursion, and we will enjoy ourselves. How often do we get to see our dearest cousin and her husband?"

"Whatever you say, bro," Berg said, nonchalantly waving Williams off.

"Calm down, boys," Robin said. "We'll need to give our tour guide a respectful amount of attention as he points out the sights."

Lennox gave a pleased hum, focusing on guiding the boat to the docks. He cut the engine a distance away, bringing them in on momentum alone. Without the engine's din, the lapping of the water against the shoreline and boat were pronounced. Williams uncoiled a rope from the aft and tossed the noose over a wooden post on the pier. He pulled until the boat bumped the wood, then he leapt out and securely wrapped the slack around the post. Robin wasted no time in disembarking, eager to feel her feet on solid ground again. The solidarity of the planks beneath her feet was only comforting until she felt them waver beneath her weight.

"Neat!" Berg exclaimed as he stepped up on the pier. "This dock floats."

Clearly, Robin thought, nauseated. *I feel like I haven't even stepped off the boat. . .* She clutched for a nearby support.

"Come along," Lennox said, checking the time as he strode up the pier. "The tour will be starting soon."

"I'm right behind you, sweetie," Robin said, recovering to trot after her 'husband.' She took up pace at his side, her pangs of nausea ebbing like the tide. The moment she stepped onto unshifting ground would be a Godsend.

"Where's the tour guide pamphlet?" Berg inquired, swinging his backpack over his arms. "I don't have it."

"We'll pick it up in the city," Lennox replied. "Come, or we'll be late."

"Wouldn't opt for that," Williams stated.

The pier ended. They walked onto hard concrete and large flat stones, which climbed as a steep ramp that curved 180° around to the only town, Vila do Corvo. As the team approached the town, Robin began to notice a few odd things. The first was that there were no streetlights, only a few tiny cars, motorcycles, and mule-drawn wagons prowling the roads. Any inhabitants that the team passed were friendly and not shy to waving and a smile.

"Beauteous," Williams uttered.

Robin felt something grab the bottom hem of her shirt. Hand twitching, she dislodged the burden of a wrist holster, palming the blade to conceal it as she looked down. An adorable little girl, no more than five years old, stood at her side, staring up at her with large eyes.

"Hello, there," Robin said, crouching down. Her right arm ducked between the shadows created by her bent legs, hiding the movements of her hand as she slipped the knife back into place.

The little girl said something in Portuguese and held out a chubby fist. A small, beaded bracelet was squeezed in the tiny fingers, faceted edges glinting blindingly in the sunlight.

"For me?" Robin said.

The little girl put the bracelet in Robin's hand, smiling widely even as the jewelry began to succumb to gravity when Robin failed to react in time. Not wishing to crush the smile, Robin caught the bracelet, stretching the thin elastic cord so it could fit on her left wrist. The yellow and black beads contrasted well with her deep tan skin.

"Thank you," Robin said, watching the beads glisten, turning her wrist to and fro. "It's beautiful. Looks like a bumblebee's coat."

The little girl giggled and scampered away, disappearing into a store.

What an adorable child, Robin thought wistfully, wondering what her own would look like, if she ever had any.

"Here we are," Lennox said, derailing Robin's thoughts. He motioned to a large wagon just up ahead. A native was chatting with some obvious tourists, making flamboyant gestures as he spoke. Nearby stood a donkey hitched to a large wooden, four-wheeled wagon with a gaping large trunk and a bench for the driver, both animal and cart appearing weathered but in good condition. Lennox called, "Is this the tour group?"

The native turned and waved. "Ah, *olá*, sir!" he said in broken and heavily accented English. "This the *O passeio pela Ilha do Corvo*. The Corvo Island Tour. You coming?"

"We have reservations," Robin said. "Are you leaving soon?"

"You just on time," the guide said. "We leaving now. Name is Simon Fresco. Come, get in wagon. I get the donkey moving."

"I don't think I've ever ridden in a donkey-towed wagon before," Berg commented as they found seats in the wagon.

Robin carefully seated herself on one of the three long wooden planks that lined the wagon. The wood creaked under her weight. "Neither have I. This will be something to remember."

"Our binoculars will come into good use on this trip," Lennox said.

Not for the wildlife or scenery, Robin thought, grasping her set. While the other tourists would do such, she and the team would be on the lookout for any signs of the Unison Order.

Fresco took the donkey's reins, and picked up a long switch. He tapped it against the donkey's rump and said something in Portuguese. With a snort, the donkey threw its weight into the harness. The wagon creaked as the wheels began moving, and Robin feared what the ride would've felt like had the path not been paved.

"We now leaving Vila do Corvo, only village on Corvo Island," Fresco began, waving vaguely over one shoulder at the town. "Vila do Corvo settled in 16th century, got town charter in 1832 as thanks from King Pedro the Fourth. . ."

While she was sure that there were plenty of little fun facts to discover, Robin tuned Fresco out. Raising her binoculars to her eyes, she focused, determined to discover any minute details of Unison Order occupation. The town might be absurdly friendly compared to the rest of the world, but the natives could easily be covering up something. Whenever she didn't have her eyes scoping the landscape, she was casually looking around at the tourists in the wagon.

There was a family of three, a middle-aged and well-dressed man, a woman in an outfit better suited for a performance stage, and a 20-something. None of them looked Unison Order-worthy, but it paid to be careful; God knew how many times that had saved her life in the past.

". . .and to left you see our cows, and on right you see more cows. Cows outnumber humans two to one. . ."

And cows are interesting. . . how? Robin thought. But, since she was the fascinated tourist, she trained her binoculars on the bovines. She got a glorious close-up of a nostril. *Yes. Fascinating. Definitely something to write home about.*

Fresco droned on. And on. And on. Robin, eyesore from the strain of scanning the fields, let her binoculars lay against her chest as she leaned on the wall of the wagon. She heaved a sigh, wondering when they would reach something more interesting.

"Up ahead, you see some windmills on hill. Those over two centuries old, built by Moors in early nineteenth century."

The windmills, built from white stone, stood like sentinels on the peak of the hill, their wooden blades slowly rotating in the constant sea wind. Robin could almost imagine the sound of the blades' creaking. The donkey plodded along, tugging the wagon past the ancient buildings.

"On other side of hill we see origin of Corvo proud wine," Fresco announced as the wagon crested the peak. "We have many grapevines in vineyards, to make brilliant wine you taste in Vila do Corvo."

Grapevines stretched over the lolling hills. The sunlight, partially blocked by shadows of clouds, abounded over the fields. Robin was impressed by the view. She was almost sorry when the wagon moved on, leaving the grape fields behind.

About 30 minutes later, Fresco finally reached the pinnacle of the tour. The wagon breached the apex of the last slope, and the view took her breath away.

"This is the crater of *Caldeirao*, cauldron," Fresco said, waving at the expanse. "Part of dormant volcano, crater walls are highest peak on Corvo. 718 meters."

He went on, but Robin wasn't listening. The steep, rocky edges of the crater descended to gently sloping fields toward three small lakes, the largest being thrice the size as the other two combined. The warm sun beamed down, creating one of the most beautiful sights Robin had ever seen.

If only I was a tourist, she thought, memorizing everything. But then she remembered her mission, and again raised her binoculars. While the other tourists were snapping pictures, Robin's thoughts remained on much more sober aspects. Retirement was looking better and better, if only so she could actually enjoy trips to places like this.

As Fresco turned the donkey around for the trip back to the village, Robin lowered the binoculars, having seen nothing out of the ordinary. She looked around at her team. Their binoculars were equipped with 300x zoom, so not even a rabbit could escape their discovery. Lennox caught their eyes one by one, and subtly shook his head.

Berg smiled. "I got some great pictures of that crater!" he exclaimed. "Wasn't that view incredible?"

Robin exhaled, leaning heavily against the wagon's wall. Dipping her right hand into a pocket, she carefully extracted a nickel-sized device. Scraping a nail along the rim to trigger a hidden switch, she hovered the device over her new, black and yellow apparel. At a single, muted *bleep*, she slid the device away and smiled.

Lois Cornette frowned at her computer monitor. Swapping pages, she stared at the screen for several moments before pressing a button on her desk. She sat back, tilting in her chair. Behind her was a camouflaged window to the outside, through which she could barely make out the ocean. She squinted, but the camouflage filters prohibited her from seeing any details.

There was a knock at her office door. Cornette straightened and placed her hands before her on the desktop. "Come in."

Gluten strode into the room. There was something different about him, but she couldn't tell what. "You summoned?" he queried.

"How much do you know about the new hacker?"

Gluten took a seat on the opposite side of her desk. "Peter Berg; no middle name. Took extracurricular self-defense classes in high school. Graduated in the top five of his class from CalTech. Was quietly discharged from Savant Technologies a year ago, after fifteen years of stellar performance. Last official records show that he is currently on extended paid leave from a nobody tech support company, Solutions, Inc. Has a wife, no dependents. Our records tell that he is a temporary member of Black Ops team 3, employed as a hacker."

"The team's current position?"

"Right above our heads, disguised as tourists. They won't find us. The natives don't even know we're here."

Cornette knew the hoops her Unison Order had to jump though in order to keep the natives' ignorance. While she had been the President, she had sent UN volcanologists to the remote island, with the instructions to distract the natives with seismic studies while construction crews used explosives to carve out the rock. The bubbling waters by the coast, caused by the creation of a submarine hanger, were explained away as natural gases escaping from a recently uncapped underwater pocket. When the base was completed, the volcanologists assured the natives that their island was again safely dormant.

She steepled her hands in front of her mouth. She thought for a long minute. "You assure me that they won't locate this base's location?"

"One hundred percent positive that they will not," Gluten stated, punctuating his words by planting his hands on her desk and leaning forward.

Her second in command had surety where she struggled. She praised him for that. Perhaps his positivity came from the knowledge that he was helping her create a safe world for the wife and daughter he had left behind.

Cornette nodded slowly. "Make preparations anyway, so that all contingencies are covered. Tell the hanger crew to keep my transport ready."

Gluten stood, bowing his head. "As you wish, Ms. Cornette."

CHAPTER TWENTY-EIGHT

The sun was going down, and Rush was well past the point of frustration. He glided along the same route he had flown all day, aching eyes painstakingly scouring the area for anything he might've missed the first few hundred times.

Hunger gnawed its nasty, little teeth at the linings of his stomach. The beast that consumed the mind if given enough time had been grabbing at his attention since midday, and was slowly sapping more energy by the moment. Stubborn to his mission, Rush hadn't taken the brief time to find a school of fish in the shallows.

"Eagle Eyes to Roost. Return to nest. Repeat, return to nest."

Rush wanted to argue, but didn't want to disobey orders. Casting a scathing glare at the cliffs and ocean, he beat his wings, forcing his body back toward Flores Island. He fought the ocean wind, pouring the last of his energy into making it back to safety.

With exhaustion upon him, Rush knew that the chances of him making it back to Flores in one sprint were negligible, at best. He managed to make it about two hundred more paces before his wing muscles felt like they were going to snap at any moment. Rush stiffened and let himself glide down to the waves.

With a surprisingly gigantic splashdown for a flier so small, he plunged into the water. His vision was cloudy beneath the swirling sea's surface. He let himself drift limply, his aching body cushioned throughout. Finally, his breath began to expire, and he forced himself to the surface. As his head broke free, rivulets of water coursed their way down his cheeks. He took a deep breath before relaxing again, and allowed the weight of his body to pull him back under.

Rush didn't know how many times he had repeated that before Robin's voice blared in his ear, only slightly muffled by the water. It was only then that he realized that the sun had set, and Lennox had called them back before dusk. Grunting with effort, he flapped his wings to get most of his body on top of the water, then doubled the exertion to get himself aloft. His muscles screamed, but the membranes of his wings caught the wind, which sent him high into the air. Rush took his time fighting the wind to make it back to Flores.

The Luna had moved from the horizon to somewhere three-quarters of the way to mid-sky when Rush arrived at the hotel. The window was open just wide enough for him to glide through. Too tired to land properly, he just aimed for Robin's bed. He limply rolled with the impact until he collided with the wall.

"There you are!" Robin said, standing above him with her hands on her hips. "Where have you been?"

Rush could only glance at her through barely-open eyelids. *Oh, this bed feels divine. . . I never want to move again.*

Assail squinted. "He's exhausted himself," he stated. "Give him some time to recover."

"Rush," Lennox said, "did you notice anything out of the ordinary?"

It took all the energy taken from a huge inhale for Rush to shake his head in the negative. Words? *Talk to me tomorrow.*

"The soldier wasn't lying," Robin said. "The Unison Order's base *must* be on Corvo! Well hidden, of course. It'll take more time to find it."

"Berg, take first watch," Lennox said. Turning, he added, "Then Williams, myself, and Conners."

Robin looked at her partner, who seemed completely dead to the world, splayed out over her bed. She glanced at his dinner, which was cold and untouched on the bedside table. Picking Rush up in both hands, she carried him over to one of the couch cushions put on the floor. Laying him on it, she laid his food next to the cushion, then went into the bathroom. She used the soap dish as a makeshift cup.

There, she thought. If her partner woke up sometime

during the night, he wouldn't starve.

"Lights out," Lennox said from under his bedsheets. He reached out and turned off the lamp above his head.

Robin tucked herself in and turned off her own lamp. Berg was the last one to turn off the last light, shutting the window and latching it before sitting down in a wicker lounge chair. The room went dark, and the moonlight peeked through cracks in the curtains. It was just enough illumination for her to see where everyone was. Williams was in the hideaway bed, Lennox was in the second single bed, and the dinosaurians were scattered on the floor on their cushions. The sound of rustling occasionally broke the calm silence as someone got comfortable, but even that died down.

The ocean wind was already pushing Rush at great velocity, and the rapid flapping of his wings enabled him to go much faster. The force of the air flow brought tears to his eyes, which overflowed and streamed toward his neck, then evaporated.

The island of Corvo was just up ahead. Somewhere on that tiny island was the Unison Order base, a base he was *determined* to find before the day was over.

"Eagle Eyes to Assail. Your birds find the worms from the air. We'll take the fishes."

"Assail to Eagle Eyes. Roger, roger that."

Rush didn't need the instructions. He was well ahead

of everyone else, having left early. He was sure that by the time he was rescanning the cliffs, they would still only be halfway to Corvo.

With some clever maneuvering, the cliffs were now directly below him. Rush turned into the wind, very slowly moving forward, but a few beats of his wings had him over the waves. Judging the depths took only a moment before he furled his wings and plummeted. Sliding into the water, he squinted through the murk of disturbed sand. The early morning sunlight painted his surroundings a beautiful blue and green combination. The nearby spires of rock were a muted gray.

It was much more difficult moving through water than his native sky. Pterodactylus were made to arch through water, entering at an angle and exiting ready to catch the wind, not swim. But with some fancy flapping, Rush managed to set himself a rhythm that propelled himself at a decent clip. He went up for air at regular intervals, taking deep breaths before diving again.

"Eagle Eyes to Roost. Check in."

Rush had just taken a breath when the call had come in. He had no intentions of answering while underwater, as all that would come out would be bubbles, anyway. While the rest of the team sounded off, he swam along the bottom of the cliff about three paces below the waves, wing-claws on one limb providing stability against the push and pull of the current.

The team finished, and there was a long pause as Rush angled toward the surface.

"Arcee to Rush. Is some–"

Rush breached with a gasp, shaking the water from his

head. "Rush to Roost. Checking in. All's well." He took a breath and submerged.

Robin sat on the boat, still dressed as a tourist. Lennox was taking the watercraft around Corvo, as if they were sightseeing. On the starboard directly opposite of her, Berg sat with his laptop open, doing something clever with codes. He had claimed that he was hacking into security cameras in Vila do Corvo. Williams was, again, at the stern, armed with an intimidating pair of binoculars.

She raised her own binoculars toward the shore. A few children were playing in the surf, with parents casually looking on. It appeared like they were having fun, splashing water at each other's faces, tackling with the intention to dislodge their footing and send both attacker and victim beneath the surface.

Be safe, and enjoy the peacefulness of Corvo while it lasts, she thought, watching them for a moment.

Swimming along the side of the cliff, Rush checked the rock for any abnormalities. He saw nothing apart from the odd crustacean or fish darting along the cracks. It was demoralizing, but Rush was nothing, if not stubborn, in his goals. He still had quite a long ways to go before his area of surveillance ended.

His eyes roved the cliffs above the surface and below, searching endlessly. Rock. Rock. More rock. Fish. Spotted rock. Ro–

He flipped around and turned headlong into the undercurrent. The section of stone below him had a rectangular shape. It was ever-so-slightly brighter than the rock around it, almost as if it was backlit. He dived. Pushing his face against the cliff, he could almost see movement.

It's a window, he realized. *A disguised window.*

Wait. If he could see in, didn't that mean that anyone could see out? Rush looked over his shoulder and saw that the sun was directly behind him, and his shadow played upon the cliff face. He quickly moved toward the surface, hoping that if whoever it was behind the window didn't think of him as anything other than a large fish.

Once he reached the surface, he hurtled himself into the air. The water dripped from his form as he fought for stability. Once he found his balance, he tilted his wings up a bit. The wind caught the membranes and sent him toward the rock. Rush braced, catching the cliffside with his feet and wing-claws.

Leaning back as far as he could without jeopardizing his fragile grasp, he scoured the cliff face with his eyes. Sure enough, he saw another oddity a few paces away, a strange discoloring so slight he might've missed it if he hadn't been looking for it. No wonder he hadn't seen it the day before.

Moving a short distance away, Rush squawked into his comm, not daring to speak in case someone was behind the opening and it wasn't soundproofed. Without meaning, his speech would resemble a seagull's far better than the rambling noises of Dinosaur-ese.

Robin raised a hand to her comm link in her ear, as if that would make the sudden rasp any more understandable. It was from one of the three Pterodactylus, that much was certain. It was too birdlike to be Shriek.

"Arcee to Birdies," she said. "Who found the worm burrow?"

"Assail to Roost. It was Rush, but it wasn't in our language.

Something is going on at his end."

"Arcee to Rush. Can you talk? Over."

Another squawk.

"One caw for yes, two for no. Have you found the worm burrow? Over."

One squawk.

Robin turned to Berg. "Triangulate Rush's location. He's found the base."

"Yes, ma'am," he replied, jumping into action.

"Finally!" Williams said, leaning back in his chair at the stern. His arms spread to embrace the boat's rim. "Those terrorists aren't surviving the week."

"I've got Rush's location," Berg stated. "Commander, drive the boat toward the cliffs on the northwest side of the island."

As they came close enough, Lennox shut the throttle and raised his binoculars to his eyes. "Those are openings, all right," he said.

"I don't see them," Robin said, frowning. She zoomed in as far as the binoculars allowed, but it took several more seconds for her to recognize the coloring of the cliffs, like shadows where there shouldn't. "Amendment: I see them."

Raising a hand to his comm, Lennox said, "Eagle Eyes to Birdies. Rendezvous at the soggy nest." He switched frequencies. "Eagle Eyes to Bald Nest. This is Eagle Eyes calling Bald Nest." He went through a complicated password verification. "Eagles

Eyes requesting operative strike team against supreme Nest. Roger, roger that."

"Arcee to Rush. Come back in."

Rush released his grasp on the cliff, battling the wind for flight. A gust against the cliff caught his wings, sending him rocketing up and over the rocks. Satisfaction bloomed in his chest as he wheeled around to rendezvous with his team.

Lois Cornette watched the security feed of a hidden camera on the cliff. The small brown reptilian pterosaur vanished from the frame, heading to where she knew not. A second later, the image of empty ocean and sky jumped and restarted to where the avian had first flown into frame, playing out in continuous repeat.

Having seen enough, she slammed her hand down onto her intercom. "Begin Red Alert, code Alpha 5-22-1-3." Almost immediately, a klaxon blared to life while small lights in the ceiling illuminated in blood red. Pressing another button, she said, "Bring me Takin. NOW."

She had no doubts that Takin would arrive without delay. Her people knew better than to stretch her patience, especially with the facade she had been producing as of late. But as she watched the seconds tick by and he still hadn't shown up. . .

A knock sounded on her door. Cornette inhaled sharply through her nose, sounding like a bull prepared to charge. "Come in."

Takin entered the office as quickly as possible, slipping through a tiny gap before he had opened the door all the way. His hair was standing on end and his skin was shiny from sweat. *Wisely, he'd run.* "Good morning, Ms. Cornette!" he said, slightly breathlessly. "You're looking exemplary today. Have you done something to your–"

"Quiet," she interrupted, staring him down. "Now, you told me that before you left you had turned the insides of their technology to burned circuits."

"Yes, ma'am," Takin said, gulping. "I did my best. Or worst, depending on your point of view. A very good job."

"Oh?" She turned her security monitor around so Takin could see. "Then you wouldn't find it too hard to explain this, darling?"

Takin paled. "I. . . They must've been sent replacements. Restocked their supplies. I wouldn't be surprised if they had brought in a replacement."

Cornette nodded slowly, again steepling her index fingers beneath her chin. "I see." She looked from the replay to the quivering man trying to appear brave. Pursing her lips, she pressed a hidden button under her desk. *I'm sorry.*

Takin stumbled as six armed men burst into the room. They surrounded him, frisked him down, and put him in cuffs.

"What– what is this?" Takin sputtered, glancing from the guards to Cornette.

She stood from her desk, smoothing out her crisp pants suit. "Guards," she said. Her tongue caught, but she recovered too quickly for anyone to take notice. "Take him to Questioning."

The blood drained from Takin's face. He put up a valiant, but useless, struggle as the guards led him down the halls. Cornette followed behind, her low heels clacking against the smooth stone floor. The steady clicks counted down the clock. When they reached their destination, in a remote section of the base, Cornette herself unlocked the door.

The guards shoved Takin into the hall beyond, then into the first room. Takin was flung haplessly into a metal chair, then cuffed to it. While the guards made sure that the man wasn't going anywhere, Cornette prowled the room, staring appraisingly at the tables and walls of varying tools and devices.

Their work done, the guards took point along the wall, becoming little more than statues in the shadows. Cornette struggled to ignore them, knowing that their presence was necessary.

"What do you want?" Takin pleaded.

Cornette ambled around the room to stop behind the chair, where Takin couldn't see her. "I want to know the procedure the Team Alpha leader will take upon learning of this location."

"He'll affirm the information, then call in an alert to headquarters," Takin blurted, his words running together in his panic. "Headquarters will probably send every spare man they can find to converge on this place. Attacks usually occur less than 24 hours after notification."

Humming, Cornette peered at Takin out of the corner of her eyes. "What are the radio frequencies the attack forces will be using?"

Takin wasted no time in naming them off.

"I'm disappointed in you. You exited too extravagantly. The rite was excellent, but in revealing your treachery you also warned them. How foolish of you."

"I should've pretended to be KIA, then?"

"No, not KIA, that would require a body and a hassle. MIA is what you should have done; leaving quietly, letting them wonder what had happened." Facing him fully, she narrowed her eyes. "It would've made them keep their codes, not be so hasty in acquiring reinforcements. Perhaps I wouldn't have lost so many squadrons of perfectly good soldiers on missions that *should* have gone perfectly because their targets hadn't seen the need to tighten and toughen up." She leaned, so close that their noses almost brushed. "If not for your actions, they wouldn't have brought in that hacker, who has helped them discover the location of this base."

Subtly biting her lip, she nodded, and one of the guards flicked a switch. Cornette watched for several seconds before nodding again. The current shut off. Takin slumped as far as allowed in the cuffs, panting heavily.

She swallowed. "The frequencies you just gave me are invalid now. You've been cut off from updates. Even your beloved computer has been denied access to their servers." She walked to a wall of bottles, selecting one and reading the label.

"I don't understand," the man panted, eyes shining. He was shaking, sweat beading on his forehead. "You. . . you promised peace."

"Yes," Cornette said gently. "You *have* done your part, and I thank you for what you did correctly. But your failure has doomed this location and delayed Peace."

"Give me another chance!" Takin begged. She was sure that, had he been free, he would've fallen onto his knees. "I'll do anything you ask, I promise. Anything. Just please, please, don't make me kill any more people. I can't... I can't... Once was too much. Set me behind a screen. I'll do whatever you want, just don't make me kill."

She wondered how Takin had ever managed to become a member of the alpha team. She couldn't fathom it.

She replied, "I know you tried, my friend. But your services are no longer required. I have other resources." She inserted a needle into the bottle, drawing into the syringe. *I have to do this. The end is worth the means, I swear to you. Goodbye, Nelson.*

"P-please..."

Setting the syringe on the counter, she went and knelt in front of him. She looked him in the eye. "You did a good job. A very good job. Thank you. You only made a few mistakes that have unfortunately cost you everything."

Takin sobbed.

Breathing deeply, she fetched the needle. He struggled as the needle neared his jugular. At a glance from Cornette, a guard moved to restrain Takin's head, fastening a strap across the forehead. Muscles and cords distended the skin in Takin's neck.

The needle slid smoothly into the flesh. Cornette hesitated briefly before pushing the plunger. *This is the kindest method in the room I can bestow, and I am a kind leader.*

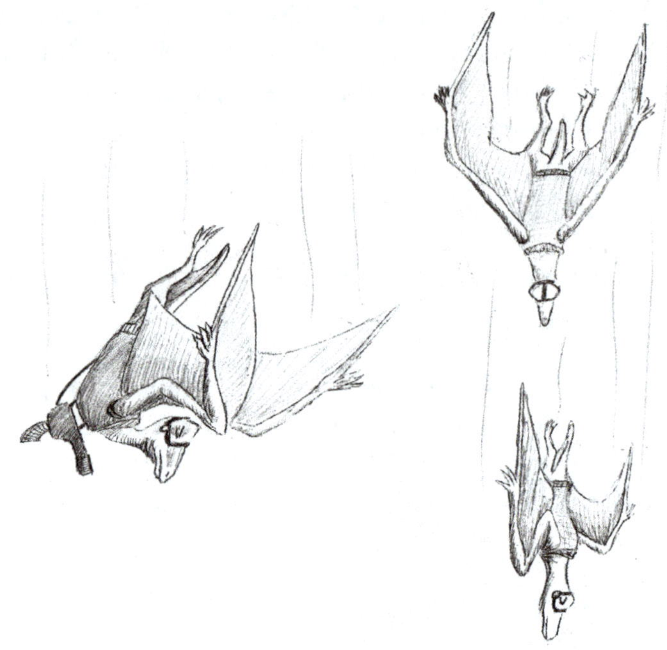

CHAPTER TWENTY-NINE

"You told me that you were *100% sure* that they would not find us!"

"Ms. Cornette, it is apparent that I erred grievously in my positivity."

Lois Cornette did not appreciate her comrade's aloofness. "Gluten, our enemies are mobilizing. There are lives at stake here. Why am I being told that evacuations, which have been practiced *regularly*, are going at a snail's pace? *Elementary children* are faster in fire and tornado drills!"

"Contrary to popular belief, our people are persons, and thought processes during drills differ from reality. They have personal effects that they want to bring with them; pictures, books, and what not. It takes time to gather–"

"*Time*? Did the French Underground wait to completely move the Jews from their homes? Did Joan of Arc cower from making the difficult decisions? I think *not*!" Cornette leveled an accusatory finger at her second in command. "Neither shall we! Mobilize our people. I want this base *emptied yesterday*."

Cornette sat back and took a breath. "I trust that my transport is ready. I will be down to the hanger momentarily."

Gluten nodded. "Understood."

Having at long last found her sea legs and iron stomach, Robin stood in the center of the little boat as it bounced merrily over the water, going airborne at the crest of each wave only to slap back down. Her rifle was clutched to her chest, her index finger hovering outside the trigger guard. The diluted pre-sunrise light cast a faint pink glow on her extensive combat gear.

Lennox halted the boat roughly a mile from Corvo. The green, dormant volcanic island was a dark mound against the vast ocean. No electric lights were visible. Williams and Lennox raised their binoculars, the two men having the best eyes of the group. Robin waited patiently as they panned over the island.

Robin turned her head just enough to see over one shoulder. Berg was on the other side of the boat, also dressed in a combat attire. Despite his helmet's visor covering the majority of his face, she could tell that he was getting pre-mission jitters. His grip was rapidly shifting on his weapon.

"Calm, Berg," she encouraged.

"Don't worry about me," he replied with a small, thin smile. "I'll be fine. Just like in the excursion. Yeah."

Williams lowered his binoculars. "All is silent, Commander," he said.

Nodding, Lennox raised a hand to his comm. "Eagle Eyes to Flock. Civvies asleep, commence mission at 0500."

Robin glanced at the glowing eastern horizon where reinforcements waited.

Rush flew in his usual position behind Assail. They were at such a high altitude, he could imagine seeing the curvature of the planet. Rush had never flown so high before, even when he had run away, and, despite his ability to fly, he felt nervous. Looking down at the distant island, he knew that Shriek was hiding somewhere in the lolling green hills, waiting for the cue.

Rush glanced at the small, flat bar Assail grasped in his feet. He had an inkling as to what it was. If Assail dropped it, hopefully it would land in the sea. He didn't want to know what would happen otherwise.

"Five mike mark," Lennox's voice broadcasted.

Rush's wings shivered, faltering in their steady beat. Almost time for H-Hour. The minutes ticked by both quickly and slowly at the same time, his interpretation of time skewed by nerves.

"Calm yourself," Assail said to Rush.

"I'm calm," Rush immediately replied. "Perfectly calm. Perfect."

"Mark."

Robin eyed the controls on the fore of the boat. The subaqueous radar detection unit registered several Manta Carriers approaching the base of the island, almost half a mile below the surface. Examination of the volcanic bedrock had revealed a single submarine hanger, which made a terrific blind bottleneck. A charge was released, and the ocean surface soon frothed as the hanger's entrance collapsed. No submarines would be escaping that way.

A small squadron of retro-choppers appeared from over the horizon, with hulls shining in the red dawn light. They careened over the island, splitting into multiple directions. Unison Order automatic missiles pursued immediately. The retro-choppers spun and dived, others came up from behind to interfere, and some of the missiles were destroyed. However, the other missiles did their work, and the more fortunate pilots bailed before their crafts exploded. The remaining retro-choppers rounded back and annihilated the launchers as they appeared until the missiles ceased. In the end, more than half of the squadron had been downed, but the fields were defenseless.

Assail abandoned his course, folding his wings and diving downward, leaving Rush and Gale above. Rush watched with anxiety as his leader's body shrank to the point of imperceptibility.

Gale flapped her wings heartily, making her bob sharply in the air. "Here we go!" she crowed in anticipation.

Rush wished he had her excitement. His heart felt like it was about to beat itself out of his chest.

He looked to the east. The sun was peeking over the ocean, casting blinding rays into his eyes. Squinting, he could just make out a multitude of miniature black dots. They were the distant shapes of dozens of Manta Carriers breaching the waves. Moments later, even smaller dots appeared; more squadrons of retro-choppers.

Robin watched through her binoculars, tracking Assail's descent. The itty bitty black speck slowly leveled out, eventually skimming the water. He reached the cliffs, slowing down, then glided to one of the openings nearest sea level. Latching onto the rock, he swung his legs over next to the opening and placed the bomb. He let go and beat a rapid pace away.

"He's clear," she reported a few seconds later.

Berg, already with his laptop open, tapped a few keys. The bomb exploded in a cloud of dust, incinerating everything within a twenty-foot radius. When the dust cleared, everything above the floor was gone. A red-lit hallway was visible past the doorway.

"Shriek to Roost. I'm hearing an alarm."

Berg nodded. "You're hearing klaxons."

A single retro-chopper leveled with the doorway from a mile-long distance. It hovered motionlessly for a single moment before a subsonic object rocketed away from a wing-mounted launcher. It slowed as it neared the breach, finally employing a parachute. The object bounced past the doorway and disappeared into the hall beyond. It exploded in a deadly cloud of shrapnel and disabling gases, to discourage any awaiting ambushes.

Robin panned her binoculars. "The troop transports

have arrived."

The Manta Carriers, held aloft in a cloud of spray by their rotors, slowed as they approached. One by one, they swiveled around so their ramps faced the hole in the cliff. Each emptied a troop of soldiers before flying away and letting the next Manta Carrier take its turn. By the time the previous Carrier had dropped its load, the second wave of retro-choppers was just arriving.

Robin took a seat as Lennox started the engine. He piloted the boat to the hole as the last Carrier pulled away. Their clothes were battered by the intense downdraft as the Carrier flew overhead, landed on the water, then safely joined its brethren beneath the surface.

Berg packed up and slung the pack over his shoulder, then checked the seal and filters on his helmet. Lennox was the first off of the boat. Once they had disembarked, the boat was given a push away from the cliff and left to drift.

Robin readied her rifle at waist level, years of experience keeping her aim true. The muzzle took corners before her body did. Her eyes were narrowed in focus. Thoughts irrelevant to the mission were gone from her mind.

"All eagles check in," Lennox said into his comm, and Robin heard the other team leaders report. Lennox turned to his team. "We're going for Cornette. Move out!"

"Hoo-ah!" Williams grunted.

The base was disturbingly barren of filth and life. Doors were left ajar. Every room they passed was given a thorough inspection, but all the team found were sagging drawers, computers left on idle screensavers, and incinerators still hot from recent taxing.

As they jogged through another hallway, having cleared the ones behind, Robin cocked her head to the side. "Do you hear that?" she mouthed, tightening her grasp on her firearm. Her index finger slid to brush the trigger guard.

Williams nodded, raising his assault rifle to eye level. Ahead of them, a pack of UO-GDs appeared from around a corner, their smooth carapaces faced the team. The heavily versatile rotors began to swing the drones into attack positions.

"Duck and cover!" Lennox shouted, throwing himself into a handily open doorway.

Bullets vanished into the wall around Robin's head as she darted for an adjacent hallway. Reaching her cover, she grabbed Berg's pack and threw him next to her. Ignoring his surprised "Oof!" and how his body rolled with momentum over the floor, she opened fire on the drones before pulling back. The other side of their hideout took a spray of bullets.

Lennox sprayed rounds, sending three drones plummeting from his wild attack. "Take them out of commission!"

"Laboring on it," Williams replied. "Eat lead, nudniks!"

A few moments later, the last UO-GD fell to the floor, clacking against the concrete. "Move out!" Lennox said.

Lois started when her office lights abruptly went out, and the incinerator hummed down to silence with the absence of power. Struggling to see with the meagre dawn light filtering through the ocean and the opaqued window, she went to the light switch, tried it, but it didn't work. Reaching for her case of files and hard drives, she went for the door. It wouldn't open. The handle turned, but the door *wouldn't open*.

Her intercom crackled, making her whirl around. *"Lois. It is apparent that it is time for the Unison Order to take a giant leap forward. You have successfully made the world cower in fear. It is time to make it surrender."*

"G-Gluten!" Lois Cornette raged. She slammed her finger down onto her intercom. "Gluten, what is the meaning–"

"I have a feeling you're ranting at me right now, but I'm not really here. Think of it as a one-way mirror.

"You are a visionary person, my old friend. However, only those with true power can finish what they start. Power is the ability to control and manipulate the people, whether one individual, or entire countries and economies. Therefore, I have taken the liberty of commandeering the Unison Order's underground bank accounts and contacts.

"Take assurance that you have not failed. You have merely passed on a legacy to those with higher intelligence and greater wisdom than yourself. May you consider your life to be whole. After all, I believe your French friends will have a personal guillotine waiting for you." The intercom light went out.

Lois collapsed into her chair.

Rush watched Assail retake his place in the lead. "You two," the black pterosaur said. "We're their eyes in the sky. Watch for any rabbit holes."

"I like rabbits on occasion," Gale cooed, squinting down at the distant island.

Assail curled a wing, tossing himself into a descending spiral. Rush and Gale quickly pursued, though Rush eschewed the spiral. They fell even faster by using their wings. The wind lashed at Rush's face, causing him to squint. He had to fight the urge to slow, because if he couldn't see. . .

One second, it looked like the ground wasn't growing any closer. The next second, it was upon them! They split off, flying the routes they had taken in the days before. Rush used his momentum to his advantage, stiffening his wings to glide and using the membranes between his legs and tail to steer.

He only gave the cliffs a cursory check, then took a diverting course over some seaside fields lined with white stone walls. Sheep interspersed with huge herds of cattle were rounding their paddocks in a swivet, remaining as far as possible from the burning carcasses of unfortunate aircraft.

Movement below caused Rush to glance downward. A huge section of a field was dividing. The livestock fled, desperately leaping over the stone walls and hedges as a crack formed in the earth. Some of the walls shook themselves apart. Pieces began tumbling into a rapidly forming cavity.

"Rush to Flock. I've found a rabbit hole big enough for a Brachiosaurus."

"Iceberg to Flock. Rush's coordinates are 39° 42' 28.9738" N, 31° 5' 11.9868" W."

The crack steadily widened in an even, square-toothed line. The sod held together, with only small clumps collapsing into the gap. The early morning light streamed into the crack, revealing a horde of UO-SHs ready to take off. The helicopters' blades were circular silver blurs casting a heavy downdraft on personnel scurrying around in an organized panic. As soon as the crack was wide enough, the helicopters in the center began to rise.

Retro-choppers, responding to Rush's coordinates, dropped upon the helicopters, machine guns spitting. Barely out of the hanger, some of the helicopters burst into flames and crashed in the fields. To escape the dogfights, Rush evacuated to a higher altitude, then circled to see where he could assist, if needed.

He veered toward a UO-SH slipping out of the gruesome melee above by kissing grass with its rails. Aiming, his foot tightened on the trigger pad, and he immediately felt the recoil bumping his underside. In satisfaction, he saw the rounds pierce the helicopter's windshield. It tripped over its own rails, somersaulting before the engine caught fire. Fully engaged, Rush swerved to encounter his next target.

Something whizzed past his ear far too fast to see. Instinct had him close his wings, making him plummet like a rock. An instant later, gray blurs pierced the air above. A helicopter broke away from the others with deadly intent. Rush flapped his wings to catch the air. Billowing, his wings caught the sea wind and sent him hurtling upward.

"Shriek to Flock! Got some choppers near me, and I'm hungry."

Rush flipped head over tail so that he was momentarily falling upside-down. His rifle aimed, he fired upon the UO-SH.

It fell away, and he took the opportunity to right himself.

Helicopters were still rising from the previously hidden hanger. Rush hugged the ground, trying to look as inconspicuous as possible in his approach. Reaching the rim, he landed. He carefully aimed, and opened fire on the idling helicopters yet to ascend. Their hulls became riddled with holes, with some of the aircraft spluttering and winding down. *Those won't be starting up again.*

Rush continued firing until his weapon clicked. He looked down at it, then remembered the procedure to reload it. Reaching into one of his many armored vest pockets, he pulled out a magazine. Awkwardly balancing on his tail and both wings, he used both feet to eject the empty magazine from his weapon, then slid in the new one until he heard the *click*.

Assuming a more comfortable position, he looked into the hanger. Personnel ran around frantically. A few guards scanned the upper rim, with weapons aimed and fingers on the trigger. Rush fled before they could spot him, taking to the air.

He screamed as a retro-chopper zoomed past, the air disturbance sending him reeling. Recovering quickly, Rush yelled again as a helicopter's blades almost chopped him in half. He darted for the open sky.

A spray of tracers and slugs streaked past. He dodged as best as he could, flipping, falling, any way he could get away. They whistled by his body as he performed extravagant evasive maneuvers. Below him, the bullets slammed into the ground, pushing up small clouds of sod and dust. His frustration peaked. No matter what maneuvers he pulled, the helicopter remained on his tail.

"I need help!" he cried into his comm, lapsing into

dinosaur-ese in his panic. Blinding pain shot through his wing. A quick glance over his shoulder displayed the neat, round hole in the membrane. "I'm wounded!" Ignoring the pain of air going through his wing, he made a tight corkscrew turn and headed for a rock rise.

"English!" came the reply. *"What's wrong?"*

Before he could respond, a helicopter ascended from behind the rise, guns pointed straight at him. Trapped from behind and ahead, with ground below, he could only go up. Flapping hard, his body tilted vertically. It would be tight. . .

I won't make it! In a move of desperation, he bent backward so that he was flying up and almost upside down. *I need to make it!*

The air from the helicopter's blades tickled his underbelly as he passed way too close. Arching his back to the point of pain, he managed to fly upside down for just long enough to curl in his wings and plummet toward the sea below.

A new sound of rockets and rotors arrived. Looking up, he saw the United States flag proudly painted on the newcomers' hulls. Looking back over his wings, he watched the Unison Order helicopters being peppered. One burst into flames and smoke, the other flipped upside down. While the upside down one ripped up the ground and itself upon crashing, the flaming helicopter had nothing but air below it.

Turning back, he took in the fast-approaching waters. Their waves frothed and crashed against the rocks of the cliff. The helicopter was falling faster now and was right above him. He could only hope that the water was deep enough.

He slammed into the water. His wings curled up close

to his body, taking advantage of his streamlined shape. The momentum from his fall cut him through the water. A little tilting of his head and feet directed him away from the point of impact above. Once his momentum faded, a few tough wing strokes propelled him faster. Air bubbles streaming up from his armor and weapons, he struggled to create enough distance between himself and the helicopter.

The sound of the impact struck his ears, followed by the shockwave of water compression. He lost his righting and spun aimlessly. When he stilled, he could see the black oil and dark hull of the helicopter before him, slowly sinking to the ocean's bottom.

With his air running out, he righted himself and surged to the surface. His beak broke the surface, and he sucked in the air. The impact of bullets in the water nearby diverted his attention back to the fight above.

The thought of staying in the water struck him. It was safe, no one could see him, and he only had to swim out to a safe distance where his survival was guaranteed. He frantically dove as a UO-SH swooped overhead, pursued closely by a strafing retro-chopper. Rush winced and curled in on himself as the slugs slammed into the sea around him. He was unharmed, the hail lasting only a moment. A dull splash in the distance had him looking to where the UO-SH sat half-submerged on the surface. A few humans entered the water, trying to swim to safety, as the helicopter sank.

Rush breached the surface again to take in another breath. Beating his wings, he managed to get enough air beneath them to lift him out of the sea. His success was immediately rewarded with a high crest of a wave, slapping him back underwater. He forced his way to the surface, breaking it with much sputtering and coughing. Recovering his breath, he tried again and soared upward.

Picking a helicopter, he broke toward it. Leveling out, his foot fisted around the trigger for his miniature, yet highly effective semi-automatic. It responded, spitting out tiny rounds. Holes pierced the helicopter's hull. Gas streamed out as the helicopter wavered in the air, the pilot struggling to hold it steady. It was a vain attempt, as it crashed moments later.

Adrenaline hummed exuberantly in Shriek's veins as she dodged aerial fire in her quest to sneak up on Unison Order soldiers emerging from an emergency exit. There was no cover on the empty hills. The ocean wind batted at her fringe as she hovered in the shadow of a stone wall.

While she had a few seconds of reprieve, she checked the status of her weapon's magazine. It didn't quite need to be replaced yet. There were two more left on her hip holster. Eighty rounds were left before she ran out.

She kept to the wall, even when the soldiers began sprinting past. They ran hunched over, keeping their gazes jumping between the distant forest and the aerial battle. She followed surreptitiously, her hands flexing on her assault rifle.

A retro-chopper crashed nearby, the force of the explosion sending Shriek tumbling while the humans stumbled. She picked herself up and ran for the safety of a wall before the soldiers could spot her. Unfortunately, she heard a shout followed by rounds kicking up the dirt around her. With a screech, she scrambled up and over the wall, landing on plush moss. There was a gap in the wall by her head, through which she could see the soldiers splitting, some heading for the trees while the rest remained behind to pursue.

Marvelous, Shriek thought. She thanked that she was so small as she used the wall as cover on her way to the same trees. It was risky, but the forest had hiding places and better chances.

The soldiers were still within hearing distance as she reached a sheltering tree trunk. Letting her rifle dangle from its strap, she planted her claws in the bark and scaled the tree. A low branch served as a decent spot to stop, where she had eyes on the soldiers with the bonus of leaves to keep them from readily spying her. With her tail waving languidly to meter her balance, she untucked her weapon and aimed.

They were gathered around a copse, chests heaving. One of the soldiers looked close to a breakdown. Another looked around, paused, then pointed at a bush. The man ripped aside the branches to reveal a girl huddled inside. Her face was pale and she made to flee, but the soldier fisted the front of her shirt and roughly pulled her out.

Shriek gritted her teeth when they started talking but she couldn't hear clearly. She decided to take another chance and sneak closer.

Before she could find a new branch on which to take post, allied ground troops appeared over a distant hill. The Unison Order soldiers took off again, dragging the girl behind them. Groaning, she followed suit.

Up ahead was a clearing. Up above was a mess of retro-choppers and helicopters. As the soldiers braved the open, Shriek shook her head but kept moving. This screamed bad idea, but she couldn't lose the civilian.

No sooner had the soldiers reached the other side of the clearing than a helicopter noticed a chicken-sized dinosaur in the tall grasses.

"Shriek calling Flock!" Rush heard over his comm. *"'Choppers all 'round me! I could use some assistance!"*

"I'm coming, Shriek!" Gale responded. *"I can see you, below me at my three o'clock."*

"Look out! There's a chopper behind you!"

"Where–?" Rush's wingbeats faltered upon hearing Gale make a gargling gasp before falling silent. The last time he'd heard that, his parents were being chomped in half by a Tyrannosaurus. He barely registered the thud of Gale's impact with the ground.

"GALE!" Shriek screamed.

Rush listened in horror as Shriek's comm picked up Unison Order soldiers' victorious cries, closely followed by gunshots.

"Shriek?" Rush called into his comm. "Shriek?!"

The helicopters were everywhere. The retro-choppers were doing the best they could, but their efforts weren't good enough against the heavier armed Unison Order aircraft. They just needed to hold off the aerial defenses for a little longer, enough for the teams inside the base to find Lois Cornette.

A retro-chopper plummeted a pace to his right, flames covering every surface. He dodged, praying to I Am that the pilot would survive. Another glance around had him adding *Please, send us help!*

"This is Red Bird Nine! Yellow team down! We're falling back, repeat, falling back!"

The retro-choppers began circling away from the island, heading back out to sea. Rush watched them leave, knowing that he was one of the only things left in the sky to shoot down.

A helicopter swiveled around, and he could see his reflection on its windscreen. Even thinking of dodging the upcoming fire was a futile hope. So, he closed his eyes, pulled his own trigger, and awaited the Light.

Robin's teeth were clenched as Lennox exercised remarkable self-restraint over the news. She had heard everything over the comms. A glance to her left showed that Williams had, too.

"Move! Move! Move!" Lennox chanted repeatedly. He led them down hall after hall, kicking open every door as they went. Every room was empty.

"Where are we?" Berg asked.

"The brig section," Lennox said. He held up a fist to halt the team as a blind corner came up. Once the coast was confirmed to be clear, he waved his hands. "Conners, Williams, take that doorway. Berg and I will continue on."

Robin took point, checking the room for any Unison Order soldiers. Her focus was so tuned on her job that it took several moments for her brain to fully absorb what her eyes were seeing. ". . .This isn't the brig section," she murmured, dropping her rifle's front. She took a few steps further to investigate the man pinned to a metal chair.

Williams' jaw tensed as he surveyed the array of torture devices on the walls and tables. "Agreed."

As much as it repulsed her, Robin bent double to check his identity, expecting to see the nameless face of a Unison Order soldier. She recoiled in horror. "*Takin!*"

Williams murmured something under his breath as he joined Robin. "Indeed," he muttered. "Williams to Flock. Nelson "Tapper" Takin has been found. He is deceased."

Robin turned away from her former colleague to survey the rest of the room. There was one computer on. When she checked it, she found it password lacking and that it was the last used item in the room. She ran through its last usage. "Six milliamperes," she stated. "That's not enough to. . ." Trailing off, she saw a clipboard nearby and flipped through the pages. "I've found a log." Near the last page, she found the last entry. "Nelson Takin. Time of death; 19:47 hours. Last night."

Lennox and Berg appeared in the doorway. Berg took one look and immediately backed out, whereupon Robin picked up on the wet sounds of heaving.

Her superior shook his head sadly. "Come," Lennox said. "We need to continue onward, back the way we came. It's a dead end further on. We'll mark this place for later retrieval."

Without any glances back, the team followed his lead out of the interrogation section. "Is there a map anywhere around here?" Robin eventually queried as they entered a new hall.

Williams panned the area. "Appears to be a base where you'd require memorization."

"It'd be nice, though," Berg added. "Like, 'You Are Here, Lois Cornette's Office This Way.'"

"Only in a perfect world," Robin grunted.

Lennox silenced them with a strict look.

Robin detoured to send a steady and powerful kick to a door. Its lock snapped, and the door swung ajar. Her rifle's muzzle followed her eyes. Another empty office, like many others. She was about to rejoin her team when she saw the computer screen alit.

An idea coming to mind, she stepped around the desk and wiggled the computer mouse. The computer flashed brighter and she entered the passcode on the sticky note taped to the monitor. The screen updated to display the desktop. Thankfully, the file names made sense. She quickly clicked on a file titled 'Maps.' It opened up to show five documents. Selecting one, it opened to show a section of grids; the base map.

"Eagle Eyes to Arcee. Where are you?"

"In one of the offices. I've found a base map. She's in Level C, Hall 16, Office 1A."

"Bravo Zulu, Arcee. Moving to coordinates."

Robin took a flash drive from a belt pouch and plugged it into the computer. She dragged everything onto it and waited for the files to copy. She removed and pocketed the flash drive, and left to find her team. Following the signs on the walls at a fast jog, she soon heard the sounds of her team up ahead. She sped up her pace, keeping her weapon at the ready.

The lights suddenly began to flicker as something in the distance snapped loudly. The halls repeatedly plunged in and out of darkness, continuing for about half a minute, until finally the lights remained off. Robin's HUD adjusted immediately, her visor illuminating the darkness of the halls.

Turning a corner, Robin saw her team up ahead, also making their way down the darkened halls. Their steps were nearly silent. They were Black-Ops after all; it was a job requirement.

She caught up, falling into step beside Berg. He glanced at her, turning away the muzzle of his rifle when he realized that it was pointing toward her leg. Robin paid little direct attention to him, her senses tuned for any sounds outside her view. A tiny radar icon on her visor's HUD showed that echolocation was active and reporting no one up ahead or down the adjacent halls.

Berg suddenly froze. When Robin turned to face him, William's hand shot up in a tight fist. The entire team stilled.

Instincts had her shout and dive into a doorway an instant before the air filled with the sharp explosions of firing automatics. It was only by pure miracle that the others managed to find cover and avoid harm in the spray of ammunition.

Ambush!

Gritting her teeth, Robin risked firing a few rounds herself before quickly pulling back again. The doorway was barely deep enough for her form, so while Lennox and Williams occupied the enemy, Robin kicked in the door behind her. The flying slab of wood smacked a Unison Order's soldier's face. She flew into action before the man could recover, swinging a knee into his gut, then slamming both arms over his back while he was bent double. She struck his skull with the butt end of her assault rifle, then quickly cuffed him to a piece of furniture and took away his weapons.

Sidling back into the doorway, she surveyed the situation. Berg was across the hall, taking cover while Lennox and Williams fired. Movement from the direction whence they had come drew her attention. Unison Order soldiers were approaching from the back. From the way her team had taken cover, they would be completely vulnerable from the other side.

Robin took aim, hoping that the soldiers hadn't seen her. She shot one, but the fallen soldier captured the awareness of the others.

"Roost! Cover!" she screamed. Robin managed to get another round off before they found her and she ducked back into shelter, but, from the sounds of it, she had only wounded her target. She shifted her rifle in her hands, but her right wouldn't respond correctly. She looked down and saw a huge bleeding gash crossing over her hand below her wrist. Quickly, before the adrenaline allowed her to feel the pain, she scooted further into cover and proceeded to dress the wound, pulling bandages from her small field kit.

Across the way, Berg scrambled to open the door next to him seconds before holes appeared where his body had been. Thankfully, Lennox and Williams had done the same, taking cover in the rooms beyond.

Tying the final knot in the gauze, Robin dropped to lay flat on the floor. It would make her more vulnerable to surprises, but her lowered position would hopefully throw off the enemy so long as they were looking higher. Peeking around the corner, she opened fire in a sweeping motion, taking down three soldiers in one pass, leaving an estimate of four. She shoved with her elbows to thrust herself back into cover again.

Taking out the last four soldiers was a trying endeavor. Senses high, Robin stole from cover. The HUD in her helmet sent echolocations down the halls, searching for standing forms.

"Clear!" Williams stated from behind her, having been investigating their previous heading.

"Clear!" Robin echoed a moment later once her HUD reported back. She glanced at an open doorway. "Iceberg, you can come out now," she added, rolling her eyes. He was a liability, but it would be rather disheartening if they lost him. She grabbed a pistol from the soldier she had eliminated, checked its ammo, then tossed it to Berg.

Berg sent her a meek smile and held the pistol in a ready position. He nodded to her.

"Move out!" Lennox ordered, pointing down the hall. "Roost to Fowl! BOLO ambushes!" he continued into the comm.

Hearing acknowledgements over her own comm, Robin took point, keeping a sharp eye on her team's tail end.

"Chickadee to Fowl! Ambush in Hall. . . Six, Level A! At least a dozen UO, requesting backup!"

"Buzzard to Chickadee! Coming you– We have our own ambush! Level B, Hall 18!"

Lennox halted their advance as reports of ambushes came in from all of the other teams. Robin adjusted her grip on her rifle uneasily. She'd *known* that it had been too easy. No normal UO personnel, not a soul in sight. . .

Ahead of her, Lennox gestured for them to remain as silent as possible before taking a few creeping steps ahead to where the hall forked. He raised a hand to adjust the sensitivity levels of his helmet's HUD. After a moment, he stepped backward and pointed down the right-hand fork, then flashed all five fingers twice for '10.'

Robin moved upward in the line, waving at Berg for him to stay back and out of harm's way. She drew alongside Lennox as Williams advanced, taking a duo of matte black orbs. Pressing a hidden button, he tossed them down the right-hand hallway and let them roll away. A bright flash of light and wisps of smoke appeared from around the corner.

At Lennox's signal, the team advanced, weapons firing into the thick, choking screen of smoke that obscured the hall. When Robin's magazine was expended, she took the opportunity in the break to reload and activate the infrared vision on her HUD. The smoke became almost transparent, revealing the heated forms of the Unison Order soldiers. The enemy fell quickly, unable to accurately retaliate.

"Sensors on high," Lennox instructed as they stepped over bodies.

They passed a signpost fastened to the wall. *Level C; Hall 15; Office Block 20A-39A.* One turn later, and they entered Hall 16. Robin began counting down the office numbers in her head, starting with 19A. They passed a small hallway, doubling back when Lennox realized that they were now entering Hall 17.

Robin took the lead as they strode down the long, doorless hall. At its end was a single door, a plaque embedded in it. The night vision on her visor made it difficult for Robin to read, but eventually made out the embossed name *Lois Cornette* on the innocuous steel door.

Williams, the largest member of her group, slid past Robin and Lennox to the door. He silently gripped the knob in one huge fist to force the knob's lock. Before he did anything, Lennox and Berg took position on either side of the doorframe out of immediate gunfire. Robin dropped to her knees and readied her weapon. Williams wrenched the knob, but to his surprise, it smoothly clicked open. Unlocked! The door swung into the room and Williams leveled his firearm.

Robin's HUD immediately flashed, a shrill whine sounded from her comm. Her night vision failed in the complete darkness, rendering her blind. From the simultaneous grunts of her team, they were all blind and helpless!

By the sound of a solid thud, Williams had been knocked to the floor. Berg shrieked like a girl.

"Make one move, darlings, and she dies."

chapter thirty

The hall lights flickered on again fluctuating wildly, dimming and brightening. Somewhere, a generator had turned on, but it apparently wasn't faring well.

With her sight recovered, Robin stared. A tall, platinum blond woman somewhere in her late 40s held a pistol to Berg's chin, the only unprotected area on his entire body. She held Berg against her wiry frame, pinning his arms and spreading his legs to devoid him of balance should he try and kick her.

"Lois Cornette, we presume?" Lennox said, unmoving.

"Astute of you, sweetie," Cornette replied.

Robin's rifle, having been leveled for the past half hour, only had to twitch a little so it was aimed at Cornette's temple. "Put the pistol down," Robin demanded.

"Whose trigger finger is faster, I wonder?" the woman murmured. "And what is this man to you? You Black-Ops are naturally suspicious and paranoid, but is that *concern* I hear in your voice? I thought that you people are supposed to have nothing to lose in such a situation as this."

"He's my teammate," Robin growled.

"Don't mind me!" Berg grunted past the indention in his chin. "Shoot her!"

"How fast are you, darling?" Cornette repeated. Robin could see her index finger beginning to tighten on the trigger. "Think quickly, now."

Rush braced himself, clenching his jaw and eyes shut tight. The morning sunlight shined on his closed eyelids, causing him to see nothing but a red glow.

But the glow vanished as the sudden darkness was punctuated by a chorus of piercing war cries. Rush's eyes flashed open to see a massive cloud of winged beasts descending from the sky, blocking the sun from view. Birds of prey of every kind, Pterodactylus, and Quetzalcoatlus swarmed the helicopters. The smaller ones found the open doors where the gunmen stood, some pecking the humans into submission while others wormed their way to the cockpit. Helicopters began dropping from the sky. Only a few pilots managed to see past their tormentors and land without crashing.

A golden eagle screeched in greeting as it flew by Rush on its way to the helicopter that had risen from behind the rock ridge. The eagle was followed by dozens of other birds, some of prey or of carrion. Rush watched in dumbfounded amazement as the helicopter he was sure was to be his death was quickly taken out of the sky. A quick glance over one shoulder showed that his pursuer was no longer there.

"Rush to Red Bird Nine! Reinforcements have arrived! Repeat, reinforcements have arrived!"

"Red Bird Nine to Rush. Nest has sent no reinforcements. Clarify."

Dodging a careening UO-SH, Rush said, "They're not from your Nest, they're from *mine*! And a lot of others."

"On our way to assist."

Whooping, Rush performed a half barrel roll and an aileron flip and darted for a loose helicopter. Finding an angle where there was no risk of hitting his avian allies, he opened fire. The windscreen covering the cockpit was riddled with holes, and the helicopter spiraled down to meet its watery grave.

The sounds of retro-chopper engines alerted the avians, who split from any remaining helicopters to open and safer skies. Rush followed behind them, hitching a ride on a Quetzalcoatlus' airstream while he watched the last of the UO-SHs crash. The retro-choppers fell into a steady circling, ready to pick off anything.

A resounding cheer rose up over the comm and from the avians. A hawk swatted its neighbor playfully, which spurred mock dogfights between many others. Rush was about to join them when he found his eyes drawn to the entrance in the cliff. Glancing at the avians patrolling nearby, looking for any other rabbit holes, he dove down to the entrance.

The lights were flickering erratically as he glided through the halls. He sniffed the air repeatedly, searching for any signs of his team. Once, he tried using the comm, but no one answered. Passing over the husks of UO-GDs, he assumed that he was going in the right direction. He flew faster, where he began to hear familiar voices.

Robin stared down the barrel of her gun. Her finger ached to pull the trigger. She could finish the woman behind the Unison Order, but was Cornette really fast enough to shoot first before death came?

"I'm waiting, sweetie," the wicked blond cooed, pressing the pistol far enough into Berg's chin to make him suck in a breath. "I'm becoming weary of waiting for you to come to a decision. Any parting words for your soon to be ex-partner?"

BANG!

Screaming, Cornette let go of Berg, grabbing her shoulder. Berg scrambled away as Cornette wailed. She re-aimed her pistol at Robin, who glared at her from behind her visor.

An echoing gunshot spurred Rush faster.

"So, you want to play it that way?" Cornette said, her words strained and tight. Williams crawled a safe distance before standing, having just shot Cornette in the leg. "Fine, then. Shoot me. Kill me. I stand before you, wearing no armor to protect myself. Take the shot and become a hero."

Robin grit her teeth. "I'm not going to kill you, Lois Cornette. Put down your weapon and surrender. No conditions."

Robin could see a differing emotion in her eyes. "Is that it, darling? I expected something more. Threats, maybe. But no matter; none of you will pull the trigger. I'm more valuable alive than dead, are I not? I have information you require. Dead men, after all, tell no tales."

"Take off the head, and the body will follow," Robin countered.

"Resulting in a power vacuum. My Unison Order will continue, with or without me. Someone else will realize my dream," Cornette said, her voice choking. "And certainly without you." Robin saw Cornette's finger start to tighten on the trigger. Training kicked in. Robin squeezed first.

Rush blurred past, as both her rifle and the pistol fired.

Robin braced for the pain as she watched Rush collide with Cornette and fall to the floor.

The pain never came. Robin lowered her barrel and added a single bullet into both of Cornette's knees. The blond woman collapsed with a pained cry. Berg skittered several yards away, shaking profusely.

"Rush!" Robin exclaimed, immediately kneeling next to him. Lennox's and Williams' movements to restrain Cornette were lost to her as she held out a hand just over Rush's hide, as if the gentlest touch would cause him to fall apart. Inside her chest, something fractured.

The little brown Pterodactylus looked up at her. Part of the skin by the corner of his stiff beak curled up in a smile. A pool of red slowly seeped out from beneath his body.

"Where are you wounded?" Robin asked.

The smile vanished, replaced by a pained grimace. "Neck," he grunted. "Angle put it in my chest, I think."

Robin gingerly picked him up, trying to block out his gasps as she slowly turned him over. Indeed, a small hole was in his neck, just outside the edge of his bulletproof vest. It was mocking. She picked him up, trying not to jostle him. Williams and Lennox made sure that Cornette couldn't escape while Berg radioed for medical assistance.

The medics and their guards arrived in an impressively short amount of time, but when Robin showed Rush, who was just barely hanging onto consciousness, they hesitated.

"We. . . have no training in veterinary medicines," the head medic said regretfully.

"How much are you willing to bet that a vet hasn't had training for a pterosaur, either?" Robin shot back, nerves beginning to fray from the stress of the situation. "Can't you do *anything* for him at all?"

The two medics exchanged a glance.

"Thank you," Robin said, gingerly handing her partner over. She cringed as an agonized groan slipped from Rush's beak as he was laid on a hastily-erected stretcher.

"Don't worry, we'll take care of him." The medics and their entourage of armed soldiers hurriedly moved off down the halls, pushing the stretcher ahead of them as they went. A second set of medics, with Lennox and Williams, lifted Cornette onto a stretcher and followed down the hall. Robin watched until she could no longer hear their footsteps.

Berg surprised her by putting a reassuring hand on her shoulder. "Come on, Arcee. Lennox and Williams have Cornette contained. Let's round up the rest of them."

Refocusing her mind from her partner's uncertain fate, Robin shifted her grip on her rifle, her expression sliding back into her game face. As she jogged down the hall, she checked her visor's HUD. It seemed to be back in operation. Whatever disabling device Cornette had used apparently was only temporary. The echolocation beamed down the paths ahead. Data appeared almost immediately. She and Berg checked every closed room, and detailed any Unison Order personnel encountered, handing them off to the nearest team.

Time was lost to her. It could have been hours or minutes, but Robin felt like the day had barely started when everyone reported that the invasion was finished. She and Berg strode to the underground helicopter hanger, where the prisoners were awaiting transport.

The prisoners were held at the corner of the hanger, surrounded by soldiers. Walking through the open double doors, Robin moved to stand beside another team. In the center was Lois Cornette, who looked as if her world had just ended.

"Searched?" Berg asked a soldier.

The soldier nodded.

"That's good," Berg said.

Robin panned her eyes over the Unison Order personnel.

"All I wanted was to see Earth at peace." Cornette sounded broken. "Was that too much? Why must you people fight peace so?"

A soldier approached the former President. "Because humanity isn't ready for slavery. One day, someone far better than you will come along, and will try to make us fall hook, line, and sinker, so we fall *hard*. Hopefully, that will never happen."

The sound of rotors accompanied by a strong wind made Robin look up. A Manta Carrier neatly descended into the hanger. Once its wheels hit the ground, the ramp lowered, and several armed men descended, holding restraining devices. The prisoners were put in the restraints and filed into the aircraft. Those too injured to move under their own power were placed on stretchers.

As the Manta Carrier lifted off, Robin watched with cool indifference. Once the aircraft reached the installation, the prisoners would be filtered and returned to their countries of origin to be punished as their governments saw fit.

Her attention was drawn to another section of sky. A massive collection of avians flew above the hanger and were blotting out the sun as they landed just out of sight. The largest of them were huge pterosaurs with manes akin to a lion's. The Quetzalcoatlus were propping themselves up on their wing-claws to peer curiously at the soldiers within the hanger.

Two forms declined to land, instead turning and descending into the hanger. When they came close enough, Robin recognized them as Assail and an albatross. The bird was awkwardly carrying Gale on its back.

Berg moved toward them and held up his arms. Somehow understanding, the albatross tilted its back so Gale could slide off. Berg caught the Pterodactylus as the bird flew away.

"We found Gale at the edge of the woods," Assail reported, alighting on the motionless rotors of a destroyed UO-SH. "We were unable to locate Shriek." He said nothing more, but his expression said enough.

Berg looked down at Gale's limp form, shivering at the sight of the still-open dark eyes. "I. . . never got to know her well," he murmured. "But I'll never forget her."

"I fathom now, Conners," Williams said quietly, looking at his empty arms. "Prithee, accept my apologies."

Robin deeply bowed her head in a nod, mouth in a thin line.

Lennox came up behind her. "How's Rush?" he asked.

Pain.

There was so much of it, Rush's thoughts couldn't mingle and join. His body *demanded* air.

There were voices hovering above him. He tried to listen, but they sounded echoey and slurred. When he tried asking them to speak clearer, all that came from his beak was a gurgling, drawn-out groan. For some reason, that made the voices sound more urgent.

Time was lost on him, but, through the disjointedness of his mind, he realized that the period of feeling numb and distant was happening more often and for longer. Something told him that this was bad.

The voices faded away to a whisper, barely audible. Rush found that floating in numbness was very strange. His gurgling breaths were beginning to become an afterthought.

Why is breathing important again? was his first coherent thought in quite a while. *Oh. It keeps me alive. . .*

The darkness was a comforting void.

EPILOGUE

Nicole and Mark worked in tandem in Weapons Development Room 7. Both stood over a tall table, scouring sets of electronic blueprints, and computer renderings and simulations. A neat stack of boxes sat nearby, holding important supplies and materials waiting to be put together into a warfare work of art.

Nicole cut herself off in the middle of defining a section of a blueprint when her phone's ringtone broke the quiet. "Sorry, Mark," she said, reaching into her pocket to check the caller ID. Unknown. Nonetheless, she flicked the screen to answer. "Hi. Who is calling, please?"

"Nicole. You need to come to the Sky Adventures airport

at once."

She frowned, worry sparking. "Pete! Is something wrong?"

"Just. . . just come. Please hurry."

"Pete?" Nicole said. "Pete!" Hearing a dial tone, she pulled her phone away from her ear and stared at it incredulously. "He hung up on me!"

"Pete?" Mark said, frowning.

"Yeah."

"Pete Berg?" At her nod, he added, "Are we talking about the same Pete?"

Nicole went to the door. "He was seriously urgent. Something's gone very wrong, and he wants me to get to the skydiving airport as quickly as possible. We'll continue this project later, Mark." Before he could open his mouth to reply, she had already slid out the door and was swinging herself down the hall, startling the posted guards.

The afternoon traffic was just beginning when she got into her lease car and pulled out onto the road. Fortunately, the traffic lights were in her favor, and she was soon in the countryside. She directed the GPS to display the route. Biting her lip, she worried as to what was wrong.

Arriving at the airport, she found only two vehicles in the parking lot. One of them was Pete's car. Quickly parking, she went to the building's front door and knocked loudly. When she received no answer, she tried the knob and found it unlocked. As she moved down the halls toward the hanger, she noticed that the building seemed abandoned.

The hanger doors were closed, and only three small planes were parked within. Nicole exited through the door that led to the runway. She squinted at the overcast sky, sighing nervously. After a few minutes, she pulled out her phone and dialed Pete's number. Holding it to her ear, she listened to the standard, monotone ringing.

"Hi, this is Pete. I'm not able to reach the phone right now, so please leave–"

Nicole hung up, recognizing Pete's legitimate recorded voicemail. Her hand dropped to her side, loosely gripping her phone. Worry gnawed at her.

Her head bolted up when she heard the rumble of engines. Out of the clouds came an aircraft. Rotors in its wings set it on the runway not far from her. A ramp on the bottom descended. Pete and three others came down, followed by Assail. Two of the four people carried small boxes decorated with the American flag.

"Pete!" Nicole exclaimed.

"Nicole," Pete said, his face uncharacteristically solemn.

"Pete, what happened?" she said, looking at him and his three companions for answers.

The shortest of the three, a man with a crew cut, moved forward. "Commander Rick Lennox. These are my teammates, Robin Conners. . ." He gestured to the red-haired woman. ". . .and Maurice Williams."

"Oh, you're the Black-Ops team," Nicole realized,

eyebrows shooting to her hairline. "What's happened?"

Pete looked at her, rubbing one arm. "Nikki, there. . . there were casualties." He slowly took the box from Lennox.

Nicole's eyes darted to the two flag-wrapped boxes, seeing them in a new light. "No. . ." she gasped. Frowning, she recounted the boxes. "Wait. There's only *two* here."

"Rush was my partner," Conners said. "And he saved my life, taking a bullet that was aimed for my head." She bit her lip before adding, "He is currently receiving medical help."

Nicole exhaled heavily.

"Shriek was mine," Williams added. "She was gunned down by UO-SHs during the base attack. Her. . . her box is empty. We were unable to locate her body."

"I was partnered with Gale," Berg said softly. "She died trying to warn Shriek. All of us were able to hear it over the comms."

Nicole reverently placed a hand on the box held by her friend. Silence dominated the runway.

"I'll inform Freedom," Nicole said eventually.

"May we come with you?" Lennox inquired. "We desire to pay our respects and participate in any events honoring our fallen partners."

Nicole took a deep breath. "Is there anything that you need to have done before I take you to her?"

"No," Lennox replied. "We have a vehicle here."

The sound of a multitude of wings drew Scope's attention from her badger dinner and to the sky, along with everyone else. It took several moments for the Quetzalcoatlus and Pterodactylus to come into view.

"What happened?" Scope called.

"We won!" a Quetzalcoatlus exclaimed, performing large barrel rolls. "The Unison Order's headquarters has been taken, and the leader is prisoner! The end of the war is in sight!"

The Squama within earshot burst into cheers, explaining to those who hadn't heard.

Scope let out a relieved breath she hadn't known she had been holding. A weight lifted from her shoulders. She smiled. "Well done," she praised.

"Thank you."

Scope whirled around. "Assail! What are you doing here?"

The black Pterodactylus shifted his wings. "My team and Nicole are on their way here."

Something in his voice sent a wave of sadness through her. "Were there deaths?" Scope asked, hoping that she had guessed wrong.

Assail slowly nodded. "They're bringing their bodies. They'll be here soon."

Scope sighed. "My heart is with yours, Assail."

Before long, a jeep came into sight, carefully weaving through the trees and bouncing heavily over dips and roots. It came to a halt at the edge of their gathering. Five humans came out, two carrying a single box each. Scope tightened her jaw, her magenta fringe drooping.

"Hi, Freedom," Nicole greeted with her English moniker.

"Hi, Nicole," Scope replied in English. "Who fell?"

"Gale and Shriek," her friend replied softly. "Rush is gravely injured, but we're trying to be hopeful." The two who carried the boxes stepped forward, holding them out. Scope closed the distance. One of them unwrapped the fabric from around the boxes before giving them to her. She placed each box on the grass and opened the lids.

"Where is Shriek?" Scope asked upon seeing that one was empty.

"We couldn't find her. We heard her death over the comms," Lennox replied.

Scope had seen much worse appearances in death, and was grateful that Gale's was peaceful. The body had even been cleaned.

"If you don't mind me asking," the second woman said slowly, "what will happen to her?"

Scope sighed. "We will burn Gale, and give her ashes to the winds to take where they please."

The tall man shifted his weight. "Are outsiders allowed to attend?"

Smiling, Scope replied, "Yes. You're all welcome." She took Gale from her box and gingerly held the Pterodactylus' stiff frame in her arms.

In the open area, the Quetzalcoatlus cleared a large space. In the center, Squama gathered large stones and erected them in neat piles that were flat on top. Scope stood at the edge and watched as wood and grasses were gathered and piled them on top of the two rock stacks. It was only when they backed away did Scope and the elder move forward.

Squama gazed from the sidelines as the two reached the rock pyres. Scope gingerly laid the boxes on the wood, making sure that they were in the center.

Sea Fern walked up, holding four stones. Two of them he gave to Scope, then they both stood before the pyres, ready to create the sparks to ignite the combustible materials.

"Wait!"

Both Utahraptors looked over their shoulders. The short man had taken a step forward, and looked like he wished to say something more. Scope nodded for him to continue.

He pursed his lips. "We usually have a eulogy for our fallen. If we could?"

Scope could see the emotions playing on the humans' faces. "Of course."

The tallest man slowly strode to Shriek's pyre and knelt next to it, putting him at near eye level with the box. "Shriek was my partner," he began. "In the time I had known her, she proved to be one of the most loyal, excited, and optimistic individuals I have ever met. I have the feeling that, if she were alive today, she would be here, grinning and playing with her kin. I have been blessed to have known her, and she will forever be in my memory." He stood, gazed a moment at the box, then plodded back to the others.

Scope looked at the red-haired woman. She was silent, but Scope could smell what wasn't seen. For a moment, it seemed that she wouldn't be saying anything. Scope waited patiently, but when nothing was done, she decided to continue.

The woman stepped forward, each stride measured as she went to the pyres. For the longest time, she did nothing but stare ahead at the forest beyond. Finally, "Rush isn't dead y– Not dead. But, I think that he could have been easily lost to us, and I would be standing before his pyre. So, I think that he needs a few words.

"Before Rush ran from his duty as a soldier, I believed him to be uncommitted, a quitter, and pessimistic. But when he came back, something had changed in him. He saved lives, and continued to honorably serve to the end." She paused. When she continued, her voice broke. "Rush was. . . is my friend in arms, and I eternally thank him for sacrificing his own life to save mine." She bowed her head, then retreated to the others.

Pete trudged to the pyre. His mouth opened and closed a few times before he finally uttered, "I wasn't able to know my partner very well, but she was certainly valiant in the line of duty. She knew what to do, performed her duty well, and did so through the end."

Scope waited for anyone else to step forward. When no one did, she and Sea Fern struck the stones they held together, and sparks flew. It took a few more tries before the pyres caught aflame. The two Utahraptors, and the humans, stepped back from the growing fire.

"I'm retiring."

Nicole couldn't see the speaker, but from the way Lennox whirled around in his seat, in shock, she assumed that it was unexpected.

"Pardon?" Lennox said.

"I'm retiring from the military," Conners repeated firmly. "When our tour's over, I'm going home."

Lennox was still, then nodded. "It was an honor serving with you, Robin Conners," he said. "May I ask why?"

"I. . . I don't wish to be fighting until I either get killed or permanently maimed in combat. I want to settle in one place, find a husband, buy a house, have two children."

There was a pause, then Nicole heard Williams say, "Having you on the team was an adventure. It was a pleasure."

"Likewise. I extend gratitude for the extensive argot succor."

Williams laughed.

Nicole remained silent, having the inkling that this was a private team moment. *May you, Conners, have a happy and fulfilled civilian life.*

The library computer slowly faded to darkness as it fell asleep. Secluded strategically in a corner where no one would see the screen, a young woman rubbed her temples. She didn't bother to wiggle the mouse, since her browsing history had already been thoroughly deleted.

Well, the RFID tag in the letter worked. Here we go, she thought, blinking at the date. She looked back to the open autobiography and used a finger to trace the words. Murmuring under her breath; "My heart pains me to know that these beautiful creatures, so fantastic beyond anything conventional history has portrayed, must still live with the blind terror lurking. If he is still on the lam, he most likely has plans in place so he can strike again at his will. This is why we must remain on alert, for if we allow a sociopath like him to win, then our world is truly lost."

Breathing deeply to stable herself, she carefully placed her small stack of books into her backpack, making sure that the paperback covers remained flat. She held back a creased notebook with wrinkled pages, scooping aside the odds and ends at the bottom of the bag before her books would fit.

The slightest glimpse of the antiquated frame had her gaze immediately shifting away, for fear that the distraction would again take hold. Despite conventional thought, she most certainly did not have all the time in the world. The lingering memories of the beloved dead shot a frigid shiver up her spine. She could not fail.

As she removed her hands to zip up the pocket, they brushed against the craggy surfaces of several of the Ores, then a stubby barrel of matte black metal.

For what choices could be made to restore a family?

ABBY BLACK

TO BE CONTINUED

ABBY BLACK

RESERVE MAPS

THE DINOSAUR RESERVE

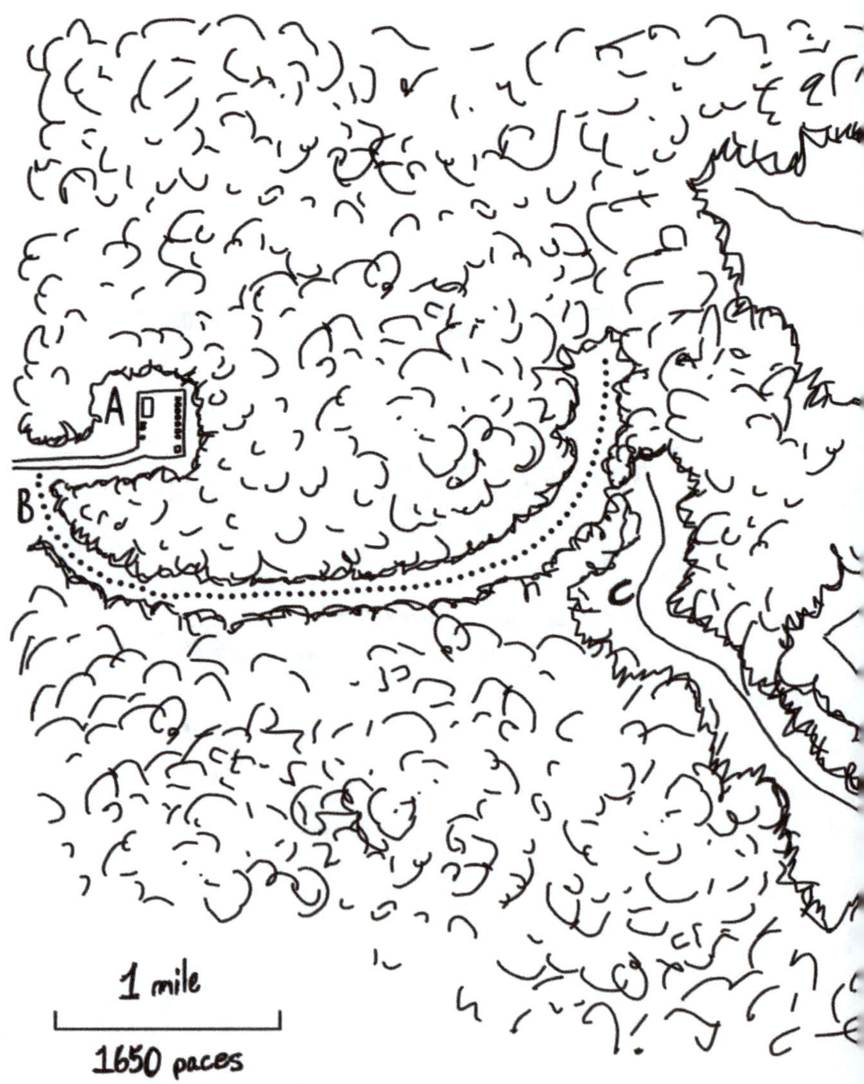

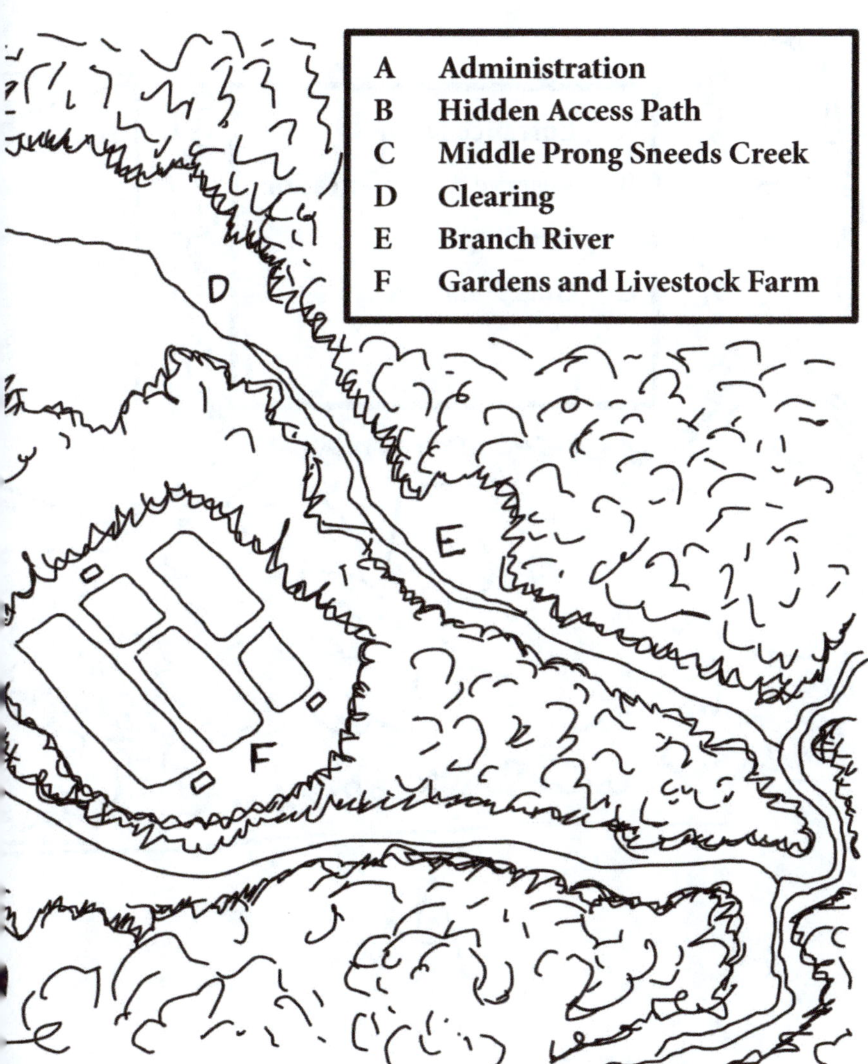
A   Administration
B   Hidden Access Path
C   Middle Prong Sneeds Creek
D   Clearing
E   Branch River
F   Gardens and Livestock Farm
D
E
F

THE DINOSAUR RESERVE

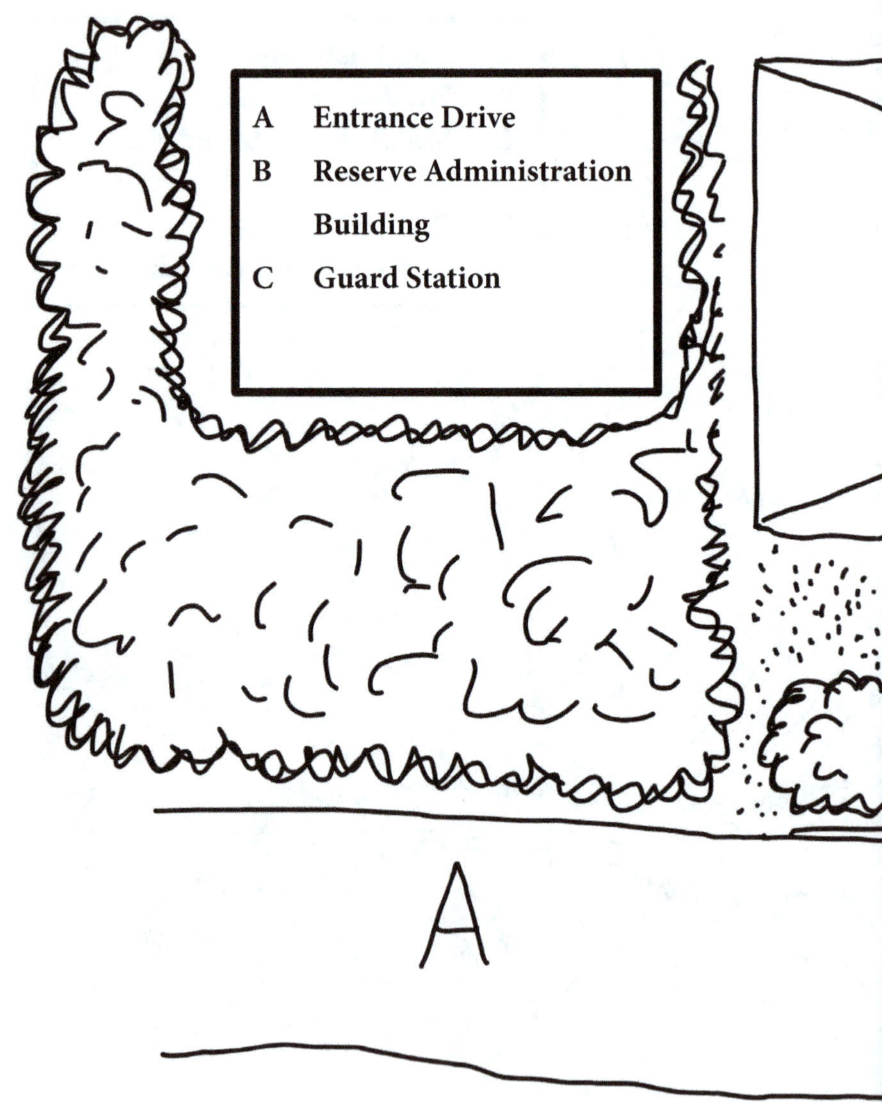

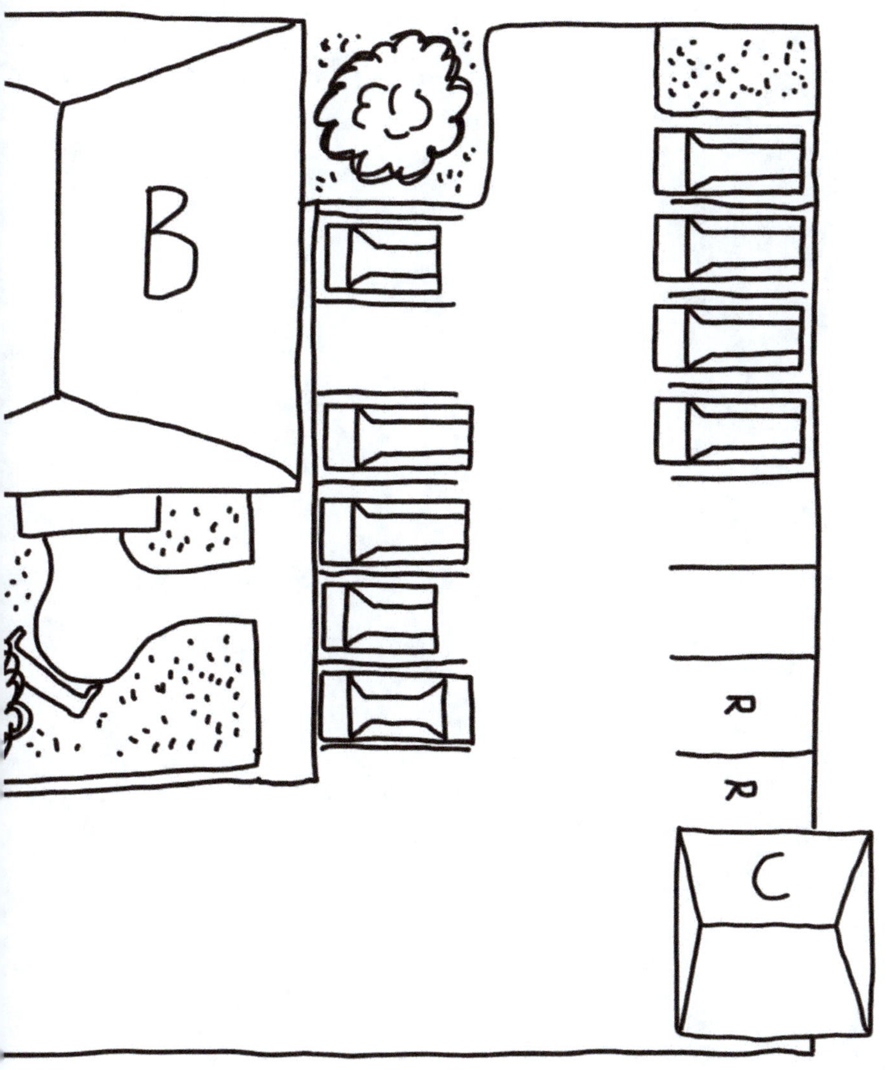
B
C
R
R

MILITARY GLOSSARY

MILITARY GLOSSARY

Military Alphabet

A = Alpha

B = Bravo

C = Charlie

D = Delta

E = Echo

F = Foxtrot

G = Golf

H = Hotel

I = India

J = Juliet

K = Kilo

L = Lima

M = Mike

N = November

O = Oscar

P = Papa

Q = Quebec

R = Romeo

S = Sierra

T = Tango

U = Uniform

V = Victor

W = Whiskey

X = X-Ray

Y = Yankee

Z = Zulu

MILITARY GLOSSARY

AMA = Against Medical Advice

Angel = A soldier killed in combat

AWOL = Away WithOut Leave

BOLO = Be On the Look Out

BZ = Slang for "Great Job"

CM = Continue Mission

COP = Combat Outpost. A small base, usually between 40 and 150 soldiers, often in a particularly hostile area. Life at a COP is often austere and demanding, with every soldier responsible for both guard duty and patrolling.

DFAC = Dining Facility, aka Chow Hall/Mess Hall

DOA = Dead On Arrival

ETA = Estimated Time of Arrival

Evac = Evacuate

FOB = Forward Operations Base

Fobbit = Servicemember who never goes outside the wire of a Forward Operations Base.

GPS = Global Positioning System

MILITARY GLOSSARY

H-Hour = The time of day when an attack, landing, or other military operation is scheduled to start.

HUD = Heads-Up Display

Inside/Outside the Wire = Describes whether you are on or off a base

KIA = Killed in Action

Klik = Kilometer

LC = Loud and Clear. Often said as "Lima Charlie"

Mike = Minute

MRE = Meals Ready to Eat. A precooked, prepackaged meal for military personnel.

POTUS = President Of The United States

RFID = Radio Frequency Idenification

"Roger, Roger That" = Understood

RTB = Return To Base

SIC = Second In Command

UAV = Unmanned Aerial Device

MILITARY GLOSSARY

Military Factory, (2003 - 2018). Military Factory - Global Defense Reference. Retrieved from www.MilitaryFactory.com

The Sixties Project, (1996). "Glossary of Military Terms & Slang from the Vietnam War". Retrieved from www2.lath.virginia.edu/sixties/HTML_docs/Resources/Glossary/Sixties_Term_Gloss_A_C.html

Sun Key Publishing, (2004 - 2018). "Military Alphabet". Retrieved from www.militaryspot.com/military-alphabet/

The ITS Crew, (January 5, 2012). "Military Acronyms, Terminology, and Slang Reference". Retrieved from www.itstactical.com/intellicom/language/military-acronymsterminology-and-slang-references/

Brody, Ben, (December 4, 2013). "U.S. Military Lingo: The (Almost) Definitive Guide". Retrieved from www.npr.org/blogs/parallels/2013/12/04/248816232/u-s-military-lingo-the-almost-definitive-guide/

GADGETS AND AIRCRAFT

GADGETS AND AIRCRAFT
RETRO - CHOPPER

Retro-choppers are a hybrid, with the streamlined fuselage/ turbine engines of a jet, and the maneuverability of a helicopter.

These aircraft are highly maneuverable, capable of navigating tightly in a combat airspace. When engaged with an enemy force, a skilled pilot can direct the craft to behave in a way similar to a wasp's flight, utilizing the full capabilities of a helicopter's rotors and a jet's speed.

To protect the pilot from redout and blackout, the Retro Chopper includes inertial dampeners and a gyroscopic cockpit with a 360 degree digital HUD. The advanced electronics require a pilot with specialized training. Consequently, the aircraft is a favorite for gamers, and a good number of the pilots were gamers.

Length: 50 feet
Width: 45 feet
Max. Speed:
    Rotor Engines: 300 mph
    Turbine Engines: 1,000 mph

Ability(ies): Vertical Takeoff and Landing

A: Cockpit
B: Turbine Intakes
C: Missile Compartments
D: Rotors
E: Turbine Exhaust

GADGETS AND AIRCRAFT
RETRO - CHOPPER

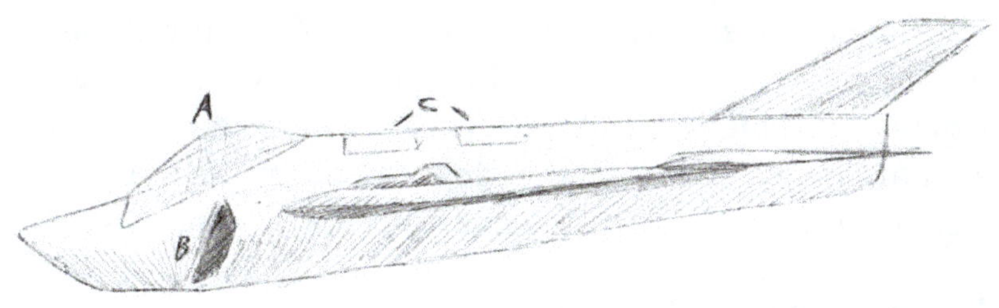

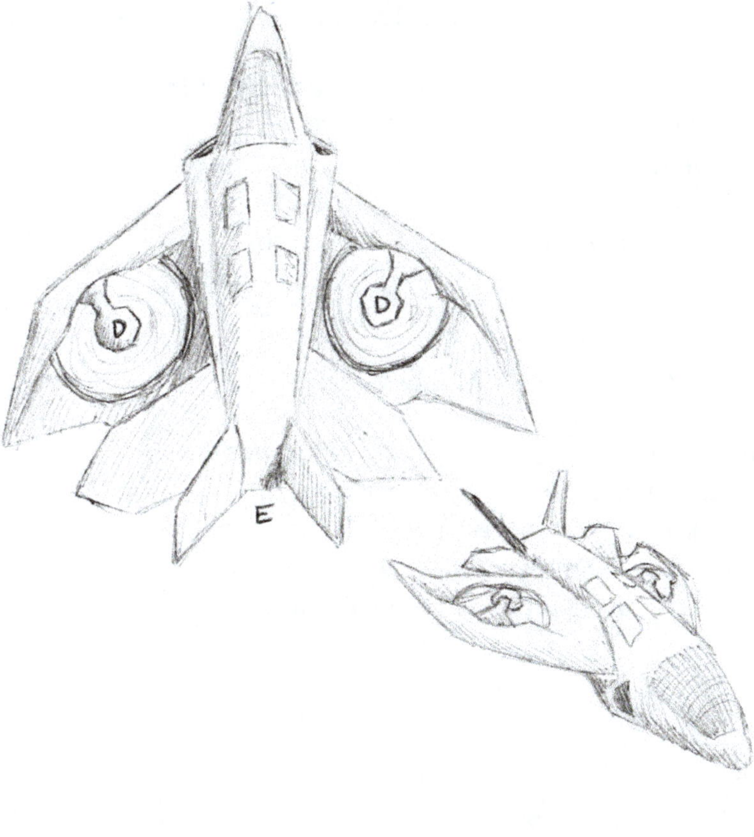

GADGETS AND AIRCRAFT
MANTA

The Manta model is capable of not only aerial travel, but is also submersible and bears a radar jammer, which renders it virtually invisible to most detection instruments. The rotors can move independently of the wing, and the blades themselves interchange between thin air blades and sturdy water ones.

There are two sizes of this model.

Manta Transport

Length: 60 feet
Width: 80 feet
Max Speed:
    Air: 400 mph
    Water: 75 mph

Max Passengers: 15
Ability(ies):
Underwater travel
Maneuverability
Stealth tech

Manta Carrier

Length: 180 feet
Width: 240 feet
Max Speed:
    Air: 200 mph
    Water: 55 mph

Max Passengers: 60
Ability(ies):
Underwater travel
Load capacity
Stealth tech

GADGETS AND AIRCRAFT
MANTA

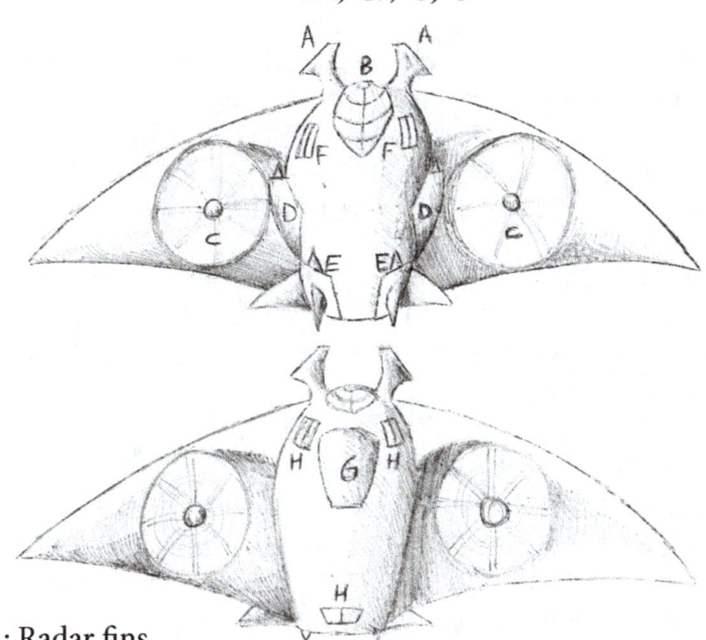

A: Radar fins

B: Cockpit

C: Rotors

D: Turbine engines

F: Weaponry holds

G: Loading ramp

H: Landing gear holds

I: Landing gear

GADGETS AND AIRCRAFT
DINOSAUR SUITS

The dinosaurian suits were designed by Nicole Nike as protection for those in the field.

The vests are worn loose for comfort, yet retain textile strength and tear resistance, lined with bulletproof shielding.

The bipedal suit version comes with an ammo belt, where magazines can been attached for easy access, while, adversely, the aerial suit version has the ammo belt incorporated into the vest chest as pockets.

As dinosaurians are not constructed anatomically the same as humans, the custom firearms are attached to lines that latch onto loops on the suits, so the firearms dangle when not in use. The aerial custom firearm takes this one step further by including a pressure pad, which acts as a trigger. This pad is attached to an anklet.

A: Firearm attachment loops
B: Headset
C: Microphone/Speaker
D: Ammo belt
E: Magazine

GADGETS AND AIRCRAFT
DINOSAUR SUITS

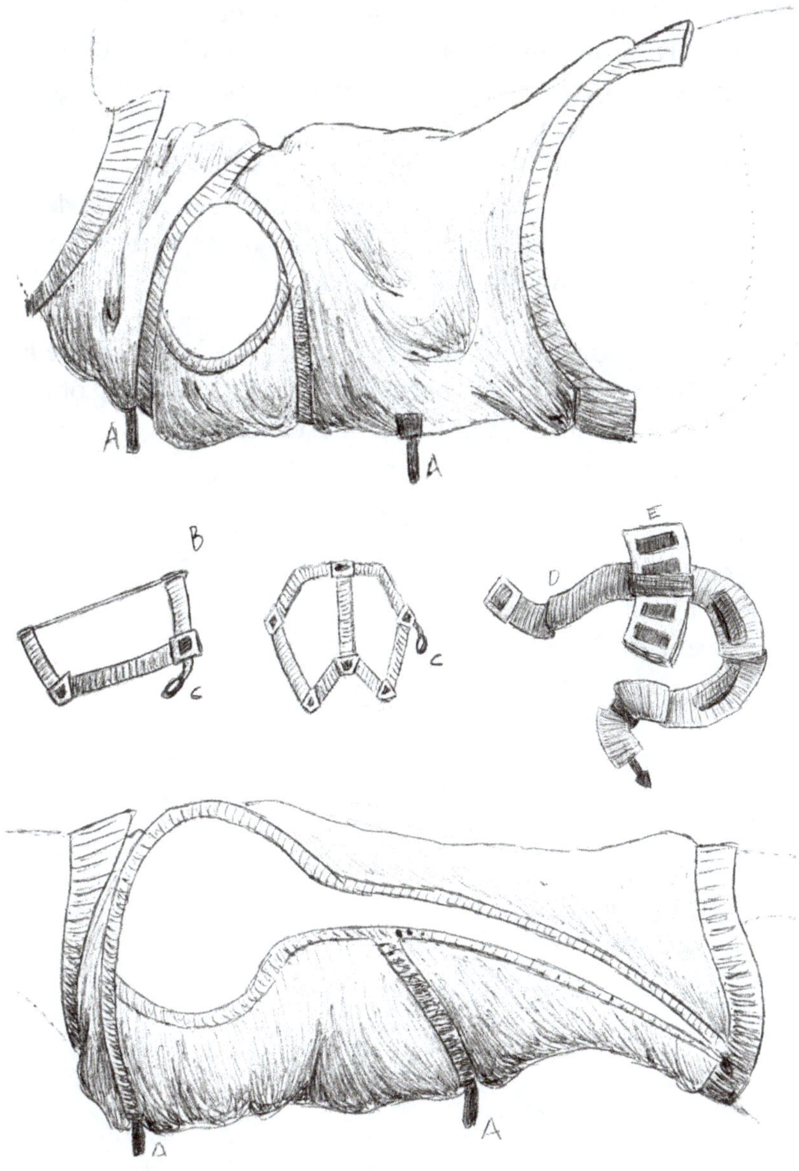

GADGETS AND AIRCRAFT
SPIDER-BOT

No larger than a quarter, this device is not officially named and is only known by the moniker "Spider-bot." It is designed specifically for reconnaissance, small and thin enough to slip into and through spaces too tiny for other drones. The drone also records video/audio, and is fitted with a compact incendiary device. The hull is outfitted with panels that detect surrounding light and color, and mimic those, rendering the device essentially invisible if immobile.

It has no ranged weapons aside from a suicide bomb. There is a tiny razor blade on the end of each leg, used for piercing objects for climbing, or slicing through an obstacle.

Length: 1 inch
Width: 1 inch
Max Speed: 0.25 mph
Ability(ies): Stealth

A: Legs
B: Blade
C: Optic panel ring
D: Storage mode

GADGETS AND AIRCRAFT
SPIDER-BOT

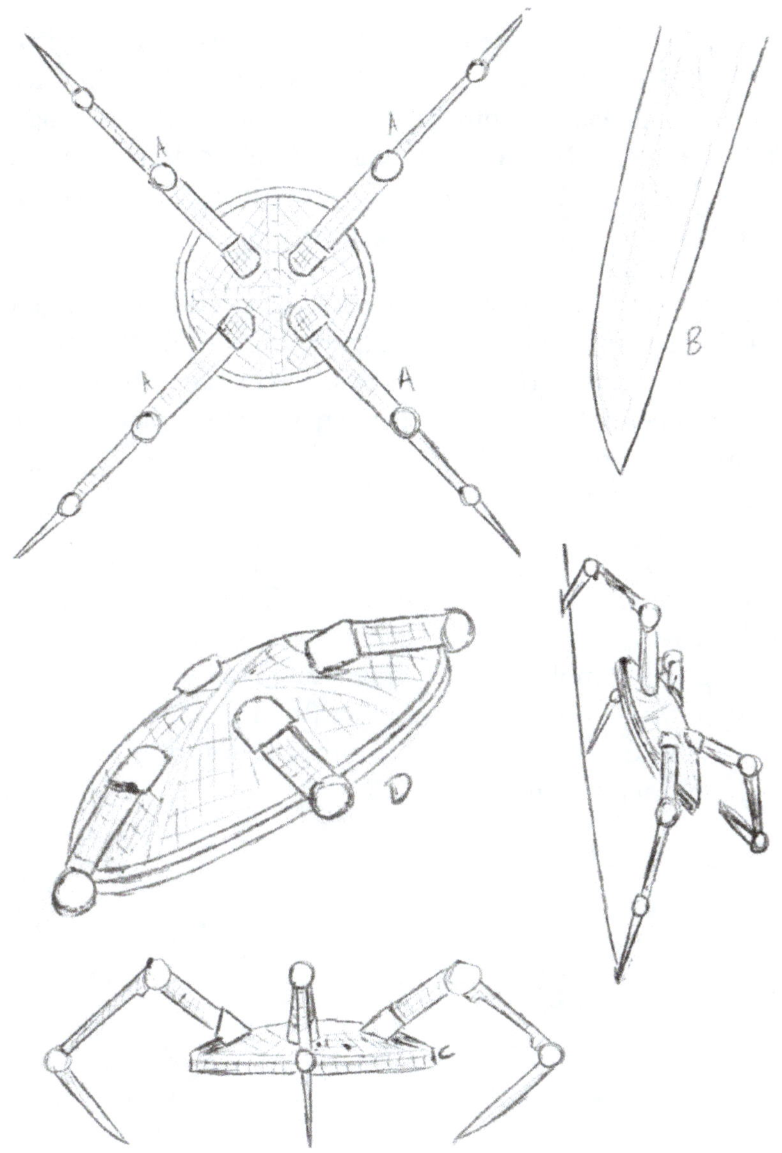

GADGETS AND AIRCRAFT
UNISON ORDER - GROUND DRONE

No bigger than an amateur enthusiast's RC helicopter, Unison Order - Ground Drones, or UO-GDs, are vicious in their programmed task of hunting down the target until it no longer retains life signs. They are extremely difficult to deactivate, and the light firearm bulletproof hull leaves only the rotors and protective sensor panel as weak points.

They are equipped with dual cannons paired with an intelligent targeting system, making them capable of learning the target's patterns and discovering weaknesses. The twin outboard rotors move independently of the fuselage, enabling tight maneuvering in close quarters.

Length: 2 feet
Width: 2 feet
Max. Speed: 12 mph
Ability(ies):
 Stealth
 Maneuverability

A: Sensor Cover Panel
B: Miniature Cannons
C: Landing Skids
D: Tail Rotor
E: Outboard Rotors

GADGETS AND AIRCRAFT
UNISON ORDER - GROUND DRONE

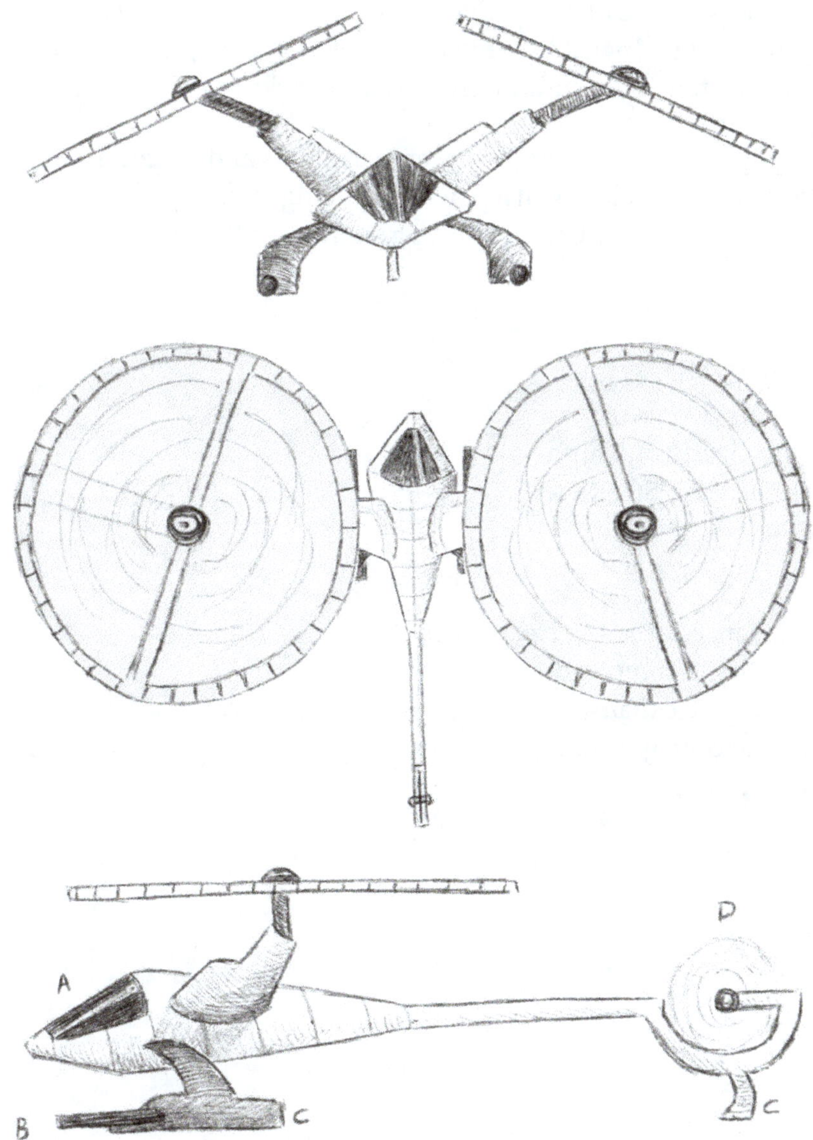

GADGETS AND AIRCRAFT
UNISON ORDER - SKY DRONE

While small, Unison Order - Sky Drones, or UO-SDs, are a powerhouse. Invisible to radar, an UO-SD can approach a target undetected. They commonly attack in packs of five or more.

Equipped with four high-powered cannons and a large amount of ranged missiles, with a powerful intelligent learning targeting system, even one UO-SD poses a significant threat.

Length: 20 feet
Width: 20 feet
Max Speed: 600 mph
Ability(ies): Stealth tech

A: Plate concealing electronics
B: Missile compartment
C: Engine exhaust
D: Landing gear compartments
E: Cannons

GADGETS AND AIRCRAFT
UNISON ORDER - SKY DRONE

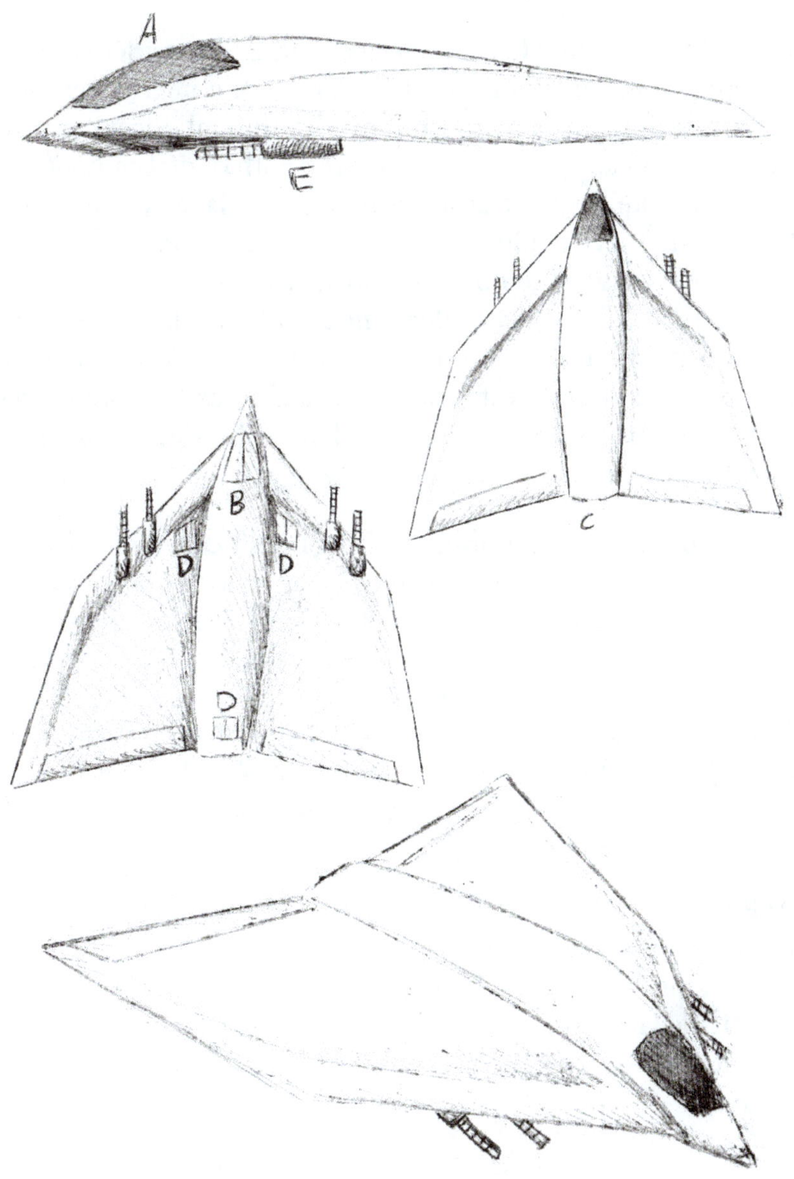

GADGETS AND AIRCRAFT
UNISON ORDER STEALTH HELICOPTER

Despite the fact that helicopters are generally considered noisy machines, the Unison Order UO-SH has the next-generation stealth technologies with improved minimal visual, radar, infra-red and acoustic signatures using both digital camouflage and an intelligent transmogrifying fuselage to improve battlefield survivability and reduced detection. The rotor blades are designed to minimize noise with sound cancellation technologies, for a near silent mode. Missile launchers and AI targetting cannons are built into the hull. A skilled pilot can make this craft extremely formidable as the projectiles and ammunition are auto-fired, balanced between maximum fatalities or maximum carnage.

As this model has been used to abduct political enemies while their families sleep, the Unison Order enforces an effective campaign of both social interdiction, and unrest suppression and prevention.

Length: 60 feet   *Width (excl. rotors):* 17 feet
Max Speed: 275 mph   *Ability(ies):* Stealth

A: Rotors
B: Rotor engine intakes
C: Cockpit
D: Missile launchers
E: Tail rotor
F: Door
G: Cannons

GADGETS AND AIRCRAFT
UNISON ORDER STEALTH HELICOPTER

DINOSAUR GLOSSARY

Dinosaur Glossary

Age

- *Hatchling* - A newly hatched dinosaur
- *Youngling* - A dinosaur one year old
- *Adult* - A mature dinosaur. Age range between youngling and adult varies with the species.

Luna

- The dinosaurian term for the moon

Pace

- The dinosaurs' term of measurement. Roughly equivalent to a meter.

Seasons

- *Green* - Spring
- *Hot* - Summer
- *Colors* - Autumn
- *White* - Winter

Squama

- What the dinosaurs collectively call themselves.

Turn

- The dinosaurian term for a year.

THE ENDANGERED DINOCTIONARY™

ALBERTOSAURUS

Pronounced: al-BERT-oh-sawr-us
Diet: Ground-dwelling carnivore
Home: Canada, Mexico, USA
Weight: 2.5 tons
Height: 10 feet
Length: 28 feet
Name Means: "Alberta Lizard"

ALLOSAURUS

Pronounced: AL-oh-sawr-us
Diet: Ground-dwelling carnivore
Home: Canada, Mexico, USA
Weight: 1 - 5 tons
Height: 14 feet
Length: 32 feet
Name Means: "Different Lizard"

BAMBIRAPTOR

Pronounced: BAM-bee-rap-tor
Diet: Ground-dwelling carnivore
Home: USA
Weight: 7 pounds
Height: 1 foot
Length: 3 feet
Name Means: "Baby Raider"

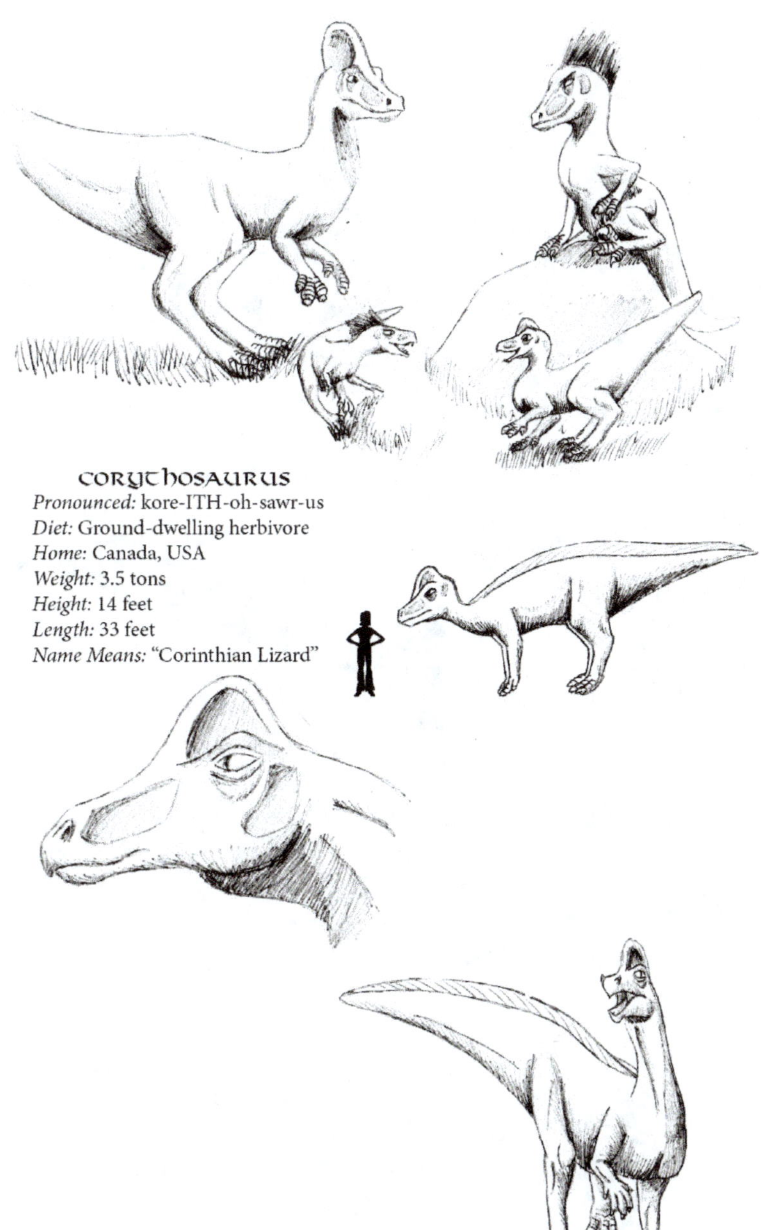

CORYTHOSAURUS

Pronounced: kore-ITH-oh-sawr-us
Diet: Ground-dwelling herbivore
Home: Canada, USA
Weight: 3.5 tons
Height: 14 feet
Length: 33 feet
Name Means: "Corinthian Lizard"

EDMONTONIA

Pronounced: ed-mon-TOH-nee-uh
Diet: Ground-dwelling herbivore
Home: Canada, USA
Weight: 4 tons
Height: 9 feet
Length: 22 feet
Name Means: "Of Edmonton"

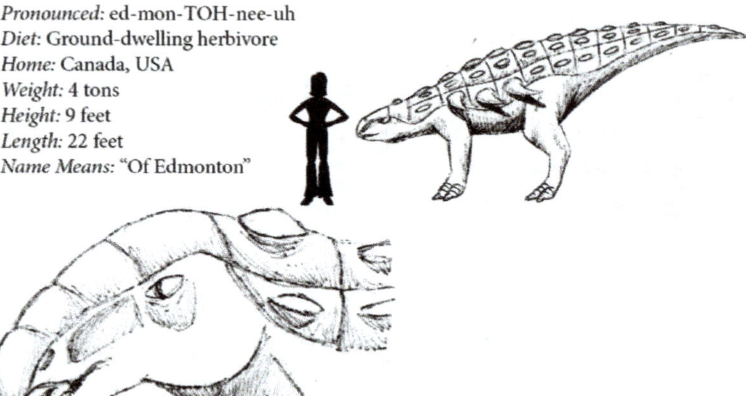

HESPERONYCUS

Pronounced: HESS-peh-RON-ih-cuss
Diet: Ground-dwelling insectivore
Home: Canada
Weight: 4 pounds
Height: 1.5 feet
Length: 3 feet
Name Means: "Western Claw"

MICROVENATOR

Pronounced: MI-crow-VEN-ah-tor
Diet: Ground-dwelling carnivore
Home: USA
Weight: 7 pounds
Height: 2 feet
Length: 4 feet
Name Means: "Small Hunter"

PTERODACTYLUS

Pronounced: TEH-roe-DACK-till-us
Diet: Aerial carnivore
Home: UK, France, Germany, Portugal
Weight: 10 pounds
Wingspan: 11 feet
Length: 6 feet
Name Means: "Wing Finger"

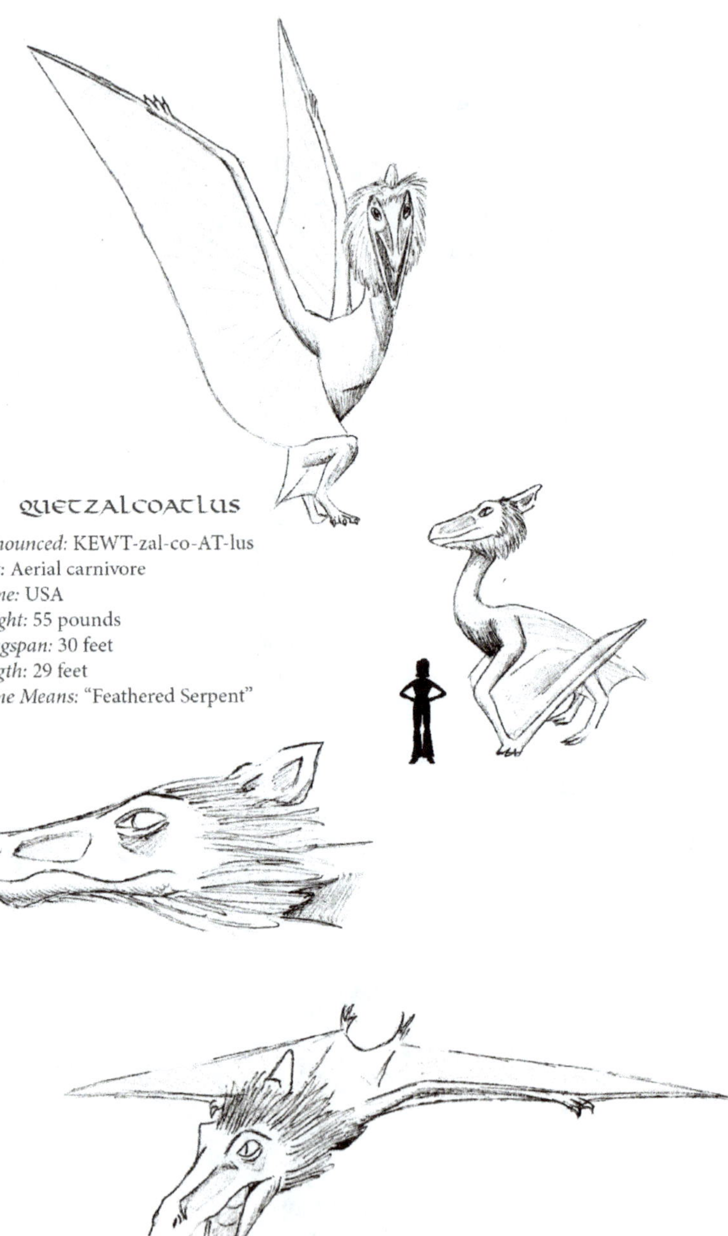

QUETZALCOATLUS

Pronounced: KEWT-zal-co-AT-lus
Diet: Aerial carnivore
Home: USA
Weight: 55 pounds
Wingspan: 30 feet
Length: 29 feet
Name Means: "Feathered Serpent"

stygimoloch

Pronounced: STIG-ee-MOE-lock
Diet: Ground-dwelling omnivore
Home: Canada, USA
Weight: 440 pounds
Height: 5 feet
Length: 10 feet
Name Means: "Styx Molcoch"

TRICERATOPS

Pronounced: try-SARE-oh-tops
Diet: Ground-dwelling herbivore
Home: Canada, Mexico, USA
Weight: 7 tons
Height: 8 feet
Length: 28 feet
Name Means: "Three Horn Face"

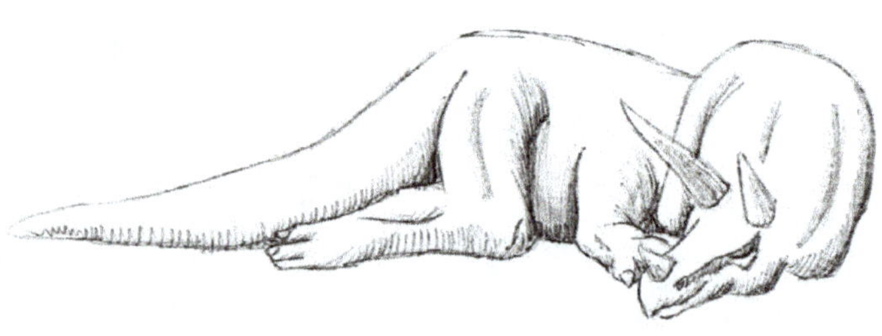

TROODON

Pronounced: TRUE-don
Diet: Ground-dwelling carnivore
Home: Canada, USA
Weight: 110 pounds
Height: 2 feet
Length: 6 feet
Name Means: "Tooth That Wounds"

Utahraptor

Pronounced: YOO-taw-rap-tor
Diet: Ground-dwelling carnivore
Home: USA
Weight: 1 ton
Height: 8 feet
Length: 23 feet
Name Means: "Utah Robber"

www.ingramcontent.com/pod-product-compliance
Lightning Source LLC
Chambersburg PA
CBHW071958110726
47910CB00005B/1571